MONSTER HUNTER HUNTER FANTOM

BAEN BOOKS IN THIS SERIES

THE MONSTER HUNTER INTERNATIONAL SERIES
Monster Hunter International by Larry Correia
Monster Hunter Vendetta by Larry Correia
Monster Hunter Alpha by Larry Correia
The Monster Hunters (compilation) by Larry Correia
Monster Hunter Legion by Larry Correia
Monster Hunter Nemesis by Larry Correia
Monster Hunter Siege by Larry Correia
The Monster Hunter Files (anthology) edited by Larry Correia and
Bryan Thomas Schmidt
Monster Hunter Guardian by Larry Correia and Sarah A. Hoyt
Monster Hunter Bloodlines by Larry Correia
Monster Hunter Fantom (anthology)
edited by Martin Fajkus and Jakub Mařík

THE MONSTER HUNTER MEMOIRS SERIES
Monster Hunter Memoirs: Grunge by Larry Correia and John Ringo
Monster Hunter Memoirs: Sinners by Larry Correia and John Ringo
Monster Hunter Memoirs: Saints by Larry Correia and John Ringo
Monster Hunter Memoirs: Fever by Larry Correia and Jason Cordova

To purchase any of these titles in e-book form, please go to www.baen.com.

MONSTER HUNTER FANTOM

A Monster Hunter Anthology

Edited by
Martin Fajkus &
Jakub Mařík

A Baen Book

Baen Publishing Enterprises
P.O. Box 1403
Riverdale, NY 10471
www.baen.com

ISBN: 978-1-6680-7253-0

Cover illustration by Petr Willert
Cover art by Lukás Tuma

First printing, January 2025

Distributed by Simon & Schuster
1230 Avenue of the Americas
New York, NY 10020

Library of Congress Control Number: 2024946668

Printed in the United States of America

10 9 8 7 6 5 4 3 2 1

CONTENTS

Foreword

DEAR HUNTERS AND HUNTRESSES, DEAR MONSTERS AND BEASTS . . .

If the preceding words have surprised you, know that I have good reasons for them. The first one is obvious. It is an undeniable fact that a properly chosen addressing is, at least in the case of a foreword, half the battle for the reader's attention, especially when it is necessary to defend the bare existence of such a text in contrast to the eleven great short stories that are impatiently waiting close behind to captivate the readers.

The second reason is based on the assumption that there are plenty of reasonably intelligent monsters on the other side of the barricade as well, so there's a definite possibility that at least a few of them might be well-read enough to enjoy this anthology. You know, "When you are throwing books long enough into the Abyss . . . the Abyss begins to read." It's admittedly a pretty hypothetical possibility, but why deprive yourself of any minority group of readers in advance? Besides, where is it written that such a monster couldn't be a real geek? Can you imagine, for example, a monster coming to a book signing to get autographs from its favorite writers? And then capture their hearts in more than just a figurative sense. But that's a whole different story.

The third reason is quite obvious: if it weren't for Hunters and monsters, this magical anthology wouldn't have been created in the first place. So why not thank them?

Now on a more serious note: the purpose of this foreword is to share a bit of the history of our *Monster Hunter Fantom* project and to reveal a few not entirely uninteresting facts connected with it. To do so, however, I must first go back more than a decade—to a time when publishers were desperately searching for a new "holy grail" that would bring them primarily wealth and secondarily some fleeting but welcomed fame. The big ones longed to discover "the next Dan Brown" or "a new J. K. Rowling," the smaller sci-fi/fantasy publishers would usually settle for "the new Kulhánek, the great Master of Czech splatterpunk." And so it happened that one day my friend and the head of the Ostrava publishing house FANTOM Print, Libor Marchlík, came to me and, with a triumphant look on his face, announced that he had discovered "the American Kulhánek," whose name was Larry Correia.

Having heard various versions of this phrase a few times already, I was quite skeptical, but upon closer inspection, strangely enough, there seemed to be some truth to his claim. Correia's Monster Hunter series, despite its originality, is in many ways in line with Kulhánek's books, be it the brutal action, a lot of spilled blood, spent bullet casings, the right amount of hyperbole and black humor, and last but not least some of the catchphrases and pop culture references. To put it simply, this was love at first read, and as the number of books published in the Czech Republic grew and Larry's world of humans and monsters developed and diversified, as new heroes, ideas and monsters were added, that feeling deepened, at least for me. The visit of Larry Correia and his lovely wife to Prague, where we not only met in person, but also had some spectacular adventures, from a truly epic meat-eating contest at the Ambiente restaurant, Larry's amazement when our small group of die-hard fans marched in front of him wearing T-shirts that featured a great caricature of him by Dan Černý, to an amazing visit to Army Museum Žižkov on Vítkov, where Correia felt like a fish in water and had an insightful discussion about various weapons.

And here we get to Jakub Mařík, a translator and Monster Hunters fan, who went on this amazing journey with us and enjoyed Correia's visit at least as much as I did. So, in 2020, not long after the publication of a collection of short stories by American authors called *Monster Hunter Files*, when I first thought that we could compile a similar anthology here in the Czech Republic, I immediately thought of him. Like any visionary, I needed a faithful sidekick who would do most of the work and let me shine. Jakub was an ideal choice for this project not only because he is the guardian and expert in the world of Monster Hunters, but also because of his enthusiasm and last but not least because of his introverted nature, which limits him quite a bit when speaking in public, but does not limit him in his writing. And time has shown that I chose well.

As soon as I presented my idea to Jakub, he immediately got excited about it, and we could start planning. Which involved some pretty heated discussions, which led to the conclusion that the anthology should be produced under the patronage of Larry Correia (and preferably with a story by him included), each story should be set in the Czech Republic, and it should involve only domestic monsters and beasts. As a bonus, the stories should be more or less connected with the hunting company Fantom based in Ostrava, which Larry Correia incorporated into *Monster Hunter Siege* after meeting some of the crew of his Czech publisher in person.

The next step was to choose the right authors, and then the real work could begin. While Jakub got the easy part, which meant convincing Larry, I had to deal with the hard part: getting Libor Marchlik excited about our project. Extracting a promise of funding out of a man whose stubbornness Scrooge McDuck would be envious of was an almost superhuman feat. But we did it. And so we could start approaching authors and luring them into our net. Oddly enough, *MHF*'s idea aroused general interest, enthusiasm, and ultimately approval. I won't enumerate here all that we had to promise and do— as the Jesuits say, the end justifies the means—but ten local fantasists embarked on the journey that led to this unique anthology.

Jakub and I were available to them practically non-stop, and we also gave them a short summary of the world of Monster Hunter and a description of the lead figures of the Fantom hunting company. (If you notice some similarities between the members of Fantom and the staff of a certain Ostrava publishing house, it is certainly no coincidence.) I'd like to elaborate a bit here, because that quartet of characters will play a sometimes larger and sometimes smaller role in the stories that follow. The most prominent one is, of course, Libor, a handsome scrooge and a business shark who can play it pretty rough. Next is Alexandra, the company's sales director, an introvert who improves her mood by detonating powerful explosives, usually in the vicinity of magical creatures. Then there's Martin, the quartermaster and the company's mad scientist with a weakness for succubus miniatures. And Petra, an archivist and a source of information on monsters and magic, who went from teaching little "monsters" at school to hunting the big ones.

Admittedly, writing stories with this formidable team was pretty easy. Though there were problems there too, especially within the usual suspects, i.e. submission deadlines. And so bargaining happened, more or less realistic reasons for delays were given, but everything was solved in time.

As editors, our main concern was that all the stories might end up similar. We were able to take care of a part of it right at the beginning—make sure the stories wouldn't be about the same monsters—but then it was up to each author and their imagination. And here, I have to admit, it came out better than I dared hope. Each story is different, and each is differently good. Whether it's the pieces by "famous" faces like Pavlovský, Kotleta or Sněgoňová, or by still evolving promising talents like Paytok or Hoza. All writers involved in this anthology really overdid themselves. What's more, it turned out that our monsters can be just as entertaining and dangerous as the American ones.

Long story short, I had a great time preparing *Monster Hunter Fantom*. And now I hope you'll enjoy these eleven stories just as much!

—Martin Fajkus

P.S.: Jakub Mařík refused to write an afterword, so anyone who feels deprived by this fact should direct their complaints to him.

MARTIN FAJKUS (* 1970)

A fan of fantasy and science-fiction, book lover, literary publicist, both editor and editor-in-chief of the magazine *Pevnost*, editor of genre collections and a fool dreaming of writing his own novel one day. A native of North Moravia, he discovered fantasy in his teens through medieval chivalric novels and *Lord of the Rings*. Although he built a solid professional career as a technical expert in the nuclear power plant field, his love of books also led him to the publishing house FANTOM Print, with whom he worked for many years selecting titles and negotiating with authors and illustrators. He started as a literary columnist for the Fantasy Planet website and also contributed to the semi-professional magazine *Ramax*. Since 2002, he has been the editor of *Pevnost* magazine, and in 2014 he became its editor-in-chief, which he still is today.

After several attempts to create his own work, he moved to the position of editor. His first work in that capacity is the anthology *Legion of the Immortals* (*Legie nesmrtelných*, FANTOM Print, 2006), a collection of fantasy short stories by an original mix of well-known local and international authors, including Steven Erikson and Raymond E. Feist.

A purely domestic anthology *Dark Times* (*Temné časy*, FANTOM Print, 2012) is mainly focused on dark fantasy. A few years later, together with Tomáš Němec, he prepared a short story collection of the best of what appeared in *Pevnost* magazine, called *Fellowship of Pevnost* (*Společenstvo pevnosti*, FANTOM Print, 2014). His latest project is *Monster Hunter: Fantom*, on which he collaborated editorially with Jakub Mařík. After what he revealed in the foreword of this book, you have to admit that his presence in *MHF* is essential!

Bulletproof
Larry Correia

Prague is a beautiful city. I've been all over the world now, and it's a stand out. It's got this unique old-world charm, and the people I knew here were really cool. So it was unfortunate that I needed to murder somebody at one of their biggest tourist attractions. In my defense, the guy I was following with intent was a member of the Sanctified Church of the Temporary Mortal Condition, and they are the worst.

A year ago those dirtbags had tried to kidnap my son. My wife had gotten our boy back, and that particular bunch of cultists had died badly—Julie is the last woman you want to piss off—but the Condition was still out there, and they were always up to no good. There's no more tiresome pest than somebody willing to sell their soul to the nefarious Old Ones. They do awful things on behalf of the most evil things in the universe in exchange for power, and I'd made it one of my missions in life to step on them whenever given the opportunity.

And somebody I believed was a cult leader had just been unlucky enough to walk right past me on the streets of Prague while I'd been waiting in line to buy a trdelnik.

Seriously, Czech street doughnuts are awesome. They cook them right there over an open fire on a stick, then cover them in sugar, coat the inside with Nutella, and fill it with ice cream. But I digress. Back to the murder.

The target of opportunity seemed to be out for a leisurely stroll. He had two young men with him—who certainly fit that sleazy dangerous vibe the Condition loved to recruit from—obviously serving as bodyguards. I stayed twenty yards behind, trying to slouch and keep my head down so I wouldn't get spotted. At six foot five, I stand out. It was a nice afternoon, so the sidewalks were crowded enough they didn't notice me.

Messing with my family made this personal. I'd bribed an MCB Agent to get us their complete file on the Condition, and I'd memorized the picture of every confirmed member. Despite the fact he was wearing a hat, sunglasses, and had grown a wispy little beard, I was pretty certain I was tailing an asshole named Fletcher Bell, who was allegedly into human sacrifice, dark magic, probably a full-fledged necromancer, and known associate of Lucinda Hood.

Only pretty certain wasn't good enough to drop the hammer on somebody. I had to be absolutely sure, which meant I needed to get closer and probably even confront him. I couldn't just do that in the open though.

Normally, killing necromancers is considered a public service. Problem was, I'd flown to Czechia for a funeral for my great aunt. I'd barely known her but had come along to support my mom, who had a lot of family here. I wasn't here on official MHI business so had no local government approval to do anything. I was unarmed. I had no backup. And even though Fletcher looked like a fat, middle-aged, lump, all necromancers were crazy dangerous.

Being sure the Czech government would frown on an American tourist snapping the neck of a British tourist on holiday, I got out my phone and searched for my contact at Fantom, the local Monster Hunting company. We'd worked with them on the siege of Severny Island, where they had proven to be solid professionals. If their laws were anything like we had in the US, Fantom could kill necromancers all day with impunity and get paid for it.

Since, "Hey it's Owen Pitt from MHI, I'm in town and I think I found an evil cult wizard you guys can shoot for money" wasn't a conversation that I wanted to have out loud, I typed a text to Libor saying basically that while I walked, added my location, and hit send.

I couldn't say that they were heading into an old part of town, because a lot of Prague was very old, but this part was a nice, peaceful, neighborhood with a lot of history. A lot of old Europe had gotten trashed during the war, but Prague hadn't, so it retained a classic central European charm that had been lost in a lot of other places. They were approaching the square with the famous astronomical clock. From the accents of the various conversations I overheard, there were locals and visitors from all over, taking pictures, eating, and chatting. Fletcher and his goons stopped walking to look at the clock. I stopped and pretended to do the same thing while I actually kept an eye on them, which was difficult, because the clock really was rather impressive looking.

They settled in to wait, like Fletcher was planning on meeting someone here. The two bodyguards kept glancing around the square, hands relaxed next to the bottoms of their untucked shirts, where they were certain to be hiding guns. He seemed nervous, which was understandable, since if he was who I thought he was, Fletcher Bell was a fugitive, wanted by the MCB and every other secret government anti-monster organization in the world. Except when a pair of cops walked through the square, Fletcher didn't even glance their way. If he was nervous right now, it wasn't because of the law.

Libor from Fantom hadn't read my text yet, so I sent another one saying exactly where we were, and that I'd keep following until I heard otherwise. I didn't say anything about how I'd kill the necromancer if the opportunity presented itself. Libor would know I would, because that's what any self-respecting Monster Hunter would do in my circumstances, and I didn't want to leave any incriminating evidence on either of our phones. I didn't know much about the local National Regulating Service, which was the Czech equivalent to the US Monster Control Bureau, but if a foreign Hunter did what I was thinking about doing in the US, the MCB would lose their friggin' minds.

When I looked back up, Fletcher seemed even more worried than before. This was clearly a meet, and being in a public place that usually meant they wanted witnesses around so nobody would try anything funny. It wasn't that warm, but the fat man was visibly sweating. Whoever he was waiting for was someone who scared him.

But what would scare a deadly necromancer?

A few minutes later an unremarkable man approached Fletcher carrying a briefcase. They began talking, but I was too far away to hear them over the noise of the crowd. Fletcher seemed relieved at who'd met him, so I got the impression that this was just the delivery boy, not whoever the necromancer was afraid of. I discreetly took a picture of all of them to send to Libor. Fletcher took the briefcase, cracked it open to look inside, and satisfied by whatever he saw, began walking away.

I started to follow, when someone said from behind me, "This is not for you."

I looked over my shoulder to see a man standing there. He was tall as I was, only lean, and there was something so unnatural about his face—like it had been chiseled from marble by a sculptor who wanted to make a handsome face but wasn't quite sure what that should look like—that it made me reflexively uneasy. I could have mistaken him for a vampire if we hadn't been standing beneath the noonday sun.

The stranger had spoken in Czech, which I understood a lot better than I could speak it, but I tried anyway.

"Do I know you?"

"You do not know me, for I am Vadim Dryak, but I know your kind."

While I had been watching Fletcher, somebody else had been watching me. It was impossible to guess his age, somewhere between twenty and fifty, but I'd bet all of those years had been hard ones. He was dressed like a businessman, only something about his stance suggested he would've been more comfortable wearing some uniform with medals and ribbons on it, instead of a jacket and no tie.

"What kind is that?"

"The kind who hunts. The one speaking to my servant is not your prey today. I require his services, so you will not take his life. You have not wronged me . . . Yet. Thus I will spare your life. You are allowed to leave in peace."

It took me a second to translate that in my head, but I didn't need to get the words exactly right to grasp the threat in that message. I had a lot of experience with this sort of thing, so I knew when I was talking to something that looked like a person but wasn't. It's the uncanny valley, mankind's visceral genetic reaction to something which looks human but isn't quite right. For us Hunters, we get to know that valley real well.

"Well that's nice of you." I switched to English. "I wonder if you're something PUFF applicable."

It turned out Dryak spoke English too. "As I wonder what the contents of your stomach would look like if I ripped open your guts and spilled them upon these stones."

"Street doughnuts probably."

I think the creature—whatever he was—took my flippant response as one of ignorance, rather than arrogance. "You have been warned."

"Warning noted and immediately disregarded." Fletcher was getting away. There were only a few feet between me and the odd stranger. I was wary but didn't expect something supernatural to make a move in front of all these regular human witnesses. Only you never know. Some of these things are really arrogant. "The only services someone like that provides are evil. What do you need a necromancer for?"

Except apparently the thing wasn't big on conversation because he just turned and walked away, in the opposite direction Fletcher had gone.

The presence of something inhuman confirmed my hunch had been right, and the man I had been following really was Fletcher Bell. I hurried and checked my phone to see if I'd gotten a response from Fantom—nothing yet—and by the time I looked up, the stranger had somehow vanished into the crowd, so seamlessly that it was downright unnerving.

I called Libor as I went after Fletcher.

He picked up. "Owen Pitt, I just saw your texts. Why didn't you tell me you were here? I would have thrown a party. We would have gotten dinner."

I had to keep my voice low, but Fletcher was pretty far ahead so I hoped he wouldn't hear an obvious American. "I'm only in town for a funeral."

"And now you're gonna kill a cultist? Was one funeral not enough for you?"

"I know, I know. I'm following them now."

"Some of my guys are already on the way. Don't do anything until they get there."

"Yeah, I don't want to go to Czech prison."

Libor laughed. "You have been in worse prisons."

"True. There's somebody or something else here too, it just talked to me and tried to warn me away."

"A monster?" I could hear the excitement in his voice. "What kind?"

"I'm not sure that he was. He was a tall, kind of intimidating, odd looking fellow. Threatened to disembowel me if I messed with our friend. Then he vanished. He's probably still around here somewhere."

"We have lots of things that look like people, until they don't."

"He said his name was Vadim Dryak."

"Oh fuck that guy!" Libor shouted in my ear. "I'm surprised he didn't kill you already. He's fext."

That wasn't comforting. "A what?"

"It's from German, *kugelfest*. Bulletproof. Undead warriors, indestructible. Very rare. Which is good, because they are cursed and very angry, that sort of thing. He's been around since the Thirty Years' War."

That had been in the sixteen hundreds, which was the extent of my knowledge on the subject, and I only knew that because of a Jeopardy question. Something like that making a deal with the Condition was bad news. "How indestructible are we talking?"

"Very. It is said they can only be killed by glass bullets."

Well that was unfortunately specific. "Any chance your guys you sent have glass bullets on them?"

"I doubt it. I just told you fexts are rare. We haven't fought with one since Samuel Österling returned from the dead to menace Jihlava."

I didn't know what any of that meant. "Okay?"

"Doesn't matter. Improvise. Help us catch these guys and I'll give you a finder's percentage on the bounty."

I'd have taken out Condition for free, but I wasn't going to turn down money. I'm a devout capitalist like that. "If I break any laws, will you tell your government I was working for Fantom the whole time?"

"Sure. Welcome aboard. Don't do anything too stupid. "

"Deal." Then I read off the nearest street sign, and the name of the store I was walking past. Then one of the bodyguards looked back my way. "Got to go." And I hung up.

Except the cultist must have been suspicious of my lackluster spycraft, because he said something to the other goon, who also looked at me. Then that one kept hurrying Fletcher along, while the first one started walking back toward me . . . Crap.

Condition cultists usually weren't bright, but I doubted he'd be brazen enough to just shoot me in the street. However, he didn't need to. All he had to do was stall me long enough to lose sight of Fletcher. Any sort of conflict would be enough to draw the attention of the law.

"Hey, buddy, what're you looking at?" he demanded as he got closer. "You got a problem?"

Yeah, too many witnesses. There was a narrow alley just ahead, so I turned into it, hoping he'd follow. And sure enough, since cult muscle tended to be cocky and belligerent, he did. He caught up to me and grabbed me by the shoulder. "What's—"

I turned and sucker punched him right in the nose. He stumbled back, stunned but reaching for his waist. I trapped his arm before he could draw his gun and spun him hard into the wall. That hit must have cracked some ribs, but the dude was tough and kept fighting for his gun. I slugged him in the teeth. The back of his head bounced off the bricks, and that was it for him. He slid to the ground, riding the express train to concussion town.

Looking both ways, no pedestrians were yelling so they'd missed our one-sided scuffle. I took his gun, a CZ P07—appropriate considering our location—chamber checked—loaded—and tucked it into my waistband beneath my shirt. It's stupid to carry without a holster, but you do what you've got to do in circumstances like this, but at least with a double action trigger I probably wouldn't blow my junk off on accident. I should have gotten out of there then, so some passersby wouldn't see this and think I was robbing him, but I took the time to check his neck, and sure enough he was wearing one of the Condition's squid god necklaces. That confirmed who I was dealing with.

Back on the street, there was no sign of Fletcher so I hurried in the direction I'd last seen him. I rounded the corner and looked around. I was in front of a store that sold fancy chandeliers. This was a busier street, and I spotted the necromancer fifty yards away, just as his bodyguard was opening the door of a waiting car. I started in that direction.

"I warned you."

The crowd parted, and Vadim Dryak had appeared seemingly out of nowhere, blocking my way.

We stood there on the sidewalk, a few feet apart, Hunter versus fext, in some kind of standoff as tourists walked around us obliviously. Fletcher was getting away. I could pull the stolen CZ and shoot him, but this monster's name was literally bulletproof, so it probably wouldn't work, and if I missed there were innocent bystanders behind him. So I'd have to do this the old-fashioned way.

Except when I tried to hit him, Dryak easily dodged my hook, and promptly hurled me through the window of the chandelier store.

I lay there on the floor, dizzy and covered in broken glass. Libor had warned me fexts were nearly indestructible. He hadn't mentioned that they moved vampire speeds and hit like Agent Franks.

Dryak stepped through the broken window and started toward me, glass crunching beneath his shoes. "It was a simple transaction. I gave him some money and trinkets in exchange for performing a spell. You should not have interrupted."

"Yeah, well..." I stood up. I'd been cut, but nothing was squirting. "Decisions got made."

The employees of the store had come running when they'd heard the noise, but then they turned and went back the other way when they saw me pick the pistol off the ground. Of course it had fallen out when I'd gotten tossed. That's why we use holsters.

Now that Dryak was walking in front of a brick wall instead of a bunch of bodies I was happy to test out just how kugelfest he really was. I raised the CZ and put two in Dryak's chest.

He stopped, reached up, and plucked the bullet out of his suit, then held it up to show me the mushroomed hollow point. Like that would scare me or something...Well, actually it kind of did. But then he started to say something—which I'd been hoping for—so I shot him in the mouth.

Dryak struck me as a talker, so I'd been hoping to see if his insides were as bulletproof as the outside. The bullet hit a tooth on the way in, then slammed into his palate, and hopefully his brain. Not a bad shot for a stolen gun that I'd only had for a minute. But the Czechs make great pistols.

Unfortunately, my brilliant idea didn't work, because Dryak just shook his head, then rolled his tongue around, and spit the bullet out. He was kugelfest through and through.

Well shit.

Outside I saw the car with the necromancer in it take off. People were fleeing the gunfire. The police would be on their way. Hopefully Fantom would get here first.

The fext rushed me. This time I dodged, but he still managed to knock me into a counter. The display items got scattered everywhere. I rolled out of the way just before his fist punched a hole in two inches of wood where my head had just been. I scrambled away, crashing between the chandeliers that had been hung low for customers to look at. Dryak followed me through the swinging chandeliers.

I didn't have glass bullets, but I was in the best place ever to improvise a glass knife.

There was a chandelier that had a bunch of long bits, so I grabbed one and snapped it off. It was round so I didn't cut my palm, and the broken end looked nice and jagged. With pistol in my right, and glass in my left, I turned to face Dryak.

The fext scoffed at my little shiv. "By sword, lance, and gun I have made war through the centuries. I have survived bombs and cannon and fire, and you think can defeat me with that?"

Only I didn't need to kill him. I just needed to survive long enough for help to arrive with more firepower. "I've killed bigger with less."

That actually seemed to offend the fext and he charged.

Only I didn't lead with the shiv. I used the gun he assumed to be useless, aiming for his eyes.

The bullets bounced off, but he'd been human once, and humans flinch when they get hit in the eyes. Luckily for me centuries of immortality hadn't caused that reflex to go away, and Dryak closed his eyes.

Sidestepping the blind charge I jabbed the glass deep into his side. It snapped off in my hand.

We parted.

Dryak looked down at his abdomen, where red was rapidly spreading across his white dress shirt. He seemed really surprised as he said, "I bleed."

"You know what that means!" I said gleefully as I picked up an even bigger glass rod that had fallen on the floor.

A car stopped in front of the shop. Hopefully that was the Czech Hunters.

Dryak looked that direction, then back at me. "We will meet again, Hunter. You will pay for this."

"Dude, get in line."

Except the fext was already fleeing out the back of the store, way faster than I could hope to chase it.

Two men ran into the shop, and the one in the lead had a big FK

Brno hand cannon, which told me these were Hunters rather than cops. "You're MHI?"

"Yeah." I pointed at his gun. "Does that thing have glass bullets in it?"

"Yes."

I pointed. "The fext went that way."

It took a few days to sort out the mess. Mom got mad at me for messing up the rest of her trip, since I was getting stitches and doing paperwork rather than visiting relatives with her.

Vadim Dryak had gotten away. You can't win them all. I have no doubt we'll run into him again. But Fantom had caught Fletcher Bell and turned him over to the authorities for a nice reward, of which I got a percentage.

However, that percentage wasn't nearly enough to cover all the damages. Fantom covered for me with the cops, but I was on the hook to pay for a dozen chandeliers. It turns out Czech chandeliers are very nice and priced accordingly!

When Libor took me out for lunch I finally got my street doughnut though.

LARRY CORREIA (* 1977)

American writer and a lucky man, because he's fulfilled several of his lifelong dreams. He grew up at a small farm in California, yet did not become a farmer, but studied economics at university. Then he made a living as a bookseller, a shooting instructor and a gun shop owner, which is almost a dream job for a fan of guns like him. Correia, however, knew of an even better job. He had been trying his hand at writing since his university days, but it wasn't until 2007's *Monster Hunter International* that he was satisfied with his novel. So satisfied, even, that when publishers rejected it, he ended up self-publishing it. That's when the book was noticed by Baen Books and, as they say, the rest is history. Correia's first novel became a bestseller. It was also a gateway to a world where humans and monsters live side by side, and to avoid many tragedies, there are also professionals who hunt said monsters for a living.

The Monster Hunter series currently includes eight books in the main series, plus a spin-off called Monster Hunters Memoirs, where Larry wrote the first trilogy with John Ringo and collaborated with Jason Cordova on the second, and many short stories. Larry Correia hasn't limited himself to action-packed Hunter stories, however; he's also written the three-volume noir-tinged Grimnoir Chronicles (Baen Books, 2011-2013), as well as the almost classical fantasy *Saga of the Forgotten Warrior* (Baen Books, 2015). In addition, he writes books about a secret unit called the Dead Six (Baen Books, 2014-2016) with Mike Kupari, and the trench fantasy *The Age of Ravens* (Baen Books, 2022) with Steven Diamond, and the list of his books doesn't end there.

And because he likes his peace of mind, he bought a mountain with the royalties from the books he sold, built a house on it and lives there happily. It's only a small mountain, but it's his!

The Homecoming
Alex Drescher

The date started out great. Candles, unobtrusive music, a three-course dinner prepared right at the table by a professional Michelin-starred chef, and finally, red rose petals scattered from the dining table to the lavishly furnished bedroom.

By the time they got there, the chef was gone, of course, but she didn't know then that it would have been better if he'd stayed.

In fact, she hadn't even suspected it later, after they'd moved, as part of the artful foreplay, into a light marble-tiled bathroom with a tub so spacious it would be a sin if they didn't both end up in it.

They did, and it was still great.

She hadn't even realized when foreplay became lovemaking, but she wasn't complaining. It, too, was very imaginative and ultimately more than satisfying.

Only then he'd shoved her head under the water and held her there with a force she wouldn't have expected from him.

And it was at that exact moment that she would have appreciated the chef's presence.

She tried to kick him, to rip his hands off her neck and get her head above the surface. Desperately, she clutched at the edges of the tub, but its smooth walls were slipping under her increasingly clumsy fingers.

Eventually, she stopped trying.

✧ ✧ ✧

Candles and unobtrusive music remained, as well as the perfectly set table with Meissen porcelain, gold cutlery and crystal wine service. Candle flames reflected off the surface of the perfectly cut decanter, illuminating its deep red contents.

She popped the last piece of toast into her mouth and, careful not to wipe the bright red lipstick from her lips, dabbed them dry with a napkin.

Then she turned to the waiting chef. "Steak tartare from *cerebellum* and *georgiadis medulla*, my dear Herbert, you know how to surprise. So delicate, so sinful..."

The chef in question was flushed. "Even a dilettante can make a good dish with fresh ingredients, my lady," he replied.

"Oh, no," she disagreed with a smile. "Your skills are unmatched. Who would have guessed how much a fading orgasm would affect the taste? All that dopamine, it's like pouring the finest French champagne through a brain."

She turned to the other late-dinner attendee. "And of course, my thanks to you, Sebastien. After all, you're the one who prepared that girl so well for a slaughter. Good thing you have no problem mating with humans. What was once frowned upon is now very useful. Who was it, anyway?"

He decided not to respond to her condescension. Herbert had really outdone himself, so why spoil his evening?

It wasn't just the sex that flooded their food with hormones tonight. Herbert had insisted on serving the woman only fresh seafood and lightly cooked freshwater fish before drowning, along with the seaweed so adored by macrobiotics, blanched in twenty-year-old port wine.

If Herbert was right, the other courses, like the starter, would be unforgettable.

"A young healthy female of the human species," he replied just before she could interpret his silence as impoliteness. "She practiced a healthy lifestyle—regular sleep, sports, no drugs, alcohol or cigarettes."

She was about to say something, but was interrupted by the arrival of Herbert serving another course.

"Lungs," he uttered in a tone as if no further description were necessary, but then added: "The drowning was done in a bath of rosemary and bergamot, with a subtle hint of thirty-year-old Orkney single malt whisky."

"Interesting choice of bath ingredients," she remarked amusedly to Sebastien.

"For you, only the best," he replied.

She bit into them eagerly, and they were exactly as she'd hoped. Fresh, young and full of water absorbed during the drowning process. As fragile as a young girl's soul, yet as full of flavor as a grown woman's body.

She delicately wiped her mouth, stained with bright red blood, and clapped enthusiastically as Herbert placed a plate in front of her, adorned with oysters and seaweed stained with fresh salmon blood, a barely three-inch piece of pale flesh looming in the center.

"An unexpected highlight of the evening I had not hoped for," said Herbert with trembling voice, "a human fetus, no more than ten weeks old, topped with a thimbleful of blood from its mother's pericardium, flavored with fifty-year-old Madeira Terrantez."

Although she was entranced by the delicacy offered, she nevertheless asked cautiously: "Will anyone miss her?"

Sebastien grinned. "She lived alone and lost her job a month ago. No one will miss her, and I'll take care of her remains."

"That's good," she replied, taking a discreet bite of the offered delicacy.

When she finished, she gestured the chef away and glanced at Sebastien. "It's time to proceed with the mating."

Sebastien immediately began to undress.

Having friends in the city incinerator plant is an incredible advantage. Especially if you bring in anything other than monsters falling under the B016 form whose discreet disposal is in the state's interest.

I was unloading crates of foil-wrapped bodies from the van when the night shift boss arrived. "Howdy, Felix," I greeted him and handed him the delivery paper.

He pocketed it without looking at it and asked me: "What have you brought me?"

"Our brave government—with regard to the energy crisis—has decided to resume coal mining in Ostrava. And what a surprise, no one realized that the abandoned mines could be inhabited by permoniks. So when they sent in the technicians, all that returned were gnawed bones. And so the minister's underlings came to the boss with an offer that couldn't be refused."

"How many have you got?" he asked me.

"One hundred and thirty-two. I only cleaned the CSM mine, but the next batch of those little buggers will be brought to you by the people who were in charge of clearing out Darkov and Paskov."

"Then we should ask Brussels for an extra supply of gas, ha, ha, ha," Felix laughed.

Then his eyes flicked to the three much larger packages I hadn't yet unloaded from the van. "What about these?"

"Wrong time, wrong place."

"And the papers?"

Sometimes you just need to get rid of something that doesn't fit any government-approved form. I handed Felix three five-thousand-crowns bills.

When the money changed hands, I helped him load the bodies onto the cart and then we moved to his office.

Felix fell on the armchair that had been brought in for burning years ago and pulled a flask and two glasses from under his desk. Good thing alcohol disinfects because they hadn't seen water in a long time. But his slivovitz was first-rate with such a high-octane number, even Russian fighter jets could fly on it.

"Busy?" I commented on the stacks of papers that covered his desk.

Felix smirked. "We buy indulgences from the Union for burning waste, and we pay the state an income tax, a special environmental tax, and an even more special war tax. There's plenty of work, but a lot less money to pay for it."

When I shook my head, he reached into his pocket and pulled out my bills.

"If we had no side income, we'd starve to death. It's disgusting. All the foreign-language mafias here have a flat rate for eliminating inconvenient witnesses. I get paid by a dozen sects whose image would be damaged by evidence of their bloody rituals, and by gnomes who settle scores in a way that would shame businessmen from the nineties."

Felix slowly rose from his chair and walked out of the office. When he returned, he was carrying a black plastic bag. "And now this arrived here," he said, tossing it at my feet.

"A new client," he added, taking ten dull but undeniably gold coins from his pocket.

"Yeah, old Spanish doubloons. Smell them," he urged me.

I did, wrinkling my nose in surprise. "Sea mud?"

He nodded. "Exactly."

I opened the bag and promptly threw up in it.

"Shit," I groaned, wiping my mouth with a sleeve.

Felix pointed to a wet spot in one corner of his office. "That's where I threw it. Welcome to the club. A young girl was cooked and eaten, and her poorly gnawed bones were brought here by that son of a bitch."

"I'll give you thirty grand if you leave me that bag and describe the bastard who brought it," I offered.

He didn't refuse.

"I'm not a pathologist," Martin informed me as I made my way to the third basement floor—where he had his kingdom—upon returning to the headquarters.

Although the boss is known for his thriftiness, it didn't show here. All the secret services of the world would have no scruples about invoking World War III for Martin's equipment.

He had everything, including a cluster of powerful computers linked by a high-speed network, things that had only been whispered about in the editorial offices of professional journals, and artifacts we'd captured on our expeditions.

For me, it's all Greek, but no other department of Fantom produces such damn effective toys.

It does have one downside, though, and that's Martin. Despite his undeniable genius, and even if you follow the unwritten rules, such as not making eye contact and not using the imperative mood, he's as hard to handle as a whale washed up on a beach.

"I know you're not a pathologist," I agreed, adding a bit of psycho-sugar. "But no one can analyze these remains as quickly and flawlessly as you can. I need to find out her name and who did this to her, so why go to a blacksmith when I can go to, why not say it, a supersmith."

Martin, who was busily fiddling with some device that was likely to explode or implode and take at least half the block to hell with it, grinned. "Sugarcoating and a mention of the lack of time. All that's missing is guilt-tripping."

"If you don't help me, that bastard will murder someone else."

"And there it is. Thanks," he replied.

"You're welcome," I said, reaching into my pocket and pulling out a small, copper-wire-covered device I'd taken from the permoniks who'd founded a new civilization in the abandoned tunnels of the CSM mine.

"How about a bribe?" I asked.

"Corruption is bad, of course," he began, staring at the thing in my palm. "But it's also effective," he added. "That's a nice little thing. Will you give it to me?"

I pointed to the black plastic bag I'd placed on his examination table. "Sure, but..."

"Sure, sure, there's always a but," he snapped at me, holding his hand out, palm up. "I'll identify the victim in ten minutes."

"It's ugly here," Petra said when she arrived at Martin's lab.

"Dark and musty," added Alexandra, who had been pulled out of a meeting with representatives of the Hyundai factory in Nošovice who had a problem with a *hu li* fox, a demonic version of the kitsune that had been set upon them by their Chinese competitors.

"I reject the request to paint this place in pastel colors immediately," the boss responded, sprawled contentedly on a wheeled office chair he'd dragged over from a nearby desk.

This guy is a legend in the industry, and as the head of a Hunter company, he's personally participated in missions, even though he could be lying on a beach in the Caribbean.

When the communists disappeared in the dustbin of history, he reinstated Fantom and Hunters went from underground to a market economy, with all the pros and cons that entailed. He averted twelve attempts to abolish Fantom by decisions of the government or ministers bribed by competitors. He uses petitions from monster rights activists to insulate his house and he supposedly put a stop to activists gluing themselves to the road in front of the headquarters by starting to drive a tank to work.

It is thanks to him that the status quo exists—the state, through the secret European fund TEFLON [1], pays us bounties for the monsters we hunt, but it also collects taxes from us and buries us in secret decrees, regulations and measures that regulate everything from ecology to maintaining the diversity of the harmless monster population to gender equality in our teams.

In fact, monsters are in the same situation as the public awareness of their existence—both are strictly regulated. The former is handled by us, and the latter by agents of the State Regulatory Service, compared to whom KGB agents look like amateur hacks. Witnesses to monster attacks are intimidated or bribed, and when that doesn't work, there is social discrediting and public execution on social media.

And Fantom grows, gets stronger and, most importantly, makes money. We are the leader in the industry, a company with equipment rivaling the armies of smaller countries, and our boss spends his days in meetings with bowing politicians from Brussels and Prague.

Petra, our archivist, gives them presentations with lots of cute kittens to lift their mood and Alexandra crushes them with hard data and disgusted looks. So the entire Fantom board was in this hastily called meeting, plus little old me.

Yes, I am Hunter, but until a year ago I was a clerk at the Job Centre. Two things changed my life—the first was the feeling that it wasn't the job for me, and the second was a striga who came to claim housing benefits without bothering to maintain her human form.

So I guess it's clear that I'm pretty low on the Fantom food chain.

Fortunately, it was Martin and the results of the analysis that brought us here. They may have made fun of me, but they didn't dare look him in the eye. As far as I know, there was a noonwraith who did just that 20 years ago, and none of us want to end up like her.

Martin pointed to the remains lying on the examination table.

"This was a woman, twenty, twenty-five years old at most, of Indo-European ethnicity. Well, more European than Indian, since she was a natural blonde. Given what's left of her, that's about all I can tell you about her. And now the interesting part..."

He grabbed a remote from the table and displayed detailed pictures

---

[1] *Tajný* (Secret) *Evropský* (European) *Fond* (Fund) *Loveckých* (for Hunter) *Odměn* (Bounties) and *Náhrad* (Reparations)

of bones, diagrams and black and white columns of detected DNA on the monitors lining the walls of the lab.

"Note the dents on the large bones. Here and here," he said, using his laser pointer, its red dot gradually coming to rest on shallow grooves in the femur and humerus.

"It looked like the work of a cannibal," Martin continued his explanation, "until I found this," he announced, parking the red dot on an image made up of a bunch of black rectangles representing nucleic bases.

"What are we looking at?" boss asked.

"Inhuman DNA," Martin replied.

"And what does it belong to?" snapped Alexandra impatiently, but the boss immediately gave her a withering look, because you never raise your voice at Martin.

"And what does it belong to?" she repeated in a whisper, rolling her eyes.

Martin tapped the keyboard with one finger and the answer appeared on the monitor directly in front of them.

"A vodnik? You're kidding," Petra breathed. "There aren't any left in the Czech Republic."

"Maybe some arrived here with refugees, like the ifrits did," the boss said thoughtfully. "Or something made them migrate. What do we have in the archives?"

Petra cleared her throat. This was her moment and she decided to seize it. "There are several species confined to Europe. However, they show significant differences in physical structure and intelligence. The Baltic anchutka looks like a small, toeless, fingerless devil. The Russian bolotyanik has frog-like eyes and bulbous fingers, and the ocheretyanik, for a change, has a strikingly large belly, a bald head and goose legs. Humanoid features and the ability to blend in with the human population are found in the Slovenian voden or the Norwegian nix. Of course, also in the Czech hastrman, but the last one was caught by K. J. Erben[2] in the summer of 1851 and TEFLON lists them as

---

[2] Karel Jaromír Erben (1811–1870)—One of the most important Czech poets and folklorists of the 19th century. His best known work is *Kytice* (*A Bouquet of Folk Legends*), a collection of dark ballads with many horror elements, and all of his hunting achievements mentioned in this short story are based on this book. In 2000, *Kytice* was made into a movie called *Wild Flowers*.

extinct. We also know of the Tatra Mountains subspecies, which was supposedly covered with moss, but the last one was killed by partisans in the 1940s. Supposedly it tasted like carp."

"Fine," said Alexandra. "So which one is it?"

Martin shrugged. "The sample taken from the victim's body wasn't very good. Based on comparing the DNA profile with the profiles from the comparison samples, there's a partial match to a voden, a nix, and a hastrman."

"Well, that will be interesting," Petra said thoughtfully, her fingers running over the screen of her mobile phone with the bravura of a piano virtuoso. "The reward for an introduced vodnik is seven hundred thousand. Eight times that for a female, because vodniks usually breed through water elementals, like a water lady or rusalka, or human girls."

"And how much for a hastrman?" I asked her.

She grinned. "They're extinct, so I have to base it on the last price list for them from the days of the Austria-Hungary." She paused for a moment. "Well, after converting from the Austrian gulden, and taking into account inflation and other considerations, the reward for him would jump like a baby goat crossed with a rocket to somewhere near twenty-two million euros."

"You should have started with that rocket goat," the boss snapped. "The problem is that all of our teams are fulfilling contracts, and if we call them off, we'll expose ourselves to contractual penalties, which I'd hate to do. These are established customers and I don't want to throw money away on outsourcing either."

"Then assign it to me," Alexandra offered.

"You're the financial director," he objected. "You are negotiating with new clients, pulling money from old ones, keeping track of inventory, arguing with suppliers, handling employee complaints, signing off on their vacations..."

"You used to do that, so I'm sure you can do it again for a few days," she replied.

"But, what if..."

"I said you can handle it!" she yelled. "I'm taking a break. I keep dealing with idiots who are so stupid they don't even know they're idiots. I need to go hunting or my head is going to explode like an overripe watermelon!"

Knowing that a woman's "I need" was a whole order of magnitude more intense than a generic "I want," the boss gave in.

"All right," he told her, "but don't think you're returning to hunting. Think of it as, ahem, I really hate that word, a *vacation*. You'll hunt for a few days, and then it's right back in the office with you. I'm not checking those stacks of reports for you!"

"I hope you didn't drag me here just for the fun," Alexandra growled as she joined me in the car.

"I've got a lot on my plate. Right now we're evaluating satellite images taken across the entire visible and invisible spectrum. Reservoirs, lakes, rivers, even swimming pools behind houses. Martin's supercomputer's using so much electricity that we got a call from the power plant asking if we're trying to create a new Frankenstein's monster. We've paid a fortune for all the CCTV footage around the incinerator plant, and we're trying to identify the car that brought in that unfortunate woman, and besides that I'm getting more people on the team, arranging insurance policies for them, and signing off on stacks of stockpile orders for gear and equipment."

I waited for her to finish, then pointed to the house I was standing by. "Simona Stránská, the girl I found in the incinerator plant, arrived here a week ago. She was working at the City Hall, but she got fired because her work position was cancelled, and she broke up with her boyfriend a month ago. That's why no one missed her. She created a profile on a dating site and went on three dates, each time with the same guy. I got her phone number and checked her movements. It didn't cost me as much as satellite images, but I know that on the last date she went here and then her cell phone turned off or was turned off."

Alexandra stared at me, apparently running out of words for the first time in her life.

Great, I could go on. "I've done a little snooping around the house and had a few friends watch it," I said, pointing through the glass at a homeless man sitting on a bench, holding a bag with a bottle of rum in his hand. Then I pointed to a cop walking a little further on, chowing down on a hot dog. "That's Franta, he works the beat here," I added, waving at him.

He noticed us and waved back with a smile.

"So I know that house belongs to a German company with Caribbean owners. They bought it three years ago and just finished the renovations this year. According to the company that did them, the owner ordered a really big pool built in the basement. No fancy modern stuff, just natural materials—stone, sand, reeds and water lilies here and there. The workers thought the contractor must have been eco-crazy, but he was paying in cash, so they kept their opinions to themselves."

"How did you find all this out?" she blurted out.

"Professional deformation. Don't you know what I used to do?"

It took her a moment, but then she remembered.

I'd been paid to uncover benefit fraud, and she'd been the leader of the Hunter team that, after I'd uncovered too much, had hidden me from the State Regulatory Service agents in a safe place until all the formalities were completed. I reckon if they hadn't done that, I'd have ended up like poor Simona.

"You know...I...," she began, but then regained her composure and continued in the same factual manner she always does, "...I have a position on the team. It'd be nice if you...the hell...I'd be happy if you took it."

"That's good," I replied with a smirk, "because I was just about to tell you that Simona's boyfriend is still in the house."

"I hope you're satisfied?" Sebastien asked her.

"The water is at a pleasant temperature," she replied, running her hands over the surface of the pool in satisfaction, "and the decoration really evokes that I am somewhere in South Bohemia. Everybody praises that region."

"We'll go back one day," he said. "Times are changing. If the local nobility can come back from exile, so can we."

She nodded, then arched her back with a groan. Her belly already resembled half of a very large ball that some modern artist had glued to her otherwise slender body. "They are kicking, brats," she said. "I hope you won't quote me."

"I wouldn't dare," he replied, dipping the washcloth into a bowl of cold water and beginning to wipe her neck and shoulders.

"That feels good," she responded. "Please continue."

"I've contacted several politicians," he informed her. "Discreetly, of course, but they have given their tentative approval, under financially favorable conditions, of our intention to resettle Czechia."

"Czechia, what a stupid word, isn't it?"

"Czechs are like that," he replied, amused. "In any case, when the time comes, we'll move this brood into natural environment away from humans. I mean, humans will be there, which will be a necessity given their appetite, but they won't be disturbed in the early tadpole stages. And because we'll also protect them from natural predators, they'll have the perfect conditions for growth."

"And when they grow to a more intelligent stage . . . ," she began.

". . . we'll come for them and they'll get the best education possible," he added for her.

She smiled at him and let him kiss her on the cheek.

Then he caressed her pregnant body with a cold washcloth for a long, long time, and she enjoyed it.

"We have no cover," I tried to argue. "Maybe we should . . ."

She silenced me with a firm wave of her hand. But I hadn't expected anything else. She didn't dwell on plans and she didn't believe in PowerPoint presentations. She was able to shout potential clients down, and when she had meetings at the Ministry of the Interior, officials would fake illness or cause themselves work-related injuries and then run off to get treatment.

"Okay," I said, reaching across the seats in the back and pulling close a sports bag that couldn't be heavier if I were smuggling gold bars.

The zipper rattled discontentedly, and the bowels of the bag revealed the nightmare of all pacifists. In addition to a bunch of loaded magazines, I had a nicely folded CZ BREN 2 5.56×45 8" carbine, several Glock 36 in .45 ACP, a Benelli M3 tactical shotgun, and two UTON II assault knives that Mikov had specially modified—blades forged under a full moon and hardened in goblin blood, and a couple of Martin's gadgets in the handle. What the customer wants is what the customer gets.

And just to be sure, I also put in . . .

"Oh, my God, an MP5. What an antique. Where'd you dig it up?" Alexandra said when she came across the submachine gun in question.

"It's my favorite toy," I replied, offended. "It has an EOTECH EXPS3 collimator, a tuned trigger, and composite ammunition mixed with silver alloy and white oak sawdust, dipped in mistletoe broth and blessed by the Bishop of Ostrava-Opava."

"Great, if you're planning to close a hellgate," she said, returning the submachine gun to the bag and grabbing one Glock and a knife. "Listen, no collateral damage! Anyone who isn't a monster or a servant is a civilian, and therefore a potential voter. Do you have anything less lethal?"

With a smirk, I handed her the other bag from the back seat. This one was considerably lighter.

She eagerly began to rummage through its contents.

"Tasers, pepper sprays, bottles of holy water, holy mistletoe, stun guns, electric batons," she commented on her findings. "And look, an infrared heater. We could use that to dry him. He could die... And what kind of rope is this?"

"I had it made by Erben's notes. It's made of bast fiber and has the hair of drowned girls woven into it. They say it works like a silver chain on a werewolf."

She handed it to me with a grin.

I stashed it in my thigh pocket and retrieved a UTON II and my 9mm Luger submachine gun from the bag. No matter how much Alexandra may turn up her nose at it, I have nothing but praise for it.

I definitely had less trouble slipping it under my jacket than attaching the knife to my belt. Damned Christmas sweets!

After a moment's thought, I also took the taser and immediately felt like a Hunter with a human face.

"Let's go!" she shouted, then kicked the door open.

The screeching of the alarm could not go unnoticed.

Sebastien grabbed a robe from the lounger and handed it to her to hide her nakedness.

"We have uninvited guests," he announced. "They're armed, so we'd better move you. You can get to the underground parking lot on the next street. I have an escape vehicle there with everything you need."

"What about our plan?"

He tried to smile. "The plan still stands. The intruders will be taken care of by a hired security company and you'll move to the hatchery.

No need to worry, everything is ready there and Herbert will see to your comfort until I arrive."

"And you?"

He stroked her. "I'll join you as soon as I've sorted things out. I don't intend to miss our first clutch."

She stroked him, too. "Please try to survive. I'm afraid when our spawn hit puberty, I will climb the walls."

"So will everyone, my dear," he assured her, "but don't worry, I'll be there with you."

While she, accompanied by the chef, ran off to the basement, he headed in the opposite direction.

As soon as we walked through the door, three men armed with telescopic batons rushed at us. They were classic brawlers of the kind offered by security agencies—sculpted musculature visible even over a jacket, shaved heads, surprisingly small compared to the rest of their bodies, and they were determined to play us hard.

But sometimes determination isn't enough.

Even though they had the advantage in height and weight, we had speed, tight space and Alexandra on our side.

Because of the first two reasons, I couldn't get involved in the fight properly. On the other hand, I was able to enjoy the bright blue glare of the stun gun Alexandra thrust under the first guy's chin.

She hadn't waited to see how he'd handle a two million volt hit, and she was already on the second one. She first threw the depleted stun gun in his face, then ducked under the baton he'd tried to hit her with.

He never got to a second blow. She kicked him expertly in the knee, and when he collapsed to the ground with a painful cry, she cancelled his dentist's card with her heel.

And then it was my turn—the third security guard's eyes bulged with shock, but that didn't stop him from dropping the baton and reaching under his jacket.

Of course, there was a chance that he would pull out bread and salt to give us the traditional Czech welcome, but it wasn't very high.

I pointed the taser at him and pulled the trigger. It clicked, the fast unwinding wires rattled, and two electrodes stabbed into his chest.

Whatever he wanted to pull out from under his jacket, that plan failed, as did his efforts to maintain control over his own body.

He was twitching convulsively in a very nice way, but I missed the lighting effects that Alexandra's stun gun was producing. The only effect was a rapidly spreading stain on his pants.

"We should cuff them," I suggested.

"Let's keep going!" she yelled, running deeper into the house.

There was a large two-story hall with staircases leading up on either side, and between them was a spacious entrance to what looked like an Art Nouveau dining room, with oil paintings in massive gilded frames hanging on the walls. Not modern, but romantic Victorian landscapes with sunsets, lakes and rivers.

I would have appreciated the owner's taste if his employees hadn't started shooting at me.

A long burst from a submachine gun bit into the wooden door frames and wall, and the individual shots from several pistols mingled with its clatter.

Running, I slid to the floor and missed an artfully made sideboard, which was blown to pieces by a crude shot.

A loud click-clack let me know that the owner of the pumping shotgun had reloaded, and as confirmation another load of splinters showered behind my collar.

Continuing to slide with inertia, I pointed the MP5 in the direction the buckshot was coming from and squeezed the trigger.

The submachine gun barked and a flood of brass shells erupted from its ejection port. An antique my ass, I thought to myself at Alexandra's address. A submachine gun set on a burst isn't one of the most accurate weapons, but when you shoot blind, it's like buying multiple raffle tickets.

A pained cry told me one of them was the winning one.

"Fire in the hole!" Alexandra yelled at that moment, and a small metal egg with a pink stripe flew past my head.

Pink?!

I immediately rolled as far away as I could.

The grenade exploded just as I pressed my hands to my ears to keep the pressure wave from blowing the stirrup and anvil out of them.

It's hard to describe what followed, but our company grenades are what the military ones want to be when they grow up.

The beautifully equipped mess hall was instantly transformed into an Ostrava pub on payday. The original oil paintings burned before they could hit the floor, and even the long dark wood dining table looked like something they'd put under Jan Hus before they burned him at the stake.

I slowly stood up to find four bodies lying on the other side of the dining room, transformed by the explosion into a big pathological puzzle.

"Clear self-defense," Alexandra commented.

A grenade blast knocked Sebastien to the ground. Apart from a few cuts and ringing in his ears, nothing else happened.

Unlike those he rushed to help.

Lifting himself up from the ground in a daze, he saw their torn bodies and his mind immediately began to flit between his anger at the money wasted on incompetent security with his desire to offer himself a bite of that tempting smelling buffet.

Such a waste, he thought, and his thoughts immediately turned to the house.

When he moved here from Hamburg, he was determined to succeed. The first returnee in nearly two centuries, despite the fearful whispers that spread among the exiles.

Then he met Herbert, who lived in the ponds around Třeboň in Southern Bohemia, and learned from him that typical Czech ability not to stand out. If they were lucky, they ate a drowner, and if they had to hunt, they were careful not to let their hunting expeditions show up too much in the police statistics through an increase in drowned or missing persons, which might draw unwelcome attention to them.

But now it was useless to worry about further secrecy. If he wanted to see his brood hatch, he had to act.

When that guy lunged at us, Alexandra and I became heroes in slow motion. He was like a lightning.

It was clear he wasn't human, so we were in the right place. But the question was whether we were also on the right side of the gun.

Reacting to someone ten times faster than you is just impossible.

While I was trying to shove a new magazine into the MP5, he hit me like a battering ram and sent me to the opposite side of the room.

The impact with a wall knocked the wind out of me, but I still managed to replace the magazine, rack the slide, and point the gun where I thought that bastard would be.

Only he wasn't there. It took me a moment to realize, through black spots in front of my eyes, that he was with Alexandra, and that it didn't look good.

She was trying to keep him off her body and doing a kung-fu ethno-dance accompanied by shooting and knife slashing, but that bastard was just too fast.

I really wanted to know what kind of vodnik K. J. Erben was fighting back then. After all, he was a skilled Hunter—he killed a noonwraith, a revenant, the ghost of a mad mother rising from the grave and harassing a couple of kids and a vodnik, and he wrote poems about it. So why didn't he mention the vodnik's speed in the hunting diary Petra found in the National Museum's depository? His vodnik was probably old, obese, or suicidal.

Alexandra fired five shots in three seconds, but didn't hit him. She was equally unsuccessful with the knife. She sliced the air around her again and again, and the vodnik was darting around her so fast he looked like a blur.

Then she fired for the sixth time, the slide of her gun remaining vulgarly open, and I couldn't shoot because she was standing in my line of sight.

I shifted position, but before I could pull the trigger and send that son of a bitch to hell, several flash bangs exploded in the room, turning us into completely incapacitated rag dolls.

Then a SWAT team burst into the room, dressed in as many layers of Kevlar as if they were expecting an attack from Godzilla's husband. One of the pseudo-commandos flipped me onto my stomach and, with a skill you only get after a thousand tries, handcuffed me.

I raised my head above the charred pile of the Persian rug and watched as another pacified Alexandra in the same manner and the other three tended to the vodnik.

But unlike us, they had wrapped him with a rope from bast fibers. The big plus was that it made him scream like a soul in purgatory.

"Dagger one, clear!" came the call.

"Dagger two and three . . . clear. We got 'em, sir," someone else barked, and then the man who haunts small children, inconvenient witnesses, and newbie Hunters came into my field of vision—Kurt Gromsky, head of the State Regulatory Service.

There's no situation in which I could meet his eyes and say that I was glad to see him. For one, he only has one eye because he lost the other one, along with half his face and most of his hair, when he fought a basilisk, and for another, because he screwed us over once.

By us, I mean Fantom, of course, because he was in charge of one of our teams until four years ago. When that basilisk messed him up, he refused to let himself be reassigned, had a fierce argument with our boss, and then slammed the door behind him in a big style.

At first he tried to get a job with rival companies, who also turned him down because of his handicap, but he got it in his head that it was the boss's long fingers that were to blame and joined the State Regulatory Service, where of course he soon won his spurs.

"Some law-abiding citizen reported a break-in and shooting," he told us. "We were in the neighborhood, so we rushed to help the valiant police officers of the local department, and who does my eye see—the all-powerful financial director and her eternal underling, Artur Klega, beaten by some civilian."

"Some civilian?" I grunted derisively. "That's why you've wrapped him in bast? How do you know he's a vodnik?"

"We were bugged," Alexandra answered for Gromsky.

"As if we could do that without a warrant," agent Gromsky responded, adding snidely: "And I object to the past tense."

To my surprise, Alexandra laughed. "You got the invoice for the permoniks, so the minister ordered you to whip us into submission, huh?"

Gromsky nodded. "When we found out that Fantom was on the lookout for a hastrman, the highest places decided we should stop it because you want to milk the state, even though people have to wear two sweaters now to save public finances and the government party voters even wear three."

"The bounties come from TEFLON, not the state budget," I argued.

"The government is looking for reserves," he replied, "and since the Minister of the Interior is eyeing the PM's seat, he'll be happy to use a billion earmarked for monster bounties for fireworks, sandwiches and steamer parties."

"Let me go," grunted the vodnik. "I'll give you a lot of money. I'm rich . . . and I know where others like me are . . ."

I'm sure he would have continued, but at that moment our UTON knife plunged up to the hilt into his throat.

As the vodnik collapsed to the floor with a grunt, agent Gromsky looked at Alexandra, who had somehow managed to free herself from her cuffs.

Then, with a sigh, he said, "Who missed that knife? Forget your Christmas bonuses, idiots."

"So, to summarize it," said JUDr. Krahujec, PhD, LLM, MBA, glancing around at the gathered people, then briefly studying his notes and continuing, "we have a breach of contract with the Fantom company and two cases of illegal restraint. Am I forgetting something?"

"Illegal wiretapping by a government-funded institution," our boss suggested.

"Oh yes, the illegal wiretapping," the former minister of three governments, honorary president of the Czech Bar Association and senior partner of the renowned law firm Krahujec, Felon and Scottfree nodded, "I'd almost forgotten about that." But his voice proved that he was well aware of it.

"We're not conducting a proceeding here in which you can represent anyone," Agent Gromsky objected.

In retrospect, I can't remember if it was our boss or Dr. Krahujec who started laughing first.

Kurt Gromsky looked at Alexandra and me and figured it out.

"Uncuff them, damn it," he barked at the agents who were chaperoning us in full combat gear. "And go away," he added.

When it happened, he sighed wearily. "All right, this one didn't go well. Let's all calm down. You forget about the alleged wiretaps, and I'll cover up that your financial director eliminated an innocent civilian."

"An innocent civilian?" the boss shot back. "He was a hastrman."

"Unfortunately, it's an allegation without a shred of evidence."

Our boss put his cell phone on the table and sent it toward the agent with his index finger. The latter looked incredulously at the text displayed on the screen.

"What's that?"

"The result of a DNA analysis," the boss replied. "And it's got a message from Martin attached. Yeah, down there, it starts by addressing you..."

"Asshole," Gromsky read it. "Nice, but I don't buy it. You didn't have a chance to get a sample from that creature."

"So the civilian has already become a creature," the boss commented with a sly smile.

"That knife!" Agent Gromsky gasped suddenly. "Shit on my tits."

"With pleasure," I said.

"Shut your face!" Gromsky snapped, turning to our boss, "Martin built a DNA scanner into it?"

"Yeah," the boss nodded. "The request for a payment of the twenty-two million euros should be in your mail. He was officially an extinct Czech hastrman. Congratulations."

There was a ping of an incoming message.

"That'll be it," the boss commented sardonically.

Agent Gromsky collapsed in his chair, his face hidden in his hands.

"I guess you can go now," Dr. Krahujec said.

"Thank you," our boss told him. "Send me the invoice."

"That won't be necessary," Dr. Krahujec replied. "I still owe you for disposing of that witch those sharp-elbowed young hawks who are running for the Bar Association sent after me..."

The boss shook his head. "That was just a friendly favor."

"Then this was an equally friendly favor on my part," the lawyer replied.

"I...can't...stand it, Herbert," she moaned, her hands cupping her big belly. "You have to...stop!"

He looked up from the steering wheel he was struggling with and tried to reassure her, "We'll be there soon, my lady. If the little ones take after Sebastien, they're going to be real hungry. There are bags of chilled blood in the minibar. It should help."

"What about...Sebastien?" she groaned.

"Don't worry, he'll be fine. I'm sure they were just some robbers. He'll join us when he's done with them."

"I have a...bad...feeling..."

"Take the blood," he ordered her, and to her surprise, she obeyed him. "Stress seems to have hastened their growth," he added.

His knowledge surprised her. In the expat community she came from, the circumstances of *how the roaches did it* had to be explained to her by other females.

At the time, she had found the whole thing of joined cloacas extremely distasteful, but she had remembered that, among other things, pregnancy could actually be shortened by feeling threatened.

She finished her third bag of blood, burped discreetly, and wiped her lips on a batiste handkerchief.

The erratic movement of the tadpoles in her womb ceased and she realized they had fallen asleep. She sensed the images of blood, fighting and killing each other and knew they were happy dreams.

"They'll want out soon," Herbert said.

"Sebastien claimed you have a hatchery ready for me."

He nodded. "We picked a great place where we don't have to worry about being discovered. There will be no leaving the tadpoles to natural selection this time. Even if there are a thousand in your brood, we have enough carcasses for them to feast on until they are able to come ashore."

"Carcasses?" she repeated, astonished.

"Yes, in various stages of decomposition. We were thinking of the milk teeth of the little tadpoles," he added.

"You are full of surprises," she replied. "Sebastien is held in high esteem among the exiles, but if they had known the care with which he had made preparations, they might have sent a much higher ranking female than myself to mate with him. And as for you, if you ever carve out your own territory on the Rio Ebro, our elite will be delighted with you as well."

He couldn't help but grin.

"There's a third Michelin star waiting for me in a restaurant I'm going to open in Prague," he replied. "Then I'm going to make a lot of tadpoles with some local human girl. They can't be lured by red ribbons anymore, but when they see the latest iPhone floating on the river..."

Martin's TCV, or Tactical Command Vehicle, cost his boss tens of millions. He entered the payment order believing that he would get it back one day, and happy that he didn't have to explain to Martin why he wouldn't give him the money.

The Volvo FH16 truck, with 750 stallions neighing under its hood, was pulling a specially modified trailer festooned with satellite dishes, quadcopter drone ejection ports, and a dozen Generation IV solar panels so powerful that the Chinese government wouldn't hesitate to offer the boss Hong Kong and its adjacent land for them.

Since Martin also liked his comforts, the trailer's interior wasn't just a bunch of monitors, holoprojectors, and all sorts of other gadgets. It also had a very comfortable couch, a plasma screen for movie nights, and a refrigerator filled with ham baguettes and cans of Master Mind energy drink.

"Do you have beer?" I asked.

He was currently occupied with a program analyzing all the available camera footage, so he just pointed to a plastic box next to the couch.

"Be my guest," he said, and was back to full attention on what he'd managed to download without the owners' knowledge.

"There they are," he finally said triumphantly, and a shot of a black SUV pulling out of the underground garage gate appeared on one of the monitors.

I recognized the garage; it was in the neighborhood of the hastrman's house.

Suddenly, the image changed. This time it was a camera mounted on some kind of toll gate. A black SUV came around the bend, drove through the gate and disappeared from view.

The image changed again, to footage taken by cameras located in a small village. The black SUV slowed down before the intersection and then pulled off the main road with its blinker flashing brightly.

"Is that water on the horizon?" the boss asked.

Without saying a word, Martin displayed a map on the second monitor, and with a flick of his sensor glove, he traced a red line around the blue blob of a reservoir.

"I don't believe it," Alexandra gasped when she realized what she was looking at. "Is that the Žermanice Reservoir?"

A table appeared on the third monitor instead of an answer.

"I checked the police databases and these are the missing persons for the last ten years," Martin informed us. "As you can see, there's been an increase in the last five years. Not significant, they were cautious and they always focused on non-resident fishermen or vacationers."

"Great, so we know where they've been going," the boss said. "Now all you have to do is tell us where they are now."

The answer was a picture of a house and a couple getting out of an equally black SUV. The man's image wasn't sharp enough, but the woman's was better because her bulging, pregnant belly occupied a few hundred pixels.

"Increase the contrast," Petra ordered Martin.

The boss gave her a quizzical look. "What's going on?"

"That woman," she uttered while furiously flipping through some bound manuscript.

It took me a moment to realize it was J. K. Erben's hunting journal.

"Yes, here it is—look at the striking paleness of her skin," she told us. "Also the asthenic build and the dull hair, probably of a greenish hue."

She paused for a moment, then continued triumphantly, "This is a female vodnik in a high stage of pregnancy."

"And what will she give birth to? Little vodniks? Roes?" Alexandra interrupted.

"Tadpoles," she replied. "Small and frighteningly voracious. If they release them into that reservoir, even suicidal people will be afraid to go in for the next few years."

I reached for another beer and gave Martin a conspiratorial wink in an unguarded moment. "Maybe you'll get a chance to try one of your inventions."

He didn't answer, but it was obvious he was intrigued by my remark.

"I only have two questions," the boss spoke up. "How many of these tadpoles will they release and how much are we getting for them?"

Petra grinned contentedly.

Surprisingly enough, the boss was satisfied with that much.

"It's much worse than that," said the chief analyst, placing several sheets of text densely interspersed with tables and graphs in front of Kurt Gromsky.

"I doubt it could get any worse," Gromsky muttered as he pulled the sheets closer. After reading the first page, he realized he had been wrong.

"How relevant is that data?"

"It's from two equally official sources," the head of the analytical department replied. "Unfortunately, I should say..."

They stared at each other across the table in silence for a moment.

Gromsky regained the gift of speech first: "Here, Southern Bohemia. Twenty years ago, the number of missing persons in the vicinity of water bodies suddenly began to increase, and held at an essentially constant level until five years ago. Then the situation reverted to twenty years ago, and we can see the same increase here," he said, jabbing his finger at the chart on the third sheet.

"That's North Moravia," the analyst offered.

"Just because I have only one eye doesn't mean I'm blind," agent Gromsky snapped at him. "It's just that this missing persons count only refers to one place."

The chief analyst leaned over the table, studied the chart in question for a moment, and then he nodded. "Žermanice Reservoir."

Kurt Gromsky picked up the papers, tapped them against the tabletop to line them up, and shoved them into a leather bag, which he promptly locked and coded.

"The Minister of the Interior needs to see this."

The chief analyst gave him a questioning look. "With all due respect, sir, people from Fantom have already got that vodnik."

Kurt Gromsky grinned, his disfigured face taking on such a frightening appearance that the analyst unconsciously pulled away. "That vodnik, Sebastien Worms by passport, a citizen of the Federal Republic of Germany, moved to the Czech Republic five years ago when his company won a competition to revitalize the Ostrava coal lagoons. Until then, he had been moving around Europe. Thank goodness for social networks... Which means he can't be responsible for those missing in Southern Bohemia."

"He has a partner," the analyst replied in understanding.

"And they'll probably be in the Žermanice Reservoir. It is too large for our organization; I will need a police task force and a bunch of cops from the districts to surround that reservoir so not a mouse escapes."

"I'll send in the drones to do a full scan. I'll probably be able to get my hands on some spy satellite data as well. Maybe I can get something out of it."

Kurt Gromsky nodded. "Focus on the area where Fantom got Worms. I have a hunch..."

Žermanice Reservoir is a paradise for fishermen and recreationists who don't mind sharing the toilet with a hundred other like-minded people on vacation. Some stay in bungalows, others live in tents. But all of them indiscriminately occupy the benches in front of every pub that has decided to tap beer and spill liquor, and since it was Friday, the vast majority of the visitors to the reservoir was not afraid of alcohol.

The same thing that usually makes our job easier did just the opposite here, and we were a welcome distraction for dozens of drunks who would have otherwise been minding their own business. Or more precisely, Martin's TCV was—they accompanied the launch of each drone with enthusiastic shouts, and when the last one left the recharge bed, they started chanting, "One more... one more!"

"If you don't jump, you're not Czech!"[3] Alexandra said into the microphone, her voice carrying to all corners of the world.

"It's working," she said in surprise as we saw, through the tinted glass of the trailer, dozens of people jumping so enthusiastically that beer was splashing out of their cups.

"Never underestimate the power of crowds and alcohol," our boss said. "What's the situation?" asked Martin.

The latter looked up from the command console and shook his head. "The reservoir is clear. No underwater structures like water castles."

"Mentioned in Erben's journal," Petra promptly answered the unspoken question.

"So nothing interesting?"

"Well, I found three cars with a dead body either behind the wheel or in the trunk, and a couple of suspicious looking barrels."

The boss shook his head understandingly. "Check the bounties posted, if it's worth reporting. Money doesn't grow on trees."

"It will one day," Martin muttered absently, writing something down on a piece of paper.

---

[3] One of the most popular slogans used to encourage Czech sports fans.

"So they're still in the house," I said, "and since we have a confirmed sighting of at least one monster, we don't have to wait for a search warrant."

"Exactly," Alexandra said, pulling a Glock from her thigh holster and giving the slide a sharp jerk.

Since I saw the pictures from the drone, calling the hacienda a house was pure understatement on my part.

It didn't look big just because it was buried in the trees. But it had two floors, and according to the plans Martin had salvaged from the archives, it had at least as many floors underground. Twelve rooms, two bathrooms, a huge living room, and a pool or fallout shelter in the basement.

Normally, we'd raid something like that with at least two teams with a third one waiting as backup.

We were like the fingers on the hand of a careless woodsman.

At least we managed to convince the boss to come with us as number three. It cost Alexandra a short speech and me a promise to let him blast the door lock with his 12/76 caliber Remington 870 Express shotgun. But if we hadn't intervened, he'd have been scrambling for the lead like he was back in the wild nineties, driving rival Russian Hunters out of the country.

We were just about to attack when a pair of helicopters whizzed overhead. They circled over the reservoir for a while, and then divers started jumping out.

"Police maneuvers?" Alexandra asked our boss.

"I don't know of any," he replied. "This is related to us."

"They're trying to steal our bounty!" Petra yelled from the TCV doorway. "It's like Time Square on all the frequencies. Gromsky's got more than a hundred cops at his disposal. He must have shown the Minister of the Interior that file he has on the Prime Minister."

"That wouldn't make him act like that, he's only a quarter orc," Alexandra argued disapprovingly. "There are worse cases in the government..."

"Whatever," the boss cut off her musings. "They're after our bounty!"

Just as he finished, he pointed the shotgun at the designer fittings of the front door and blasted them in all directions. "Let's go! Let's go!

Let's go!" he yelled, and even though the original plan was different, he ran in first.

"No, no, no," she screamed as Herbert dragged her through the corridors of the house. "I . . . I have to . . . It's . . . time."

"Time maybe, but not the place," he told her, forcing her to continue on down the stairs to the basement. They passed the magnificent pool Sebastien had so carefully prepared for her brood, and the other two, where the bodies of several drowners were already at the bottom, waiting for her kids to be safely fed upon in their earliest days.

"Here! Stop . . . I have to," she tried to protest.

"No, my lady," he told her firmly. "They found us. Believe me, we must go on. Sebastien and I have thought of everything. Your offspring will be taken care of. We are nearly there, please come."

She followed him stumblingly until they reached another pool, much smaller compared to the previous ones.

The water in it was murky and smelled like fish.

"What's that?"

"A way to safety," he replied. "It leads to the backup feeding station at the bottom of the reservoir."

"I . . . have to . . . ," she squealed, her body twisting in spasm. "They . . . already . . ."

"Yes," he nodded, "they . . . already . . ."

She was surprised when he stroked her hair in a fatherly manner, and then again when he opened her stomach with a single slash of the knife drawn from beneath his jacket.

She screamed in pain and tried to pull away from him, but he held her too tightly.

"There's no other way," he whispered in her ear as a stream of offspring rushed from her bowels into the murky waters of the pool.

"The survival of the species is everything," he added when she stopped struggling and let herself be laid on the floor like a puppet.

Herbert put down the knife and plunged his palm into her bowels.

When he took it out again, his bloody palm held a small, shuffling tadpole that couldn't keep up with its more agile brethren.

It was then that he smiled for the first time; slowly dipping his hand into the pool and watching that tiny creature furiously flick its arrow-like tail in an attempt to swim as far away from him as possible.

"That's right, just run, little one," he whispered.

"Only ten divers for the whole reservoir?" agent Gromsky growled, glancing at the pale police captain who had the misfortune of being in charge.

"You can thank budget cuts for that," the captain replied. "We've only got enough diesel to get us here and back, and the only thing I've managed to get a hold of are a couple of obsolete sonars that escaped the stock sales. My men are loading them into boats and will cruise the reservoir until they find something."

Kurt Gromsky sighed. "I'll add two agents to each boat, armed to fight monsters."

Within moments, the whine of engines was heard over the water and eight yellow boats with a dozen passengers headed toward the divers waiting in the middle of the dam.

"When they find something, and I don't mean if, but when," Gromsky announced to the captain, "you will inform me immediately. I will not tolerate failure. I want patrols on all entry points to the reservoir. Have them report if they encounter any Hunters, especially from Fantom. They must be delayed as long as possible."

The captain cleared his throat nervously and, his eyes darting from side to side as if he were looking for someone to help, said, "That's pointless."

"What?"

"About an hour and a half ago, a truck and a trailer with a bunch of satellite dishes and other junk on the roof drove by. It had Fantom's logo on it."

"That's their command vehicle," Gromsky snapped. "It's got enough electronics in it to give your technicians wet dreams till next Christmas. Do we know where it went and who was in it?"

"No and no," the captain replied laconically.

"Shit," Gromsky swore. "We've got to find those vodniks first."

A thousand tadpoles rushed out of the mouth of the tunnel, and a school of bream that got in their way was gnawed to the bone in a second.

It was hardly an appetizer from their point of view, so the wild, unexpectedly born and hungry tadpoles set off in search of more food.

They were not picky, as long as there was enough to eat.

Then they noticed the divers and the yellow things heading their way.

"You'll never get me!" came from behind the open door we had run to, the declaration accompanied by several shots.

The bullets missed us harmlessly, but even so, we ended up kneeling just in case, our heads bowed as if in prayer. In this case, for a long life on Earth.

The boss fired first, and after two more shots, all that was left of the door was a pile of splinters.

The dark shadow that hid behind them retreated in a flash.

But not fast enough, because Alexandra managed to fire a shot at him and there was a pained yelp.

"After him!" I yelled, and was the first to go on the offensive.

I flew through the doorway, ran through two rooms in succession, dodged the corpse of the woman I'd seen in the pictures taken by the drone, her belly brutally sliced open, and tripped over a three feet tall wall that, as it eventually turned out, was the edge of some kind of pool.

I fell headfirst into water so murky that even the water company would be embarrassed to take money for it, thanking my training for forcing me to rip the Velcro fasteners of my ballistic vest without thinking and pull out my UTON knife from the holster on my thigh.

At that precise moment, the attack came. Even though I had a decent amount of training, and I don't mean some online course on the internet, I had a hard time defending myself.

I took three devastating blows to the chest, which left me with air bubbles coming out of me like burst bagpipes, and then that bastard tried to rip the tailpiece out of my neck.

Fortunately, I've seen enough Chinese kung-fu movies to know what to do.

Fighting underwater has one undeniable advantage—on land, opponents circle around each other and hit each other with insults that include their parents' sexual habits and information about how often their grave will be pissed on. But with a mouth full of water, no such thing is possible.

So we fought in comfortable silence. It would have been nice if I could say that a punch followed a punch or that an attempted choking was followed by another attempted choking, except that I had a dagger in my right hand and clapping isn't the only thing you can't do with only one hand.

So I at least tried to stab that son of a bitch. You don't want to know how many attempts I made. There was a little blood in the water, so I must have hit the mark a couple of times, but it wasn't anything I'd consider a success.

After two minutes of struggling, I realized something was wrong—we were underwater and he, unlike me, didn't need to breathe.

A minute later he knocked the knife out of my hand.

They say that in the last moment people's lives flash before their eyes. As it would have been quite boring for me, all I could think was: Shit, shit, shit!

But instead of a plethora of memories, a tunnel with a light at the end, and smiling ancestors with "Welcome!" signs, I achieved enlightenment—I reached into my thigh pocket and pulled out the forgotten bast rope.

When the vodnik jumped at me, I managed to wrap it around his neck.

He instantly froze as a statue. To his own detriment, because I immediately started tightening the noose.

The effects of a bast rope with drowned virgin hair on a vodnik were truly comparable to a silver chain on a werewolf.

First the vodnik's eyes popped out of their sockets, then his tongue out of his mouth, and finally the contents of his bowels out of his guts. And then his head fell off.

I probably would have celebrated the victory if something hadn't bitten me at that moment. It was a three-inch-long bastard with a tail and a mouth full of small, sharp teeth.

I instinctively swung at it and hit it with the frayed end of the rope. It had the same effect as if I'd sent a couple of thousand volts into it, and the little bugger instantly turned belly up.

When I surfaced, leaning on the edge of the pool, I started shouting at the top of my lungs, "Everybody over here! We're in deep shit!"

✦ ✦ ✦

When Kurt Gromsky saw the water around the divers and boats begin to boil, as if some camper had thrown a gigantic immersion cooker into it, they wouldn't have drawn a single drop of a blood out of him even if they had cut very deep.

The divers were thrashing about like they were hit by Saint Vitus' dance, but there was no holiness in it as the water around them was rapidly turning red with blood.

Then whatever was eating the divers began to destroy the police rafts, which one by one lost air, sinking, and the desperate screams of their crews mingled with the screams of the dying divers.

Watching it was like getting a voucher for a visit to Dante's Inferno.

Right about then, I finally ran up to him. I would have made it sooner, but my boss was running at my heels and I didn't dare increase my lead too much.

He had a very sour look on his face. He didn't like my idea of talking to Gromsky, nor my statement that I had a plan. Fortunately, Martin took my side, and you really don't want to argue with him.

"Those are baby vodniks," I informed Gromsky.

"They're tadpoles and there could be a thousand of them," Petra joined in. "The size of the brood varies according to the quality of the female."

"And... male," the boss grunted breathlessly.

"Erben didn't write about that," Petra objected.

"We don't have time to argue," I pointed out. Given my position in the corporate food chain, it was pretty daring, but there was no time for consideration.

Surprisingly though, I got many a nod. Except, of course, from Petra, whom I interrupted.

"We need to get all the people out of the water immediately," I continued.

"A little late," agent Gromsky said, staring at the bodies still floating on the surface, quivering under a staccato of bites.

"The vacationers, I mean," I replied. "If they get to them, you won't be able to hide it even if you blackmail the head of Czech News Agency."

"Those tadpoles," Petra echoed, "are going to be even more voracious. Until..."

"Until what?" asked Gromsky.

"Until they come out of the water. Then they'll be not only voracious, but inventive too."

"We must, er, you must stop them," Gromsky sputtered.

"I have a plan," I echoed, "and all I need are a few cows and five minutes with Martin."

While no plan survives contact with the enemy, mine went down the tubes a lot sooner.

"You can't throw cows in the water because that would be animal cruelty."

"Just dead ones," I suggested.

"They produce methane, so you'd buy two giraffes for the price of one, and besides, there are only pigs slaughtered in slaughterhouses within a two-hundred-kilometer radius."

"Then let's throw pigs there. Dead, so it's not a cruelty."

"We won't get any," I was immediately enlightened. "Oktoberfest is coming up, and since the green vegans are in power in Germany, Bavarian sausages have to be made with Czech meat."

If our boss hadn't pulled out his cell phone, my plan would have ended up where the sun doesn't shine and the doctor only looks when he has to.

Conversation with the person whom our boss called "Papa Nguyen" lasted exactly one minute, and after another thirty, a rickety V3S truck arrived with two barrels full of bloody remains that would be refused even in a rendering plant, and a laughing Vietnamese man sitting behind the wheel asked me in perfect Ostravan dialect: "Whayer tuh, boss?"

With the help of agents, we moved the barrels onto a ferryboat, which Gromsky had commandeered for a change.

Unlike the rubber rafts, which the tadpoles had easily chewed through, it was fiberglass, and besides the barrels it could also hold the little me, Alexandra and Gromsky.

That was important, because I wouldn't touch that bloody slop for all the money in the world.

"You know," Alexandra grunted as she poured another stinking portion into the water, "it reminds me of a scene from *Jaws.*"

"I'd hate to...end up like...that captain," Gromsky swore, suppressing the urge to vomit.

The bloodstain had already spread nicely from us. It was enough for the little bastards to notice...

"I've got them on sonar," came Martin's voice on the earpiece. "They're heading your way."

"They're here," I yelled.

Alexandra dropped the scoop and picked up a flamethrower from the floor of the ferryboat. It was a useful toy for fighting in confined spaces, but if the water-dwelling tadpoles wanted to imitate flying fish, you'd be hard pressed to find a more suitable weapon.

Suddenly, a dark blur appeared. The flock circled us and then headed off to see if there might be bigger chunks of meat than what we had offered them.

The ferryboat rocked several times, and the tapping on its walls sounded like a death toll.

Then the first enthusiastic tadpoles jumped above the surface.

"Eat flames!" Alexandra yelled, letting her flamethrower roar.

A tongue of fire licked the edge of the boat and the smell of grilled mackerel filled the air.

"I'd like a snack," agent Gromsky commented as he used his Kevlar helmet to beat the tadpoles escaping the flames at the bottom of the ferry.

As the rower, I was a spectator, but even so, the events drew me into the action more than was healthy. The ferryboat was no longer rocking, it was shaking under the incessant attacks of the hungry spawn, and in several places cracks were beginning to run down the thick layer of fiberglass.

A batch of flames was now alternately licking port and starboard sides, and the smell of roasting fish was turning into an annoying stench.

Suddenly, the ferryboat rocked so much that we almost fell out of it.

"Martin!" I yelled. "If you've been waiting for the right moment, it's now!"

"The edge of the knot is still too far from you," came his, for my taste, too uninvolved reply in my earphones.

"Eat this!" I shouted, grabbing the edge of one of the barrels and tipping it over into the water.

The bloodstain on the surface darkened and immediately afterwards stirred with the frenetic activity of hungry tadpoles.

"For God's sake, just start it already!" I yelled, tearing a tadpole that had arrived for the tasting off my forearm.

The whirring of the incoming drones seemed like heavenly music. Immediately afterwards, small cylinders were released from beneath their wings, and bluish discharges erupted from them as they hit the surface.

"Mr. Gromsky informed me that there were some problems," the Minister of the Interior said, fidgeting in his designer chair. "Surely we can find some reasonable solution."

"I'm sure we will," the boss nodded and placed a fascicle as thick as my thigh in front of him.

"We've got a thousand sixty-two confirmed tadpoles. I suggest you read the analysis of Professor Čmela from Charles University and Professors Zweig and Hermann from the University of Heidelberg. There is no doubt that the species is the Czech hastrman."

The Minister skimmed through the documents. "That is possible, but the sum is ridiculous," he said, and then added: "We paid you for the adults. So how about, since tadpoles were never listed on the price list, we settle this by reimbursing the cost of catching them plus some bonus. Maybe I could get you into the honors list and the President will give you some state decoration," he added for the boss.

"Sounds tempting," the boss admitted, "except we drove an aspen stake through the Chancellor's heart during the last purge of the Prague Castle. So I don't think the President will oblige you."

"The government agrees with me," replied the Minister. "We simply won't pay you that sum."

The boss was about to object, but was stopped by Alexandra walking up to the Minister, who unconsciously pulled away from her.

Placing two business cards on the table in front of him, Alexandra said with a smile: "We'll let our lawyers handle this. As you can see, one of them is your party colleague and the other was in charge of your doctoral studies. So we'll meet at the secret chamber of the Supreme Administrative Court. I'm sure it'll be a nice pastime for them..."

It reassured me of why I had voted for him—we were already at the elevator and he was still cursing.

"It's going to drag on for years," the boss complained.

"No problem for us," Alexandra said cheekily. "Results just came in. The ripped up female from the house by the reservoir came from the Rio Ebro region of Spain. According to Petra, there should be a colony of exiled hastrman there. The bounty for the tadpoles will be pocket change compared them. So I suggest a full company holiday."

The boss laughed. "In a warm climate and with the prospect of drawing rewards directly from the Brussels fund for elimination of supernatural creatures? Who could resist..."

ALEX DRESCHER (* 1972)

A native of the harsh Ostrava region, writing under a pen name, he has a law degree and is putting his hard-earned knowledge to good use serving the state in hope of a solid retirement pension. At the same time, as an avid fan of Jiří Kulhánek's work and of Czech action fiction in general, he is a prime example of the fact that fantasy knows no boundaries, same as hard action. Alex started writing fantasy in high school and completed his first novel in college, but it wasn't until a trio of novels collectively titled *The Perfect Deal* (*Dokonalý obchod*, Leonardo 2007) that he made his debut in a compelling combination of fantasy and action, featuring royal prosecutor Klopp Yggredd who investigates the most difficult crimes for his king, often involving magic and the supernatural.

The author subsequently used this original hero in a pair of other books—*What Goes Around* (*S čím kdo zachází*, Leonardo 2008) and *There Are No Other Ways* (*Není jiných cest*, Leonardo 2010)—before plunging headlong into the turbulent waters of modern action fiction. First, with a pair of novels in the *Permeation* series—*The Journeyman* (*Tovaryš*, Leonardo, 2010) and *One of Nine* (*Jeden z devíti*, Leonardo 2012), where the world of science meets the world of magic. They were followed by another pair of novels from same world, *Lights in the Darkness* (*Světla v temnotách*, FANTOM Print, 2017), which was published as a sequel on the author's website prior to the print version, and finally with the similarly conceived *Creators of Worlds* (*Tvůrci světů*, FANTOM Print, 2019). In each of these stories, the author offers a brisk, action-packed adventure that doesn't lack suspense, hyperbole, or black humor and clever punchlines. It's just a shame that, due to too much work, this up-and-coming author hasn't been publishing in recent years. But the *MHF* anthology was too tempting not to take this chance.

The Dragon of Brno
Kristýna Sněgoňová

The monster moved.

It took an interminable amount of time before it turned its head towards Lucie Jahodová, and she watched it, motionless, to not miss the right moment.

"NOW!"

Marek pressed the lever of the sprayer, and water hit the snail. The monster immediately retracted its eyestalks and remained motionless at the bottom of the aquarium.

"Was that all?" Marek asked in disappointment.

"It made him happy," Lucie tried to hide that her expectations had not been met either. "He likes water."

The boy put down the sprayer and looked around the room unenthusiastically, as if considering what to do for entertainment instead of playing with the ugly snail.

Lucie hated her afternoon shift. The children group closed at six, and the kids had to be picked up at least ten minutes early so the tutor could take out the trash, wash the tables, tidy up the learning materials, and do everything a paid cleaner should do, except the owner didn't pay one. Instead, the owner incorporated taking care of the premises into the tutors' job description, so that Lucie finished at 6:30 every afternoon, with everything after 6:00 being the unpaid consequence of not having time to clean up during the handover of the children to their parents. It was only made worse by Marek's parents who, despite repeated reminders, pleas, and even threats, would pick up their son after six, sometimes after six-thirty, and whenever Lucie called them, would tell her *do you understand how busy we are* in a tone that made it clear she will never understand that with her working position.

"Shall we watch the moss ball for a while?" Lucie offered desperately, while trying for the fifth time to piss off Marek's father. Probably literally, because he refused her call twice, so her attempts began to fall into voicemail. She mentally berated him all sorts of things, but that was little consolation.

The boy gave her a sad look.

She understood him, because the moss ball was even more boring than a snail, but she couldn't say it out loud. There was definitely something educational about having these two creatures here, though she hadn't figured out what yet. The green orb lay in the bowl, not moving. She watched it alone for a while, but when her head started to drop, she moved with Marek to the reading corner to a book about large machines.

Just as she got the impression that she knew more about the Bagger 288 wheeled excavator than any tutor in a children group would ever have, the bell rang. She got up, said *Marek, Daddy's here*, and went out into the hallway, between the shoe racks, only one of which remained occupied. She opened the door with an expression that clearly announced to the newcomer that the school fees were not nearly enough to do what she had to do for their payer. Unfortunately, the newcomer couldn't read that in Lucie's face, because he wasn't paying any tuition.

"Hello, Strawberry," Petr Schiller greeted her with a smile.

One of the things Lucie appreciated about her current job was the fact that, unlike the previous one, she didn't share it with him. "What do you want here?!"

Petr pushed off the door frame. "May I come in?"

"Only if you're going to pick up the kid."

Marek peeked out of the playroom. A long green string snot hung down to his lower lip, but he sucked it back up his nose in one expert pull.

Petr shivered. "We can talk in the hallway."

"I don't have the time and I don't have anything to talk about, especially not with you."

Lucie tried to slam the door, but Petr stuck his foot in it with swiftness that would have made any peddler of God's Word envious. She ignored his pained groan and returned to the playroom.

She was just forcing Marek to use a handkerchief when Petr limped in.

"I got a call from Ostrava. They called you too."

Lucie didn't turn around. "I don't have the time to pick up calls from unknown numbers."

"If you hadn't erased them, they wouldn't be unknown," Petr argued, carefully sitting down in the reading nook and opening a book about large machines. "They sent you an e-mail, too."

"It must have fallen into spam." Lucie finally stopped, handkerchief in hand. "And how do you know about that?"

"When they couldn't get in touch with you, they asked me to come see you."

"I thought you didn't even know where I was working. I *was hoping* you didn't know where I was working."

Petr looked around critically and finally his gaze landed on Marek, who was smearing snot over his face with his sleeve. "No wonder."

"It's not bad at all," Lucie argued firmly and began straightening the remaining books on the shelf. "And as I recall, we weren't given a choice back then."

"They offered us a transfer to Ostrava," Petr reminded her.

Lucie folded her arms. The memory of the closing of the Brno branch of Fantom, a Czech monster hunting company, angered her even a year later. Monsters were dwindling all over the country, which was bittersweet for the Hunters, but she couldn't forgive Fantom for firing the people from Brno. Though deep down, she knew it made sense—they'd been getting the least amount of contracts long before their cancellation, unless it was to help out elsewhere. If anything threatened Brno, it was burning stumps, not monsters. Most of the ones they didn't hunt toed the line, so Fantom left them alone.

Perhaps the sad end of Jakub Holý, the third member of the Brno Fantom, contributed to their dissolution, because in his case, there were too many monsters for him. It took them a while to notice that his behavior was no longer just peculiar. All Hunters were a bit weird— if they weren't, they would be working behind the cash register at a supermarket or at the Office for the Control of Political Parties'

Finances—but when Jakub started to claim that Voices were talking to him through electrical sockets, they realized they were not *that* weird. They had to send him to the Černovice asylum after he spent an entire night running away from them through Brno, removing license plates from random people's cars because he believed the numbers on them were capable of summoning a demon. Luckily, running with the plates slowed him down so much that Petr took him down in a car park behind a supermarket just before dawn. It was actually the last hunt of the Brno Fantom branch.

Then came the sad months, during which Lucie cleaned the office twice a day to keep herself occupied until she thought of trying online English tutoring, and Petr was going to a pub called Glass Meadow to get drunk, and then slept at his desk until noon, because he lived in Jehnice and getting to the office in the city center was easier than driving home in the morning. Lucie was avoiding him at first, but then she got used to ignoring him and he stopped apologizing for the fact that the office constantly smelled of stale beer.

They lived in that depressing status quo for another month, and when Libor, the director of Fantom, arrived in Brno to personally thank them for all they had done not only for Fantom, but especially for the Czech Republic, presenting them with commemorative certificates and a voucher for a purchase at a bookstore in Ostrava, it took them both by surprise. They didn't resist, because it wouldn't have done them any good; the Hunters didn't have a union, and even if they had, they could hardly hide the fact that they hadn't had a job for a long time. But Lucie couldn't shake the bitter aftertaste of the end of their collaboration. She hadn't seen either of her colleagues for a year— she hadn't heard from Jakub since winter, when he had called her excitedly to say that he was off the pills because he was feeling better and would call her again when he had finished collecting all the license plates, and she had no idea what Petr was doing.

"They did offer that," she agreed. "But I was born here."

"And I didn't want to learn a new language," Petr said, and when Lucie looked surprised, he added: "It was just a joke."

"Haha," Lucie didn't appreciate it. "Why are you here, anyway?"

Petr checked Marek with a glance, then lowered his voice, "Ostrava offered us a job."

Lucie squinted her eyes. In the past, Ostrava would call them in to help when monsters were causing too much trouble in another city, but this was not the case—the Brno branch was no more, she had become a tutor in a children group, and Petr...

"Where do you work?" she asked, kind of against her will.

"I'm a CNC operator." Petr smiled, "but maybe not for long."

Lucie shook her head. "Whatever Ostrava wants us to do, we're not doing it anymore."

"Maybe not now, but you don't forget the hunt. It's like..."

"Riding a bike?"

"Sex."

This time, Lucie was the one to shoot a glance at Marek. Then she grabbed Petr by the arm and pulled him out into the hallway. "I'm done with Fantom."

"But they're not done with you."

"I'll delete that spam and forget I saw you."

"Aren't you wondering why they called?" Petr asked. "You were born here, Strawberry, I'd think you'd want to know what's going on."

Lucie curled her lip. "If there was something going on, I'd know even without Fantom. I watch TV."

"Someone's killing monsters," Petr said.

Silence fell down the corridor.

Lucie watched Petr for a few seconds, then laughed dryly. "Oh, no!"

"I'm serious."

"That's what we were paid for."

"But now it's done by someone who's not being paid to do it. At least not by Fantom."

"They should be happy to save money."

"But they're not. Bodies have started turning up, and the ways they've killed them..." Petr shook his head. "It was brutal."

"How...brutal?" Lucie asked reluctantly. She mentally berated herself for it, but Petr's words intrigued her. Maybe she'd been reading *Green Eggs and Ham* for too many times.

"It looks like ritual murders. Something... about it seems familiar, but I can't remember what."

"Are you hoping I'll remember?"

Petr smiled again. "We had a good time together, Strawberry."

"That was a long time ago," Lucie stopped him before he could get to their last big hunt, a success that had been talked about throughout

Fantom, after which their little celebration had twisted in a way she didn't want to think about because workplace relationships had always been taboo for her. Petr hadn't stopped smiling, which meant that he remembered that evening very well too, and it was clear to him that she hadn't forgotten either, so she decided to wipe that smile off his face. "We're both different people. You literally, because I can see at least twenty pounds that I don't remember."

Petr shrugged. "You don't exactly outdo yourself at CNC."

A bell rang down the corridor.

"Thank goodness," Lucie muttered and opened the door. A man in a suit stood on the threshold, his eyes fixed on his wristwatch.

"Well, finally!" he said without greeting, as if he wasn't the one they'd been waiting for, and pushed past Lucie into the hallway.

"Hello, Mr. Jonáš," Lucie restrained herself and closed the door. Then she gestured with her hand for Marek to come and get dressed. "I called you."

"I don't have time to answer the phone," Jonáš snapped.

Perhaps because she couldn't control her irritation from the previous conversation, she snapped too, "And I don't have time to stay here until six-thirty just for you."

Jonáš turned to her, surprised and annoyed at the same time, while Marek put on his sneakers, sucked in green snot and watched them with interest.

"This isn't your leisure activity, it's your work."

"On the contrary. My work ended almost three quarters of an hour ago. I have no problem staying here if you call you will be late, but..."

Jonáš pointed a thumb at Petr. "I'm not the last one here, so what's the big deal?"

"But... That's..."

Petr didn't wait to see what he'd come up with. He pulled a paper tissue out of the box on the shelf, gave it to the boy and said: "I'm her boyfriend. I waited for her at home, and then I came over to see if she was okay, because she's really not getting paid to be your private nanny."

Jonáš's face stiffened. "We'll see what your boss has to say about you bringing visitors here."

"He's not my boyfriend," Lucie objected.

"Dad, what's sex?" Marek asked loudly.

Jonáš paused, looked at Lucie, and barked, "I'll complain about you!" and dragged Marek out.

Lucie only recovered when Petr closed the door again. "Are you normal!?"

"I am, but you must have a screw loose when you, out of all the possible jobs, chose this one," he claimed, handing Lucie a piece of paper.

She took it and ran her eyes over it, but one side was blank and the other was just a number with a bunch of zeros on it.

"What's this?" she asked angrily.

"The reward that Ostrava is offering. Either I get it all or we share it; that depends on you. And on whether you'd rather keep wiping snot for free or take a year's worth of vacation."

They stared at each other for a moment.

Lucie stood there, holding the note in her hand, Jonáš's voice echoing in her ears. If he complained, the headmistress wouldn't let her off the hook. It wasn't in her job description to stand up for tutors in front of parents and their often impossible demands.

"If," Lucie spoke slowly, "we can find out what's going on."

"Why kindergarten?" Petr asked as Lucie got into his blue Toyota and he headed down the main road to Řečkovice.

"I guess I needed to surround myself with someone intelligent for a change. And it's a children group, not a kindergarten."

"You wipe their asses differently in there?"

Lucie clenched her fingers, resting on the thighs of her jeans, and silently counted to ten. Petr had been getting on her nerves since they'd started working together, mostly because of how flippantly he approached monster hunting, and worse, how good he was at it, despite the fact that he was often plagued by hangovers while doing it. She barely kept pace with him, even though she was trying much harder than he was, and that drove her crazy. She didn't think he could irritate her more, but it had gotten worse since the night they'd celebrated their successful vampire hunt at the Tech Museum, when Lucie had gotten carried away with her enthusiasm, a few glasses of gin and tonic, and, though she'd never admit it out loud, Petr's scent. She just hoped that if he really wanted to cooperate, he wouldn't start talking about it.

"Why exactly . . ." Lucie paused. She had completely forgotten what Petr was doing. Even in the past, all she cared about was how good a Hunter he was. Unlike Jakub, who was a great analyst but a lousy operative. Even before he went insane.

"CNC operator?" Petr finished, shrugging. "I'm a machinist by trade, and this job is so easy, even you could do it. It lets me clear my head. Which I guess I needed after everything that happened."

Lucie understood that. Switching from the *"I know what lives among us and I kill it for money"* mode to the normal world, living in the everyday and pretending to herself and others that nothing more ever happened, was hard even for her. For the first few months, at every unusual sound from outside, she would rush to the safe where she kept her cache, and in kindergarten she knew which kitchen drawer held the biggest and sharpest knives.

"You don't mind coming back, though? Now that you have a new life?" she asked instead of coming up with some creative insult.

Petr shook his head without taking his eyes off the road ahead. "I don't have a new life, just the same one as before. Maybe with a new job, but . . ."

He hesitated, and Lucie narrowed her eyes. "You're hoping they'll take us back."

"You think I want monsters running around again so I can kill them?"

"Yeah."

Petr smiled wryly, but said nothing.

When they pulled up in front of his house, Lucie got out and looked around curiously. She didn't know Jehnice too well, but she liked the house in front of her. The well-kept garden suggested that Petr didn't live here alone, because they never even had a cactus in the office—every plant wilted around Lucie, even though she watered them regularly, and Petr certainly wouldn't water anything.

"I'm taking care of my Grandma," he said, as if he knew what she was thinking.

"Poor Grandma."

But either he took better care of her than he did of everything else, or she was much tougher than expected, because when she came out of the house—attracted by the sound of the engine—she didn't look like some poor thing.

"Oh, Petr." She clapped her hands together and eyed Lucie happily. "Why didn't you tell me you were going to have a visitor? I'd have baked a cake for your girlfriend."

"She's just a friend, Grandma," Petr stopped her, wincing when he caught Lucie's amused expression out of the corner of his eye. "And with her figure, she shouldn't eat anything sweet."

"She'll know you're bullshitting," Lucie whispered. "A man like you doesn't have any friends."

Grandma let them into the house and, despite their refusal, set about making coffee, tea and something good to go with it.

Petr sighed, but he didn't comment on it.

He led Lucie upstairs, shoved her into his study, and she giggled the moment she crossed the threshold. She too had missed her time with Fantom, but here it felt like the last year hadn't happened at all. She'd thought that when they were finished, the people from Ostrava had taken all the binders, either archived or shredded their contents, and erased former Hunters from their mind after the last paycheck, but here the Brno branch of Fantom was still alive.

There was a huge map of Brno on the wall. The first few cases they stuck pins into and connected them with red thread, but then they stopped being able to read it and the map became a rather unaesthetically pierced decoration. There were familiar binders on the shelf, and when Lucie pulled one out—she realized she was holding her breath with suspense—and opened it, she found paper folders, each labeled with the number of the hunt and the codename under which they'd spoken about it.

"*Playing with fire,*" she read half aloud.

She remembered that case—a *plivnik* had taken up residence in the newly built apartment building, and getting it out was a real pain in the ass. Maybe some of the tenants would have welcomed him, but since he demanded a soul in return for his services—at least according to the rules, although this one claimed he would help in exchange for booze and cigarettes, and Jakub insisted he remembered him from the bench on the main station, that he was not a *plivnik*, but a homeless man, and his offer to mop the hallways was nice, but the rent included cleaning service—Petr and Lucie had evicted him without mercy. They only got a couple of thousand from TEFLON for it, and when Alexandra called them, instead of congratulating them, she didn't hide her suspicion that Jakub was right and they had just shamelessly taken money for evicting some bum from the basement.

"Wow," Lucie muttered.

Petr glanced at her out of the corner of his eye, as if he wasn't sure if she was appraising his office approvingly or derisively. She wasn't really sure either, but in the end, nostalgia got the better of her. Those years under Fantom had been...

She put down the binder. "Why are we here? Other than to make your grandmother happy and give her the false impression that you have a girlfriend."

"I certainly wouldn't use you for that," Petr objected, handing Lucie a paper folder. "I didn't know if you were going to do it, so I didn't want to carry it around with me."

When Lucie opened the folder, the photos fell out onto the floor. "Ugh!"

The photographs showed a disfigured girl, definitely pretty in life, but in death her skin was grey, streaked with wounds and bloodstains. Her long hair was matted and thinning because someone had ripped some of it out—it hung around her dented head like silver decorations on a Christmas tree. A bluish tongue stuck out of the girl's open mouth, one eye was bulging out, the other was cracked and only an empty socket stared into the lens. But the worst thing was that she was broken and braided in the Brno wheel hanging on the wall of the new City Hall. Unknown symbols were painted around it, in what appeared to be her blood.

"This is..." Lucie bent down, picked up the top photo and looked at the dead woman closely, though that sight made her stomach churn. "A *slibka*?"

Petr nodded, as if waiting to see if Lucie would notice, among all the brutal violence, the unmistakable signs that the dead woman was not human, but a supernatural being, mistaken by people for a wraith. According to legends, a slibka was an unfaithful girl, but in reality it was a monster in human form, an ethereal woman with silver hair who liked to attack drunken students on their way to their nightly binge. She prowled around bus stops and side streets, and when she managed to drag a boy into a dark corner, she snapped his neck and ate his guts.

"Who did this to her?" Lucie asked.

Petr rolled his eyes. "If I'd known, I'd have found him and take your share from TEFLON for myself."

There was a knock and Grandma stuck her head in the room. "Would you like some green, black or fruit tea, miss..."

"Just Lucie," Lucie smiled politely. "And I'd love to have..."

"She won't have any, Grandma." Petr pushed his grandmother out into the hallway, then he leaned against the door. "What do you think?"

"You're very rude to your Grandma. I'm not even talking about me."

"I'm not talking about you either, I'm talking about that slibka."

Lucie focused on the symbols on the wall.

They looked familiar to her too, but at the same time she was sure she didn't know what they meant. "Something about them...But I've never seen them before."

"Just like me," Petr agreed. "It's like I can't remember the word, and yet it's on my tongue. I don't know the symbols, but at the same time it's like..."

"How come I haven't heard of it? Something like that must have been all over the media."

"The police are covering it up at the insistence of the SRS, with the explanation that it could be a serial killer."

"Because of the symbols?"

"Because that slibka there is the third victim."

Lucie was taken aback. "What?"

Petr tapped on the other two folders on the table.

Lucie skimmed through them. Different monsters, different places, same symbols around them. "City Hall, St. James Church, villa Tugendhat..."

"The Tugendhat murder got out, but luckily the media accepted the suicide story. Though few could write such a litany with their guts."

Lucie put down the files. "*Obviously* it's a serial killer."

"And the symbols are the same every time, so it's hard to tell if they're going to stop at five or twenty victims."

"If they're going to stop at all."

"Until we know what they mean, we won't know for sure...So time is of the essence at this point."

"No one in Ostrava can read them?"

"Strangely enough, no." Petr ruffled his hair. "I was thinking..."

"No." Lucie shook her head decisively. "I know what you want to say, and the answer is no."

"She's not a monster in the true sense of the word."

"She's an evil witch."

"Every other woman is."

"Maybe just to you. And no wonder. Consulting a striga about a serial killer..."

"About black magic," Petr interrupted Lucie. "Because this is obviously black magic."

"She'll want something for it," Lucie reminded him.

Petr grimaced. "Yeah, money. She does tarot readings now. Normally, for a trade in Líšeň."

"The striga?" Lucie frowned. "Where did she get her permit?"

"You can ask her yourself." Petr put his ear to the door, and when he was sure his grandmother had given up, he grabbed all three files and opened the door to the hallway. "I booked us in for eight o'clock, so we've got to hurry."

The striga not only lived, but also ran her business in a 2+1 apartment in a panel building in the Death Valley in Líšen. At least, that's what Lucie's mother called that place. She used to go there to visit a friend and was always stressed by the fact that after getting off the bus she was on the level of the last floor of the house below her.

Since the elevator didn't work, Lucie and Petr climbed up to the fifth floor and stopped in front of a door with a name tag that read *"Madame Black"* and information that the person in question did *horoscope and tarot*, all surrounded by stickers with the symbols of the zodiac signs.

"Madame *Black*," Lucie snorted. "Of course."

Petr rang the doorbell. Unlike Lucie, he'd taken a shoulder holster with his favorite Glock 18, but he hadn't offered any gun to her, though he certainly had more of them at home, and maybe that was why he wasn't as nervous as she was.

It took about half a minute before there were shuffling footsteps heard in the hallway, the jangling of a safety chain, and finally a squeaky voice: "Welcome to my humble..."

The words died on her parted lips as she recognized her visitors.

The striga hadn't changed much in the two years Lucie hadn't seen her—she was still morbidly obese, a wonder she could fit into the frame of the front door, her hair was disheveled around her head as if she'd just been electrocuted, and her long yellowed nails, the polish peeling off them, suggested she hadn't quit smoking. The smell of cigarette smoke enveloped her more than the aura of mystery she must have been striving for with a good dozen necklaces, talismans and bracelets with the tree of life, the ankh, the hand of Fatima, the eye of Horus, the dharmachakra and a host of other symbols that were lost in the fat folds.

She placed one hand on the door frame, making it clear that she was *definitely not inviting* them in. "I'm clean. I have a deal with Fantom."

Petr held up his hands. "We know that, we helped make that deal."

"You helped," Lucie reminded. "I disagreed."

The striga flashed black eyes at her. "So what do you want here?"

Petr pointed to the sign on the door.

The striga paused. "To get a horoscope?"

"A tarot reading. We're interested in what's coming up in the near future," Petr smiled.

"I can tell you myself. For free," Lucie muttered, moving her hand involuntarily before remembering she didn't have a gun on her. "Once we cross that threshold..."

"You'll only get what you pay for," the striga objected. "I've been clean since the deal was made."

They looked at each other for a moment, then Lucie sighed and shrugged.

"Come in," the striga said curtly and hobbled off into the hall. "And take off your shoes, I cleaned the carpets yesterday."

Lucie and Petr looked at each other and both shook their heads slightly.

If something went wrong, they didn't want to face it barefoot. Plus, the carpet looked like it hadn't been cleaned in a long time.

On her way through the hallway, Lucie didn't notice any traces of the striga's previous life—but that didn't mean she had really left it all behind. She remembered all too well how she had fallen into their hands as part of another case, and since they hadn't been able to prove that the black magic items they had found then had come from her, she had made a deal with Fantom. Lucie regretted to this day that during the last hunts, all of the Brno staff had gone half throttle, albeit each for different reasons, and hadn't worked too hard when they could have proven that the striga wasn't quite harmless.

They passed through a beaded curtain into a room that smelled of scented sticks so pervasive that they almost overpowered the ever-present smell of cigarette smoke. There was blue wallpaper with constellation symbols on the walls, and a Himalayan salt crystal lamp and a ritual cauldron with a chakra flower of life on a shelf full of books on the practical uses of the divining pendulum, magical numbers and angels. In the center of the room was a round table surrounded by chairs and a huge cushioned armchair, above which hung an almost equally huge decorative mandala. On the table was what else but a crystal ball and next to it a deck of tarot cards. On the windowsill, colored candles of varying heights burned.

The striga slumped into an armchair, steepled her meaty fingers, and gestured to the chairs. "Sit down."

Lucie and Petr sat down. While Petr looked around the room curiously, Lucie squinted suspiciously at the giantess in front of her. The striga took the ball off the table and set it down on the floor, her back cracking so hard Lucie jerked. Then she picked up the deck, made herself comfortable in the chair, some of her body overflowing over the armrests, and slowly began to shuffle the cards.

"So you want to know about your future?"

Petr nodded. "Especially if it contains a lot of luck, wealth, and love."

Lucie couldn't help a contemptuous snort.

"Shuffle the deck," the striga prompted Petr, and when he did as she told him, she turned to Lucie. "And you cut the deck."

"Come on, cut the deck," Petr supported the striga when Lucie didn't move.

"If I'm gonna cut something, I'm gonna cut you," Lucie said through her teeth, but when the silence in the room became almost as thick as incense smoke, she obeyed with a sigh.

Painfully slowly, the striga unfolded the cards in an intricate interpretive pattern. Even as her sharp black eyes flicked from card to card, Lucie felt like the whole thing had taken a good quarter of an hour.

She was about to protest that she didn't have that much time, even though no one but Paclik the cat was waiting for her in the empty apartment in Kohoutovice, when the striga finally spoke, "I see...a lot of children."

"That's possible," Petr concluded, pointing at Lucie. "She works at the kindergarten."

Lucie kicked him hard in the ankle. The striga didn't need to know more about her than was necessary, ideally nothing.

The old woman shook her head. "It's not work-related." Then she smiled wickedly. "These are your children. All five of them."

"Whose? Mine?"

"No, yours. Both of you. *Your* children."

Petr smirked. "I've been always thinking big."

"Bullshit!" Lucie snapped, searching in her purse for the files. Then she opened the top one and threw it between her and the striga so violently that it swept most of her cards to the floor. "Have you ever seen this before?" The top photo had symbols written in blood, specifically those from the murder in the garden of Villa Tugendhat.

The striga transformed in front of their eyes. She had sunk into herself, but her black eyes had almost fallen out of their sockets. A stream of curses rolled from her parted lips in a language Lucie and Petr didn't know. A sudden wind swept through the room, though the windows were closed, and blew out all the candles.

Lucie turned sharply to Petr, who, unlike her, was armed, but clearly didn't see striga as a threat and stayed in his chair. She therefore walked over to the shelf and grabbed the ritual dagger that was leaning against the books.

The striga fell silent.

For a few seconds, she just breathed sharply, fleshy fingers gripping the edge of the table. Her massive breast rose and fell wildly beneath the black silk.

"Where did you...." Her voice screeched like fingernails on a pane of glass. "Where did you get that?"

Petr reached out slowly and closed the folder again while Lucie stood behind him, knife ready so she could use it if the striga decided to attack them. "From the police."

"These symbols..."

"...haven't been deciphered yet, which is why we came here. You've seen them before, haven't you?"

Shaken striga licked her lower lip, then shook her head.

"No."

"Don't lie to us," Petr demanded. "For one thing, you're on probation, so you are harming yourself, and for another, we're not leaving until we know what you know, and neither you nor we want to spend any more time here than necessary."

"I've already said what I know. Nothing."

"That's possible, at least as far as the tarot is concerned. But not when it comes to the symbols. And while you're mumbling, I'm mentally calculating how much we'd get for catching someone who practices black magic..."

Lucie realized that she used to be the voice of reason for the Brno branch of Fantom, and felt a stab of anger. Not only did Petr have a gun, unlike her, but he didn't even need one, because working on the CNC obviously added +10 to his charisma and intelligence.

She slowly put the dagger down and asked the striga, "Is this black magic? At least you can tell us that."

"That ritual. It is so horrible that it defies the usual division of magic. Was there a ... body involved?"

Petr nodded. "A noonwraith. In this case."

"How many ... How many have ..."

Lucie shook her head. "Tell us what it means first."

The striga opened and closed her mouth idly for a moment, then suddenly froze. "No." With shaking hands, she arranged the rest of the cards in a deck. "I don't want anything to do with this. After all, you're the Hunters, I'm just the card reader."

"If we don't know who we're hunting, it's going to be harder."

"You'll do fine, as you always do. I can only tell you what's in store for you."

"Five children, and that's not something I want to hear."

"But that's all I can tell you. I didn't perform this ritual. You can try to pin it on me, but unless the other Hunters are completely stupid, they'll know this is beyond my abilities."

Lucie folded her hands. "We can make you talk, you know that."

The striga grinned. She had managed to suppress her fear, and if she felt any sympathy, not for the Hunters, but for their money, it was gone. Petr sighed and looked reproachfully at Lucie. But she was fed up with it.

She pointed to the folder Petr had picked up from the table. "It's obviously black magic and you're the last evil witch in Brno."

"Apparently you don't go to town much, my dear," the striga claimed bitingly. "Last time I was at the post office, some old hag ran over my leg with a shopping bag, and then..."

"A real wicked witch," Lucie corrected herself. "Maybe you really do read cards for a living now, though I doubt it after what I've heard, but that doesn't mean you couldn't have gone off to braid a slibka in the wheel during the night."

Striga stiffened. "Someone braided her in the wheel? And left behind similar symbols?"

Lucie nodded.

The striga pondered that for a few seconds, absently shuffling the deck of cards as she did so. Then she set it down and stared at Petr. "Go to the Central Cemetery. Talk to the deadlings. They know everything that's going on in the city."

Petr shuddered. "I hate them."

The striga smiled vindictively. "So do I, but if anyone can tell you who's responsible for the killings, it's those little..."

As a tutor in a children's group, Lucie felt the need to stop next word before it was spoken. "Thank you. See you."

"I would rather not," the striga told her. "You know where the door is, I presume."

"Sure," Lucie replied, and she and Petr made their way down the hall, pursued by the muffled cursing of striga, who not only then realized that she hadn't been paid for her service, but couldn't get out of her chair fast enough to stop the leaving Hunters.

"It's dark now," Lucie said as they exited the apartment building. "We could check them out."

"Deadlings only show up at noon and midnight," Petr reminded her, and Lucie felt blood rush to her cheeks, because she should have known something like that. Reading nursery rhymes, wiping butts and scraping scabs off the walls didn't do her brain any good. "But we could grab a dinner in the meantime, what do you say, Strawberry? Noodles?"

Lucie was about to argue that she didn't have the time, or rather the inclination, but then she realized that if she was to be ready at midnight, there was no point in going home, and besides, she was really hungry. She knew which noodle store Petr meant, and was surprised to realize that she hadn't gone there since she'd left Fantom.

She opened the car door and said, "Noodles."

When they sat down by a plastic table in an Asian restaurant, Lucie felt more nostalgic than when she saw the wall map of Brno in Petr's home. This was where they came after every closed case and hunt. They used to sit at a table next to a strip of running sushi, even though Jakub was the only one who ate sushi, and each time he'd talked them into trying it too, without success. Lucie and Petr were loyal to one dish, though—Lucie to Cantonese noodles with chicken and Petr to crispy duck—so the waiter never asked them what they wanted and just brought their food straight away. They once helped the owner when a basilisk took up residence in her warehouse, and since then they've kind of considered that restaurant their own.

Lucie was disappointed when a waiter she'd never seen before placed menus in front of them. She felt as if she'd come home after her first semester at college to find that they'd moved all her stuff out of her room because she didn't need it anymore. She noted with exasperation that the menu contents had changed as well, and was almost afraid to order the Cantonese noodles, lest she accidentally discover that they didn't even taste like she remembered, and that part of their charm was due to the simple fact that they symbolized a job well done and a bounty from TEFLON to her.

When the waiter left with the menus, Petr asked, "Don't you miss it a bit, Strawberry?"

"What?" Lucie asked into her glass of soda.

Petr sat down on a chair. "Hunting."

Lucie watched the popping bubbles and wondered. There was no easy answer to that question. "Even if... I couldn't change it then. Except for moving, which I didn't want to do. And maybe that was a sign... that it was time to quit. Find something normal, a job that doesn't involve killing, a place they'll keep for me when I get back after maternity leave..." She remembered what the striga had told them and quickly set the glass down. "What about you? When we find whoever is responsible for all this, will you move to Ostrava?"

Petr run his index finger on the rim of his glass. "Maybe."

"Or it was a good thing we quit before we ended up like Jakub," Lucie reminded.

Petr shook his head. "Jakub was mentally ill."

"And it probably didn't help that he was doing what he was doing. I bet that wouldn't have happened to him in some office."

"Or it would have happened to him sooner."

They started eating in silence.

The noodles tasted half like glutamate and half like memories. But neither was bad, and Lucie found herself enjoying it again—the silence between her and Petr was not oppressive, but soft as cotton wool. Time passed faster than she'd thought, so when the waiter warned them before eleven that they'd be closing soon, it took them both by surprise. Petr insisted on paying, not out of excessive gentlemanliness, but out of concern that one dinner would ruin Lucie's finances for the rest of the month, which, while insulting, wasn't that far from the truth. She concluded that she deserved at least a little compensation after all she'd had to endure with him during her time at Fantom, and didn't resist for long.

They left the car in the parking lot across the cemetery, walked through the underpass and along the high cemetery wall. A red-faced drunk slept at the bus stop, a young man walked along the sidewalk opposite them, his hands in the pockets of his pulled-up sweatshirt, but anyone they met might have thought of them as lovers on a night walk, though they kept their distance and the surroundings of the Central cemetery weren't exactly romantic.

They stopped by the wall, checked that the air was clear, and then Petr cupped his hands, Lucie put her arms around his neck, stepped into his clasped hands and he lifted her up. She caught the wall, swung her leg over to the other side, and before she could ask if he needed help, Petr jumped up behind her with a groan. Lucie smirked in the darkness—those extra pounds took a toll on him. They jumped down in sync like water jumpers and froze for a moment, though by this time the cemetery gate was long closed and no one was supposed to be among the graves. But of course, since they had gotten there so easily, they might not have been the only ones alive there.

"Do you know where we can find them?" Lucie whispered.

Petr shook his head and unholstered his pistol, just in case. Jakub had been the one to speak to the deadlings in the past—it drove Petr crazy that unless one spoke to them in reverse word order, they started to wail hysterically. "We'll have to take a look around."

They made their way side by side among the graves.

Places of remembrance never gave Lucie a sense of dread, quite the opposite. She seemed to encounter more monsters, supernatural or human, in the streets. These creatures weren't even monsters in the true sense of the word, because if they harmed people, it was only by being annoying. As far as Lucie remembered from Jakub's first encounter with them, rumor had it that the deadlings coveted a shirt made of flax sown at the new moon, but in reality they preferred begging for cigars and making inappropriate offers to women.

"Do you have a cigarette?" Lucie asked in a whisper.

"I can give you something much better, honey."

The voice came from behind a time-worn tombstone to their right. They walked around it and stopped in front of an approximately sixteen-year-old kid sprawled on the tombstone. Lucie knew that the creatures liked to take on a form that was close to their behavior, even though they were often several centuries old. The second puberty was clearly never going to end for them, and it was even more annoying than the first. Out of the darkness behind the tombstone emerged a second deadling, a pimply young man with greasy hair and a sunken chest beneath an unbuttoned marijuana-patterned shirt.

Lucie elbowed Petr in the ribs. "Offer them a cigarette."

"Maybe you should talk to them," he said out of the corner of his mouth. "You're good with kids."

"What kids?" the deadling objected, rising from the marble tombstone. He hadn't noticed that he'd swept away the lantern in the process.

Petr reached into the breast pocket of his jacket, pulled out a packet and stubbed out two cigarettes. "Would you like some, boys?"

"Boys, some like you would?" Lucie blurted out, and when Petr shot her an annoyed look, she stuck her chin out defiantly. She was determined to avoid the wailing.

The deadling's eyes skipped from the offered cigarettes to Petr and then to Lucie. "Oh yeah, thanks."

The teen reached for a smoke, stuck it in the corner of his mouth, and held up a thumb. Lucie thought he meant to acknowledge their generosity, so when a flame shot out of the end of the teenager's finger, she yelped. The pimply deadling chuckled, took a second cigarette and let his thumb light his friend's. Simultaneously, like gourmets, they both blew smoke into the darkness.

"Nice to have someone come visit us."

"Yeah, we're pretty lonely here." The adolescent slid his gaze over Lucie's breasts. Nervously, she pulled her jacket closer to her body, which he didn't mind at all—maybe the creatures could see through the fabric. "If you know what I mean."

"I'm sure she knows," the pimply teenager reasoned. "Even if she is at least forty."

"So? An old barn burns best."

"Who's an old barn, you brat? And I'm twenty-eight, even though it's none of your business!" Lucie blurted out, but Petr stopped her immediately:

"Word order."

As if it were a sign, the adolescent opened his mouth so wide that "his jaw dropped to his chest" took on a whole new meaning, and then let out a wail so horrifying that Lucie's blood ran cold in her veins. She wrung her hands and covered her ears as Petr screamed into the scream: "Thank you so much!" The pimply teenager obviously couldn't pass up the opportunity and joined in on the wailing. His unfinished cigarette landed on the tombstone and his chin almost did too. The sound penetrated to the marrow of her bones, ripping and tearing at everything he could reach. Lucie realized her nose was bleeding.

It was only when Petr reached into his holster, drew his pistol and pointed it at the teenager's wide-open mouth that the wailing immediately stopped.

"Ordinary bullets won't hurt us," the teenager said nervously.

"If I were you, I'd hope I didn't know that when I loaded the magazine this afternoon," Petr said.

"Afternoon this magazine the loaded I...," Lucie began, but fell silent as Petr put his index finger on the trigger. She stomped the burning end of the lost cigarette with her heel and said, "You're right, forget it."

"Already did, I don't have the patience to talk like a retard all night. We want to ask you some questions."

The teenager stared down the barrel of Petr's gun for a few seconds, then asked hesitantly, "What kind of questions?"

"Something's going on," Petr began.

The pimply deadling shrugged. "This is Brno, there's always something going on."

"Recently a group of nudists caught a bike thief near the Brno reservoir and kept him surrounded by their dicks until the police arrived."

"Dude, that would make a great headline!"

As if forgetting about the gun for a moment, the two deadlings giggled.

Lucie didn't find it amusing. Pulling a handkerchief from her pocket, she wiped the blood from under her nose and announced, "Someone's killing monsters. And it's not us."

"I don't know anything about that."

Petr grinned. "But you do know. The witch ratted you out."

The teenager spat. "Bitch."

The pimply deadling bristled. "Look, our turf is this graveyard. We don't want to meddle in anything outside."

"Whoever's doing this probably won't ask whether or not you want to have your guts used for scribbling on the walls. They'll just take them."

The deadlings looked at each other indecisively.

Then one of them smoothed his hair. "Could you put the gun away, buddy?"

"I could, but I don't want to, *buddy*."

"Come on, we're not hurting anyone."

Petr shrugged. "Maybe. But maybe you're more than just dead teens pissing people by whining, and you're behind all of this."

The pimply teenager chuckled nervously. "No way. We couldn't do something like that. And we wouldn't want to."

"Then who are we looking for?" Petr asked.

The teenager narrowed his eyes. "The Brno Dragon."

"There's supposedly only one dragon left in the world," Lucie reminded Petr. "And I doubt he hid in Brno after that Vegas incident. Maybe he means a wyvern?"

"No, he probably keeps bullshitting," Petr decided, moving his index finger on the trigger.

The teenager immediately raised his hands and the pimply deadling jumped so fast that he tripped over a tombstone and fell to the ground. His teeth clicked together, but instead of wailing, he just grunted, "Fucking hell!"

"I have no idea who or what he is, but he calls himself the Brno Dragon," the adolescent muttered quickly. "Or maybe that's what the others call him ... Everybody knows it's not a good idea to hang around the Giraffe on Moravian Square or to go see what time it is on Onderka's penis[4]."

"That is never a good idea." Petr lowered his gun. "What is this Brno Dragon, a man, or a monster?"

The teenager took a breath, but then, as if changing his mind, just shook his head. "From what I've heard ... he's a bigger monster than any of us."

What she saw in the files gave Lucie a similar impression, but she didn't say anything out loud. Petr was pretty good at questioning without her. "What else do you know about him?"

The pimply teenager scratched under his chin. "Nothing you couldn't find out for yourself if you went downtown. Two or three nights of sightseeing and I'll bet, you'll see him at work."

"Shut up," the second deadling advised him, and the other obediently fell silent.

Lucie knew that deadlings couldn't get very far from the cemetery they were connected to, so even if they wanted to, they wouldn't leave Brno. On the other hand, maybe being tied to a place with none of the Brno symbols nearby protected them from the unwanted attention of the Brno Dragon. Whoever that creature was.

"Thanks for your help," Petr grinned, holstering his pistol and tossing the teenager a pack of cigarettes.

The creature quickly caught it and nodded, though Lucie could feel his suspicious gaze on her back until they disappeared behind the wall.

"Now what?" she asked as she wiped her palms on the thighs of her pants.

"Shall we look downtown?" Petr suggested.

Lucie had another afternoon shift tomorrow so she didn't have to get up so early, but the idea of just stumbling upon the perpetrator of

---

[4] Brno astronomical clock, unveiled by Mayor Onderka in 2010. The six-meter-high block of black granite is cigar-shaped and regularly releases a commemorative glass ball at 11:00 a.m., which is why it took less than an hour before it gained several colorful nicknames.

so many horrific murders didn't seem very likely. "Do you think we'll run into him trying to stuff that Svratka voden into the ball hole in the astronomical clock? That would be a real stroke of luck..."

But maybe the reunion after a year brought them luck, because that's exactly what happened.

This time they left the car on Moravian Square and went to Česká Street. After a few steps, Lucie realized how suddenly cold it had become.

The cold had penetrated her jacket and blouse, pinching her skin. She hadn't experienced such a cold night at the end of September for a long time. She wrapped her arms around herself and rubbed them together, but it didn't help warm her up.

"Can you feel it?" she gasped, surprised to notice her breath steamed in the icy air. Sand crunched under the soles of her boots—then she remembered which way they were going and realized there was no sand on the ground.

"Frost," Petr whispered, reaching for his gun and speeding up.

Lucie felt like she was naked next to him—not because of the sudden chill, but because she didn't even have a damn pepper spray on her—yet she stayed with him. She took krav maga classes for three years, after all. When she was coming back from a lesson, she'd been attacked by a werewolf, and she'd defended herself, and Fantom had offered her a job. Even though the Brno Dragon terrified her in a new way, she was driven forward by curiosity and desire, which she had almost forgotten in the last few months.

The hunt.

"Have you noticed..."

"...that no one is here?" she finished for Petr.

It was 00:30 a.m. and the center of Brno, at other times full of students looking for still open pubs, was empty. Something had turned it into a ghostly place, and Lucie wasn't surprised when icy mist began to roll around her feet. She'd wager that none of the security cameras on the buildings or in the surrounding shops were working now.

"There," she gritted her teeth as they walked out into Liberty Square.

"I see it," Petr whispered. "Although I don't know what it is..."

Lucie knew that he wasn't talking about the failed attempt at an artistic rendering of a clock with symbolic overtones, but about what was at its base. The dark outline of the Brno astronomical clock was rising out of a fog so thick it could be cut, and something seemed to disappear and reappear in front of it.

A sharp scream cut through the silence, and then it was as if the fog flowed into the mouth of whoever did it and silenced him again.

Petr started running, and Lucie followed him.

"Police, freeze!" Petr yelled, pointing his gun into the fog.

Something flickered in it—at first it seemed to have retreated behind the astronomical clock, then it swept past Petr. He promptly turned and began to chase it. For a moment, Lucie felt a whiff of something she couldn't describe, and then she slid across the icy ground toward the astronomical clock, like she'd slid into home base in high school softball.

In front of the black stone sculpture, a voden, a representative of the Slovenian subspecies of European vodnik, lay moaning. He had moved to Brno shortly after Fantom established a branch there, and if he had known what awaited him, he might have changed his mind about immigrating. Neither Lucie nor Petr ever came into conflict with him—if he drowned people, he did it so skillfully that no one found out. But now he seemed half dead himself. Black veins shone through his otherwise greenish skin, his bulging frog eyes were sunken in their sockets; almost white blood trickled from the corner of his mouth. He was twitching as if he had a seizure, shirt torn and a long cut on his bare chest. The wound was deep, but then something—or rather someone—interrupted the perpetrator and he stopped what they were doing.

Lucie looked around, her gaze falling on the knife blade gleaming on the ground, drops of blood all around. She ripped the silk scarf from her neck, crumpled it and pressed it against the wound. It might have been too deep to heal on its own, but maybe water could help the voden. Footsteps echoed through the square—two sets of them, which meant that the Brno Dragon was not some intangible entity that had merged with the fog, making pursuit impossible. The perpetrator was running towards the Constitutional Court, with Petr hot on his heels.

"I'll be right back," Lucie whispered to the voden, but since only his whites continued to glisten in the mist, she had no idea if he could hear her.

She ran to the bronze fountain decorated with Jan Skácel's verses. She hoped she wouldn't miss it in the thick fog, and when she felt the metal grate beneath her feet, she breathed a sigh of relief. Bending down, she stretched her shawl between two rods and no sooner had it been soaked with water than she pulled it out and walked fast back to the voden. He was lying where she had left him, grunting and spurting white blood.

Lucie knelt down beside him and slowly wrung most of the water out of the scarf on the open wound. Then she let the rest drip into his open mouth. As the voden coughed and gasped, she looked back into the fog behind her. The sounds of running feet had long since died away, and the square was plunged into a silence disturbed only by grunts of the wounded monster.

Lucie wrung the scarf on the wound again, then took the voden's hand and pressed it on it hard. "Hold on to it, I'll be back in a minute."

She didn't wait to see if he would answer her, and headed in the direction Petr had disappeared.

Lucie kept her gaze fixed on the fog in front of her, straining her hearing. She reached blindly into her pocket for her cell phone. She allowed herself to blink at the display as she dialed Petr's number. Thankfully, she never deleted it, though she had been tempted many times. Perhaps she knew this connection to her former life would come in handy. She listened to the silence, but the ringing of Petr's phone came from neither near nor far, or maybe it did, but the fog engulfed it like quicksand, not letting a single tone reach Lucie.

She made it as far as to the Jošt statue, but there she just looked around helplessly. She saw no traces of the Brno Dragon that could help her guess which way they had gone, and she heard no sign that the pursuit was continuing. Her best option was to rescue the voden and hope he knew who had attacked him and could tell her. Petr had to fend for himself, at least for now.

She quickly returned to the clock. The ground beneath it was empty, leaving only blood and a knife that no one had picked up.

"Shit," Lucie cursed.

Saying it out loud was a relief, though at the same time she felt a little guilty, since she had to watch her tongue constantly because of her job. But there was no one here now, let alone the kids, so she added a few more curses and then she walked around the stone sculpture. She shone her cell phone flashlight on the ground, and it was only through a beam of light that made the fog swirl like specks of dust in the summer sun that she noticed that the Brno Dragon had started writing after all.

Familiar symbols could be seen at the very base of the clock. They almost disappeared on the black surface, and yet, once she saw them, they drew her gaze to them in a strange way.

She squatted down and just watched them intently for a moment. Something about them struck her as familiar again, but it was as if two pages had been stuck together in the filing cabinet of her memories and she couldn't see what was written on them. An insistent feeling came over her, like something itching under her skin that couldn't be scratched.

"Come on . . . Come on . . . ," she repeated to herself, forgetting for a moment that there was even something around, perhaps quite close, that could kill her.

And then she remembered.

The thought was unexpected and sudden, and it was the only thing that made everything fall into place.

"It's not *what* is written," Lucie breathed, "it's *how* it is written."

She reached for her phone again and found Petr's number. But once again he didn't pick up.

"Shit," she huffed, but then straightened up.

She knew exactly where to go with her questions, and suddenly a horrible feeling came over her that she couldn't wait another minute to get the answers. She gripped her phone a little tighter and started running.

Petr raced through the night, sounds of running steps echoing through the fog ahead of him, but he did not see the one he was chasing.

His heart was pounding wildly, blood was rushing in his ears, and a slow but insistent stabbing pain started in his side. He hadn't chased anyone in a long time, and he'd been only talking about going to the gym for the last year rather than actually doing it more than twice—and it showed. He tripped over his own foot and caught a road sign in his fall. He didn't fall, but he'd lost the seconds he'd needed—a moment ago he'd thought he could just reach out and grab the Brno Dragon by the shoulder, but now he couldn't hear their breathing. He had a gun in his hand, only he didn't dare fire lest he hit some innocent human, though the streets of Brno still looked empty.

He gritted his teeth and sped up.

He felt that he was running not on reserves but on the last of his strength, and he realized that if he didn't catch the Brno Dragon in a minute, he wouldn't catch them at all.

At the end of the street, he ran out of breath.

He slowed down, took two steps, then stopped. A chill ran down his back that couldn't be blamed on the sweat sticking to his skin under the jacket. The chill in the air didn't let up.

The surrounding silence was almost deafening. No voices, no car engines, as if the entirety of Brno was just a theater stage on which Petr acted out his role for a while. And his part wasn't over yet.

Something crackled to his left. He turned slowly in that direction, but he couldn't see through the thick fog. He squinted and slid his index finger to the trigger of his Glock. He couldn't shake the feeling that someone was watching him, as he stood there surrounded by the fog, lost in his own city, confused by everything that had happened... And they were not about to attack him; they were just enjoying his helplessness.

He took a deep breath of the cold air, then held his breath so he wouldn't miss the slightest sound. Only he heard nothing but the wild beating of his own heart.

Until...

"I met a friend of mine at the garbage this morning..."

The call rang out through the silence like a shot from a starter's pistol.

"Shit!" Petr began frantically searching his pockets for his cell phone.

"... throwing an old jacket in the trash."

He finally felt the phone and muted the sound with his thumb, not even looking to see who was calling.

Then he lifted his head sharply, but the feeling of being watched was gone.

He holstered his pistol, then braced his hands on his thighs and just breathed raspingly for a moment. Sweat stung in his eyes, his lungs burned, and his legs shook like jelly. He spat, disgusted at his own weakness. In front of Lucie, he'd acted as if the extra pounds weren't a problem, but he felt his flabby muscles more now than ever.

He straightened up and stared into the fog. It was beginning to dissolve, but that was hardly good news—he had no doubt that the Brno Dragon was behind the unnatural fog, and the fact that it was dissipating before his eyes could only mean that they were well out of his reach.

He wiped his sweaty forehead, turned around and returned to the square. He had no idea which way he had followed the Brno Dragon until the fog parted enough for him to make out the back of the Brno City Theatre. Then he realized Lucie must have called him, and he pulled out his phone, only to find two missed calls from her.

When he called back, she didn't answer.

Despite the stabbing pain in his side, he sped up again. There was no sign of the fog on Česká Street, but people had returned to it. There weren't many, but he did see two young men staggering to a tram stop. He raced towards the astronomical clock, realizing with horror with each passing yard that Lucie was not there. He reached the knife that lay on the ground and the drops of blood that trailed from it . . .

He followed the bloody trail to the mouth of Kobližná Street and up Kozí Street. He walked through a passage, his eyes on the ground to make sure not a drop escaped.

And then he saw him in the park in front of Janáček Theatre.

He was sitting on the edge of a fountain, against the backdrop of the illuminated water scenery.

Petr walked up to him as quietly as he could, and then grabbed him firmly by his coat. The voden bent over in horror, but his injury was so serious that, though he was soaked, he was not yet at full strength. To leave the creature within reach of water would have been stupid, so Petr began to drag him into the park. The voden struggled, flailing his arms and kicking, but Petr threw him to the ground, knelt down and grabbed him by the flaps of his coat.

"Who did this to you?" he asked quietly.

The voden resisted for a moment longer, but when he realized that he couldn't get out of Petr's grasp, he went limp and just kept darting his eyes back and forth, as if wondering how to get out of the trap.

"Who was it?" Petr repeated.

The voden stopped looking for an escape route, bared his sharp teeth and stammered in a slight Slovenian accent, "If you're here to finish me off, go ahead."

"Why would I do that? I want to find out who attacked you."

"As if you don't know..."

"If I knew, I wouldn't have asked."

"You should ask your friend."

Petr frowned. "What are you talking about, you idiot?"

"You're the idiot!" snapped the voden. "If you got paid for me..."

"Enough!" Petr stopped the creature. "Are you telling me that a human did this to you?"

"The other fellow," the voden grimaced hatefully. "So why don't you stop playing dumb and do what you have to do?"

They stared at each other for a few more seconds, and then Petr let go of him and sat back down. "I don't know which one of us is nuts."

"I do..."

The voden sat up with a grunt and pulled his coat to his bloodied shirt. He waited a moment to see if Petr would change his mind and finish what the Brno Dragon had started, then carefully stood up and began a slow retreat into the darkness. After a few yards he looked over his shoulder, and when Petr still didn't get up, with a squeak of "You're both nuts!" he ran into the darkness.

Petr let out a gasp, as if he'd been punched in the stomach by the voden as a parting shot. He understood what the voden was saying, but it didn't make sense.

As if in a daze, he walked to his car, got behind the wheel and started it. Then he hit the gas and sped off down the night street. Even after a year since the end of his career as a Hunter, he hadn't forgotten where the other members of the Brno branch of Fantom lived and how to get to them quickly by any means possible, so it didn't take him long to stop in front of Jakub's house in Žabovřesky.

Only a few windows were lit in the low brick house, but Petr couldn't remember which ones belonged to his former colleague. For a moment he thought that if he had visited Jakub after he'd been released from the asylum for the second time, he might have known. He hadn't called him once, and hadn't even responded to his Christmas card—though perhaps that was because it was written in a clumsy verse and implied that Jakub would be happy if Petr invited him to his place to celebrate the end of the year. He didn't; instead he celebrated New Year's Eve by drinking beer tapped into a two-liter PET bottle in the beer store across the street and watching the New Year's Eve show from 1975. Anything associated with Jakub reminded him that he and Lucie should have done more for him, but they were only thinking about themselves and the end of the Brno Hunters at the time. Then, when he could hear from him, the first months at his new job were consumed by remorse, and he cowardly decided it was best to forget about Jakub.

He paused with his finger over the bell with *Jakub Holý* listed on it, then pulled a set of lockpicks from his pocket. It took him longer than he expected to open the front door, but thankfully no one was coming home at this time of night. The light above the entrance did try to come on, but he made sure it wouldn't anyway, and his actions remained shrouded in darkness.

When he pushed the door and it opened, Petr's relief was almost palpable. He blinked to get the sweat out of his eyes and pushed his way into a cold hallway. The light didn't automatically turn on in there, so he hid his flashlight in his hand, letting just a sliver of light pass between his fingers so he wouldn't trip on the stairs. He vaguely remembered that Jakub lived on the second floor, and was relieved when he found his name on the door to his left.

He pressed his ear to the door for a moment.

It was as if he had been hit by lighting. He was seized by an uncontrollable urge to rush down the stairs, run out of the house, jump into his car and stop at the other end of Brno. But something had pinned him in place.

That whisper.

A monotonous mumbling, an indistinct stream of words, a hissing sound that seemed to suddenly surround him on all sides.

The hairs on the back of his neck stood on end, and goose bumps appeared on his arms. His stomach clenched, and for a moment he thought he couldn't breathe, that he would suffocate in that corridor stinking of damp plaster. Whispered words rushed down his throat like ice water and flooded his lungs.

He took a step back.

Then another.

Two words pounded in his temples:

GO AWAY.

He stumbled over his own feet, and took two steps backwards and down. He'd never felt such fear before.

GO AWAY.

He put a sweaty hand on the railing and tried to grip it, but his fingers were cold and limp. Two more steps.

GO AWAY.

And then something unexpected appeared at the very edge of his perception.

It was just a glimpse, as if he'd seen something out of the corner of his eye, and before he could move his head, it was gone.

It was Lucie.

He remembered exactly when and where—one lazy Monday afternoon in their old office. They'd been filling out paperwork for the SRS and it seemed to Petr that it would never end, that the State Regulatory Service known for its adherence to bureaucracy would send in form after form just to see how long they could keep them entertained. While Jakub had already finished and was patiently explaining to them what belonged in which box, Lucie raised her head, looked at Petr and, aware that no one else could see her, began to silently parody Jakub. Usually she didn't do anything like that; it was more often him clowning around and her letting him know how childish it was, and he was all the more surprised by the sudden harmony. In that moment, as sunlight bounced through Lucie's hair and she mimicked Jakub' serious expression perfectly, he realized that this was the girl he wanted to spend as much time with as possible. Not just hunting, actually, more like anything else, as long as it was with her. But there were just too many loose ends between them and he didn't know which one to grasp, and when he finally did, of course he picked the wrong one, and rather than try to patch things up with Lucie, he was perhaps glad that the Brno branch of Fantom had been broken up and he could run away and tell himself that if they'd continued, they'd definitely have ended up together, but what the hell...

Pussy.

He rushed up the stairs, but instead of one, he ran up two flights. He reached the apartment above Jakub's, hit the light switch, and leaned his full weight on the bell. After a moment, shuffling footsteps and muffled swearing sounded in the hallway, then the peephole cover moved. Petr used a trick he rarely resorted to, for many good reasons, and lifted his case with a fake police badge in front of the peephole.

"Police! Open up!" he demanded firmly.

There were a few seconds of silence, during which his mind whirled with all the horrible scenes he could imagine, but then came the sound of a door being unlocked and a shaky voice: "Jesus Christ, I hope nothing has happened to our Karel..."

When the door opened, Petr wasted no time in kicking it open just enough to avoid hitting the pensioner in striped pajamas who was squinting at him with swollen eyes.

"Sorry, Karel is fine, but I have to use your balcony!" he shouted over his shoulder, raced through the living room where he knocked a lamp over, swore, and burst into the bedroom.

In the bed, he sensed rather than saw the outline of a human body—the woman screamed and pulled the covers up under her chin—but he didn't stop, opened the balcony door and ran out. He swung himself over the metal railing and landed on the balcony below. His heart was pounding wildly, and for a moment he thanked God that despite a year of doing nothing, his muscle memory hadn't let him down—but maybe it was mostly desperation and adrenaline that drove him.

He spun around and rammed his shoulder into the door with all his strength. It gave way, flew open and hit the wall so hard that the bottom half cracked and the glass spilled out onto the floor. But by that time Petr had already burst into the living room, pistol in hand.

The sight in front of him took his breath away for a moment.

Lucie was lying on the floor in the middle of a pentagram that was not painted on the worn parquet floor, but floated in the air like haze over a hot road in the middle of a hot summer. Lit candles hung at its points, dangling on invisible threads. The surrounding walls were coated with frost; the air in the room was icy. Although Jakub could not arrive long before Petr, he immediately set about the ritual.

"Are you mad?" Petr yelled.

His former colleague stood at the head of the pentagram, dagger in hand. He was no longer muttering, but an unnatural darkness seemed to continue to creep towards the drawing from the corners of the room. Jakub brushed overgrown hair out of his face—he was sickly pale and much thinner than before.

His eyes glittered feverishly as he pointed the dagger at Petr. "That's what you thought! And you wanted to convince me of it! Only I'm fine, I've been fine the whole time!"

"Except for the fact that you're the Brno Dragon."

"No, it's not just me. The Brno Dragon is *so much more*."

"You tried to kill that voden and kidnapped Lucie," Petr stated the obvious.

Jakub shook his head. His nostrils quivered and sweat trickled down his temples. "She came alone. Said *I recognized your handwriting, the loop you make instead of an S.* I'm surprised you noticed how I write. I'm surprised you noticed I ever existed!"

"Jakub . . . ," Petr began, but Jakub stopped him.

"It's true! You thought you didn't need me. That I was just an accountant who once accidentally killed a rusalka and is now of no use to you! I know that very well! But the Voices that spoke to me knew the potential I had. They told me I had to show it to you. I must show it to everyone!"

"The voices are . . . ," Petr tried again.

Lucie groaned in the pentagram and shook her head feebly. A trickle of blood ran down her temple; Jakub must have hit her with something, but she didn't seem hurt otherwise.

"My friends, unlike you!" Jakub yelled. "You have no idea what's really going on here. About all those who live here with us. But I do, I studied the books, I searched, I listened . . . The voices told me to kill all the monsters. And then you. And in the end . . ."

Jakub waved his dagger towards Lucie, perhaps just to indicate that the whole world would be next.

But Petr didn't wait for that.

He pulled the trigger.

The projectile left the barrel of his Glock and just before it could hit Jakub's arm, it stopped mid-air and slowly began to rotate on its longer axis.

Jakub grinned. His teeth were suddenly inhumanly sharp, his pupils dilated like a cat's.

"You think you can stop ME with a simple weapon?" he hissed, and the same feeling that had gripped Petr on the stairs took over.

The cold bit into him in full force, paralyzing his lungs, heart and brain. It was as if something had frozen him in time and he could only stand and watch helplessly . . .

"Yeah, that's what I think," Lucie grunted, rising from the floor in a daze and pressing a lit candle to Jakub' ear.

Jakub screamed, the projectile fell on the floor and the grip Petr felt on him loosened.

"Now!" cried Lucie.

Petr pulled the trigger again.

Jakub only managed to widen his eyes in surprise when the bullet hit him in the heart. He stood for a moment, watching Petr in puzzlement, then gasped *finally, silence* and slowly collapsed to the ground. Blood bubbled in his mouth for a moment longer, but then he went limp and breathed his last with a barely noticeable, surprised smile.

Petr walked over to Lucie and helped her stand up. "Are you okay, Strawberry?"

"As okay as one can be when they try to ritually sacrifice you to the Voices..."

"You think he was talking about...," Petr began, but despite the fact that Jakub was lying dead on the ground, he didn't dare finish the question.

Lucie, however, understood what he was asking and shook her head gently. "I think they're gone. At least for now."

They just stood for a moment, looking at the body in front of them as the frost on the walls slowly crackled and faded. It wouldn't be long before everything returned to normal, well, except for the dead Jakub.

"We'll have to call Ostrava," Lucie said. "Tell them what happened here. Jakub... he may have been babbling, but if any of it was true, it's far from over."

"Someone will have to find out what that Brno Dragon actually was," Petr reminded her.

"That's true."

They looked at each other with an unspoken question in their eyes.

Maybe they'd solve the case, get paid, and get back to their jobs. But maybe they'd just opened the door to something much bigger, something they could do if Fantom gave them permission. And if they stayed together.

Petr took Lucie's hand. "But now we have to get out of here fast, before that grandpa upstairs calls the real police."

KRISTÝNA SNĚGOŇOVÁ (* 1986)

One of the brightest stars in the sky of Czech fiction, she is a writer with a unique talent for telling fascinating stories from both her own and shared worlds. It is fitting that her literary career was launched by winning the Fallout fan fiction award The Brahmin Udder in 2009, where she excelled with her short story "Monsters Should Stick Together." She subsequently developed her talents in genre anthologies, to name but a few: *Fantasy 2014* (Klub Julese Vernea, 2015); the trio of unique anthologies *In the Shadow of the Reich* (*Ve stínu říše*, Epocha, 2017), *In the Shadow of the Apocalypse* (*Ve stínu apokalypsy*, Epocha, 2018), and *In the Shadow of Magic* (*Ve stínu magie*, Epocha, 2019).

From short stories, it was only a small step to more extensive texts. The first novel notch on her authorial belt was a noir urban fantasy *Blood for the Rusalka* (*Krev pro rusalku*, Epocha, 2018), one of the bestseller books of 2018, followed a year later by another urban fantasy *The Sources* (*Zřídla*, Epocha, 2019), where she tried a new take on her storytelling and style. Among Kristýna Sněgoňová's most notable projects is The Cities series, including the novels *City in the Clouds* (*Město v oblacích*, Epocha, 2020), *Earth in Ruins* (*Země v troskách*, Epocha, 2021), and *World in Storm* (*Svět v bouři*, Epocha, 2022), where she tackled the theme of post-apocalypse in her original way. From 2020, she has been venturing into space with František Kotleta in an action space opera series Legion, to which she has so far contributed books *Amanda* (*Amanda*, Epocha, 2020), *Nerds and Hotshots* (*Šprti a frajeři*, Epocha, 2021), *Lord of the Mountains* (*Pán hor*, Epocha, 2022), and *Dead Drop* (*Mrtvá schránka*, Epocha, 2022). In 2023, she also tried her hand as an editor (together with Lukáš Vavrečka) in the anthology *Depths of the City* (*Hlubiny města*, Epocha, 2023), which focused on urban fantasy.

Given the number of monsters and beasts that have appeared in Kristýna's stories so far, and the innovative ways in which they have been disposed of, she was an ideal candidate for *MHF*. The fact that she lives in Brno—the second biggest Czech city and the biggest Czech village where nothing ever happens, which is why only a local can write a believable action story set there—played a part in this too...

The Call of the Forest
Jakub Mařík

When Stefan woke up, he could smell the scent of pine needles and damp moss. That surprised him, because he was pretty sure that kind of scent had no place in his bedroom. He thought he could hear someone's voice too, but if anyone was there with him, they had gone silent. Stefan opened his eyes. There was a full moon where his ceiling should be.

"What the..." he muttered, slowly standing up and looking around.

He was surrounded by trees. Lots of trees. And since that was the case, he leaned against one and tried to remember how he got here.

The last thing he could recall was sitting with his brothers. Tobias was furious that Stefan and Klaus had left him out of something. Did they sign some deal without him? Stefan couldn't remember signing anything recently. Besides, it would have to be something about the house or estate because he wouldn't need his brother's signature for anything else. They must have been able to explain it to Tobias, because they opened a bottle of slivovitz, Tobias calmed down, and then...

And then nothing.

Could this be that infamous blacking out drunk which he's managed to avoid—despite his wild university years—to this day?

But then how did he end up in a forest?

"Hey, hey, hey, the dice are rolled, play!"

Stefan nearly jumped out of his skin at the sound before he realized it was coming from the pocket of his jeans. It was a cell phone; the alarm had just gone off. The phone was his, but he had no idea why he would set an alarm for 1:30 a.m. And that horrible pop song instead of a normal ringtone . . . He turned it off before he'd have to listen to it a second time.

His brothers were definitely pranking him. They saw he was as drunk as a skunk and took him behind the house and into the woods. Now they were either hiding somewhere nearby or sleeping at home.

"Hey!" Stefan shouted, just in case Tobias and Klaus were hiding in the bushes somewhere, waiting for that stupid alarm to wake him up. "Where are you, you bastards?"

His only answer were the sounds of the night forest—before the alarm drowned them out again.

"Hey, hey, hey, the dice are rolled, play!"

Stefan angrily turned it off. He wanted to throw the phone away. Fortunately, he realized in time how stupid that would be. Opening his contact list, he dialed Klaus's number. There was no ringtone, and when he checked the screen, there was an empty line where the signal strength indicator should be. Where had these idiots taken him that he had no signal? He shoved the phone back into his pocket.

"HEY, HEY, HEY?"

Stefan froze. Those weren't his brothers. No way. It sounded like an animal, something between a bear and a Rottweiler, and it unerringly strummed the strings of his oldest instincts, which screamed at him to run and not stop at any cost. Stefan would have gladly obeyed them if he knew exactly where the sound came from. For now, he could only back up and hope he was heading in the right direction.

Maybe if he stayed quiet, it would go away . . .

"Hey, hey, hey, the dice are rolled, play!"

Something howled deep in the woods and began to push its way through the bushes so loudly that Stefan had no more trouble determining where it was coming from. The moon offered enough light to keep him from tripping over the first root, so he ran as fast as possible. When the path tilted to a slope, he instinctively headed down.

The sounds behind him grew louder and closer. He didn't know what was chasing him, but there must have been more of them, because the deep, hoarse *hey*-ing was joined by several other voices.

Stefan's phone encouraged them relentlessly, the trio of singers reliably guiding his pursuers. Hadn't it been in his pocket, Stefan would have thrown the phone away.

The gentle slope suddenly became steep. Stefan cursed as his boots sunk into dusty dirt, desperately trying to keep his balance as he ran down. He made it all the way down without falling, but he was unable to avoid the massive tree. He crashed into the trunk, tripped over a root and ended up on his ass.

"*Scheiße!*" he cursed desperately and scrambled quickly back to his feet before he noticed three stripes on the tree trunk.

Two white ones and a dark blue one in the middle.

A hiking sign!

Stefan only now realized that he was standing on a trodden path. He had moved to Czechia three years ago and had already walked most of the nearby hiking trails. The blue trail led above Mikulášovice, but he could be several kilometers away from town. But maybe . . .

He glanced around again, and then he looked up.

It was there.

The peak of the Dancer loomed above the treetops in the moonlight and couldn't have been more than a kilometer away. If he made it to the stone lookout tower, he could hide in the restaurant. He'd been there twice before and didn't recall it having bars on the windows. He'd get in, barricade himself in the restroom and wait for the owner.

Stefan started running again.

Something hit him so hard that he fell off the road and rolled down the slope until a few boulders stopped him. He must have broken his leg; something definitely snapped. Before he could check, the pain in his leg was overshadowed by a much worse pain in his chest as his pursuer jumped on him and broke half of his ribs.

The creature lowered its head, inspecting him. Its face was disturbingly human; only the nose was too flattened and the mouth too wide. Green eyes were so bright they almost glowed. Short grey fur covered its face and a long mane of hair as thick as horsehair crowned the head. Its nostrils flared as it took in the scent of its prey.

Stefan didn't dare breathe. He doubted that playing dead would help, but there was nothing better he could do.

Five smaller creatures scrambled down the slope, perfect copies of the giant that had Stefan pinned to the ground, only their manes were much shorter and thinner.

"Hey, hey, hey, the dice are rolled, play!"

The creature jerked its head sharply and frowned at the pocket hiding Stefan's cell phone. Apparently surprised, it cocked its head to the side, almost as if it was considering something. Then the creature tapped Stephan's pocket with a claw and grunted disdainfully, almost as if it knew what was inside. The ringing didn't stop, but the creature lost interest in it completely. It leaned toward Stefan, bared its teeth, and growled.

"HEY, HEY, HEY?"

Stefan swallowed hard and wheezed: "Hey?"

If he'd known that would be his last word, he might have said something wittier.

Richard Janda was sitting on the bench in front of the Dancer, frowning at the patch on his right shoulder. A picture of a hare returned his gaze defiantly. A hare . . . Why couldn't his new team have a better sign? HE did his rookie rounds in Budějovice, where the local team used a patch with the White Lady in a classic pin-up girl style, wearing white bikini. He really liked her—who didn't—but then he got transferred to Rezek's team, where he ended up with a hare. True, it was a tough-looking hare with an eye patch and a cigar, but it was far from a proper hunting emblem.

"What, you don't like our mascot?" came a voice from behind him.

Jaromír Klapka wore his hare proudly on the back of his leather jacket. With a grey beard and his hair pulled back in a ponytail, he looked like an old hippie who had converted to the Hell's Angels. This impression was enhanced by his leather gloves, which he hadn't removed since they first met. He must have been well into his sixties, but he also was that sinewy Eastwood type who wouldn't admit his age until he was in his eighties. Jaromír pulled a flask from his breast pocket, took a small sip, and offered it to Richard.

"No, thanks," Richard declined. "It's not that I don't like it, but a rabbit doesn't really suit the Hunters."

Jaromír choked a little. "Did you say the R-word? You want Boleslav to kick you off the team on your first day?"

"A rabbit, a hare, does it matter?"

"Damn right it matters. It's his family crest." When Richard looked at him in puzzlement, Jaromír added: "You didn't check who your new team leader was?"

"When would I have the time to do that?" Richard sighed. "Yesterday evening I was enjoying a Budvar from a freshly tapped keg—you know, since Fantom saved their brewer, their beer's free for any Hunter—and then I spent the night on the train. Didn't even have time to pack."

"Yeah, it happened fast with Hana, but I guarantee you that she's more pissed about her inflamed appendix than you are. But Boleslav is cautious, he always sends at least three hunters, and there's way too many of you guys in Budějovice anyway." Jaromír gave Richard a questioning look. "You really don't know anything?"

Richard just shrugged.

"In that case, it is my great honor to inform you that our team leader is a direct descendant of House Zajíc of Hazmburk[5] , one of the oldest hunting families in Bohemia."

"Wait, wait. That medieval noble family? They were Hunters?"

"You bet they were. Zbynek Zajíc got Hazmburk as a reward for saving young Charles IV from a basilisk in Italy. Then when his great-great-grandson killed another one in Palestine, he had it stuffed and hung in Budyně. But it had to be replaced by a crocodile during the Josephine reforms, and that one nearly burned to the ashes a few years later anyway."

"So Boleslav is a nobleman?" Richard turned to look at the leader of their little team. Boleslav Rezek was leaning against the van, fiddling with his phone and trying to coax information from local police. His old contact had recently retired and the rest of the local cops were intimidated by a recent call from the SRS.

"It's complicated," Jaromír said. "His ancestor . . . how shall I put it . . . was *born out of wedlock*, and his mother was supposedly not of an entirely human lineage. Which doesn't change the fact that his family's been hunting monsters since the Middle Ages, and his several-greats-grandfather was one of the founders of Fantom."

Richard still had more questions to ask, but then he heard footsteps

---

[5] The Zajíc family (Hares in English) was one of the most influential noble families in the Czech Kingdom from the 13th to the 17th century.

and someone cleared their throat behind him. He turned around. Boleslav Rezek of House Zajíc was standing directly behind him. He was in his early forties, tall with broad shoulders, short blond hair, and wore a long coat despite the early summer. His icy blue eyes were piercing.

"Sorry about that rabbit . . . er . . . sire?" Richard blurted out.

"See what you're doing, Jaromír?" Boleslav frowned. "How am I supposed to work with the newbie after your little introduction?"

"I didn't say anything that wasn't true," Jaromír objected.

"Really? And of what inhuman origin was my dear ancestor's mother this time? A forest nymph? Or perhaps an elven queen?"

"Okay, I may have embellished a few details here and there but I wasn't lying about your magic sword."

Richard slid his gaze to a bulge under the long coat. Boleslav's gaze shifted from piercing to an *I'll-slice-you-to-pieces* one.

"Damn, I didn't even get to that part, did I?" grinned Jaromír.

"Laugh for now, Jaromír, but when Libor raises the question of mandatory retirement age again, the number I'll suggest won't be so funny."

"You wouldn't betray me like that."

"Maybe I would, maybe I wouldn't. You never know with those inhuman genes of mine." Boleslav finally looked at Richard. "And you, stand up."

Richard stood up.

"Now hold out your hand."

Richard held out his hand.

"I'm Boleslav," his new boss told him as he shook his hand. "I'm no lord, sire, or whatever else this Judas will come up with. And to make it clear, nobody calls me any pet names either. Understood?"

"Yes . . . Boleslav."

"Good. Now move, the crime scene awaits."

The crime scene was located a few yards away from a path, marked out by police tape wrapped around four trees. According to the coroner, the body had been lying there for two days before it was found by a hiker who was not deterred by the miserable weather. For the past three days, violent storms have raged in the Šluknov region and the sky only cleared today.

Boleslav cautiously climbed down the steep slope. Pine needles were trashed around as if wild boars had been on a rampage here, and the trunks of all four trees were covered with blood spatter. Someone tried to scrub it, no doubt on the orders of the State Regulatory Service—which, as Boleslav informed them, had not yet arrived—but soon gave up.

"It wasn't much bigger than a human," Boleslav guessed from the bloodstains. "The victim was lying on the ground and the assailant was slashing him with claws for some time before finally ripping his throat out." He looked at the trees again. "One killed him, but then others joined in. The smaller splashes will be them feeding on him."

"That fits," Jaromír confirmed. He walked around the slope, looking at his cell phone and studying photos which Boleslav finally managed to coax out of someone at the police station. "The pics are crappy, but the bites seem to be different sizes. At least three sets."

"Can you tell what did it?"

"It was definitely not a werewolf; judging by the shape, the mouth was roughly human."

"That doesn't narrow it down much. Any mention of missing organs in the autopsy report?"

Jaromír quickly found the photo in question and squinted at the tiny letters. "No. They gutted him like a fish, but they were more interested in flesh than guts. There's hardly anything missing except liver, but every other monster loves good liver."

Boleslav grunted, dissatisfied. Picky monsters were easier to identify.

"Why he was there? I mean the victim," Richard asked. He stayed on the path and was keeping watch. People might have been officially banned from entering the forest due to trees damaged by the storm, but the Hunters were still only armed with modified CZ 600 Range hunting rifles. Neither of the three looked like a typical hunter, but it was the most acceptable compromise for the sake of 'not attracting attention,' something the SRS loved to use as an excuse to bully everyone. Each of them also had a pistol hidden under their jacket, and if Jaromír wasn't lying, Boleslav had a magic sword.

Boleslav looked at the pine needles as if the corpse was still lying there. "Stefan Haas, 31 years old, German, lived in Velký Šenov for the last three years. His father got some land in the Šluknov region in restitution, but he and his brothers had only returned to the Czech Republic recently. Single, no children, degree in economics. Alexandra is already looking him up."

"Velký Šenov is on the other side of the hills, isn't it?"

"Yup."

"So what was he doing here last night?"

"Wait, the cops have a theory about that." Jaromír took up the fight with his new cell phone again. He didn't say it out loud so he wouldn't have to listen to mentions about his age later, but he hated the smartphone and its stack of useless apps. If he had his way, he would still be using a Nokia brick. "There it is. When they searched the area, they found a doe cut down about a mile deeper in the woods. It's been gnawed on worse than Haas, so they couldn't tell if it had been shot before it was cut down, but they thought Haas was a poacher."

"Was Haas armed?" Boleslav asked.

"Wait a minute . . . No weapons were found. If he had a rifle and a knife, he lost them on the run."

Boleslav stood up and looked behind Jaromír. On the steeper slope above the road, Haas' footprints were still visible. They wouldn't find clear tracks among pine needles in the forest after two days' worth of downpour, but they could still get a decent idea of the direction Haas had come running from. Panicking people stumbling through a forest don't usually take many turns.

"The cops searched the place for less than an hour before the SRS pulled them off and started intimidating them. With a little luck, there'll be clues that didn't make it in the official report."

They climbed the slope, went around the longer way where the road wasn't so steep like the cops before them, and started retracing Haas' steps in a wedge formation. Richard and Jaromír walked on the sides, keeping watch with rifles ready, while Boleslav walked in front, looking for tracks. Every once in a while, he bent down and pointed out the way to go. Richard didn't usually see anything in the fallen needles, but then again, he grew up in the city and came closest to tracking anything when he was at a summer camp looking for arrows pointing to a treasure. On the other hand, the scion of one of the oldest hunting families in Czechia may have been tracking monsters before Richard's parents first allowed him to touch an air rifle at a fair. More disturbing, however, was that all the tracks Boleslav has found so far belonged to Haas. Whatever had killed him moved through the woods carefully enough that the rain covered its presence.

"How long till the SRS shows up?" Richard asked. While talking would scare off regular game, talking now might instead attract monsters and save them some legwork.

"My guess is tomorrow morning," Jaromír replied. "Boris isn't the youngest anymore, and it takes a while to get him ready."

"Boris?"

"You don't know Boris? Oh, that's right, you started in Budějovice, there's not much work for him there," Jaromír laughed. "Boris is the best agent the SRS's ever had. Always ready. Never complains. He's never said a bad word about the Hunters. And if you give him some whipped cream, he'll even let you scratch his head."

"Scratch his . . . what?"

Boleslav sighed again. Richard already noticed that this particular sigh was reserved for Jaromír. "Boris is a bear," he replied without turning around. "Every time something happens in the mountains, the SRS brings him in and lets him run around a bit. Boris roars loudly a few times, scares off the mushroom pickers and takes a shit in the middle of the main hiking trail. The SRS airs a report about a bear sighting and the locals stop going in the woods for a few days. For the last couple of years, they've been also deploying a cougar that supposedly escaped from its owner, but that one runs away for real every once in a while."

Richard shook his head in amusement. As he did so, out of the corner of his eye he saw something glistening in the moss.

"I've got something," he told the others and went to inspect it. It was a cell phone. It looked expensive, but it was covered in so many scratches that its current price would be in cents by now. Richard picked it up and showed it to Boleslav. "Couldn't it belong to Haas?"

Jaromír took the cell phone and turned it over in his hands. "I wouldn't be surprised. From the scratches, it looks like it was held by something with sharp claws. It probably liked the way it glistened, but then it lost interest." He tried to turn the phone on. The scratched screen displayed a German prompt for a code, and then the battery died and the phone shut down.

"Take it," Boleslav said. "If we don't find anything better, Martin can tell you how to crack it open. Maybe the guy took a picture of our monster before he realized he'd better run away from it."

"Yeah, right," Jaromír grumbled, shoving the phone in his pocket. He had no doubt that their techno-mage could get in it, but Martin was in Ostrava right now, which meant that Jaromír would have to do it himself while Martin would instruct him through a call. Martin, however, lived under the assumption that everyone understood his technical gibberish, and he could describe the simple hammering of a nail in such a crazy way that even a professional carpenter would stare at him cluelessly.

Boleslav led them another three hundred meters further before he stopped and got down on one knee. "Do you see it too, Jaromír?"

"Yeah," Jaromír nodded, though he didn't look like he would be able to expand on that sentence and add what he was supposed to be seeing. "How about you, rookie?"

"I don't see anything," Richard admitted truthfully.

Boleslav pointed to a tiny depression in the pine needles and moss. "Haas was lying there. On his back. See that dent? That's where he leaned on his hand before he stood up. And then he took a few slow steps, so he still felt safe. Which leads us to an interesting question."

Boleslav looked at Richard. He wasn't surprised. It was only a matter of time before the new team leader started testing him. He outright dismissed the most obvious question: why Haas would be lying in the woods at night. It took him a moment to figure it out.

"We didn't see any lost weapons. If he was attacked here, he must have lost them on the way to the Dancer."

"Exactly," Boleslav agreed. "Not only that, we didn't even see that doe he supposedly killed. Either someone was here with him, or the doe was killed by someone else."

"Another victim?"

"I wouldn't be surprised. We'd better search the place properly. They must be somewhere nearby. Haas would've run immediately if someone else was being murdered on the other side of the hill."

Boleslav stood up, looked around again, and then pointed to some bushes in the distance. "Jaromír, go check there. Those branches look like they broke off recently, and some of those shrubs were uprooted. Richard, you go to the other side. I'll try to find some tracks. That bastard must've left something behind."

They split up. This deep in the woods, they could drop all pretense and, with the exception of the crouching Boleslav, advance with their rifles ready to fire. Richard walked around the pile of stones, stopped at the edge of the slope, and looked around. It was all spruce, moss and an occasional old fallen tree; the only bright color in sight were red toadstools. He didn't even find that damn doe.

"I've got something." Jaromír pulled a long hair out of the shrubs. Black, thick and good forty centimeters long. "And I see a few shorter ones." He sniffed the hair lightly and ran it between his fingers. "Gentlemen, we have a winner. Only heykals have a mane like this."

"A pack of heykals who've had a taste of human flesh." Boleslav cursed under his breath. "Once they start, they won't stop."

There was a whole separate lecture about heykals during the training, although Richard thought they didn't deserve such attention. They mostly stayed away from humans, had no special abilities, there weren't many left, and the rewards TEFLON paid for them were among the significantly smaller ones. They were, however, an endemite of Czechia, and all Hunters loved stories about monsters unknown to other countries.

Officially, they were classified as Fey, a broad category of intelligent monsters that could often successfully impersonate people, but heykals were closer to animals than humans. The most popular theory was that the Fey had released them in the Bohemian Basin as an experiment during the ancient wars with elves, but that heykals turned out to be too uncontrollable. They ruled the night forests till Middle Ages, when technological advances stopped their rampage. Crossbows, and later firearms, slowly turned the tide in favor of humans, and the heykals, who could live up to nearly two hundred years, quickly realized that such armed people were best avoided. The last major clash between humans and heykals occurred in late 1920s, when an artillery range was established in Brdy Mountains, the result of which was complete extermination of local heykals.

These days heykals lived in the most remote mountain areas, sleeping in caves or dug-out burrows during the day and hunting overpopulated boars and deer during the night. When humans were attacked, it was usually by an old outcast or by an angry young male who lost a fight with his alpha and stayed alive. Then there were the rare cases when someone wandered through the woods at night and hollered "Hey!" which happened to sound just like a challenge to a fight that the highly territorial heykals couldn't refuse. Under the communist regime, a few border guards paid the highest price for this.

But a whole pack attacking . . . that hasn't happened in decades.

"Maybe they moved here after the forest fire in the Giants Mountains," Jaromír suggested as they returned to the parking lot near the Dancer. It was too late to look for the heykals' den; the sun would set in less than four hours. Hunting nocturnal creatures at night was too risky. "The pack must have moved on and now it's consolidating its position in new territory."

"I don't think so." Boleslav shook his head. "That fire in the Giant Mountains happened last year, so they would have had one wintering over by now. Something must have provoked them."

"Or someone," Jaromír added. "We still don't know who killed that doe."

They eventually found the gnawed animal near Haas's semi-final resting place. It was lying in a shallow depression where it couldn't be seen from a distance, but that didn't stop the smell of blood from spreading. Even Boleslav didn't find any traces there.

Of course, the team mascot had to be on the van too, although the painter decided to be more creative this time. This hare had muscles like it grew up in a bodybuilder's nutritional supplement shop, was spitting fire and had a half-naked Amazon on its back to which even Frank Frazetta would nod approvingly. Richard suspected that Jaromír, rather than Boleslav, was behind this original concept.

Once they were in the van, Boleslav pulled out his cell phone and called Fantom.

"Alexandra, it's Boleslav. I need you to do something for me."

"*You and all the other Hunters in the field,*" Alexandra replied, still bitter that Libor made her the vice-president few years back, which was a fancy way to say that he'd dumped all of the company paperwork on her. "*I'm assuming it's not physical assistance.*"

"Oh, come on, you know that if I ever need to blow something up, I'll only call you. Did you forget about Kosov?"

"*That was two years ago, Boleslav.*"

"That's true, but the locals were so impressed by your explosion that the mayors of all nearby villages have to keep reassuring them that mining won't be resumed."

Back then, a *skalnik*, essentially a naturally formed golem, took up residence in the abandoned Kosov quarry. Since shooting at a moving pile of rocks was pointless, Boleslav enlisted the help of Alexandra, a notorious lover of explosives of all types. The resulting blast was so powerful that gravel from the skalnik rained down as far away as Hradec Králové, a town situated a few miles away.

"Oh, the good old days," Alexandra sighed wistfully. "All right, so what do you need from me?"

"First and foremost, I'm reporting that a pack of heykals is behind that attack. Since we're near the German border, they might have their burrows on the other side, so I need a cross-border hunting permit for our newbie. Also, let the Grimms know we might show up there, so they don't think we're stepping on their toes."

"I'll take care of it. What else?"

"We found the victim's smartphone in the woods. I need Martin to coach Jaromír on how to access it."

"I'm sure Jaromír is looking forward to that conversation."

"He is so excited that he's not been talking about anything else for the last hour."

"I'll tell him to give Jaromír a call. Is that all?"

"And I need to find out which lands the Haas family owns or used to own around these parts in the last hundred and fifty years."

Alexandra's voice grew colder by another few degrees. "In other words, you're asking me to dig through crappy scans of land registry from the Austro-Hungarian era."

"Look, it's not my fault. Haas was killed by a pack with one very large male, maybe even an alpha, so it must have been over a hundred years old. If it recognized Haas by scent as a descendant of a local land owner, they might have moved to the newly conquered territory. You know how territorial those bastards are."

"Well, I'm looking forward to it about as much as Jaromír is looking forward to Martin's instructions."

"Look on the bright side. Since a whole pack was involved, we will have to wipe out an entire clan and destroy their burrows. I've heard they tend to be very deep, well reinforced, and require a lot of explosives to destroy."

"Why didn't you start with that instead of burying me in land books?" Alexandra cheered up. "I'll try to find it for you as soon as possible, but I can't guarantee it'd be today."

"Thanks."

Boleslav hung up and patted the driver's armrest. "You'll hear from Martin."

"So no more phone calls for now?" Jaromír asked.

"For now," Boleslav confirmed. Jaromír immediately reached for the player, but Boleslav stopped him before he could select a playlist. "But if memory serves me well, I'm choosing the music today."

"Oh, come on. We listened to those little girls of yours all the way here. I'm sure the rookie would appreciate a little change too. Isn't that right, Richard? Would you like some proper metal?"

"Don't drag Richard into this, he can have his pick tomorrow," Boleslav stopped him. "Put on *Rock a Little* by Stevie Nicks."

"Girly rock," Jaromír grumbled, but did as told.

Boleslav leaned back, listened in silence for a moment, and then he looked at Richard. "Are you just going to watch, or do you want to touch too?"

Richard tore his eyes away from Boleslav's belt. "What? I ... I didn't mean to ..."

"See what you've done, Jaromír?" Boleslav sighed, though this time it sounded overly theatrical. "He can't even talk to me normally."

"Look, you're already punishing me with *the rocker* here, so how about you guys work it out yourselves and leave me out of it?"

Boleslav unbuttoned his coat, unbuckled the sheath from his belt, and handed it to over. Richard was expecting a classic sword, perhaps with just a little extravagant hilt, but the scabbard was too wide for that and the hilt was made of plain wood. When he pulled it out, it turned out to be a machete. He noticed the symbols carved into the blade and burned into the smoothed hilt. Some looked familiar, but others he didn't recognize in the slightest.

"Is it really ... magical?"

"Define magical." Boleslav shrugged. "My grandfather brought it from Cuba in the 60's when something was killing Czechoslovakian workers building a cement factory there. The local soldiers and our government Hunters failed so spectacularly that the commies had no choice but to come begging to Libor's grandfather because they didn't want to embarrass themselves internationally. Fantom had been shut down for almost twenty years by then; the communist regime would never have allowed so many armed people with undesirable opinions.

But he negotiated a special deal with them to unofficially restart the company under state supervision.

My grandfather, in his search for the source of the monsters, met a local houngan, a voodoo priest, who told him that he was hunting a *baccoo*, a half-wooden creature working for a vengeful Batista supporter, and even gave him a blessed machete, because that bastard pissed him too. I don't know if it's magical, but it worked on the *baccoo*. Two years later my grandfather had it blessed by a dervish in Syria and since then he, my dad, and I have added the blessings of twenty-one holy men and women from all over the world, and I've yet to meet something it couldn't decapitate."

With almost sacred awe, Richard tucked the machete back in its sheath and returned it to Boleslav. He was clipping it back onto his belt when the van came to an abrupt stop.

At the intersection, an old Škoda car pulled in front of them, its owner leaning out the window and yelling something at Jaromír. His words may have been drowned out by Stevie Nicks, who had just conveniently repeated that she can't wait, but the content was easy to guess.

Jaromír listened to him for a moment before calmly pulling off his glove and showing the driver a middle finger so scarred it looked like a souvenir from a mummy. Early in his Hunter's career, he had encountered a *fayermon* near Olomouc, and when he drowned it in a trough behind a cowshed, he got grave burns on both hands. The eyes of the Škoda driver bulged, and then he stepped on the gas and disappeared as fast as the thirty-year-old car could. Jaromír slowly pulled his glove back on, winked at Richard, and started off again toward Mikulášovice.

When they wanted to enjoy a long-delayed lunch in Mikulášovice, they were welcomed by such a hostile mood inside the restaurant that they opted for the outside seating. Either the driver of the old wreck managed to drive around the whole village and thoroughly slandered them, or the locals downright hated strangers who didn't look like tourists. Richard felt like he was in one of those horror towns in America, where every outsider was seen as an intruder or a potential sacrifice to the local dark deity.

Were there cults that worshipped heykals? Richard hoped for the opposite, but human stupidity had no limits.

They were sitting by one of the outside tables for nearly twenty minutes before the waitress decided they weren't leaving and came to ask them what they wanted to drink. Then she wrote down their order, reluctantly supplied a menu from which they picked something right away just to be on the safe side, and her departure marked the beginning of another long wait.

Boleslav, who meanwhile got an email with the first bits of information from Alexandra, began to mark the Haas' lands on a map. Since the heykals would not move into fields, he focused on forests and marked six small plots in the vicinity of Mikulášovice, Velký Šenov and Vilémov. At first glance it was clear that the small bits of land scattered around weren't all that the Haas family had owned in the past, but only the crumbs given to back them by a restitution court. Alexandra promised to deliver the older data soon, and as a consolation prize, she sent them the Haas brothers' contact info. Boleslav called each of them three times, but neither answered.

Jaromír got an email too, though it didn't make him happy at all. Martin was preparing for a mission and didn't have time for a phone call, so he sent Jaromír an app of his own making and some "simple" instructions on how to hack the phone they found. Which meant that Jaromír has been spending the last twenty minutes threatening the two cable-connected smartphones and thoroughly cursing Martin, Haas, and the manufacturers of both devices.

"How's it going?" asked Boleslav after another futile attempt to contact Klaus Haas.

"How can it possibly go?" Jaromír growled, tapping the touchscreen of phone furiously like it was a fishbowl with a deaf fish in it. "So far and I managed was to feed that thing half my battery, and Martin's app keeps telling me to wait. Apparently, I'm not the first person to play with this piece of crap. Well, if I wait another half an hour, my phone will die and then the rookie can try it."

The waitress came out of the restaurant, slammed three small, overly foaming mugs of beer on the table without a word, and disappeared before they could comment on the quality of her service.

"Are they always so hostile here?" Richard asked.

Boleslav shrugged. "So far we had no problems with anyone in the Šluknov region. I think we even stopped by to eat here before, and I don't remember such attitude."

"Maybe they're all bothered by the closure of the Dancer?" Jaromír suggested, before checking that the cable connecting the phones was firmly seated in both sockets. "It won't do the local tourism business much good."

"I doubt they'd make such a fuss over—"

"You should be ashamed!"

The three of them looked in surprise at a scowling fat granny with pastel-dyed hair who had come up to their table and was pointing her finger at them menacingly. Two other women stayed in front of the seating area, nodding in agreement.

"What?" Jaromír blurted out.

The extended finger, as if it heard him, immediately pointed at his nose.

"Especially you, sir!" snapped the granny. "At your age you should be more mature!"

Jaromír narrowed his eyes. He hated reminders of his age. On the other hand, the decent chance that he was older than all the hags present gave him a nice excuse to ditch the "honor your elders" rule, which such lecturing grandmothers often relied on. He smiled brightly at her.

"But you and your squadron matured like milk forgotten in the sun," he said loudly enough for her close support to hear it.

"What . . . what?!"

The granny was about to start a tirade in response when Jaromír pulled off his glove, flipped her a scarred bird, and derailed her the same way as he'd done with the driver they'd met on the road. The granny opened and closed her mouth like a half-choked fish a few times before turning around and quickly shuffling away. The remaining pensioners took her between them and led her away while trying to figure out a way to complain about someone who could no longer be called "a youngster these days."

"Did you see that? Unbelievable." Jaromír shook his head as he put on his glove.

At that moment, the waitress came out of the restaurant and threw plates with the food they ordered in front of everyone. Jaromír's plate landed so hard that some of the sauce and rice splashed on the table; a meat roll nearly followed.

That was the last straw.

"That's enough!" Jaromír exploded. "Would you kindly explain what is it you've got against us? Why does everyone here treat us as if we were lepers?"

The waitress pressed her lips together tightly and was about to retreat into the restaurant, but Jaromír's behavior was clearly the last straw for her as well. "And what were you thinking? That we were going to welcome some techno heads here with open arms?"

The Hunters exchanged puzzled looks. "Techno heads?"

"Try that on someone else!" spat the waitress. "Everyone here knows about that little party of yours!"

"Miss, we're no techno heads," Richard quickly interjected, noticing that Jaromír was about to use his hand argument again. The last thing he wanted right now was to be thrown out of the restaurant when the steak he had ordered was finally in front of him. "We're from the State Veterinary Administration."

The waitress looked at Jaromír's clothes and then at the van with its dragon rabbit painting. "The State Veterinary Administration?"

"Yes, exactly," Boleslav nodded. "Maybe you've heard about the bear near the Dancer?"

"Yeah, the guys have been—" The waitress swallowed hard as she realized that the trio chased outside weren't any quiet hours disturbers, but customers who would be deciding the size of her tip. "Oh. Gentlemen, I'm terribly sorry. I thought you were with them. I . . . would you like to order something else?"

"Nothing yet," Boleslav replied soothingly, letting her retreat into the restaurant. A few regulars inside looked like they wanted to get up and throw them out, but the waitress quickly explained the situation and they calmly returned to their beers.

"Techno head . . ." Jaromír frowned, as if bit into a lemon. "Do I look like . . . Yes. Yes! I'm in!"

The program from Martin finally broke through and let them into Haas' phone. Jaromír immediately picked it up and started clicking on the icons.

"His last calls were four hours before he died, both outgoing, first to Tobias and then to Klaus."

"His brothers," Boleslav added.

"And there's a text from Tobias. Well, my German is far from perfect, but calling someone a *schweinehund* doesn't sound very brotherly. Apparently the brothers rented some land without his consent." Jaromír left the safety of the familiar icons and tried the others that were on the top bar. "Hey, Haas got twenty-five alarms set here, three minutes apart. And the first one is at quarter to two at night?"

"That's the lower end of the estimated time of death." Boleslav thoughtfully skewered a potato and quickly chewed and swallowed it. "Twenty-five alarms . . . Jaromír, play the ringtone. You'll find it—"

"I know where it is," Jaromír lied, looked at the current time, changed the final six to a seven and entered the resulting number as a new alarm.

"Hey, hey, hey, the dice are rolled, play!"

Jaromír quickly turned the alarm clock off, and the Hunters looked at the cell phone for a moment as if a venomous snake was hiding in it. It wouldn't be far from the truth.

"I guess it's clear to everyone what happened to Haas," Boleslav said quietly.

"Yeah," Jaromír nodded. "This was clearly a murder. Someone knew about the heykals, dragged Haas off into the woods, and let them do the dirty work for him. That doe must have attracted them, and then this pop song whipped them into a frenzy, which I don't blame them for."

"But why so complicated?" asked Richard.

"If the killer knew about the heykals, they could have known about the SRS, and that the investigation would be taken over and frozen immediately," Boleslav said. "Then they'll put a car accident or a fall off a cliff on Haas' death certificate and no one will look for the killer."

"But that doesn't make sense," Richard opposed him. "I know their agents are far from geniuses, but if they found the cell phone, even they would figure out it was murder. And someone using monsters to kill, that would be reason for an investigation."

"The rookie is right," Jaromír supported him. "This phone is a smoking gun. The killer didn't care that it would end up labeled a murder. It's too complicated."

Boleslav nodded in agreement and cut off a piece of fried gouda cheese. The waitress may have treated them like lepers, but if the chef thought he was serving some techno heads, professional pride prevented him from preparing a led than perfect fry.

"Maybe it wasn't about Haas, but about the heykals," Richard suggested. "Couldn't he have been a sacrifice or something?"

Bóleslav stopped chewing and swallowed the boiled potato almost whole. "I think you're onto something."

"Who would sacrifice people to heykals?" Jaromír asked doubtfully. "What would they get out of it? A heykal won't grant your wish, and you don't have to keep it away either, because it won't even go near a human house."

"No, I mean that it was about the heykals."

Boleslav waved at the waitress when she was passing the door. This time she came right up and with a smile. "More beer?"

"No, thanks." Boleslav pushed a map in front of her. "Could you show me where they're planning to have that techno party?" When her smile faded at the suggestion that techno heads and the State Veterinary Administration might not be entirely mutually exclusive, he quickly added: "I thought we could maybe check the noise levels there, and if they would cross the limit, we could sic the police on them."

"You can do that?" The waitress asked with hope in her voice.

"Don't doubt it," Jaromír said with a straight face.

The waitress tapped her finger on the wooded hills northeast of Mikulášovice. "Somewhere here, below the Fox Stones. Take a detour through Vilémov and at Šenov, then take a turn towards the outdoor forest pool. I'm sure you could hear them from there."

"Thank you, and we'll pay for food." Boleslav took out his wallet and pulled out a thousand crowns bill. "Keep the change."

As soon as the waitress, surprised to see a decent tip despite the initial misunderstanding, disappeared into the restaurant, Boleslav tapped the spot she had marked for them. It was located inside one of Haas' marked lots. "We have a problem."

"We might have a problem, but the techno heads are in deep shit," Jaromír elaborated. "If the heykals move there, they won't like the night disturbance."

"They'll definitely go there," Boleslav said. "First that text message, and two days later a forest technoparty on his property? If any of you think that's a coincidence, you should change jobs. Someone's been sending those heykals after them, and I'm sure they made sure that the heykals would pick this particular piece of the Haas estate."

"But who is that someone?"

"A local lover of peace and nature?" Boleslav shrugged. "As the three old ladies and our waitress proved, they don't like techno heads around here. It wouldn't be the first giant monster trouble caused by one hateful idiot."

Boleslav got up from the table, folded the map and put it in his pocket.

"Wait, we're going to leave right now?" Jaromír looked wistfully at his late lunch and dinner merged into one. "It's not like the heykals are going to come out as soon as the sun goes down."

"You should take a lesson from Richard here," Boleslav grinned, gesturing to the newbie, who quickly tossed in a couple of croquettes and took the steak away in his hand. Boleslav then pressed the half-eaten fried cheese on its untouched compatriot, picked it up off the plate and took another provocative bite. "A wise Hunter only orders food that can either be eaten quickly or easily taken away."

Jaromír looked at his departing companions and then at his meet roll drowned in a mixture of rice and sauce. "Fuck this job," he cursed, fishing the roll out of the sauce and hurrying after them.

The van started from Mikulášovice, but instead of taking the detour recommended by the waitress, they picked a shorter route through the fields. Jaromír took the wheel and tried to prove to everyone that his van has the soul of a racing car. Richard and Boleslav sat in the back, checking their guns. It was getting dark slowly, but if their theory about the relocation of the heykal pack was correct, they would be on high alert around their new den in order to take on any intruders, especially if the singers or techno heads use the H-word.

Fortunately, heykals had only limited regenerative abilities and standard ammo worked on them; Hunters usually only needed a good aim or a few extra shots. Their biggest advantage was their thick skin, which could stop most standard hunting weapons, and their speed. So Boleslav pulled three CZ 806 Bren assault rifles and magazines of armor piercing ammo from the hidden space under the floor. These heykals were in for another bloody lesson in the advances of the arms industry.

Boleslav's cell rang; Alexandra's number appeared on the display. He accepted the call. It wasn't Alexandra.

"Why the hell didn't you tell me you were headed to a magical place?

If I didn't happen to see what Alex was looking up in the register, I wouldn't even know about it!"

Petra, as a former teacher, usually operated in two basic modes— a kind source of information for inquisitive students, or the nightmare of rude teenagers having fun in class and spoiling the delivery of literary classics. Eight years ago, her strictness nearly cost her her life when she let three great-grandchildren of a gypsy witch repeat a grade. After vain attempts at persuasion, the witch tried to curse Petra in her office. However, Petra had been collecting dream catchers, crystals and talismans for many years, for which her office was nicknamed the cabinet of esotericism. These not only stopped the curse, but the spell was amplified by several crystals, the dreamcatcher with amethyst beads deflected it back at the witch, and to both women's surprise, the witch's being much greater of course, the ancient sorceress exploded and turned the room into a cabinet of carnage. And since there wasn't much interest in a teacher blowing up students' great-grandmothers and the SRS wasn't entirely convinced that the whole incident was a coincidence and kept breathing down Petra's neck, Libor eventually hired her as Fantom's archivist, where she could study real magic.

Right now she was screaming at him as if he'd said that Poe's most famous poem was called *Robin*.

"Hey, calm down, Petra. I wasn't checking out any magical place," Boleslav defended himself. "I just wanted to know what land belongs to our victim."

"So the Fox Stones are just a coincidence?!"

"The Fox Stones?" Boleslav repeated. "But that's just a local hill with a stone field. Or are there some fallen menhirs?"

"There aren't," Petra replied. *"Or at least that's what an online article said in 2020. And before that in 2014 . . . and 2007 . . . and 2001 . . . and 1996. And before that, I found newspaper articles from 1994 and 1989. I probably don't need to explain what that means."*

If the SRS has been churning out such regular denial reports through the media, there must have been something far worse than foxes roaming around the Fox Stones at some point, and the SRS has never been able to clean the place up properly.

"Did you find out something in the archives?"

"There was nothing in the digital archive, and there's no time to dig through the books. So I had to call Malenthiada."

Boleslav whistled softly. Queen Malenthiada ruled a small community of Czech elves in the satellite town Háj near Prague. Her estate now consisted of just forty-two family houses she had wrested from the post-Cold War government when the Coexistence Treaty was renewed, and before that her clan crammed in a panel building on the outskirts of Kladno where the communists had shuffled them for fifty years, but she still acted as if her empire spanned five continents.

"Another unpleasant call?"

"*Not at all. It started out as usual, but as soon as I mentioned the Fox Stones, she was suddenly as matter-of-fact as an Ikea manual. According to her, that hill used to be a Fey gathering place and a portal to their world. The elves shut it down and it cost them dearly. She indirectly hinted that this was the reason why the Czech clan is one of the smallest in Europe. But that's not the worst of it, Boleslav. She didn't even haggle about the price of her services. I wouldn't be surprised if she packed her bags after hanging up, just in case.*"

"I see. You'd better call the SRS. Someone is throwing a techno party under the Fox Stones tonight, which means a lot of witnesses at best." Boleslav didn't need to add that at worst they'd have to cover up a huge massacre. In magical places, even the more intelligent monsters lost their sanity, and heykals were half-animals. "I gotta hang up now."

Boleslav cut off the call, sighed, and punched the driver's seat. "Did you hear that, Jaromír?"

"I've heard enough."

"Then step on it."

"And what do you think I've been doing?" Jaromír grumbled, but still pulled a bit of hidden horsepower out of the tortured engine.

Richard bit his lip nervously. "So, a Fey portal?"

"Exactly." Boleslav frowned at him. "Something come to mind? Then out with it now while we can do something about it."

"Heykals are Fey. Lower and feral, but still Fey. If they massacre the techno heads there, couldn't the portal see it as a blood sacrifice and open up?" Richard cautiously returned to his sacrifice theory.

Boleslav just kept staring at him for a few seconds while he thought that possibility over. Then he pounded on the seat again. "Did you hear that, Jaromír?"

"I heard and I'm stepping on the gas, but do me a favor and spare me any more good news or I'll stomp that pedal through the floor!"

When they reached the forest, the sun was setting behind the distant mountains. The mud on the forest path was rutted and reliably guided them to their destination. Jaromír heard the music first. He opened the window and stuck his head out. "That's not techno," he grunted in surprise. "That's metal!" Then he listened more carefully. "And crappy one."

"I don't think the heykals will care what style of music gets them out of their lair," Boleslav replied. He'd already checked his rifle and was now turning his attention to his Laugo Arms Alien pistol. Richard already noticed that when it came to gear, Boleslav was a patriot.

The van's lights pulled out of the shadows a roughly built wooden barrier and a stocky guy in a black T-shirt with yellow VP CREW print on it that looked like someone had made it recently. The security guard looked at the van with a picture of an Amazon on a hare, figured the right kind of people were coming, and let them pass.

Beyond the barrier, the forest gave way to a larger clearing. At one end stood a podium made of wooden planks, with a few speakers and a large light board, turned off for now, and a large sign reading VIIMEINEN PIMENNYS between two small Finnish flags. A few cars and eight minibuses were parked on the edges, including a mobile chicken grill, as some locals figured that since they already had techno heads here, they might as well try to make some money out of it. The fans had a few tents set up in front of the cars; one elderly couple had even set up chairs, had a kettle on a portable stove, and they were both nibbling on some pastries. Richard was surprised that they were so far from the stage, but judging by Jaromír's disapproving expression, the metal band currently performing on the stage probably wasn't very good.

"The opening act," he commented. "And if not, no wonder they are performing in the woods."

"Stay in the van with the guns," Boleslav told him. "Richard and I will find out who's in charge and try to convince them to cancel the concert."

"If it's not Czechs, try telling them you're from the National Park Service," Jaromír advised him. "The Giant Mountains are not far away, maybe they'll fall for it. And if not, try it the SRS style."

Boleslav and Richard covered their pistol holsters and climbed out of the van. Meanwhile, the band on the stage acknowledged that they wouldn't find any fame for themselves today and cleared the area, which was followed by weak applause. The trio that replaced them were a different league. They all wore black leather suits, had their heads shaved and their faces blackened with an oval of white glow-in-the-dark paint on the edges. Their every movement showed that a stage was their life.

The singer spoke into a microphone. Richard couldn't understand a word he said, but the crowd roared with excitement. That could be a problem. If the audience was full of Finns and panic broke out, it would be damn hard to calm them down and coordinate.

Boleslav led them around the crowd of fans to the backstage area. The failure of an opening act was getting off the stage and retreating unobtrusively to their tent. Richard tried to catch a glimpse of the promoter or the band's manager, but he saw no one else around. Hopefully the Finns weren't representing themselves. He didn't feel like going on stage to see them.

The guitarist and drummer rocked it out, accompanied by enthusiastic cheers of the fans, and the singer joined them soon. His voice was hoarse, as if he'd spent all his life in a coal mine, and the foreign words gave Richard a slight headache. He shook his head and then bumped into Boleslav, who stopped abruptly.

"Oh shit," Boleslav swore softly. "This isn't Finnish."

"You speak Finnish?"

"No." Boleslav reached for his holster, and when he moved again, he walked noticeably faster. "But I've heard this language a few times, and for every bastard who used it we got reward from TEFLON afterwards."

They were about five meters away from the stage when the light board came to life. Three words appeared on it, which even Richard could read with no problem. "Oh, shit," he quoted Boleslav.

The fans did what their idols wanted and started chanting at the top of their lungs.

"HEY! HEY! HEY!"

And Richard could have sworn he heard a not-too-distant reply from the forest.

✦ ✦ ✦

They ran behind the stage, and as soon as the audience was out of sight, they pulled out their guns. Boleslav went first, slowly ascending the stairs, when Richard stopped him and pointed to the edge of the stage. Carved into the edges of the planks was a string of runic symbols that glowed faintly, as if the wood beneath was rotten and luminous.

"I noticed. Must be a protective circle," Boleslav said. The Finns were obviously making sure the heykals wouldn't tear them apart as well. "We'll have to get everyone in here and hope it works."

Boleslav walked up on the stage and crouched behind a giant speaker.

"We'll give them one chance to surrender, just in case someone is using them," he told Richard. "But if they try anything fishy, we need to neutralize them quickly so the audience doesn't have time to start panicking."

"Understood."

"You take the left side and I'll—"

The guitarist turned around right then, noticing them. He tilted his blackened head to the side in surprise before his eyes widened in recognition. "*Metsästäjät!*" he yelled, dropping his guitar and reaching in his jacket with his right hand.

A concealed gun during a performance? That was enough of an admission of guilt for Boleslav. His Alien barked three times, the guitarist spun on his heel and fell face first on the floorboards.

Now that he was exposed, Boleslav turned to face the rest of the band on autopilot. The drummer dropped his drumsticks and picked up a short shotgun propped behind the drums. *Bang, bang, bang.* The drummer fell off his stool, fired skyward, kicked the drum with one foot, and clanked the cymbal with the galvanized toe of his other shoe.

The singer turned slowly and looked at the Hunter pointing a gun at him.

"Get down on the ground!" Boleslav yelled at him, nodding with the barrel towards the boards to cross the language barrier.

The singer smiled and shook his hands slightly. Short strings studded with bones and shiny stones slipped from his sleeves. Sparks skipped between the strings as they swung closer to each other.

Boleslav didn't bother with a second warning and fired three shots.

Three flashes appeared in front of the singer's chest, like small meteors entering the atmosphere and burning to nothing. The unharmed singer's smile widened. He swung the strings, then threw his arms out violently toward Boleslav. The space above the stage rippled like air over hot desert sand. It would have been easy to miss if not for the cloud of splinters rising behind it. Boleslav ducked to the right, the blast of air missed him and shredded the tarp behind the stage.

Richard quickly came out from behind the speaker and fired his Beretta twice. Two hits to the head accomplished little more than some twitching, but the Finn stopped paying attention to the lying Boleslav and turned to his new opponent. Richard leapt on the stairs. A speaker hit by magic flew through the tarp in a shower of sparks. Richard peered cautiously over the edge of the stage.

The singer was laughing loudly, like a child who'd just discovered how a new toy worked. The sparkly strings twisted as if he held the severed head of Medusa in each hand. He was about to swing them again when gunfire sounded in the distance and several fiery flowers bloomed on his back. Jaromír climbed on top of the van and shot him with a Bren.

The magical aura protected the singer from the bullets, but some of the kinetic energy must have passed through because he flinched a little with each hit. The Finn turned, stretched his arms out and froze at the sight of the crowd of fans. Some of them had figured out something was wrong, but most were still shouting excitedly, thinking it was all part of the show. The singer took a step back as a shot from the Bren hit him in the chest, but he didn't return the attack. Whatever he had planned for the audience, he clearly needed more of them than would be left alive after a magical attack over their heads.

"You want magic, you'll get magic."

Richard turned his head and saw Boleslav getting up and drawing the family machete. As soon as the blade appeared, all Richard's doubts about its magical nature evaporated. Half of the engraved symbols glowed, irritated by the nearby burst of powerful dark magic, and the hilt pulsed blue under his fingers.

"Hey, bastard!"

The singer turned automatically, and Boleslav slashed him across the neck.

The machete collided with the protective shell, and the Finn was suddenly surrounded by a glowing scarlet web. The blade of the machete flared, penetrated the glittering threads, and slipped out the other side, coated in sparks and burning blood. The magical shield flickered and disappeared. The singer fell on his back into the audience. Concert instincts kicked in for a few spectators who caught the falling body, only to have the ones behind them being hit by a geyser of blood as the severed head fell between outstretched hands.

For a moment there was complete silence as even the most oblivious fans realized that this wasn't a part of the show. Before panic could fully kick in, Jaromír sent a long burst skyward, and all the spectators instinctively crouched where they stood.

Boleslav picked up the dropped mic, tapped it, and when the appropriate response came from the surviving speaker, he addressed the audience.

"I'll be brief. Monsters exist, and they've just been summoned here to tear you all apart. The only safe place is on the stage, so for your own sake, move on it quickly." Then he repeated the whole thing in English.

Several people moved hesitantly towards the steps of the stage. The others just looked around in confusion, the crowd humming in muffled conversations as the more linguistically proficient individuals translated to the others what they'd just heard, though most of it was probably variations on, "Those freaks who shot *Viimeinen Pimennys* are babbling about monsters, and they're definitely going to kill us too."

"HEEEEEEY! HEEEEEY! HEEEEEY!"

A long howl brought the audience to the ground more effectively than Jaromír's gunfire. Even the most rational ones instinctively knew that such a sound could not have been made by either animal or man.

At the farthest edge of the clearing, a massive figure with a black mane emerged from the forest. The alpha heykal walked on all fours, but when it stopped, it reared up on its hind legs, thumped its chest like a gorilla, and roared again menacingly. Behind him, other males, of comparable size and smaller, females with shorter manes and more mature cubs, came out of the forest.

There must have been more than fifty, maybe more than sixty heykals, and Richard suddenly realized why the Haas brothers hadn't answered their phones. Both Tobias and Klaus must have been lying in a different Šluknov forest, chewed to the bone, while not one, but three packs of heykals moved to their new home under the Fox Stones.

"So what are you waiting for?" Boleslav shouted at the hesitating crowd.

The loud shout snapped most of them out of their stupor. The crowd scurried to the stage, people running for the stairs or trying to climb the wooden construction. Jaromír jumped down from the van and, festooned with Brens and a bag of spare magazines, raced after them.

The alpha heykal dropped to all fours, grunted hoarsely, and the first wave of heykals ran to the stage as well.

Boleslav and Richard stood in the corners of the stage so they wouldn't be knocked down by the panicking crowd, and watched out for the first eight heykals. The massive males ran along the edge of the forest at first, and only began to approach the stage when parked cars and tents stood between them and the Hunters. Just as was mentioned in training, heykals knew all too well what firearms were. Jaromír had been cut off by the spectators swarming onto the stage, so for now they only had pistols and three spare magazines on their belts.

"Only shoot them when they get close to people!" Boleslav shouted over the crowd. "We need to save ammo until Jaromír gets here!"

The first heykal leapt on a parked BMW, heyed belligerently and jumped over the roofs of two minibuses before disappearing behind them again. Another ran between the tents, a quick shadow against the bright background. Richard followed them with the barrel of his Beretta, but his eyes were flitting to other cars as well. The heykals were provoking them, either knowing their guns wouldn't be very accurate at this distance or they were distracting them from something else. The rest of the pack, including the alpha, kept near the edge of the woods.

A young blonde in the back of the crowd had fallen and the two heykals immediately seized the opportunity, jumped over the cars and ran on all fours towards the easy prey. Richard quickly fired twice, missing once, but the second bullet hit a heykal in the front leg. The male misstepped, fell in an unplanned roll and quickly retreated back to cover. Boleslav waited until the second heykal was almost upon the blonde and put a single bullet through its eye. The heykal's legs buckled and it slid on its belly up to the blonde, who screamed, stood up, and raced to the stage.

Unfortunately, not everyone in the audience sought safety with the Hunters. While they were rescuing the blonde from two heykals, the other six were attacking anyone who tried to hide between the cars.

The owner of the mobile grill was just pulling the blinds down when a heykal jumped through his delivery window and hit him with such force that the small van flipped on its side. Screams echoed from the tent, where the opening band had retreated after its lackluster performance, and blood spattered the bright blue fabric. The guy with a shaved head and the same black makeup as the band jumped in a car. He only managed to go half the distance between the parking lot and the road before a huge heykal caught up with him, ripped the door off, dragged him out and threw him into the darkness. The rest of the heykals were bouncing around on the roofs of two minibuses, trying to get to the drivers.

There was nothing the Hunters could do for most of them, but the drivers still had a chance. They gave up on saving bullets—the minibuses were too far away for that—and emptied their magazines at the heykals around cars. One yelped and fell out of a minibus, but another, even with a bloody back, crashed in through a window. Hearing his colleague's screams, the other driver ran out and raced toward the stage. Apparently he hadn't noticed that the two Hunters onstage were in the process of changing magazines. He ran almost twenty meters before a heykal landed on his back and grabbed his neck.

Running, Jaromír turned and blasted it with a short burst from his Bren. The driver crawled out from under a limp paw and ran toward the rest of the crowd.

"Help! Help!"

The fat security guy, who'd been manning the barrier and was hiding behind trees after the first round of shots, finally figured out he would be safer on the stage and rushed toward the Hunters. The heykals among the tents noticed prey that would not escape them easily, and went after him.

Jaromír immediately aimed at them, but the guy ran in front of them, staggering from side to side. "Move aside, you idiot!" VP CREW didn't hear him and continued to stumble along the same trajectory. Jaromír cursed, took careful aim, waited for the security guy to start staggering the other way, and fired low over the ground. A triple burst peppered the grass in front of the heykal, and one bullet smoothly blew off several of its fingers. The whimpering heykal limped into the woods on three legs. Then all the saints smiled at the security guy and sent a root hidden in the grass his way. He fell to the ground, the heykal ten steps behind him suddenly offered itself as if on a silver platter, and Jaromír rebuilt its face with another burst.

The VP CREW got up and ran to Jaromír. "Thanks, d—"

Jaromír thrust the bag with magazines in his hands. "Take it to the stage!" he shouted at him, backing up quickly, rifle ready to fire.

Metallic bangs echoed from the overturned grill, and indistinct shadows were moving between the tents and inside a minibus, but the other heykals retreated from sight. Richard looked toward the edge of forest. The line of heykals amongst the trees was nervous, the males in particular were angrily heying and shifting in place, but the alpha kept turning his head from side to side and growling to keep them in place.

What the hell was it waiting for?

By the time the security guy reached the stage, all other survivors were already crowded on it; there must have been over a hundred of them. Richard took his backpack from the last straggler and then helped him up. Jaromír arrived a moment later, tossed each Hunter a rifle and climbed onstage. When he turned around, from their elevated position he could finally see all of the heykals on the other side of the clearing.

"Well, that doesn't look good. I've never seen such a big pack—"

There was a loud crash behind the stage, the lights went out, and the clearing was plunged into darkness, broken only by a light in the car with the torn off door and a fallen tent that had just caught fire from a stove. The full moon, which had been shining like a spotlight on the meadow till now, had of course decided to hide behind thick clouds a moment ago.

Boleslav immediately ran over to the back and shone a flashlight into a hole left by the blown loudspeaker. The generator was lying on the ground; the cables had been ripped out and the heykal whom Jaromír had deprived of his fingers was persistently pounding it with its good paw. Apparently firearms weren't the only technology they were familiar with.

When the light hit it, it heyed and lunged for Boleslav, only to be stopped half a meter from the stage by an invisible barrier. There was a flash, the boards under Boleslav shook slightly, and the shrieking heykal bounced back, half of his majestic mane ending up burned to cinders. Boleslav finished him.

As soon as the lights went out, the rest of the heykals started moving. They were in no hurry, knowing damn well that humans, unlike them, could not see in the dark.

"You didn't bring an NVD, did you?" Boleslav asked.

"And would you like to have a flamethrower too?" retorted Jaromír.

"I would, but you probably didn't bring that either."

Sudden shouts came from the cars. Several shouts. Someone stayed there.

Richard searched the dark and noticed the lights of smartphones in one car. However, one of the heykals from the first wave spotted them as well. It jumped on the hood and started pounding on the windshield. Richard pointed his flashlight at it, but the car was facing the stage, the heykal was just an indistinct shadow, and he couldn't see the people behind him at all.

"Shit."

Richard quickly unbuckled his flashlight and reached for his belt. Česká zbrojovka, same as the most of bigger arms manufactures, was not only familiar with the existence of monsters, but also ready to help the Hunters, who were regular customers, when their weapons needed a little modification; his CZ 806 Bren deserved a few extra letters in its name because of them. Thanks to one of those modifications, Richard could now fit an extra-long custom bayonet with a silver-plated lower blade that, with a little skill, could decapitate a werewolf, a vampire, and a host of other humanoid monsters in one fell swoop when it came to resorting to the old disposal classics.

"Cover me!" he shouted to Jaromír and jumped off the stage.

The fire spread from one tent to two others. Richard ran to the car in a slight arc so that any attackers would have to run in front of the burning tents to offer themselves to the Hunters on the stage. One tried it; by the limp it must have been the male he had shot before. Three bullets from a Bren hit it in the side and the heykal ended up right in the burning fabric instead of going around the tent. It screamed briefly, but couldn't stand up again, and the flames really loved its thick mane.

The heykal on the hood didn't even notice anyone running towards it, focused solely on the three young girls crouched in the back seat.

Richard plunged the bayonet in its back. The heykal shrieked when Richard lifted it on its toes. With a hard pull, Richard forced it to turn sideways, and as he swung it away from the windshield, he twisted the bayonet to the left, aligning the barrel with the spine and shattering the thoracic vertebrae with a short burst. The heykal went limp and slid off the silver-plated blade.

The girls didn't wait for prompting, they jumped out of the car and ran to the stage. Richard gave them a small head start before following them.

"Watch out, cubs!" Jaromír shouted at him.

Little heykals ran under the minibuses. Their manes were so short that they looked like a failed afro, and they were no bigger than a pit bull, but that did not make them any less dangerous than their adult counterparts. In the Middle Ages, they were just as feared as adults, but often considered a separate species because of their different attacks. They would usually run up behind someone, jump on their neck, and either strangle them themselves or keep them occupied long enough for an adult heykal to arrive, earning them the nickname the stranglers.

Richard could hear the shrieking heying as Jaromír hit one, but the tiny heykals were too fast for him to repeat it regularly. Richard heard one that couldn't contain its excitement and heyed a bit right behind him. He immediately dodged to the left and blindly slashed with his bayonet. The little strangler practically cut itself in half in flight. Richard took advantage of the fact that he was already half-turned and blasted the two nearest cubs. Then he looked towards the minibuses and immediately regretted it.

The pack reached the cars, climbing over and under them, dozens of heykals rolling over the vehicles like a tsunami. The sight was enough for Richard to find reserves in his legs that he hadn't known he had until then, and in the last twenty meters he broke all his previous speed records. Boleslav and Jaromír were shooting at the approaching mass, but the older metal fan who had first helped the girls stayed on the edge of the stage and pulled Richard onto it as well.

The heykals crossed the clearing and crashed into the protective barrier like a flood into a rock. The wooden structure shook and the magical shield sparkled so wildly that the entire dome could be seen with the naked eye. The Hunters had to step back from the edge, lest they lose their balance and fall off. The heykals shrieked in pain upon contact with the barrier, their stream shattering, and the burned monsters quickly disappeared in the darkness at the edge of the clearing, where they heyed loudly and circled the magical shelter.

Jaromír walked closer to Boleslav and quietly remarked: "The stage cannot withstand another attack like this. It will collapse, the protective circle will break, and then we are all screwed."

As if the stage had heard him, the boards disturbed by the magical attack creaked so loudly that the metalheads on them stepped away in fear.

"I know," Boleslav replied as he searched the darkness with the barrel of his Bren. "Our only chance is to kill as many of them as we can as quickly as possible. They won't fight to the last, even with that Fey portal nearby."

"Thanks for the reminder," Jaromír said. "Up until now I was only thinking about our lives and theirs, and now I have to worry about an alien invasion too. No stress... Watch out!"

A big heykal ran out of the darkness, crashed into the stage and disappeared before Jaromír could fire. The next one immediately repeated it on the other side. The collision with the barrier must have hurt like hell, but the heykals were too riled up to pay attention to such trifles.

"Let's form a triangle!" Boleslav shouted, so that the more distant Richard could hear him. "We've got four spare magazines each, so don't hold back. We'll have to kill at least twenty of them before they give up, and the more males the better."

The Hunters took up new positions and looked out for the heykals. The monsters continued to charge against the shield, the males alternating with the females, but this time the Hunters were ready for them, and after ten attacks, three heykals were left dead in front of the stage and two other limped off into the darkness. Their willingness to attack was waning, but they weren't about to give up. For them, this was a battle for the forest below the Fox Stones, a new territory that they clearly fell in love with.

"Look, I don't want to be Cassandra, but we've got another problem!" Jaromír yelled, nodding his head towards the parking lot.

The tents were all on fire now, and as a second wave of heykals ran between them, one flew off to the overturned grill. The small van caught in the flames too, and the heykal that had been hiding in it quickly jumped out with a mouth full of grilled chicken.

Richard didn't know how big the propane tank inside was, but if it exploded, especially if the slain owner had a spare in there too, the shockwave would knock down the stage and the people on it like rag dolls. It was starting to look like they might make it, only for bloodthirsty fate to suck most of the sand of their hourglass.

"HEY! HEY! HEY!"

The alpha heykal, who had kept his distance till now, jumped on the car with the torn off door so that the Hunters could clearly see him. The whole pack around him came out of the shadows, standing on minibuses and in front of burning tents, keeping their eyes on the stage. The alpha thumped his chest again, heyed loudly, and pointed at the Hunters.

He was challenging them.

"Now that the snake has kindly shown us its head, we can finally blow it off," Jaromír growled, pointing his gun at the alpha.

The pack heyed loudly, and Boleslav quickly knocked the barrel to the ground. "They know what rifles can do. Shoot that alpha after a challenge to a duel and it'll drive the pack mad."

"We might have no other option, because I'm not going to wrestle with him."

The alpha heykal seemed to hear them, as he confidently puffed up his chest and goaded them to try and shoot him.

Boleslav bit his lip. "There is a story told in our family that when Vilém Zajíc hosted King Ludwig, they were ambushed on a hunt by a pack of heykals, forced to hunt during the day by an early arrival of winter. The heykals killed their horses and dogs, and most of the royal retinue ended up dead or wounded, so Vilém bet everything on one card and challenged their alpha to a duel. When he defeated him, the pack retreated and let them go."

"And you think that because your ancestor could beat up a heykal, you can do it too?" Jaromír asked doubtfully.

"He didn't beat him with his bare hands," Boleslav corrected him. "He killed him with a boar spear, and if the heykals didn't mind a spear in those days..."

Boleslav stepped on the edge of the stage, unbuckled his machete and showed it to the heykal. A few of the younger heykals heyed again in protest, but the older ones silenced them with grunts. The alpha snorted contemptuously and jumped down from the car.

The challenge was accepted.

The alpha watched his opponent jump off the stage. The opponent... That man was weak. All humans were weak, even the Hunters. The days when they could wield swords and spears were long gone; these days humans relied only on metal-spitting sticks. He would kill him, and if his pack wouldn't submit, he'd kill them too...

No, he couldn't let them go. He will not let them go.

He had to kill them. The new home demanded it. The rocks screamed it at him. The trees hissed it at him. There was a smell in the air he didn't recognize, but something deep inside him knew it. This place belonged to him. He'd owned this place before he'd come here. Only ancient traditions prevented him from attacking the Hunter right away.

The Hunter drew his sword and tossed the scabbard aside. The blade sparkled with light and magic.

The alpha blinked in surprise. He realized he'd made a mistake.

The weapon the Hunter was holding was powerful. Weak people don't carry powerful weapons they don't know how to use. The Hunter would be a stronger opponent than he thought.

But he couldn't back down, not today.

As he moved his pack to its new home, two more alphas claimed the same territory. The forest was too small for three leaders, and on the second night after the move, there was a battle for leadership over all packs. The alpha won, defeating and killing his rivals and then a young challenger who hoped that a tired and injured leader would not make it through the next fight. He was wrong.

The Alpha led the largest pack he had seen in his long life, but his position was still precarious. The males of his own pack wouldn't dare disobey him, they knew him too well for that, but among the newcomers he noticed several strong heykals who would soon challenge him to a duel. So he sent them all in battle first, hoping the Hunters would take care of them for him, but nearly half of them escaped without a scratch.

He couldn't retreat.

He had to fight.

He had to kill him and then all the others.

✦ ✦ ✦

When Boleslav drew the family machete, the alpha heykal hesitated but quickly masked it with another battle heying. He approached Boleslav on all fours, baring his teeth and puffing out his chest, but caution flickered through the exaggerated confidence. When only a few steps separated them, the heykal snapped his teeth in a feigned attack.

Boleslav quickly ducked.

The alpha snorted disdainfully and repeated it.

Boleslav backed away again.

The alpha bared his teeth in a disturbingly human smile. Derisive heying came from the semicircle of heykals that surrounded the warriors. The alpha decided to try a third time.

Boleslav, however, didn't move an inch and slashed at his throat in a lightning-fast move. Machete ran through mane, the sharpened blade slicing smoothly through matted hair, but it didn't reach the neck. This time it was the heykal's turn to jump away quickly. He had lost the lower quarter of his mane and was showing off his bald neck. Several females turned their heads towards their neighbors and heyed softly at them. The heykals had more in common with humans than met the eye.

The alpha was enraged by such unexpected humiliation. He snarled and charged towards Boleslav. The Hunter swung his machete at him, but the heykal ducked his head, ran under the whizzing blade, and, when he was behind Boleslav, kicked out with his hind leg and struck the Hunter in the hip. Boleslav was lifted in the air and crashed into the car from which a heykal had jumped out earlier. He hit the back door hard and fell to the ground.

"Screw it," Jaromír growled, pointing his gun at the heykal.

"Don't interfere!" Boleslav shouted at him, then quickly rolled to the side before the running alpha came crashing down on him. His shoulder slammed into the torn-off door. He lifted it in front of him and stopped another attack.

The alpha slammed his fist in the door, and if Boleslav hadn't had his knee pressed against it on top of his hands, the improvised shield would have crushed him like a machine press. The second blow shattered the window and showered him with glass. The heykal was determined to squash him like a bug and pounded relentlessly on the door, while Boleslav's tired arms sank a little lower with each blow. He knew that if he didn't go on the offensive quickly, he wouldn't be able to resist for very long.

As the alpha swung for another blow, Boleslav took a gamble, leaving the door propped with his left hand only, and slashed his machete at the heykal's leg. This time he reached him. The blade went over his shin. With a startled yelp, the alpha jumped back, stood on his rear and examined the wound, thin smoke rising from the bloodied leg. Heykals might have been a Czech endemic species, but at least one of the holy men who had blessed the machete must have hated the Fey as a whole.

Boleslav took advantage of the alpha's brief distraction as he looked at the disproportionately painful wound, picked himself up, and threw the car door at him. The heykal registered the movement out of the corner of his eye and instinctively caught the door in his outstretched hands. But by then Boleslav was already in motion, and with a leap he stabbed at the popped-out window. The machete ran across the heykal's face, leaving a deep, smoking wound.

The alpha roared in pain, swung the door at the Hunter and threw him back against the car. Boleslav almost ended up inside it, but at the last moment he grabbed the frame of the torn-off door and pulled himself back up. The heykal threw the door away and touched his wounded face, in which only one eye now shone. He had either lost the other or it was completely covered in blood. He heyed angrily and ran towards the car.

Boleslav jumped up, pressed his back against the roof of the car, lifted his legs and quickly rolled aside. The alpha hit the side of the car and pushed it in front of him for a good five meters before he realized that he was only crushing the bodywork beneath his body. He looked around in confusion. When he looked up, he saw a kneeling Boleslav and a falling machete. The tip lodged between his shoulder and neck, and Boleslav pushed half of the blade into his opponent with both hands before the shrieking alpha pushed himself away from the car and staggered back a few steps, the machete still in his body. He looked like he was going to collapse on the ground at any moment, but found enough strength in himself to jump on the car roof. Boleslav didn't have time to dodge and they both disappeared behind the car.

"Shit!" Jaromír ran the flashlight beam over and around the car. "Do you see him?"

"No!" Richard replied, but he thought he could hear muffled cursing from behind the car in addition to the heykal's wailing.

Most of the heykals couldn't see what was going on either, craning their necks like meerkats and trying to see behind the car.

The sounds of the fight died down.

The head of a heykal appeared above the hood, followed by Boleslav, who held its bloody mane. With obvious trouble, he scrambled up on the car, showed the trophy to the shocked heykals, and then, like Conan with Thulsa's head, threw it at their feet before taking a deep breath and roaring mightily:

"HEEEEEEEY! HEEEEEEEEEY! HEEEEEEEEEY!"

At that moment, the propane inside the mobile grill reached critical temperature and the van exploded. The nearest heykals disappeared in a fireball and others were thrown several meters away by the explosion. Boleslav was swept off the van by the shockwave and rolled along the ground almost to the stage. The force of the explosion threw most of the metalheads against the tarp at the back of the stage, which snapped under their weight, and a clump of screaming, tangled people fell to the ground on the other side. The entire wooden structure creaked painfully and collapsed.

Richard, who had held on to the wreckage of the stage, scrambled to his feet and ran a flashlight beam over the heykals. He was ready to open fire as soon as they moved toward the civilians, but there was no need. Without their alpha and scared by blast, the heykals panicked, picking themselves up off the ground in a daze before running into the woods. Some had their manes on fire and Richard could follow them deep into the forest. A minute passed, and the only heykals that remained in the clearing were either dead or badly injured and stunned, a condition that the Hunters would soon reclassify as dead as well.

Angry cursing came from the human huddle. A battered Jaromír emerged from under the tarp and rushed to the lying Boleslav.

"Hey, Boleslav, are you okay?"

Boleslav raised his head and looked at Jaromír with contempt. "Couldn't have start that question with a dumber word, could you?" he grunted, slumping back on the grass.

As soon as all the surviving heykals who couldn't escape into the forest were finished, Jaromír retrieved a first aid kit from the team van and checked on Boleslav. He disinfected the cuts on his chest and arms, bandaged the larger ones, and helped him hobble to a seat in the van. It was clear to both of them that he also had several broken ribs, but there was nothing they could do about that now. The metalheads ended only with scratches and bruises, the debris from the grill fortunately not hitting anyone. Boleslav ordered them to stay on the ruins of the stage. The protective runes were extinguished after the explosion when the boards broke, but the metalheads didn't know that, and with a little luck, neither would the heykals if a few suicidally inclined ones decided to come back.

While Jaromír treated Boleslav, Richard searched a van marked VIIMEINEN PIMENNYS on the side that was parked behind the stage. In addition to the things one would expect inside a metal band' van, he found a lot of papers covered with runes and notes in Finnish. He discovered the real treasure in the glove compartment. One of the cultists not only kept a diary, but he even kept it in Czech; the group was obviously international. Richard brought it to Boleslav, who immediately confiscated it to distract his brain from his aching body by reading it until reinforcements would arrive. While he was being treated, he contacted Alexandra and she confirmed that the State Regulatory Service had taken their warning seriously for once and was on its way.

The SRS finally arrived two hours later, with the closest response team joining the convoy bringing Boris. The agents reached the clearing, found the heykals dispersed, and began attending to the witnesses.

Richard expected the usual intimidation by jail and suggestions that prison was the better option, but the agents were all smiles, reassuring the metal fans and generally being nice to them. It was so unexpected that he unwittingly placed a Bren in his lap in case the portal actually opened and some masked Fey arrived instead of SRS agents.

The agents checked all survivors and began rounding them up for "vaccinations" because they came in contact with dangerous creatures carrying many contagious diseases. When the first vaccinated person began to nod off, Richard finally calmed down. The survivors were being given a special cocktail of sedatives and chemicals that would reliably erase the last five hours of their memories. The SRS only used it rarely because witnesses with memory loss tended to question what happened during their blackout, but an illegal metal concert offered several sufficient possible explanations.

Once all the survivors were asleep, the smiles immediately disappeared and the agents got down to the real work. Because the best way to get people to accept a short memory loss was to make sure they didn't want to remember the missing moments, the agents began to compete who would put the sleeping witnesses in the most embarrassing situation.

Selected pairs, ideally of a large age difference or of the same sex, were stripped naked and slipped into sleeping bags found in the minibuses. A middle-aged man who looked like a walking healthy lifestyle ad ended up leaning against the remnants of the stage, a tourniquet on one arm and an empty syringe in the other. More syringes, along with empty hard liquor bottles and stripped clothing, were strewn across the meadow. Richard watched in disbelief as one agent dragged a young man in shorts to the edge of the meadow, pulled on a latex glove, stuck finger down the witness's throat with a perfectly indifferent expression, waited for the metalhead to throw up the last of his food, and then laid his head in a puddle of his own vomit. Then he looked at the man for a moment like an artist who just finished a painting, and after a brief moment of reflection, he pulled off the man's shorts and underwear and threw both into the woods. When they were finished, the agents settled down on the stage and discussed the charges they would slap the metalheads with after they woke up and how many dead heykals would the collected fines pay for.

The SRS managed to bring the phrase "cynical beasts" to a whole new level.

While the agents were carefully setting up several mental breakdowns and many therapy sessions, a truck with a covered trailer backed into the meadow. The SRS section responsible for covering up monster attacks loaded it with the wreckage of a mobile grill, the cultists' van, the most damaged minivan, and all the dead people, including the *Viimeinen Pimennys* trio. There would undoubtedly be a report about a tragic car crash in today's news, and the SRS may even pay an "expert" to give a lecture on the dangers of mobile grills. The dead heykals were loaded into an unmarked van to be taken to a government lab where, after examination, they would be incinerated, and Boleslav personally oversaw that Fantom got a receipt for TEFLON for each carcass.

"I've got good news and bad news," Boleslav announced to the rest of the team as he limped back to the van and slumped in a seat. "The good news is that I managed to read the diary and I know what happened here."

"You read the whole thing in two hours?" Jaromír asked dubiously.

"I didn't have to," Boleslav replied. "The beginning was a classic about a misunderstood child, unloving parents and cruel girls. It didn't get interesting until the end. Our drummer, Otakar Mach by his civil name, was born not far from here in Vilémov, picked up an interest in the occult in high school and at twenty decided to join a small Czech cell of the Condition in Pardubice. However, he only managed to make his first contact before that cell was exposed and exterminated."

"Wait, wasn't it Fantom who took them all out?" Jaromír remembered.

"It was, don't interrupt me," Boleslav said. "So Mach got scared and fled to the far north, to Finland, where he met Jani Korpela, the singer of *Viimeinen Pimennys*. As he demonstrated today, Jani knew a lot more about magic. According to Otakar, he was obsessed with the Fey, and during his research he came across an old ritual that could open a portal to their world."

"And of course he had to do it right away, even though he had no idea what would be on the other side," Jaromír grumbled. "These idiots are unteachable."

Boleslav looked at him wearily. "Jaromír . . ."

"I'm shutting up, I'm shutting up."

"But Jani had a problem. Not only he did not know of any Fey portal he could open, but he needed real Fey to take care of the human sacrifices. And here comes our bullied-by-everyone Otakar to save the day. Having grown up here, he knew both about heykals and the Fox Stones. So Jani kicked out his old drummer, brought in Otakar, planned a small concert for selected fans near the Fox Stones, the *Viimeinen Pimennys* came to Czechia, and you all know the rest."

"So they were lone gunmen? Yeah, that's good news. I was worried we'd be tripping over SRS agents at every step for at least a year here because of them. And the bad news?"

"I talked to Alexandra. The SRS was pretty spooked by the threat of the portal opening, and they're going to completely wipe out every heykal that was here today, just in case their proximity to the portal awakened memories of the good old days. And knowing the SRS, any heykals they will find in the woods, even those dead because of us, they're going to declare their own kills and Fantom won't get a dime for them, not to mention the bonus for destroying their burrows."

"Wait, wait," Jaromír interrupted him. "You're telling me we have to go back to the forest?"

"Not me. Libor. We had over sixty heykals here, but there's only what, nineteen corpses left? He didn't like that outcome. He's sending in a team from Ústí to help us, but in the meantime you're to search nearby woods, claim all corpses and wounded stragglers, and if you have any time left, find their burrows."

"You this, you that... Why do I get the feeling you're not going to trudge through the woods with us?" Jaromír said suspiciously.

"I have broken ribs, and according to company regulations, I can't go into the field right now."

"Yeah, right," Jaromír snorted. "Suddenly the regulations come in handy. We're going to hike this whole forest while you will be ogling nurses at a hospital."

"Well, the pack is without an alpha now, so there's also a good chance it will break up into the original ones and everyone will go back to their old hunting grounds."

"So it's not just *this* forest, it's the *whole* Šluknov region?" Jaromír cocked his head and looked reproachfully at the stars. "I haven't eaten properly all day, now I won't even get any sleep... never quote me, but I'm really getting too old for this." Jaromír leaned into the van and pulled out a spray bottle of whipped cream from his backpack. "Come on, rookie; let's go give Boris a few pats, because that's the only good thing that's coming our way today."

JAKUB MAŘÍK (* 1981)

An enthusiastic writer with introverted tendencies he studied legal administration but forced himself to sit in an office for only a few years. As soon as he could, he moved full-time on to activities he enjoyed much more—translating and writing his own stories set in fantastic worlds.

He started as a short story writer, which earned him a reputation as a chameleon who enjoys switching between different genres of science fiction and fantasy. You can come across his stories in several anthologies—a detective urban fantasy in *Mlok 2008* (*Nová vlna*, 2008), a ghost story in *Rags of Shroud* (*Cáry rubáše*, Epocha, 2013), a spy urban fantasy in *In the Shadow of the Reich* (*Ve stínu říše*, Epocha, 2017), or a military sci-fi in *The Law of the Gene* (*Zákon genu*, Epocha, 2023), but his work has long been connected with the magazine *Pevnost*, to which he has contributed with a historical fantasy short story "Koboué" (12/2008), a light cyberpunk story "Red Fields of Elysium" (08/2011), or a humorous series about Ming Duo, a captain of a space freighter (2017-2023).

His first book was part of a shared urban fantasy series Hammer of Wizards (*Kladivo na čaroděje*, Epocha, 2012-2018) where his *Hard Dreams* (*Drsné sny*, Epocha, 2014) generated quite the reader interest.

It took another six years for the author to take his next step. In doing so, he surprised once again when he plunged into space in the first adventure of the spaceship UTSS *Salamis*, titled *In the Shadow of the Sun* (*Ve stínu slunce*, Mystery Press, 2020), a well-received space military sci-fi laced with a decent amount of detective elements. It was followed by novels *In the Embrace of Ice* (*V ledovém sevření*, Mystery Press, 2021), *In the Blood Belt* (*V Krvavém pásu*, Mystery Press, 2022), and *In the Dead Zone* (*V mrtvé zoně*, Mystery Press, 2023). He is currently working on the final installment: *In the Lion's Den*.

You can read about Jakub's path to becoming one of the editors of *MHF* in the foreword. It should be noted, however, that even here he managed to pleasantly surprise us.

Sweet Dreams
Karel Doležal

Mr. Jarušek fell backwards on the bed. He couldn't feel his arms, he couldn't feel his legs and his head was throbbing. That he wouldn't give up this life! In the morning, he pours coffee into himself and goes to Semtín to juggle with explosives. Hýsek and Křížek have been sick for a week now, so he's doing the job of three men, not to mention that explosion in the building next door today. His ears were still ringing, and he was also hauled over the coals because the evacuation took ten seconds longer than regulations were demanding.

Yeah, the pay was good, but he'd be better off as a garbage man in Pardubice or Bohdaneč. He's been dead tired for the last month, squeezed like a lemon. Everything hurt, and he got some rash from work. He scratched his chest, but he felt that it only made the itching worse. He'll try to ignore it.

His eyes were closing relentlessly. He will brush his teeth in the morning; he doesn't want to get up. He would just switch off the lamp.

He barely peeled his eyelids apart and then immediately jerked. What was that? Something was moving to his left . . .

Oh.

All the more reason to turn it off. A *mura*—a nocturnal butterfly— was flying around the lamp on the nightstand, performing a shadow show.

Click.

Fly wherever you want, mura.

Mr. Jarušek closed his eyes again. Sleep, that blissful state. Those moments when he could be whoever he wished to be. The big boss who would yell at Hýsek for coming in late and then tell Křížek that if he wanted a raise, he shouldn't be slacking off.

Sleep has crept into the fantasy of a successful manager's life and slowly turned it into a dream. A beautiful dream. Jarušek, an engineer dressed in an expensive suit, was sprawled in a comfortable office chair, watching what was going on in the factory on a monitor. Whenever someone was slacking off, he could just touch a button, turn on the microphone and shout at them.

A pleasant scent tickled his nose. Coffee. But proper coffee, not like that instant slop he would normally drink every morning. The door creaked open and he fixed his gaze on his secretary carrying a steaming cup. He couldn't even remember her name. After all, he didn't care. The important thing were her perfect curves, the wavy blonde hair reaching her mid-back and the face of a Barbie doll.

He greeted her with a smile, which she returned. When she set the coffee on the table, he didn't even have the time to say thank you. She straddled him immediately. The expensive chair worked and tilted back. The engineer Jarušek, trapped on one side by the padding and on the other by the girl's hot body, didn't protest. After all, he's the big boss, this comes with it.

A hot kiss on his neck made him shiver. The assistant slid her mouth a little lower. Her golden mane was right in front of his eyes and he sniffed it like a gourmet.

Ugh.

Something wasn't right. He expected fragrant shampoo, but instead his nose was assaulted by an iron smell he remembered well from his childhood, when he helped his grandfather butcher during a pig slaughter. The smell of blood.

He tried to rise in his chair, but couldn't. The secretary with a wasp waist must have weighed over a ton. The moment he opened his mouth to ask her for some space, he couldn't catch his breath. As she lay on top of him, she squeezed the last of the air out of his lungs and the pressure made it impossible for him to breathe again.

However, the foul smell of blood remained in his nose and seemed to grow stronger. Where was it coming from?

Mr. Jarušek woke up from his sleep with a gasp. He wanted to take a breath, but he still felt heaviness in his chest. Heaviness and stabbing pain. And cold. His blanket was on the floor, but he didn't have the strength to pick it up.

He turned his gaze to his chest.

Two embers rose from the darkness, staring straight into his face.

"Really?" I said, shaking my head in disapproval. "Does anyone have any solid evidence? How do I know you're not sending me on some wild goose chase?"

Alexandra, who had clearly pulled the shortest straw today, sighed. Years ago, she'd sent me on a hunt that had turned out to be simple mass hysteria, not a monster. But explain something like that to a hundred villagers while you stand with a smoking rifle over a dying mare that, despite the claims of a dozen people, has its head firmly planted on its neck, and also belongs to a successful Prague manager who comes here on the weekends to ride it.

I hope that's enough to make you understand that unless I have at least a picture of the monster, I don't really want to go on a job.

"Listen, I know it's quite unusual for Czechia, but our informant reports so many cases that it can't be a coincidence anymore," our beloved business director explained patiently, as always very excited to personally talk to people instead of being holed up in an office somewhere and only sending emails.

"How many people live there? Four hundred? And there are about thirty cases? Christ, an epidemic, something in the local water supply, allergies! It's all chemical factories near Pardubice, did you take that into consideration? As far as I know, there's a leak at least once a year. Sudden weakness and exhaustion aren't necessarily caused by blood loss, no matter what that doctor says. A vampire in such small village sounds like the least likely option at the moment."

"It doesn't necessarily have to be a vampire. Blood tests for vampirism came back negative."

"Then what?" I threw my hands up in a desperate gesture. "You're saying it sucks blood, right? But so do mosquitoes! They pay us for the monsters we catch. How are we supposed to equip ourselves and decide how many people to send if we don't even know what's going on?"

"We have a strigoi as a working theory. Some might think that a strigoi and a vampire are one and the same, but a strigoi is a more primitive creature from earlier times. A restless and cursed soul rising from the dead. It also thirsts for blood, but it doesn't spread its curse by biting."

"Aren't they supposed to be from Romania?" I interjected. "And as far as I know, they're so decimated by us that they'd rather not stick their noses out of the Southern Carpathians."

"That's not so far from us, don't you think? It would only take one Romanian witch who moved to Czechia and cursed someone. It may sound unlikely, but from the evidence gathered so far, a strigoi seems to be the most likely option."

I grumbled something in protest and took a breath to make another point.

"Consider your mission field reconnaissance, yes?" Alexandra cut me off and stood up. "This has happened to you before too, hasn't it? You were searching for an imp and ended up with three dead gnomes."

I was about to answer when she placed two folders in front of me.

"I think these two will make good teammates for the task at hand."

Not a single syllable came out of me. The photo of the woman on the first folder didn't mean anything to me. However, at the sight of the round face with a genuine smile grinning at me from the second, I had to snort softly. Man, I haven't seen you in a while. All right, I'll do it, if only for you.

"Okay, you convinced me."

The team will meet on site, with accommodation provided by a local man who has converted an old brick barn into "rustic housing."

When I heard these details, I was terrified of what was in store for me. In the end, it wasn't such a horror. Two small rooms separated by a narrow hallway, plus a bathroom. Flushable toilet, lights, even two electric sockets by each bed. Luxurious. And the smell of manure that occasionally wafted from the nearby pigsties gave it proper countryside atmosphere. What else could you want from a village called Dolany, halfway between Pardubice and Hradec Králové.

I stood on the doorstep and wondered what to do now, when Láda's round face appeared above the fence.

"Hey, dude!" he called and rushed to the gate.

"Howdy," I smiled back at him and let my palm get crushed by his gorilla paw.

"So, shall we do Volary again?"

"Sure, but this time without naked occultist hiding under my bed, please."

Láďa started laughing, which caught the attention of our landlord, Mr. Osička, who started peeking curiously out the door. Damn, I guess we shouldn't yell like that.

The best thing about our job is that if we take a tape recorder and a camera and declare ourselves ghost hunters, most people will buy it. Check any collection of local folk tales. We're overflowing with ghosts.

Then they think we're harmless fools wandering around the graveyard. Even so, there's little in our work that we can talk about out loud in the public.

We sat down on a bench and moved on to more neutral topics. How are you, what are you doing, all wrapped up in euphemisms, of course. I commented on Láďa's elephant-smuggling-sized suitcase, saying that he had traveled light.

"You know, we're just supposed to scout the terrain," he shrugged. "I only packed the essentials." He squinted towards the door of the landlord's house and added quietly: "And sharpened spikes can be made anywhere."

I rolled my eyes.

"So you believe it?"

"In our work? Look, nothing surprises me anymore. By the way, what about that woman, Jiřina? You know her?"

Jiřina Dostálová, the prototype of a skinny math teacher with greasy blonde hair in a ponytail and her grandfather's framed glasses. That kind of girl next door who gets a makeover from a more attractive friend halfway through the movie and ends up named the cheerleading captain. Or she gets hacked to death with a machete at the 30th minute. I prefer the latter kind of movies.

"I took a look at her file. Apparently, she's not exactly a Hunter, more like a researcher."

So she's got a chance to survive right up to the moment when she wants to give the audience a key piece of information about the monster. That's when said monster breaks through the wall and bites her head off.

"So if it gets rough, we'll throw her as far away as possible from us and we will do Volary again," Láďa grumbles.

He looked into the distance at an approaching car. The wind blew a chicken feather from somewhere and it caught on his cheek. He didn't bat an eyelash. That was a remnant from his army days. He said he'd been in ops where you had to wait motionless for an order and nobody cared that you were standing in an anthill. I'd have blown that down a long time ago, but I don't have the same level of discipline as Láďa. Just like I miss the few dozen pounds of muscle that wrap around his massive frame.

The car, a shiny black Audi Q8, began to slow down. Was it her? Sure enough, there must have been a checkered flag stuck on the rock ahead, according to the GPS, because the driver gracefully turned through the open gate into the yard. The owner peered curiously out of the door. Jiřina Dostálová got out of the car.

"I think I just fell in love," Láďa breathed out tenderly.

"I don't know, a bit too ordinary for me," I grumbled.

"With that car, dude."

Yeah, that made sense.

Our teammate ostentatiously ignored us and went straight to the landlord, with whom she exchanged a few words. He just nodded obligingly at every word she said and grinned like an idiot, which she returned with a professional fake smile. Could this woman reel even an elephant in on boiled spaghetti? We've paid for our stay, but maybe she'll arrange a discount?

When she was done with that yokel, she headed straight for us.

"Šubert and Beránek, right?" she began with a question. "Jiřina Dostálová, nice to meet you. Please come to the car. The situation has changed."

I hadn't even had time to speak when the driver's side door slammed behind her.

"Nice to meet you too, babe," Láďa mumbled and went to sit in the back.

No sooner had I got on than the smell of petrol hit my nose. Of course, her company car and fuel are paid for, so she carries a "just in case" canister in the trunk which usually means she pours it into her own car at home. Judging by the intensity, though, I'd expect that if she didn't spill it outright, she's got a leaking cap at least.

"I read your files," Jiřina spoke first. "Ctibor Šubert, Ladislav

Beránek, both of you have a nice row of notches on your belts. It will be an honor to work with you."

I grumbled something vague, preferring not to imagine the look on Láďa's face. So she read our files, fine. She might also know that I was the group leader. So later, I'm getting an explanation as to why I had to take a bus while she got a company car.

"Nice to meet you," I squeezed out when Láďa nudged me through the seat with his knee. "I've read about you having quite a bit of experience with research and such and..."

I almost turned and grunted when I felt the knee in my back again.

Yeah, yeah, I got it.

"Where are we headed, anyway?" I went straight to the point for a change. Meanwhile, the landscape with meadows, forests and ponds, all colored in autumn yellows and browns, had been replaced by the first houses of the town of Lázně Bohdaneč.

"To see our informant. He called me an hour ago."

"Any good news?" Láďa finally spoke from behind.

"Sort of," Jiřina shrugged. "We finally have something to work with. The first dead victim."

Oh shit.

When it comes to informants, usually former Hunters, the best profession for them is one in which they come into contact with as many people as possible. The waiter who listens to the regulars in a pub, the hairdresser to whom every old lady confides that the neighbors are haunted. Or, in our case, the local doctor, Kabelka M.D., an elderly gentleman with remnants of grey hair around his ears and glasses resembling the bottoms of beer mugs.

"I bent a few rules for this," he said as he led us to the morgue. "The coroner and police chief are our people, so we delayed the usual procedures so you could examine the body."

"Did you find anything new?" I asked.

The doctor threw up his hands in a futile gesture and began fishing a key from his pocket.

"Nothing that would make me any wiser. Basically the same thing I reported at the beginning and what locals came to me with. Like something was sucking his blood. I've sent a blood sample to the SRS, just in case, but I expect a negative result for vampirism again. Anyway, you'll see for yourself."

The key clicked in the lock and the door opened. There was a chill and the fluorescent lights flickered. We stared at the table and the bare feet peeking out from under a sheet.

"Martin Jarušek, thirty-eight years old, production operator at Explosia Inc."

"So a worker," Láďa translated the doctor's statement into human language.

"Exactly," nodded the doctor. "He'd been my patient for over ten years. I've prescribed antibiotics for him twice, and I couldn't find anything more interesting in his chart. That guy was as healthy as a turnip."

And big as a mountain, I thought as I pulled the sheet off the dead man. All muscle, six-pack abs. Yeah, he had a manual job and probably worked out in his spare time.

I immediately looked at his neck.

"You won't find any bites," the doctor told me. "I'd report that, don't worry. I've examined him completely."

"And what's that?" pointed Jiřina at the dead man's chest. Although the body had already turned deathly pale, we could clearly see a reddened swollen spot around the left nipple.

"Inflammation," explained doctor Kabelka. "It is possible that he had an epidermoid cyst there and by an unprofessional attempt to remove it, he had carried infection there."

I glanced at our researcher, Jiřina. She met my eyes with the same questioning look.

"He squeezed out a pimple in a wrong way," Láďa translated.

"In layman's terms, but to the point," the doctor agreed. "Anyway, the place does show signs of injury, but the likely reason for that is that he scratched it. The cause of death is undoubtedly blood loss. The inflammation may have been unpleasant, but it doesn't look like anything life-threatening."

Jiřina took notes while I examined the body once more. Láďa was nervously stretching the index finger of his right hand. He was clearly not enjoying this and would rather shoot something.

"No bite doesn't mean anything yet. A strigoi can also be modern and draw blood through a syringe," I speculated.

"For someone to die from blood loss, it'd have to draw it out pretty quickly," countered Jiřina. "We have to take into account the number of people with the same symptoms. Does it suck blood out of them every night? Where is it sucking it from? After a few nights, people would notice they have punctures in their elbow sockets, right?"

"Or it scratches the victim's nipple and nurses blood," Láďa echoed from the back seat, but somehow I didn't have the energy to answer him. Holy shit, what gave him that idea?

"But more people would have the same problem, wouldn't they? They would have noticed it," Jiřina was more active than me.

"Oh right, so all we have to do is go around the village, banging on doors and saying 'Hello, may I see your tits?'"

"Láďa, stop," I groaned, shaking my head. On the other hand, maybe people noticed it, but they didn't think it was anything serious.

"This one is luxurious!" Láďa assessed the Dolany cemetery. "For a modern bloodsucker, it's perfect. Away from the village, a proper wall, even a parking lot in front of the gate!"

His words were accompanied by a constant *snip-snip* as he was sharpening a wooden stake with his knife. Yeah, apparently certain methods work on multiple kinds of bloodsuckers. Jiřina sat a bit away from him, poking a stick into the fire we had lighted behind the chapel. The smell of the smoke, along with the red setting sun and the whipping November wind, reminded me of some poem about shepherds roasting potatoes. I wondered if they were also watching thick mist slowly approaching them from a pond beyond the field. That kind of mist where a monster hides like it's nothing.

I found some work gloves in our landlord's shed, and I'd just dragged a dog rose bush I'd cut in front of the graveyard onto Jiřina's campfire.

"Do you really think this will work?" I asked Jiřina doubtfully.

"It's already burning properly. It'll catch on fire."

"I'm not talking about that. Is the smoke from a thorny flower really going to drift right down to an undead's grave?"

"There's a lot of bullshit about them, but I've tested this one."

"How about not being able to cross running water? We crossed a stream on the way."

"Yeah, that's why they built the Opatovice Canal," Láďa interjected, waving his knife towards the cemetery gate, which was the direction he suspected it flowed. "The water for the ponds was just a cover."

Jiřina shrugged and raked the burning wood.

"Bridges are probably fine. And a bat will fly over anything. Throw it in, Ctibor."

I happily threw a load of thorns into the flames, feeling them puncture my gloves in a few places.

"There was a dry one, wouldn't that be better?" I offered, looking at the still green tendrils of the dog rose.

"We need the smoke, wet branches will be better," Jiřina replied, trying to poke as much of the natural barbed wire as she could in the center of the fire.

Snip-snip, Láďa continued his work. He stood up holding one of the finished stakes, gave it a try and hit the first O in IN LOVING MEMORY on a wreath five yards away.

"Good one," I commented.

"Hardly," Láďa waved his hand at that. "I was aiming for the angel's gloriola," he pointed to a nearby grave.

"Let me try it," I prompted, and he threw me another stake.

Okay, straddle, aim, and throw!

The tip of the stake lodged between the marble head and the iron halo.

"I prefer guns," Láďa growled, tucking the knife into a holster at his waist. Then he turned his attention to Jiřina and her fully biological bloodsucker smoke detector.

There was plenty of smoke rising skyward. It snuggled nicely against the small tower on the chapel and then dissipated. Which was exactly what we didn't want.

I glanced at Jiřina, ready to ask a question, but noticing her grim expression, I preferred to keep my mouth shut. It really wasn't working out the way she wanted.

"Does a strigoi know someone is walking on their grave?" I suggested instead. "Like they'd rather pretend they're not home and not go out?"

"Even if they do, I hope they won't know who we are," she murmured in reply. "But they can't ward off the smoke. It really ought to find them!"

"Is there another method?" I wondered.

"Do you have a seven-year-old boy in white clothes sitting on a white horse? They say that at high noon, that horse is guaranteed to recognize the right grave."

"Well, a campfire sounds easier."

The sun had set by then. Láďa shivered with cold and looked around. It was clear that if he didn't see a strigoi in three minutes, he was going somewhere warm.

"I said it from the beginning," I shrugged. "A strigoi in such village? Unlikely."

"How about we put it out and go home?" echoed Láďa, fishing his gloves out of his pocket. "Let's sleep on it."

Without a word, Jiřina pulled a watering can from behind a nearby grave and tossed it to him.

"You noticed the pump by the gate, didn't you?"

The attitude of Czechs towards monsters is clear. Check out any fairy tale. Everyone makes fun of the devils, the will-o'-wisps are depressed that everyone thinks they're just rotten stumps, and the rusalkas supposedly joined the ballet.

Besides, this isn't America with a lot of empty space where a pagan cult can easily hide. Even Volary, which Láďa and I reminisced about, was a rather fun experience. The case of occultists hanging around the primordial nature of Durandel the Wood Sprite has gone down in history. I still vividly remember Láďa shooting down cultists fleeing down the hillside with short bursts, while I was luring their half-tree, half-animal pet right into a small minefield.

Once it was on its back, it was easy to get to its brain with an axe. I wasn't surprised it looked like a walnut.

But that was a notorious beast. People knew it from fairy tales and old stories about local glassmakers. This one? Well, who knows.

"Maybe someone brought a chupacabra from Mexico?" Láďa suggested.

"I saw a goat at the neighbors' place and it looked fine," I shook my head dismissively while looking over Jiřina's shoulder at my laptop. "And don't you dare tell some joke about sucking boobs."

"That's what you get for picking up a little Spanish," my teammate chuckled.

Jiřina was going through the company database, but after a

moment she sighed, and I nearly sputtered when she moved on to Wikipedia.

"You're kidding, right? If the teacher finds out where you downloaded your essay from, you will get an F!" I lectured her in the best nerd voice I could muster.

"It's possible we're dealing with something we've never fought before," Jiřina retorted. "I've always liked mythology, but Slavic and especially Czech mythology is terribly fragmented. Every region has a different version of the same monster. And our Slavic myths are mixed with Germanic ones."

"Also, don't forget that it may be something no one has ever seen! A new species," Láďa remarked from his bed as he inspected the AR-15 assault rifle he had pulled from his suitcase.

"I feel so much better now," muttered Jiřina, then looked up at me as I put on my jacket. "Where are you going?"

"Field work. If there's something flying around at night, there's good chance I'll see it. You search the net, Láďa gets his arsenal ready."

The door slammed behind me and the November night frost bit into me. First of all, I needed some peace to think, and that's impossible with Láďa's remarks in background.

Compared to the rush of a big city, I would call the nighttime atmosphere of a small village like Dolany peaceful. Quiet and calm, a dog barked here and there, but even they preferred to crawl into their kennels in this cold.

A fire tank, a chapel, the municipal office, a memorial to the victims of the First World War, the church, a pub, a general store, all this was drowned in the darkness and quiet of the night. I decided to go left at the next junction so as not to unnecessarily return to the cemetery.

The sidewalk was empty. If I were just a few miles further, in Lázně Bohdaneč, I would probably meet someone, but here? If any old ladies suffer from insomnia, I'll be the subject of gossip tomorrow. A vandal, or maybe a robber. And it was definitely the one who killed Mr. Jarušek!

I shuddered. A thicker fog rolled into the village, rising from the nearby ponds. Soon it would engulf the whole village and it would be like wading through milk. Even worse than the cold is a cold and wet weather at the same time; it was the kind of weather in which even a monster's ass would freeze.

I thought I'd turn around soon. Not only I was cold, but I wouldn't be able to see more than two yards.

Just as I had that thought, an outline of a human figure emerged from the fog on the other sidewalk, walking in the opposite direction. Hey, I'm not alone. But if I turn around now, it'll look bad. Like I'm stalking them.

I kept walking for a while, but the freeze made me change my mind. Damn it, I'll turn around, they might not even see me in this fog.

Yeah, fog in front of me, fog behind me. But after just a few steps back towards our lodgings, something came out of it right in front of me. Another human outline. Damn it, there's traffic!

She was bundled up in a thick winter jacket and had her hood pulled up over her head. I could barely get any closer before I could see the features of her unhealthily pale face. I also noticed the pregnant belly she was holding on to.

"Good evening," I blurted out. I wanted to look like a good guy.

We stood facing each other and she just stared at me with her dark eyes. The circles around them made them look even bigger. A large freckle on her chin formed a triumvirate with them.

She nodded silently in greeting. Well, hallelujah, I was afraid she'd dissolve into more fog without another word.

I smiled and continued on my way. I met a pregnant young woman on the street at night. Unusual, but maybe she was just going home. And she was shy. Nothing suspicious.

After a few steps, I realized she was following me like a shadow. I stopped, so did she.

"Do you need anything? Maybe a ride somewhere?" I asked, but again she just stared at me and didn't say anything. Okay, this wasn't normal anymore.

"Are you alright?" I kept trying.

She nodded. At least some reaction.

She squeezed her round belly a little tighter and looked down at it. I had a feeling she'd whispered something silently.

"Excuse me?"

"Where do you live?" she said. Hey, she can talk. And even in Czech.

"At Mr. Osička's pension," I replied uncertainly. That's a question. I wonder how many people provide housing here, huh?

Another nod.

"Do you need a place to stay? Do you have somewhere to go?"

She shook her head negatively at first, then affirmatively.

"I'm sorry, but I have to go," I smiled nervously and took a step away from her. "Goodbye."

She nodded. Then she propped her stomach up and ran away. How far along was she? Could she still be able to run like this? Damn it, I should have found out her name and asked Dr. Kabelka about her! Maybe she's in his records.

I walked a few steps and looked back again. The wind was blowing, bringing a cloud of particularly thick fog from the fields. For a moment, I thought I saw someone inside it.

I sped up and checked if I could quickly draw my concealed knife and gun.

Stupid paranoia.

Just as I locked the door behind me, the sound of an approaching earthquake caught my attention. I'd almost forgotten how badly Láďa snores. Jiřina came out of the other room, using her cell phone as a flashlight. Judging by the direction she took, she was heading for the bathroom. She looked at me, obviously expecting a reaction.

"So how was the field work?" she muttered when none came.

"Nothing. I couldn't see the tip of my nose in this fog. I met this weird woman, but she didn't look like a strigoi. Could an undead be pregnant?"

"I doubt it. I guess it's too much to ask to crack this in one evening, huh?" Jiřina yawned, continuing on her way. "Good night."

"Good night."

I opened the door to mine and Láďa's room. My buddy was sleeping like a little kid. On his back, limbs in all directions and with the blanket kicked off.

A maternal feeling awoke in me and I went to cover him. In the process I almost tripped over his belt with a gun and a knife, which he had left lying on the floor with his trousers. He's got a chair next to him, damn it! That's what I get for my goodness...

I threw a blanket over him. Good night, buddy.

✦   ✦   ✦

I felt quite nervous on the way to Alexandra's office. I was tempted to turn around and flee because I wasn't sure why she had called me. It all happened so suddenly, so unexpectedly. Plus, everyone was staring at me. I could feel their stares on my back, but whenever I turned around, they looked like nothing happened.

Why are there so many people here? Where did they come from?

I passed more and more faces. They all know who I am, they are all judging me. He's the one who's going to be hauled over the coals.

The dreaded door loomed in front of me. When I grasped the handle, I felt so weak I couldn't even open it. Eventually, however, it gave way and I was able to enter the lion's den.

Alexandra was smiling. I hadn't expected that.

She motioned for me to sit down. The otherwise uncomfortable chair accepted me into its surprisingly soft embrace until I almost expected it to start stroking my ass.

"Have I ever told you, Ctibor, what an asset you are to us?" she began to speak in honeyed words. The chair beneath me was suddenly even more comfortable. I sank deeper into it. At the same time, however, I felt a sense of an outside force pushing me into it.

"You will receive an extraordinary reward for your accomplishments," Alexandra announced, placing a briefcase on the table. The locks clicked and I saw green bills.

"What kind of bullshit is this?" I giggled. "A generic scene from an American movie? My money goes into my account, no such cliché."

I looked in that briefcase. Sure enough, the numbers on the money were impossible to read properly, and even the portrait of the statesman seemed to refuse to steady before my gaze.

Realizing I was in a dream had happened more than once in my life. Lucid dreaming is fun, but unfortunately, I usually fall asleep harder or wake up sooner.

The pressure increased and I fell into the chair again. The cushioning inflated as if it wanted to absorb me. Oh no, nothing like that! This is my dream, I'm its master.

I reached to my side. My hand grasped the hilt of a bayonet. Unlike Láďa, I keep a blade in my bed.

With my thumb, I pushed the snap button and freed the blade. Steel glinted in the fluorescent light.

Wait, that's not really necessary. It's my dream! I thought to myself that the chair should cease its actions.

Nothing. The mysterious force pushed me in even more. You want it? You got it! Looks like I will need my knife after all.

I stuck it in the padding. If it doesn't deflate, I'll cut my way out of it.

Alexandra backed away from me with fear in her eyes. Why did I keep seeing her as standing behind a desk? It wasn't until now that I realized my eyes were deceiving me. She had been standing in front of me the whole time, pressing against my chest.

The pressure stopped. She took a few steps back and began to walk around me. Oh, right, you want to get the door. Too bad it's locked.

Because this is my dream, remember?

She grabbed the doorknob and yanked it in vain. She gave it a worried look, but immediately turned her attention back to me.

I got up from my chair. Damn, it was actually as uncomfortable as ever. I held out my hand with the bayonet and watched as Alexandra stared fearfully at its tip.

This was getting weird. Too long for a lucid dream. Knowing me, I should be waking up any minute now.

And it's just a dream in the first place, so what the hell? What can a dream version of my boss do to me?

I'll never know. She put her hand to the keyhole and it literally sucked her in. Alexandra turned into black slime and ran through the keyhole.

A clear sign to my mind that I should wake up.

I opened my eyes. The light of a street lamp glinted on the blade of the bayonet I was clutching in my hand. Yeah, I keep it with me for emergencies, but this truly was the first time I've ever drawn it in my dreams. Pretty dangerous.

I sat up in bed and put the blade on the nightstand. I had no idea what time it might be, but I didn't feel the least bit tired after such a bizarre dream. I just felt need to pee.

On my way to the bathroom, I noticed a light coming from the opposite door. After I finished, I knocked on the door.

"Come in," I heard Jiřina say.

I entered. My teammate was sitting at the coffee table, her hands tucked under her chin, reading something on her laptop.

"Can't sleep?"

"It literally won't let me sleep," she replied, rubbing her eyes. "I decided to look directly for Dolany, but there is more than one village with that name. And I had to be skipping all those Dolan's Cadillac references or bad paintings of Donald Duck. It didn't lead anywhere. I do have one tip, though. A *mura*."

"I'd expect more of a mosquito."

"Not the insect. A mura as a mythological creature. But that's the problem. It's just a rumor, we don't have any records of an actual mura. There are stories about them in Slavic and Germanic mythology, and each tale mentions them differently. Sometimes it is a cursed person, sometimes a monster, or a mischievous house imp. And there's more; it is often supposed to be a soul leaving the body and masquerading as a white cat, straw or horse."

"So anything around us can be a mura?"

Jiřina nodded.

"Exactly. And as soon as you're not paying attention, it sits on you and sucks. But blood loss and an inflamed nipple are the only things that match one hundred percent so far. The ways to defend yourself are as chaotic as descriptions of the mura. Anoint your chest with pitch, draw a pentagram on the door, keep something sharp in bed..."

"That doesn't sound very safe."

"Sort of. And I think if we start scribbling stars on people's doors, we'll be cast out as Satanists. But for now, the best part. Do you want to know how to kill her? Nail it to the wall or cut it in half."

I smiled. Sounds trivial.

"Okay, so the identification is the hard part, then even a kid can handle the disposal."

She nodded.

"I'd better go to bed or I won't be able to get up tomorrow. I'll summarize my research for the both of you then."

"Sounds reasonable," I nodded. "Good night, then. Again."

In the morning we were greeted by fog again. I like autumn, but I hate mornings like this. You get the feeling from the start that the cold is going to completely overcome you within a minute. It's disgusting.

I stood on the doorstep with a cup of coffee and watched the white wisps roll over. Judging by the sounds from inside, Jiřina must have gotten up, but Láďa was still cutting wood with a chainsaw.

A message dinged on my cell phone. Dr. Kabelka. Tests on the deceased Mr. Jarušek came back negative. As expected.

Every now and then, someone would walk by and everyone looked like someone was sucking their blood in the night. Of course, on a morning like this, I'd chalk it up to a natural reluctance to get up and go out.

But how many of them were really victims?

I walked closer to the fence to get a better view of the passers-by. It wasn't the same hustle as in the city. I had plenty of time to focus on everyone and wonder if this young...

The coffee cup stopped halfway to my mouth. I recognize this woman! I saw her last night and she disappeared into the fog! You'd think you would notice a pregnant woman, but that was the problem. I clearly recognized her, but she had obviously forgotten her belly somewhere. She was wearing a hood and we met in the twilight, but I recognized those dark eyes with the circles and the freckle on her chin right away. What now? Run up to her and congratulate her on the kid? Or was it her sister?

She noticed me staring at her and returned my gaze. A very neutral look. I smiled and nodded in greeting. She looked away and minded her own business.

And I stood there like an idiot, staring at her back and sipping my coffee again. Maybe she had a dog under her jacket last night?

The door creaked open behind me. Láďa, the hard-ass, came out on the doorstep, wearing nothing but shorts and a T-shirt.

"Hey," he said, leaning against the fence next to me. A granny on the opposite sidewalk, wrapped in coat like a mummy, looked offended that he was exposing himself to the deadly cold. Láďa scowled at her, scratched his chest, turned up his collar provocatively, and waved his other hand to expel the excess heat.

I just grunted something in greeting. My mind was processing that woman I met last night.

"Jiřina is calling you in. She wants to recap her research for us."

I nodded silently and followed him. Our teammate was waiting for us, sitting behind her laptop. I sat down on the couch next to Láďa and didn't listen to Jiřina too much as she started her lecture just like the night before.

A mura can change shape, I know that now. But who says I saw a mura? The girl might not be connected to the case at all. On the other hand, why would she ask me where we were staying at night and then pretend she didn't know me in the morning? There's something weird about this village. Maybe not a monster, but definitely a few freaks.

Láďa somehow couldn't settle down and almost elbowed me a couple of times when he was tugging on his shirt. Again! For at least the third time.

"Ctibor here is the only such freak," he suddenly interrupted Jiřina's explanation, which brought me out of my reverie.

"What?" I blurted out, and it was obvious I hadn't been listening.

"How to fight off a mura. You have to have something sharp in your bed. Only you sleep with a knife," he almost taunted me.

"Compared to you, whose guns are thrown on the ground for me to trip over, huh?" I grinned in return.

He shrugged and scratched his stomach.

"May I continue?" Jiřina broke in between us. "A mura will start by causing you a pleasant dream. It will lull you to sleep. Then it'll sit on you, you might even feel like it's suffocating you. Then it starts sucking blood from your chest."

My thoughts flew with lightning speed.

A pleasant dream. Like one about a lot of money. The weight pushing down. Rescue in the form of a sharp object.

Then all I had to do was look at Láďa rubbing his chest. The same Láďa who ants can crawl all over and he wouldn't mind.

"Láďa, take off your shirt," I said as calmly as I could, though I didn't feel like it.

"What?"

"Take your shirt off, I'm afraid our operation is compromised."

The silence was as thick as molasses. And I mentally cursed to myself that I had quite definitely told the mura where we were staying.

Láďa pulled off his shirt.

There was a bit dried blood around his left nipple.

✦ ✦ ✦

Láďa bore it bravely. He lay on the sofa and let Jiřina look at the wound. Meanwhile, I was pacing back and forth in the corridor, because as soon as I started doing it in the room, she chased me out.

I'm such an idiot! This is just not possible!

"You can come in!" shouted Jiřina. I came back and sat down next to my friend who was getting dressed.

"So, is he going to turn into a mura?"

"Yeah," Láďa chimed in, "turn off the light bulb or I'll be flying around it."

"He shouldn't," Jiřina corrected him. "But that wound is really strange. At first I thought it was capillary bleeding. As if the mura sucked it out with a vacuum. But then I noticed there are actually tiny punctures lined up in several circles."

"I've seen that before," I broke in, trying in vain to remember the case in question. Then it dawned on me. It wasn't a case. It was a book about aquatic animals that I had as a child.

I looked at Jiřina with an extra skeptical eye.

"Lampreys?" I suggested.

She nodded.

"Exactly. It looks like a lamprey bite."

"And a mura bite is supposed to look like what?"

"I don't know, I haven't read anything about that. Like I said, there are a million variations mentioned, but none of them mention this."

"If we've never really encountered this mura and every description says it's supposed to look different, we'll have to go straight to the main source for information!"

"And what is that, Mr. Smart?" she retorted sarcastically.

"Maybe there's a library in the town hall, no?"

Jiřina said she would try to pirate some book online. But although it may seem absurd to some nowadays, not everything is on the net. Consider me old-fashioned, but Google will never replace a librarian.

One might think that a tiny library in a local town hall would hardly be a sufficient source of information. But on the other hand, where else to look for local history and lore enthusiasts?

I knocked, opened the door, said hello . . . and froze.

The brown-haired lady behind the counter looked at me wearily with big dark eyes that, together with the freckle on her chin, formed a small constellation.

Shit. I hate these coincidences.

"Hello," she greeted in return and smiled. "What do you need?"

I stared at her and remained silent. What now? In the face of a mura, even a harmless story about paranormal investigators is dangerous.

"Do you have any books about local lore, please?" I began neutrally. "I'm mapping Czech mythology and focusing more on regional folklore."

The girl bit her lower lip. I expected her to leap over the counter and bite into me at any moment.

"Well, that's not exactly something the local grandmothers read," she replied after a moment's thought. "To tell you the truth, I mostly have romance and mystery novels. But I know of a book you'd appreciate. I have it at home. You live in Osička's house, don't you? I saw you there this morning. The gossips here make you out to be a detective or a spy, by the way. Anyway, I have the book at home, and I live across from the playground. If you wander there around 6:30, I'll lend it to you."

I carried on a little more casual talk with her for a while. I waited for her to slip some information, but no luck. In fact, all I've learned was that her name was Marie.

Okay, I have a date at 6:30.

"When she comes out, do I have to sit on that swing and pretend I'm ten years old?" Láďa teased me as we walked to the meeting place.

"Do what you want, but watch my back. And the kids are past their bedtime!"

Láďa was grumbling all the way. He'd spent the day walking around the village, looking for anything suspicious. Considering his years of experience in detecting monsters, he declared that he had never seen a more ordinary village.

Jiřina spent the whole day reading. What do we have her for? Wouldn't home office be enough? She's got my phone number.

"I don't like this. That girl looks like a shot in the dark to me. Everything you're describing seems like a coincidence," Láďa continued to play the skeptic.

"First of all, I'm going to borrow a book from her. She may have nothing to do with the case, but if she gives us information, that's a good thing."

We arrived at the place. Wisps of fog rolled into the village as they had yesterday, dimming the already meager light coming from the surrounding houses. This side street could only dream of street lights; only the main ones in Dolany got them. Still, I could see enough of Marie's house. A two-story new building, obviously insulated, plastic windows, tiled roof. Nice house, where did she get the money for it?

In the end, Láďa just walked a short distance and disappeared into the fog. Just in time, the silhouette of Marie appeared in the opposite direction.

"Good evening, so here I am," I smiled at her like friendliness itself, but in my mind I was crouched and ready to dodge an attack.

"Hello," she nodded back and huddled a little more into her scarf. "I'll get it for you right away."

So what's it going to be? Invite me in and try to kill me? Or will she throw her arms around my neck because I'm the hero she's always wanted?

As soon as we reached the door, she asked me to wait a moment and disappeared into the house. Sure, she wants to get ready. Sharpen her fangs, powder her nose...

She opened the door again and handed me a leather-bound book. "Here you go. When do you think you could give it back?"

"Well, tomorrow, perhaps," I stammered out, surprised by the unexpected turn of events.

"Then bring it to me at work, will you? I'm off to cook, I'm hungry as a wolf. Bye!"

"Bye..."

The door slammed in my face.

"Dude, that was really anticlimactic," Láďa claimed behind me, pretending to be a random passerby.

Jiřina glanced at the book. "*Tales from Pardubice and Hradec region*," she read the title in golden letters and flipped through it. "Where did you leave Láďa?"

"He said he was going to bed right away."

As if on cue, the sound of cutting wood came from his room.

"That was fast," Jiřina assessed her teammate's performance, then she stuck her finger in the book. "A mura! It's here. So, where... Oh my God! *At the end of a village called Dolany lived...* The very first sentence!"

"You know who can, does."

"It's less than two pages."

Jiřina read while I sank down on the couch. I'm curious to see what I'll learn.

"A lamprey-like mouth would be mentioned here. Literally," Jiřina spoke up a moment later. "However, the rest of the description makes me wonder what our ancestors smoked. A barrel-shaped body, glowing eyes, duck feet, cat claws... What are whynges?"

"Wings," I pulled an obscure piece of knowledge from the depths of my brain. "That sounds like a real bizarro. I think a more likely image is a woman who..."

I didn't finish. I was sitting across from a window facing the street. The lamp there was fighting desperately with the fog, but it was still enough to illuminate the figure that had climbed over the fence and jumped into the garden.

Marie.

With a pregnant belly.

I flew off the couch and ran for the front door. I slammed the handle. Shit, Láďa locked it! Come on, here's his jacket. Something's jingling, but which pocket is it? Shit, the zipper's stuck!

I tugged. The stitches holding the zipper weren't as tight as the stuck teeth, so I got into the pocket. Unlock it, fast.

"What's wrong?" I heard Jiřina behind my back.

"The librarian is here," I replied, finally unlocking the door. A fog rolled in.

"Marie!" I shouted.

She was just hopping over the fence, this time toward the street.

The pregnant belly was gone.

I ran to the gate, but before I could unlock it, Marie disappeared into the fog. No, I'm not going after her alone. There's gotta be more of us for that.

"Jiřina, get ready. We'll take the car, I'll just go get Láďa."

He'll be pissed that I'm waking him up.

✦ ✦ ✦

"Láďa, emergency!" I yelled and turned on the light... and froze immediately.

My buddy had his shirt rolled up and something looking like a winged barrel was sitting on his bare chest. Like a little elephant with its trunk attached to his left nipple.

It was like a fucking joke.

The mura broke away. Unswallowed blood gushed from its trunk and splashed Láďa.

By that point, I had a bayonet in my hand. You can't run, you bitch.

It tried to, but duck legs aren't exactly made for running. When it tried to slip past me, I kicked it across the room. Then I slammed the door behind me and lunged at it.

Feathers rustled. The mura flapped its wings and jumped. The target? My chest.

I flinched and felt the leathery flesh brush against me. Its feet, with their floating membranes, slapped me, and the sharp pain in my arm showed that the rumor didn't lie about the cat's claws either.

Plus, the creature had torn my favorite shirt.

I took a swing at it. The tip of the blade struck the mura in the wing, disrupting its flight plan. With a thud, the fat creature crashed into the wall.

I got you!

One step, two steps, ready to slash...

If I didn't see it with my own two eyes, I wouldn't believe it.

One moment a lifeless pile of misery buried its snout in the corner, sticking its butt out at me. The next, there was a hissing beast that shot its trunk towards me, full of circles of teeth.

The mura didn't turn around. It just... changed. It crawled through itself to face me, its already glowing eyes now blazing with rage.

I jumped back, took a step to avoid the trunk... and tripped over Láďa's pants, his belt festooned with weapons.

Oh, shit.

I slammed the table with my wrist and dropped the bayonet. In the fall, I rolled over and fell flat on my back. Immediately, I felt the mura land on my chest and sink its claws into me. It was heavier than it looked.

The trunk came into my field of vision. The leathery, sphincter-like membrane contracted several times, loosening around a black hole surrounded by needle-like teeth. Guessing its target, I instinctively covered my eyes.

A shot rang out. The mura wobbled, fell off me onto its side, and rolled under the table.

"You okay?" I heard Láďa's voice.

"Just fine, Sleeping Beauty," I replied, accepting a helping hand.

"I'm sorry, but that bitch is not only sucking on you, she's like … hypnotizing you. I knew you were fighting, but I was still in a dream and couldn't snap out of it."

I looked at my teammate's hand. He was clutching a small revolver. It almost disappeared in his huge paw.

He noticed my look and immediately explained, "You know, I'm not like you, sleeping with a knife in my bed. I prefer to have a real gun under my pillow."

I didn't comment on that and instead pushed the table away.

Nothing. There was just a bloodstain on the carpet under the table. Could it have rolled away?

The furthest tip curved and the mura popped out from under the completely flat carpet. There wasn't even a bump! It immediately ran for the door, leaving a trail of blood in its wake.

I wasn't playing the hero and got out of Láďa's way.

Two shots rang out. The first missed, the second hit the mura in the leg. It staggered, but still bounced and made it to the door.

Suddenly, it turned into a shapeless dark blob, stretched into a string and jumped through the keyhole in a flash. I immediately remembered my dream in which Alexandra had done the same thing. Damn, I must have perceived more in my sleep then I thought!

There was a scream from outside the door. Láďa was the first to go, and I grabbed the dropped bayonet and followed.

Jiřina, seeing us, retreated into her room. We ran down the blood trail, but no sooner had we reached the doorstep than the chase was over.

The mura lay on its side next to the car, twitching.

"It bled to death, bitch," Láďa chimed in. "It's out of blood. My blood!"

With the blade outstretched in front of me, I bent down over the dead monster and poked it. Láďa immediately covered me with his body, for the shots had evidently awakened the landlord, who was looking fearfully out of the window.

The mura's movements were slowing. I rolled it over on its other side.

"Láďa, you hit it in the torso the first time, didn't you?"

"Oh yeah, the biggest target, I played it safe."

"This wound on its leg is quite obvious, but can you see here and here?" I rolled the mura around on the grass. "The bullet went through, but instead of a gash I see a scar."

"So it tore it up inside, right? Though, as we saw, it's amorphous."

"So that's why Marie wore it under her jacket! It doesn't like the cold! It's like a lizard, it freezes in the cold!" I deduced.

"And we don't even have to nail it to the wall or cut it."

"But why should Marie help it?" I wondered.

"Because it told her to do it?" Láďa shrugged. "Hey, if that bitch can enter your dreams, it might as well brainwash you, right? I told you it was like hypnosis."

Jiřina joined us, dressed appropriately for the cold outside.

"I think I'm going to go calm Mr. Osička down while you get your hardware ready for a visit at Miss Librarian's." she said. "I think she has a lot to explain."

Some firecrackers in Láďa's backpack accidentally blew up. He got hurt, he was bleeding, so we're taking him to the hospital. But I think the moment Jiřina pulled out her wallet and a few bills changed hands, she could have easily claimed that a herd of elephants had raided the former barn, and the landlord wouldn't have cared.

We arrived at Marie's house. The lights were on, but all the windows were drawn with heavy curtains, so we couldn't look inside.

I checked to make sure I had everything I needed. Under my jacket I hid a bayonet, a fully loaded Glock and two spare magazines. In my hands I held the borrowed book of local legends.

"It's ironic that it was the perpetrator who gave us the information about the creature," Láďa was saying while he made the final check of an assault rifle. With a cursory glance, I couldn't even tell how many weapons he had on his body, only hoping we won't need the pair of grenades he'd slipped into the pocket of his tactical vest.

"I'd call her a victim. At least I hope so," I replied, waiting for him to stand around the corner so Marie wouldn't see him right away.

Jiřina was rummaging in the trunk of the car.

"Go ahead, I'm right on your heels," we heard her say. Láďa finally admitted that he didn't see any cameras and hid.

I rang the bell. Nothing. The second time, nothing. As I reached for the bell a third time, Láďa nudged me to move.

Fortunately, the door opened inward. When an army boot fell heavily on it, it was wise and stepped back.

"We're here to stop a monster or save a victim, so it doesn't matter which she is," Láďa defended his course of action and started forward with his rifle pointed.

I put the borrowed book on the shoe rack. It had served its purpose.

The first thing that struck me was the heat in the house. Downright tropics, an unprecedented phenomenon at the current price of energy. Then the smell hit my nose; a mix of an elephant pavilion and a chemical warehouse. Not many people would voluntarily have this at home, so to me it was clear evidence that something was going on here.

Láďa peered into the living room. Well, we only suspected it was a living room, because now I'd call it more of a hatchery.

Hanging from the ceiling, covered in a mass of deep red tissue, were leathery bags the size of small backpacks on slimy stalks.

I pulled out my bayonet and opened one with a quick slash. A mucous black mass poured out and fell to the ground with a splash. Some parts looked more solid. White, not yet glowing eyeballs, a trunk with rings of teeth and hints of wings with tiny slimy feathers.

"Holy shit," Láďa commented on the situation.

"Yeah," I nodded and looked around. The house had one more floor and an attic. Maybe even a basement. I saw at least a dozen cocoons in this room alone.

With a pistol in my hand, I walked into the kitchen. I couldn't identify what Marie was cooking in the large pot sitting on the stove, but I didn't believe it was meant for human consumption. It wasn't hard to tell that the chemical component of the smell came mostly from there.

I opened the fridge in anticipation of a store of chemicals. I didn't open the PET bottles that peeked out at me, but I suspected the red content was not wine.

Five more cocoons hung above the dining table, with a thick pulsating blood vessel running between them, stuck to the ceiling like an arm.

"This house is alive," I remarked, opening the window to let in the freezing fog. Láďa joined in. Open the windows, turn off the heat. We soon found out that the terrible heat was coming from electric heaters. Two in the living room, one more in the kitchen.

I peeked into the pantry and the bedroom. More cocoons, more pulsating blood vessels.

"When I first heard the word mura, I expected a fairy-tale creature. Someone who's being helping Snow White or something," Láďa said, while unplugging another electric heater. "But this? What the hell is that, anyway?"

I'd answer him if I knew. In the meantime, I carefully poked the bayonet into the blood vessel above me. It bent, but I'd have to try harder to pierce it.

The temperature in the house was dropping and we made our way up the stairs. Another scene with cocoons, but we found something new inside a bathroom. The bathtub was filled to the brim with a volatile-smelling liquid, part of which must have been the mix that Marie was cooking downstairs. The tap was a little open, keeping the water level, and beneath its murky surface I could sense something like a heart pumping the filth into the blood vessels that crawled out of the tub like tentacles and ran to all corners of the house. I turned off the tap, but to reach under the surface to pull out the stopper—that I didn't dare.

Láďa opened the door of the next room. Here was Marie's library. A beautiful, big one. I estimated that she must have had at least a thousand books on the white shelves along the walls.

There were considerably fewer canisters of chemicals, but still more than one would expect in a library.

Gasoline, acetone, ammonia. I didn't read any further. When was the story of the mura supposed to take place? What kind of potions were they brewing back then? What were they using?

Láďa and I looked at each other in silence and went downstairs again. We still haven't found what was most important—Marie.

Meanwhile, the temperature downstairs had dropped to forty degrees. The blood vessels on the ceiling pulsed in a slower rhythm, and they shook now and then. Could it be the cold? Outside it had begun to snow, and through the wide-open window the wind blew flakes into the bedroom, forming little drifts.

The strange thing was that there were none on the bed. There they melted immediately. Moreover, why hadn't we noticed before that one particularly thick slimy tube ran directly underneath it? Accompanied by an electric cord. I bent down. Oh, yeah, there was a hole. And Marie was tiny; she could squeeze through it without moving the furniture.

I nodded to Láďa and together we pushed the bed away. The hole in the floor where the blood vessel disappeared was just enough for a person to squeeze through. Dim red light illuminated the roughly seven feet long ladder below. A fire, perhaps? It wasn't a steady glow; it flickered.

"I'm going first," I said, and climbed down the first rungs.

As I reached solid ground, something crunched softly under my boot. I looked in disgust at the completely desiccated dead rat. The light was enough to see that it wasn't the only one. Surely they'd all been drained by muras. And the husks that remained were then dried to cinders by the heat.

I looked around the walls. Stone, bricks. It looked like an old cellar, which was definitely not fitting the modern house above it. The house was probably standing at the site of an older building.

Flickering light came from around the corner from a hole cut in the wall. Light, heat and smell.

Láďa was already standing behind me, rifle ready to fire. Together we peered into the passage.

Marie. She was lying on a large flexible membrane stretched between luminous fleshy stalactites, her eyes wide open, staring at the ceiling, a mura perched on her chest. It wasn't sucking blood, just gently stroking her cheek with its trunk. There was another electric heater plugged into the extension cord she had strung here.

I quietly leaned over to the plug and unplugged it. Not that it was likely to make a difference, as most of the heat must have come from the passages leading further into the ground that we could see behind Marie.

I gestured to Láďa that we should go back. Silent like mice, we climbed the ladder back to the bedroom. In her doorway, Jiřina was waiting for us.

"If this is behind the rumors of muras, Czech mythology is wilder than I thought," she whispered, as if afraid that the cocoons would start hatching on command.

"Call for backup," I said. "More people, full gear. There's probably a bigger nest underground than what you see here. We know what's here, so our job is done."

"Yeah, the identification was successful," Láďa added. "It's a real mess."

We left the house. If the muras decided to follow us, perhaps the cold weather would be our ally. Plus, the fog and snow were playing into our hands, hiding us from prying neighbors.

We stood with Láďa in the hallway and watched as Jiřina made a long phone call in the car.

"Do you think that girl is doing this willingly?" Láďa asked.

"Hmm? Well, I don't know. Why would she give me the book that helped us? On the other hand..."

"What are you doing here? And why is it so cold here? Is that a machine gun?!"

We turned around. Marie was standing behind us, looking quite scared.

"No, an assault rifle, people often confuse the two. Don't worry, we're here to protect you from that," Láďa went straight to the point and pointed the barrel to the nearest cocoon.

Marie looked in that direction.

"From my chandelier?"

The cocoon was really hanging on the chandelier.

"Oh no, I mean that one!" my buddy pointed behind her.

She turned around.

And got a stunning blow.

"Was that necessary?"

"If she can't see what the muras have done to her house, who knows what else is in her head," Láďa defended himself, and I gave him the benefit of the doubt.

I grabbed Marie under her arms and dragged her to the car. Jiřina opened the door for me and helped me slide her inside.

The smell of gasoline inside was stronger than before. What the hell was she doing here?

A gunshot snapped me out of my reverie. And another. A short burst.

I ran back into the house. Láďa was kneeling in the living room, aiming at the bedroom door, where a mura was currently rolling around in pain. The puddle next to it suggested that its companion had tried to liquefy, but the low ambient temperature no longer allowed it to flow away.

The wounded mura soon stopped moving.

"We'll have the police here in a few minutes," I sighed, pulling my Glock from a holster as a screeching sound like two rocks grinding against each other came from the hole in the ground.

What the hell was going on?

We walked over to the hole and shone light into it. There were cracks in the walls of the cellar, and dust was pouring out of them. We heard snuffling and snorting, like a large animal wading through a river of slime.

Something told me that the idea was not far from the truth.

The floor cracked and fell somewhere into the dark depths. There was a rumble and then dozens of glowing pairs of eyes looked at us. Trunks wavered and muras, glued into a single van-sized organism similar to a giant millipede, began to claw their way to the surface.

Láďa immediately opened fire and I followed his example. Whether single shots or short bursts, all seemed futile. Blood and black liquid spurted in all directions, but the monster was only slowed by the fire. The eyes faded as the wounded muras seeped inward among the healthy ones that replaced them.

We began to retreat and change magazines. Great, even though help was probably on the way, it would be too late for us.

The magazine clicked into place and I fired into the largest cluster of eyes. The muras screeched, oozing a foul-smelling liquid at me, but they disappeared immediately. We have to lure them out into the cold and...

Then I realized. The heat! It was not only an adrenaline! It's radiating right off these creatures!

Another shot, another retreat of the muras inside. But I noticed that it wasn't just the ones that got hit that were going in. The muras were taking turns moving towards us. They'd stay on the surface for a while and then go warm up.

The tentacles reached for us; the claws slashed. Only bullets kept them out of reach. We were already in the garden. I was running low on ammunition. I know Láďa, he's got more, but...

"Get out of the way," Jiřina pushed us away and faced the monster rolling down the porch.

That's why her car smelled of gas.

And why she took the time to get ready.

We immediately took a few steps away from Jiřina, who pulled the trigger of a flamethrower. The flammable mixture spewed out onto a bunch of monsters. Then my teammate switched on the flame, which immediately jumped along the stream.

You like heat, but fire, that's different, isn't it?

The burning muras fell off and mostly lay dead. The mura colony hesitated. They were more resilient together, but also slower.

Jiřina blew out the fire again. The muras made a hasty retreat back to the house. Interestingly, the colony did not allow the burning individuals to enter. As soon as a mura started burning, the others chased it away. They even slashed a few with their claws rather than let them in.

That gave me an idea. And we had to act fast, because the whole village had to know about us by now.

"Jiřina, go to the hole and burn anything that tries to come out. Láďa, you come with me!" I shouted, ran into the house and headed upstairs.

"They burn really good," I heard Láďa say behind me.

"No surprise, when you see what they're chomping on besides blood!" I said, gesturing to the bookcase full of canisters and bottles. "Take everything that burns!"

In the end we had to go three times.

We were staring into a hole. I threw a flashlight in it. The cone of light moved away for a while, then it bounced off something and flew off somewhere we couldn't see it anymore.

"If they're bothered by the fire, we can at least do something before reinforcements arrive," I said to Jiřina as I opened the containers and lined them up.

"I still can't believe something like this made it into local lore," Jiřina shook her head. "How long has this place been around? Why are we only learning about it now?"

"Maybe the muras were sleeping underground, but the dwarves were greedy and dug too deep?" I laughed and opened a can of gasoline.

She shrugged.

Láďa, meanwhile, got into the car, ready to leave immediately in case of an emergency. We certainly didn't have time to waste.

"Ready?" I asked Jiřina.

She put on her protective goggles and nodded.

"Yeah."

I pushed on a row of canisters and bottles. They fell down like skittle pins.

"Now!"

Jiřina pulled the trigger and sent her own contribution after the regiment of flammables.

Then we ran to the car and didn't look back.

The blue beacons were coming.

I could have sworn the ground shook, but I'm sure it was just my imagination.

When I went to Alexandra's office, everyone was looking at me. Damn, déjà vu. Soon, a suitcase of money will land on the desk and the boss will trickle through the keyhole.

I knocked and entered when prompted. Alexandra was looking at something on her computer.

"Good afternoon," I began cheerfully, but her look stopped me.

Then I was settled into her uncomfortable visitor's chair by a gesture.

"You know," she began, "you've done your job well. You had to identify the threat, which you did. You also did enough to eliminate it before the reinforcements arrived. It's just that the consequences are somewhat greater than we expected."

I swallowed dryly. What was she talking about? The most the witnesses have seen was arson, and Marie is locked up in a hospital with no contact with the outside world.

"As you told me yourself the other day, it's all chemical factories around Pardubice. We can explain a lot of incidents by an explosion or a leak of dangerous substances. But this time it's going to be a bit harder."

"If it's about the house burned down, or maybe others too, then ...," I said, but Alexandra cut me off with a gesture.

"That house was a hatchery, and it's a good thing it burned down.

Fortunately the fire didn't spread, thanks to the weather. The same fog and snow that are now our allies as they are covering the traces of the muras' lair."

"Covering how? It was underground."

"And it was made of organic matter and probably alive itself," Alexandra countered. "As soon as you set it on fire, it began to move. The locals reported something like a weak earthquake."

Ah, crossed my mind, *so I didn't imagine it.*

"There were landslides, trees uprooted, that sort of thing. Then the fog lifted for a while and we were able to take aerial photographs."

She turned the monitor toward me, where a photo file was open. Mud was dripping down a low hill onto a road, revealing what looked like a huge tumor hidden underneath.

"Wow," I gasped. "I really wouldn't have expected this from the local lore."

"No one would. And you know what the best part of this situation is?"

"No?"

"That you're one of the world's leading experts on these creatures at this point. I'll email you the data, while you get ready to return to Dolany."

I looked her squarely in the eye. Oh, crap. I wish she'd rather run through the keyhole.

KAREL DOLEŽAL (* 1988)

For some people, writing has become a way of life. One of those people is Karel, who started with this hobby not long after he became the master of letters in primary school. He then returned to his own works several times until the age of twenty-one, when he finally decided to take his writing to the market. 2011 was a turning point for him, because he was nominated three times in the Karel Čapek Award for his texts *Cards Don't Lie, Square,* and *Recipient Not Reached*, which earned him the enviable Skokan Award for promising new authors and spurred him on to further writing. He also began publishing in genre magazines, as well as in anthologies. His original short story "Ashmender" about a very creative necromancer was published in the anthology *One Step Before Hell* (*Jeden krok před peklem*, Epocha, 2018) from the world of Hammer of Wizards and his text "Let's end with Adam" was published in the opulent anthology *Legends: Praga Mater Urbium* (*Legendy: Praga mater urbium*, Straky na vrbě, 2020).

The author's first novel was *Zombies, Chimeras and Rock'n'Roll* (*Zombie, chiméry a Rock'n'Roll*, Straky na vrbě, 2019), an original and somewhat bizarre adventure full of senile undead, shapeshifters, and rock bands. The same world is the setting for short stories *He Takes* "After Grandpa!" (Pevnost 5/2020), "Zmej, the Thirteenth Draconian King," which was published in anthology *Spawns of Darkness* (*Zplozenci temnoty*, Straky na vrbě, 2021), and "In the Depths Older Than Life "(Pevnost, 1/2022). And rock'n'roll is also one of the prominent themes of the loose sequel to the first novel, titled *Cosmic Wraiths, Earthly Roars* (*Zjevy kosmické, řevy pozemské*, Straky na vrbě, 2022).

Karel Doležal was invited to participate in the *MHF* project because of the short story "He Takes After Grandpa!," a great urban fantasy about a blacksmith and demon hunter in one person living in Prague, and he has rewarded us with an excellent story.

A Question of Greed and Death
Jakub Hoza

The cellar reeked of mold and something else. There was a strange metallic smell in the stale air. Like a coin rolled on a tongue.

A light bulb hanging from a cord hung perfectly still, bringing a figure sitting in a solid oak chair out of the darkness. In other circumstances it might have been considered a royal throne, if it weren't for the fact that the thin young man in the chair had his hands and feet bound with thick leather cuffs and a gag in his mouth, around which saliva was leaking. It mingled with the tears running down his cheeks to his chin. A casual observer might have noticed dark stains on the unpainted wood. They might also notice the bloody scales lying on the floor. The fingernails that were now painfully missing from the tied man's left hand.

Certainly not a picture one would expect to see in a basement under an old jewelry store and a second-hand shop merged into one. The tied man didn't expect it either, which was the very reason why he was now in this situation.

He was not alone in the cellar. His companions, however, were hiding in the shadows for now. One of the standing figures placed the pliers on the workbench with a clack. Another took a drag from a cigarette. The red eye glowed briefly.

The smoker moved closer to the light. He was a medium-sized man in a tartan-patterned flannel shirt and a black padded vest. Black hair was slicked back from a low forehead and a slightly receding chin gave him a sleazy expression. The impression was deepened by a grin out of the corner of his mouth as he stubbed out the cigarette on the tied man's forearm. A cry of pain escaped from beneath the gag.

"Well, well, boy. No need to scream. That doesn't help, you know," said the figure deepest in the shadows.

The person stepped out of the gloom. He was an old man with sparse gray hair combed over the bald spot on the top of his head. His cheeks hung like a bulldog's and he wore small reading glasses on his nose. He looked like someone's kind uncle. However, he was only saving the kind uncle façade for the customers in the shop upstairs. Down here, he had nothing but coldness in his eyes.

"Take his gag out. I think he's ready to talk."

Sleazy loosened the strap holding the gag and pulled it out of the tied man's mouth. Finally, for good measure, he added a punch to the back of the head. The tied man spurted bloody spit on his pants.

"Oh come on, Yevgeny, don't be rude to our guest!" Uncle threatened him with his finger. "In case he might be reluctant to have a friendly conversation, the soldering iron is already hot."

Yevgeny and the other minions laughed dutifully.

"Now, now, boy, tell me where you found this."

Gold glittered in Uncle's outstretched hand.

He sat huddled between two gorillas in the back seat of a big black BMW. He cradled his bandaged left hand in his arms and tried hard not to whimper in terror. He knew full well that his injured fingers had been bandaged just so he wouldn't stain the leather seats.

"That ring you brought me is a real miracle," Uncle turned to him from the passenger seat. "Fifteenth century, if I'm not mistaken. Gold and emerald. Beautiful work," he murmured with satisfaction.

The young man, his hair falling into his eyes, mumbled something.

"What did you say? Don't be shy. You're among friends here."

The young man straightened up.

"I told you the historical value of that jewel is incalculable," he blurted out, though his voice was trembling.

Uncle nodded his head in agreement.

"Who should know but a fourth-year archaeology student? That's why I was quite a surprised when you tried to offer it to me so clumsily. Well, you've learned that greed doesn't pay off."

The student fell silent. Slowly he was beginning to realize that he himself was likely to become an object of study for future generations of archaeologists.

Although their journey from Týnec nad Sázavou took only ten minutes, the sun was already setting behind the horizon. *How long have I been in that cellar?* he thought.

In the fire of the setting sun, the ruins of castle Kostelec nad Sázavou, for several centuries known only as Ruined Kostelec, appeared on a high rocky promontory behind a river bend.

The asphalt road ended just after a turn off the road that continued on to Kamenice. An old unpaved road led up to the castle. From the wheels of a powerful car climbing up the slope, small stones flew out of the clay ground. After about two-thirds of the climb, the wheels turned one last time, the car stopped and the driver pressed the electronic brake button. The engine fell silent, the doors opened.

The young archaeologist was the second-to-last to step out when Yevgeny pushed him out the door. He grazed his knee and elbow on the rocks in the road when he landed. Then he apparently whimpered too long, because Uncle hit him in the back with a walking stick.

"No stalling," he urged him jovially. "You'll lead the way. And don't try to run. I may not be able to walk very fast anymore, but Lojzik over there would send a little bee after you. He's got a hive full of them."

The aforementioned Lojzik, with a camouflage cap on his shaved head and a redneck moustache, showed him a dark 9mm CZ 75.

The student hurriedly stepped forward. With an injured knee, he dragged himself painfully up the slope. The drift soon ended and they headed further to the right. The darkness grew faster among the trees. He had to be careful where he was stepping. Fallen leaves rustled under their feet, the occasional twig snapped. Behind him he heard quickened breathing, the occasional few words, and Uncle's complaints that he was too old for such shenanigans.

He flinched as something creaked above them. But it was only the branches in the treetops.

In a short time the moat of the castle appeared before them. Beech trees with smooth greenish bark grew all around. The ground, overgrown with thick roots, was almost leafless. Like a naked corpse in the morgue, exposed to the eyes of the visitors.

They reached the foot of a simple wooden bridge with no

supporting pillars. It may have had railings for safety reasons, but otherwise it was meant to resemble the original drawbridge as closely as possible.

On their side of the moat, it rested on a low part of the original foundation. On the opposite side, it led to a much better-preserved remnant of the castle tower with a passage through which the castle was formerly entered. The foundations of the tower rose more than seven feet high from the partially buried moat, and two walls, ten feet high, on the side of the passage have been preserved from the tower itself.

The moat was now barely twenty feet deep and its walls were only gently sloped. Still, the student's stomach heaved at the sight of it and he had to grasp the railing for a moment. That was all he was allowed, for his friend Yevgeny made it clear to him with another hit that unnecessary breaks would not be tolerated.

They climbed up the gentle slope to the top of the rocky promontory on which the castle stood. The gloom, meanwhile, grew so thick that the student was almost startled when the walls of the main building of the castle appeared before them. It was the only one of the buildings that still had all four walls rising two stories high.

They bypassed the castle palace from the right, and came to a not very large courtyard. Opposite them was a wall with a large hole in it, with a building on their left and a corner remnant of one of the square guard towers on their right. Around the corner of the building grew a tree, the roots of which slithered like great snakes through the courtyard.

Approximately in the middle of the courtyard was a fire pit dug by campers and filled with charred wood. Next to the fire pit lay a whitewashed sitting log.

"Which way in?" Uncle asked. "We are not here to roast marshmallows and sing kumbaya."

The minions exchanged grins behind the student's back.

"This way," the student pointed and stepped inside through one of the holes in the palace wall.

He led them to another hole that at the bottom of one of the outer walls of the building. A chill seemed to emanate from within.

"Don't tell me you found it here. So many others have searched that basement. They've dug and dug, and all they've found was some old junk," Uncle pointed out ominously.

"It was there. I swear," the student persuaded them.

"Flashlights!" Uncle shouted. "Yevgeny goes first, our lucky finder second and then the rest of us."

Cones of light cut the darkness beneath their feet and one by one they began to lower themselves through the hole.

"I'm surprised they didn't shut this place down long ago. After all, someone could get hurt in here," Uncle groaned as the soil dug under his manicured fingernails.

Soon they were all five feet deeper. The lowest point of the ceiling vault was about eight inches above their heads. The cellar was on the slope which adjoined the west wall of the castle. Although the vault of split stone above them looked untouched except for a coating of cobwebs, none of the current visitors to the underground could shake the feeling that it was bound to collapse on them at any moment. The cellar itself was not very large. It was rectangular in plan, approximately fifteen feet by twenty.

Uncle tapped his wand on the floor. Generations of archaeologists and other (amateur, for a change) grave diggers had carried out the dirt and rubble that the cellar had originally been filled with. In doing so, they uncovered the original cellar floor, which had been smothered to a hardness rivaling a concrete slab.

"So, dear boy, where's our treasure?" Uncle looked around in the lights crisscrossing the space.

"But you won't kill me then, will you? You promised."

"No, of course not," Uncle nodded without hesitation.

The student licked his lips.

"And could I get a cut of it? Of the treasure, I mean. I won't say anything to anyone."

"Ah, my boy, you see? Greed gets everyone in the end. You needn't worry. You'll get exactly the share you deserve."

In the dark, the mobsters didn't have to hide their amused smiles. "Here it is."

The student reached one of the far corners of the dungeon. There he knelt down and pointed to one of the larger stones set into the wall.

"You'll have to scrape up a chunk of the floor to get it out," he explained.

It was easy to do now, even with a mutilated hand, but the first time he had to use a pickaxe.

"When I was here on my practice digs, I noticed that there was no mortar in the joints around the stone. I mean, you can't see it properly anywhere because it has weathered and fell out over time, but there weren't even any remnants of it. I had to wait until the work was finished and hope no one else noticed." As he spoke, a discoverer's excitement began to creep into his speech.

When, with a grunt, he finally managed to pull the stone out, the eager torchlight revealed a niche that held gold coins and jewels.

"How much is there?" Uncle asked.

His voice sounded a little strangled, while a number the size of the budget of the Prague magistrate ran through his mind.

"I don't know. I wanted to buy proper equipment and make it the discovery of the century."

Uncle sighed.

"It's damp in here. A few more minutes and my knuckles will ache."

He nodded to the driver.

"Get out. You'll help me up. Meanwhile, Yevgeny and Lojzik will help our benefactor here take out the whole stash. But before that, search the place thoroughly. It would be a shame to overlook anything. Then we'll close it all up."

At those words a chill ran down the student's back from neck to tailbone.

Uncle and Chauffeur reached the bridge, where the old mobster leaned against the railing. Chauffeur took out a cigarette and lit it.

"It's unbelievable anyway," Uncle shook his head. "What is the world coming to? How can the young be so stupid? A college boy, and he brings me a treasure like that."

Chauffeur shrugged.

"I'd say it's natural selection. How are we going to do it? Bury him here in the basement?"

"Oh, please. What if someone finds him by accident? We don't want the cops snooping around. Some of them aren't that incompetent. They might figure it out. Besides, you saw that floor yourself. It'd take forever to dig a proper hole for a dead body. It's all stone."

He paused for a moment, wondering if he should light up too. Only his pulmonologist insisted that he should cut down on smoking. Significantly.

"In the forest above Čakovice, there are a lot of old tank trenches left after the military exercises from the commie era. They're six feet deep. One corpse can disappear there like nothing. It's five minutes by car and the nearest state cops are in Kamenice."

Chauffeur nodded and rubbed his hands, cigarette in the corner of his mouth. When it was completely dark, it got noticeably colder. He didn't like it here. Something about this place was grating on his nerves like a sharp pick on the strings of a flamenco guitar.

Looking towards the ruins of the palace, he noticed that in the moonlight, wisps of mist began to creep through the ruins.

The sooner they were done with it, the better.

It took about twenty minutes before the entire treasure was taken out of its hiding place and divided into three bags because of its weight. Then they examined the stones in the walls of the cellar for another ten minutes, but found no other hiding place. They returned the stone to its original place, raked up the soil and smothered it.

"Now?" Lojzik turned to Yevgeny.

He just shook his head.

"You want to pull him out of this cellar? We'll do it outside."

"If I shoot him here, they won't hear the shots in the village."

"That's a good point," Yevgeny scratched his head. "Then we'll just strangle him outside. It's clean and noiseless."

The subject of their conversation, who had been listening to it with growing horror, ran like a hare to the entrance of the cellar.

However, as he caught the edge of the hole to pull himself out, a heavy boot landed on his right hand. A metal boot, belonging to a leg covered with plate armor.

He screamed at the top of his lungs. Compared to this, the interrogation in Uncle's basement was nothing. The tread crushed his fingers and wrist bones. He looked up at the dark figure towering over him. Something about it wasn't right, but he couldn't see it properly because of the tears in his eyes.

He didn't get the time to investigate further. A sharp broad blade came down from above. It plunged deep into his open mouth, severing his spine and coming out between his shoulder blades. A bloody flood ran down his back. The leg lifted and the student collapsed back in the cellar.

A hulking figure clad in dingy plate armor stepped into the light cones of flashlights in front of the shocked mobsters with a heavy thump and a screech of steel. In one hand it held a broad, straight sword. A chill spread through the cellar, as if it had suddenly begun to freeze.

The cones of light, along with the sights of weapons, climbed up the medieval armor until they reached his head. Then the mobsters started screaming and shooting.

At the first yell, Uncle frowned in annoyance.

"Can't they do it quietly? I'll take their bonuses for this."

After another roar, the frown disappeared from his face. Although the sound from the basement was muffled, he recognized the screams of pure terror. Then the gunfire joined in.

"Get us out of here! Quick!" Uncle shouted.

Without regard for his wand, he ran as fast as he could to the car. Chauffeur followed him after a brief hesitation. Behind them, a roar echoed into the gunfire. High-pitched, like a pig being killed. It died down only when they slammed the car door shut behind them and started the car.

Down the slope by the castle, Chauffeur backed out at suicidal speed, skidded the car around and was already hurtling through the curves towards Týnec nad Sázavou.

They reached the residence on the outskirts of the town in a few moments. It wasn't big; in any metropolis it would be considered a family house. The gate automatically slid aside and Chauffeur parked the car in front of the house. His breathing was rapid. He couldn't breathe properly the whole way.

He and Uncle entered the house together. He quickly switched the security system on and then helped his boss up the stairs to the first floor study. There, he sat his shaken boss down in a chair. Uncle, who used to inspire terror just by looking at you, now looked like a miserable old man.

"Pour me...pour us a drink," Uncle grunted, pointing to the minibar and refrigerator standing in the corner.

Chauffeur obediently walked over to the bar. He first pulled out a cut glass and then a bottle of eighteen-year-old whiskey. He didn't skimp on the amount poured. He brought one to the old man.

"What are we going to do? We should have helped them, not run away!" he growled angrily.

"What would you have done?" his boss said quietly. "They fired two magazines and they got them anyway ... and took their time. Two more guns wouldn't have done anything."

"But..."

"Tomorrow we'll get the rest of the guys together, get some real guns, and go out there and take a look. But during the daytime!"

He pulled a heavy gold ring from his pocket and turned it in his fingers. He suspected it was all that was left of his treasure.

Just as the first bottle of whisky was disrespectfully emptied, the bedroom door was pushed open. They both startled. Uncle spilled the rest of the glass in his lap, while Chauffeur's cut glass slipped from his hand and landed safely on the carpet.

A young black-haired woman walked in. That she was a woman was obvious, as she was dressed only in her underwear. Very black, very lacy and very revealing.

"Is something wrong, honey?" she asked nervously.

They stared at her like she was a ghost.

"When you didn't come in for a long time, I fell asleep in bed. If we're not doing anything tonight, I'll call for a ride."

Chauffeur had a hard time swallowing his saliva. Only the boss could afford such a luxurious whore.

"Piss off, you stupid bitch!" growled Uncle.

"Listen, you old..."

She paused and exhaled slowly. Just business, no emotions.

"So you're obviously not in the mood for our usual fun today. I see. With your permission, then, I'll get dressed and call for a ride. Let me know when you're interested in another appointment."

With that, she turned and strode back to the bedroom. She swayed as she walked, so much that Uncle almost changed his mind. Chauffeur had to bend a little to hide his erection.

Within three minutes, the bedroom door opened again. She came out in a smart suit from Louis Vuitton's latest collection, a Gucci bag slung over her shoulder.

"Show her out!" Uncle ordered without looking at her. This evening was not going at all as he planned. To hell with the student and the trouble he brought along with that ring.

"Hey, how about a quickie with me? If you'll give me a discount. At least you wouldn't come up empty," suggested Chauffeur, while they were having a cigarette together outside.

"Screw yourself," she sneered.

"You're pretty cheeky," he frowned.

"Don't try to pull rank on me, boy. You think your pathetic bunch of third-rate mobsters is going to impress anyone? Try to touch me against my will, and you'll wish someone had just put a bullet through your forehead. So shut up."

He licked his lips. And he spat. He reminded himself who was pimping her. The silence dragged uncomfortably. The cigarettes were getting shorter.

"It's getting cold," she said, looking around worriedly.

A dog barked briefly at the neighbors. Then it whimpered and fell silent.

"This is strange," Chauffeur remarked in a low voice. Steam curdled at his mouth. "Once that damned mutt starts, it can't be silenced."

The streetlights flickered on and off. Heavy footsteps hit the asphalt. They creaked and rattled. And they were getting closer.

A large shadow appeared at the gate to the property. Tortured metal groaned, a crack of solid steel echoed, loud almost like a gunshot. The gate opened with a creak. Something inhuman entered the yard. Something like the personification of darkness.

Two cigarette butts hit the ground.

The police, who were summoned by screams from worried neighbors, found in the house, in addition to a destroyed door, broken furniture and a lot of blood, the self-proclaimed head of local organized crime. Without his head, but in several pieces.

Hiding in the bushes was a young woman, scared out of her wits, who had apparently given up her sanity in the course of the events and was shouting utter nonsense. After some deliberation, she was taken to an asylum in Říčany.

The investigation was not rushed. The police quickly came to the conclusion that it was a case of settling scores within organized crime factions. No one found the gold ring with the emerald or Chauffeur. No one was looking for them.

A day passed and night fell. The light of the waxing moon reflected off the grey stones of the crumbling walls and illuminated the grassy plain in the corner of the outer wall. An old brown blanket was spread out on the ground. Beside it was a blue glowing insect trap. A lighted torch lay nearby.

Two figures were grappling with each other in front of the blanket. Or so it seemed. One of them was a young man who seemed to be about nineteen, with curly greasy hair and clearly overweight. His belly button stuck out of his unbuttoned leather jacket. A girl about the same age with a mane of blonde hair was slender and more than a head shorter. Her glossy black jacket was lying at their feet, and Curly eagerly resumed the work he had begun.

"Don't worry. There's no one here," he whispered hoarsely as he fumbled his hand under her shirt.

She squeaked and tried to push his hands away, while he tried to undo the hooks of her bra.

"Stop it, you don't even have a rubber with you!" she protested.

"You're on the pill."

The hooks finally gave up any attempts at holding out, and his hands got to work with the eagerness of a milkmaid in the morning. The T-shirt went over her head to end up on a blackthorn bush by the castle wall.

"I didn't expect it to go this far today, you asshole," she tried again, but the blanket spread out on the ground convicted her of lying.

There was a creak of metal somewhere behind them.

"Someone's here!"

"We're alone here," Curly replied absently.

He was busy unbuttoning her jeans at that moment. He couldn't see properly in the dark. He squatted down to do it.

"I'm cold and done!" she declared angrily.

"Why can't I unbutton it!"

There was a squeaky footfall.

The button finally came loose and she felt her jeans and panties being pulled down over her butt.

"Well, finally," he grunted in satisfaction.

And while he was looking between her legs, a large figure emerged from the darkness in front of her eyes. She screamed. There wasn't much more either of them could do.

✢ ✢ ✢

The following morning, the city cops vomited all over the scene. They added their contribution to the fund already set up by campers, the lucky finders of the nighttime massacre.

The state police was called and after a detailed examination of the scene found more bodies in the basement of the ruined castle. The state cops were much more resilient and professional. They didn't vomit and they carefully photographed everything. When the forensics specialists put together the individual body puzzles, they calculated the exact number of victims. Only the heads were nowhere to be found.

Rumors of a serial killer on the loose began to spread in Týnec nad Sázavou and the surrounding villages. They started calling him the Head Hunter.

Two days later, a new Land Rover Defender pulled up outside a pub in Týnec. It aroused some interest among the passers-by, because cars like that didn't usually park there. A strange group got out of the car and headed into the pub.

Although it was around midday, the pub was almost empty. It was an old watering hole, the kind one could come across in any small town. Apparently the owner had imagined that all he needed to do to modernize it was to knock out a chunk of wall, add large windows facing the street, and repaint the inside. The old dark chairs and solid wood tables successfully thwarted his plan.

The first to walk through the door was a man who, judging by the look of him, must have been nearing sixty. Yet there was nothing soft about him. He was slightly taller than average height, his athletic build standing out thanks to a perfectly tailored dark grey suit. An ascetically thin and elongated face was covered with deep wrinkles that would befit a man at least ten years older. The usual cheerful fans of wrinkles around his eyes, however, were absent from his face. The blue, extremely cold eyes would probably not bear such a thing in their vicinity.

He was carrying a large sports bag in his left hand. It didn't really fit his appearance. He looked more like the kind of businessman who plays golf. Not the kind of guy who frequents the gym. And then there were the shoes. Heavy, over-the-ankle track shoes didn't count as dress shoes.

The second one to enter was a woman, or rather a girl, who looked barely eighteen. She was slender, dressed in ripped jeans and a lightweight knee-length dress in pastel colors and with nature motifs. They were cinched at the waist with a belt of braided leather straps. She wore brown suede boots and carried an Indian-style purse with fringe over her shoulder.

Hazel eyes peeked suspiciously from beneath bangs of dark blonde wavy hair, set in a pixie-soft face. She clutched a lighter in her right hand. A good old Zippo made of polished steel.

The last to enter was thirty-something man with broad shoulders in camouflage pants tucked into tall army boots. His khaki jacket was unbuttoned and on his black T-shirt was a picture of a white bunny with teeth like a piranha and a chainsaw in its bloody paws.

His head was almost shaved, except for a short brush of dark hair on the top of it. But his massive, almost black beard could comfortably house an entire colony of bees. He ran a practiced gaze over the whole place before letting the door close.

One might say that the group of three was so diverse that it would be fit only for the beginning of a joke. A stockbroker, a hippie and a soldier walk into a bar . . .

They found a round table for five in the lounge, with a reservation sign. The grey-haired man carefully placed his bag next to the chair. The soldier leaned his elbows on the table. The girl clicked her lighter a few times. She was opening and closing the cover again and again.

A lanky young waiter, who might have been in his early twenties, rushed up to the table. From beneath his greasy manga hairstyle, he peered discreetly at the girl.

"Please, there's a reservation at this table for the mayor and his entourage. You must sit elsewhere."

"That's all right. We're his entourage," the gray-haired man replied calmly without looking at him. He had a faint accent that was not easy to place.

"Really?" the young man said doubtfully.

"Yeah," the soldier grunted. "So, how about you quit snooping around and give us three beers instead?"

"Wine for me," the girl corrected him softly.

"Sure, sweetheart," the soldier nodded hastily. "Two beers and wine, then. Red. The best you've got here. Is that right?"

The girl nodded almost imperceptibly, and the waiter hastily cleared his throat.

The ordered drinks landed in front of them in no time.

The grey-haired man barely sipped on his, as did the girl, who then nodded her head again. The soldier, on the other hand, took a big gulp and drained over half the pint in one go.

"That helped. It gets pretty hot in the fall."

The bag on the ground shuddered.

"I want a beer too," came a squeaky voice from the luggage.

Without batting an eye, the gray-haired man tugged at the zipper of his bag, picked up his nearly intact pint, and carefully placed it in the luggage. Immediately there was a loud sipping sound.

"I don't know, boss," the soldier echoed while shaking his head. "Besides it being against regulations, it doesn't seem very hygienic to me."

"You know where you can put said regs?" replied the man coldly, without moving a single wrinkle.

"Yeah."

"And do you know where my results are?"

"Yeah. All the way on the top of the board," the soldier admitted. "But I still don't know why we are carrying it with us."

"Because I'm used to him, and maybe the SRS will finally grant him an exemption. He might be more useful than you'd know."

The bag shuddered again. There was an incredibly loud burp.

"Not bad, but it needs some ink," the bag squeaked.

The soldier put his head in his hands.

The gray-haired man pulled a bottle of ink from his coat and placed it in his bag. There was the sound of a cork being pulled out, then a clunk as something in the bag hungrily added ink to the beer.

"This is really too much. Why didn't I stay in Afghanistan? There was much better company there. Just Taliban and mountain demons."

The grey-haired man raised an eyebrow. By about a millimeter.

"Because they declared you mentally unstable and locked you up in the Bohnice asylum? Pavilion twenty-four for particularly serious cases. At least that's what I read in your file."

The soldier folded his arms across his chest.

"Yeah, you remember it well. And so do I."

He shuddered. The girl, who had been silent until then, put her hand on his forearm.

"Burn?" she asked timidly.

She clicked the lighter again.

"Not yet, sweetheart," he forced a smile at her.

Another burp came from the luggage.

"I want a hot dog."

The soldier looked around to see a menu on one of the adjacent tables. No chance. He leaned over the bag.

"This is a beer pub. They don't have hot dogs here. Maybe some pickled cheese."

"Yuck!" came from the bag in a heartfelt voice.

"I'd like a hot dog, too," said the girl.

The gray-haired man took a breath.

At that moment the waiter arrived with a new pint. With a puzzled look, he searched the table for the missing empty one. Then he noticed the movement of the bag on the floor.

"Look, you can't have a dog in here. Not even in the bag."

The gray-haired man turned slowly toward him. The soldier caught little of his gaze, but a chill ran down his spine anyway. He remembered what they said about the boss. About what he did before he started working for Fantom.

The waiter froze like a mouse under a snake's gaze.

"That's not a dog. And we want four hot dogs."

"Four?" the waiter repeated, uncomprehendingly.

"You bet!" came a squeak from the bag.

The waiter jumped.

"Well . . . we don't have hot dogs," he stammered.

The girl straightened in her chair and held out her lighter menacingly.

"I'm not getting my hot dog?!" she growled softly.

The waiter crouched down and looked like he was going to cry.

"We want four hot dogs," the gray-haired man repeated. "Three with mustard and one with ketchup."

"I want one with ketchup tonight, too," the bag specified.

"So two with mustard and two with ketchup."

"They'll be here any minute, gentlemen and lady," was all the waiter could muster before staggering dazedly off in the direction of the kitchen.

✦ ✦ ✦

Just as they were wiping mustard and ketchup off their lips, the door to the pub creaked open. A clean-shaven man with square Armani glasses and a lightweight bag of by same brand came rushing to their table. To go with it, probably to be trendy, he wore light blue jeans. On his feet were a pair of half-boots and on the opposite pole of his body ruled an artistically disheveled nest of brown hair. He looked exactly like one of those young progressive bankers from the commercials. And he was just as credible.

"Here I am," he informed the seated company of the obvious, wiping his sweaty face with a recycled paper handkerchief. You could tell by the big green mark.

"I got held up at the new water treatment plant. We are having a little trouble after launch. They claim we supplied them with poor quality filter sand. It's like my cousin doesn't know what he's doing."

"Can we cut to the chase?" the gray-haired one interrupted.

"Oh, sorry," the official immediately shifted gears and put on a professional smile. "I'm Bořislav Rachota, the mayor," he added, as if expecting to be applauded.

"I know. We spoke on the phone," the gray-haired man informed him without much interest.

The mayor stopped puffing like a cooing pigeon.

"Yes, yes. So you're Petar Krstič?"

"Petar will do."

"And your partners?"

"This is Lydie," he nodded his head to the girl, who clicked her lighter in response.

"And you can call me Gunny," the soldier entered the conversation.

"Gunny?!" The mayor wrinkled his nose in disgust.

"An old nickname. I'm used to it," the bearded man grinned.

The gray-haired man sighed.

"Our names aren't important. What's important is what we have to do."

"Umm, sure," the mayor agreed. "Look, this whole situation could put me in a bad light. I'd leave it to the police, even though they seem clueless, but... How can I put this? We have, well, we *had*, a seer in town. I always thought she was a charlatan, but others swore by her. Including many members of the council. And then she suddenly declares that evil has awakened here, picks up and leaves... Ouch!"

He waved his hands so vehemently that he hit his elbow on the table. While rubbing his bruised arm, he continued.

"And she had a well-established business here. I tried calling her to tell her not to panic, and she... well, let's just say she was brusque with me. Right after that I got a call from some secret service I've never heard of in my life, saying they're going to send someone and I'm supposed to keep a lid on it, or else... But whatever."

Petar tapped his fingers on the table.

"If I understand it correctly, your psychic wasn't the first to express suspicions that supernatural forces were responsible for the deaths."

"Yes, the witness. She must be some kind of a prostitute," the mayor winced as he saw them looking at him.

"And you put her in a nuthouse!" Gunny snapped.

"She's in an institution where she'll get the best possible care," the mayor stammered out.

"I'm not familiar with the Říčany nuthouse, but the local hospital is known as a death sentence for patients with anything more serious than an inflamed splinter in their thumb."

"That's enough. Besides, someone other than the mayor probably had her locked up there," Petar settled him down. "We can deal with this later. For now, we need to examine the crime scene."

The mayor licked his lips.

"Well, Mr. Burghauf's villa is sealed by the state police, and I'd need... You understand, I need you to be as discreet as possible. Otherwise... Otherwise, I'm told they'll order an audit."

The bag wobbled. Petar nudged it with his foot.

"What's that?!" Mayor's eyes bugged out.

"Special equipment," the gray-haired man reassured him. "But to get back to the point. Actually, we're far more interested in the other crime scene. The castle."

"You think it's all about the castle? I've issued orders that it's off-limits... To think of such a massacre happening there again... It would destroy me!"

He was suddenly pale as a wall under the tan from the solarium.

"Then we shouldn't waste any more time," Petar remarked unmoved. "Are you here by car?"

"Yes, of course."

"Very well. Let's go."

As one they rose from the table. The soldier brazenly brushed off the approaching waiter, saying the bill was going on the mayor's tab. No one objected.

As they climbed up the hill to the ruins, the sun warmed them through the leaves. Gunny didn't miss the furrows dug by the car's wheels. As far as he knew, visitors usually parked beside the road below the castle. Considering the quality of the road, he wasn't surprised. Someone hadn't been paying attention to their car for the sake of convenience. It wasn't hard to guess who it might have been.

Soon they were standing by the bridge over the castle moat. They didn't have to wait for the panting mayor, who trailed behind them. They knew the way from photographs and maps. Petar walked purposefully in the lead. Gunny walked a little to the side, taking in his surroundings. He wasn't going to be caught off guard. He knew how surprises in his line of work usually ended. Lydie, on the other hand, occasionally jumped with an excited expression, and even twirled around a few times.

The mayor looked at her with utter disgust as he rested his hands on his knees, trying to catch a breath.

They crossed the bridge and continued on to the courtyard. There were still large dark patches on it.

"Is it safe?" The mayor, who had arrived behind them, looked around in alarm, as only now had some disturbing thoughts come to him.

"All the attacks happened at night. There's already a pattern," the grey-haired man remarked calmly. "Besides, our instruments aren't detecting anything yet."

He patted the side of the sports bag he'd carried all the way to the castle.

"You bet!" came a low mutter from the bag.

"What?" The mayor looked puzzled.

"Nothing. Just noise," Petar replied. "So what do you think?"

The question was clearly not directed at the mayor.

The soldier was looking closely at the spots on the ground, crossing the courtyard and the patch behind him. Finally, he glanced at a stain he found on one of the walls of the crumbled tower, a good five meters away.

"If there were only two dead here, they ended up totally FUBAR," he pursed his lips and shook his head slightly.

"What?" the mayor didn't understand.

"A special military term. Whoever did it was fast. They didn't have time to do anything. Not even to run. I'd like to see pictures of the bodies. Under different circumstances, I'd think they stepped on an anti-personnel mine."

Petar turned to the mayor.

"Are there crime scene photos available?"

"I can't just request the file. But maybe one of my guys, I mean from our city police, took some pictures on his cell phone."

"Okay. Where's the basement?"

They crawled through the opening inside the dilapidated building and soon they were standing in front of the black hole.

"You don't expect me to go in there, do you?" the mayor asked.

"No," confirmed the gray-haired man.

"You can cover us from above, so we won't be surprised from there," Gunny winked at the politician.

The mayor began to look around in alarm.

"Do you think anyone could really . . ."

But by then the soldier had disappeared in the hole.

"Clear!" came from below.

Petar climbed down without a word, then reached for the bag he had left at the edge of the hole earlier.

"Excuse me," came a quiet voice behind the mayor.

He jumped in fright, and turned to find himself staring into Lydie's hazel eyes.

He paled and his stomach clenched in fear. Once, when he visited the zoo in Prague, he looked into the eyes of a tiger, who was looking at him through the glass. He knew at once from that look that the big cat was contemplating what he might taste like.

Despite the girl's shy appearance, her gaze was unbearably similar.

He quickly shuffled aside, fumbling desperately for his pack of cigarettes. He completely forgot that he had quit smoking years ago.

Lydie softly hopped down and wrinkled her nose. She was standing right in the middle of a large brown spot.

"We have a different opinion of what's clear," she muttered.

"That's just a phrase, sweetheart," Gunny winked at her over his shoulder.

He had a flashlight in one hand, a large-caliber pistol in the other.

"It's even worse up here than upstairs. Terrible mess for only three bodies. They tried to shoot, a lot. You can still smell the cordite in the air."

"Yes," Petar nodded. "The shells were picked up by the cops, but I'd say they were also shooting for their lives. And it didn't do them any good."

"Why don't we actually request the file from the SRS?" Gunny asked.

"Because, according to Alexandra, the SRS sent out new forms for the release of a live police file. She estimates that it will take at least two days to fill them out..."

"Damned bureaucrats."

At that moment, the bag in his hand fluttered and the zipper opened from the inside.

"It's here," the thin voice said with absolute certainty. "There's a focal point in this basement. I feel like my balls are going to freeze. We'd better get out of here. And fast."

The bag closed again.

"Burn?" Lydie suggested, clicking her lighter to confirm her words.

"We know too little yet," the gray-haired one dismissed. "Now get out!"

They scrambled upstairs.

"So what did you find out?" The mayor wondered.

"You've got a wraith here," Petar informed him unenthusiastically.

The mayor had to lean against the wall.

"Sure, what else. This can only happen to me."

"Not at all," the soldier grinned at him. "It happens more often than you'd think, it just doesn't make the front page."

"What kind of wraith?" the mayor asked weakly.

"That's what we need to find out." Petar scratched his chin. "What did the witness say?"

"She was babbling something about a monster. I don't know the details. And I can't just ask the police."

"So we'll have to talk to the witness. Would you be so kind and arrange a visit?"

"Are you kidding me?! I said to be discreet!"

"Then tell them you found her family," Petar suggested. "If you push a little, they'll bite, even though they might not like it."

"All right," the mayor slumped his shoulders.

"Well, why don't you try calling them right now?" the soldier suggested with a friendly smile that would probably make even a Kodiak bear run away.

The mayor stepped aside along the wall. He pulled out his smartphone from his pocket.

The gray-haired man opened his bag.

"You can talk now."

"There's something haunting this place that cares a lot about it. But why now? Someone was doing something in the basement and disturbed it. I'd bet an ear on that."

"So it's some kind of a guardian. We need to find out more. Ordinary firearms don't seem to be working."

The others, including the bag, nodded in agreement.

He hated it. He walked down the green and white painted hallway. The old-fashioned fluorescent lights shone above his head.

I can't take it, thought Radek Trhavý, who was used to being called Gunny by his old unit. By the unit of which he was the only one left alive. He remembered pavilion twenty-four and the therapeutic methods the white coats used there.

So I'm back in a damn asylum, he groaned in his mind. Although they had a big sign over the entrance saying it was the "Sanatorium" in Říčany, he was not fooled by flowers and happy animals. Inside, it looked just like in Bohnice.

The walls were pressing against him, the fluorescent lights flickered and buzzed irregularly.

I can't take it!

He felt a gentle touch on his forearm. He lowered his gaze and saw that Lydie was stroking his arm. It was like she was reading his mind. When he looked her in the eyes, he could clearly see the fear in them. She was feeling the same way he did. Gunny felt ashamed.

"Thanks."

She just smiled at him.

"This is it," Petar echoed in front of them. "Room twenty-seven. I'd better go see her myself first."

"Thanks, boss, I mean, uncle," Gunny corrected himself.

He mentally cursed himself as he saw the older, stocky nurse who had accompanied them frown at him.

Petar shot him one more cold look and then disappeared behind the door, followed by the nurse.

The grey-haired man saw the witness as soon as he entered the room. She was dressed in hospital clothes and sitting on the bed. Her gaze was fixed on the opposite wall. About thirty centimeters to the side from a picture of flowers.

He walked slowly over to her and then sat down on the bed a short distance from her.

"Tereza? Tereza, can you hear me?"

A silly phrase, but he couldn't think of anything better.

Slowly, as if powered by clockwork, she turned to him. He noticed she was completely glassy-eyed.

"There was a monster. It was killing people," she informed him in an urgent, shaky voice.

"What kind of a monster was it? What did it look like?"

"There was a monster. It was killing people."

The nurse, standing discreetly in the corner of the room, cleared her throat.

"She keeps saying the same thing over and over."

He turned to the nurse. He was furious. Maybe the SRS bastards were doing this to him on purpose.

"What did you dope her with?" he said calmly.

He rarely showed emotion.

"The usual calming stuff."

"Sure."

This time a little anger seemed to seep into his voice.

"You didn't see the condition she was brought in. We'll gradually reduce the dose, but that's not for me to decide."

He stood up.

"Thanks for nothing."

Two orderlies were walking down the empty corridor. They were talking quietly on the way. One of them was thin but sinewy. The other was taller and must have weighed at least three hundred pounds. He looked more like something from the animal kingdom. The only thing missing was oinking. Their conversation had just reached the height of professionalism.

"Did you see that chick in twenty-seven? The tits and the ass. Real fancy bitch."

"We could try it tonight. Just a little raise of the meds. And then..."

They heard a click.

It was only then that they noticed the girl leaning against the wall of the hallway just beside the tall cabinet, watching them from under her bangs.

Skinny frowned at her.

"Why are you staring at us?"

Across the way, the door to the restroom opened. A dangerous-looking man in army clothes stepped out. With one glance, he scanned the scene before him.

"Is there a problem, sis?"

Piggy raised his hands in front of him.

"No problem. She just surprised us a little," Skinny snapped.

They hurried down the hallway at a quickened pace.

Lydie pushed off the wall and looked seriously in Gunny's eyes.

"We have work to do here," she said firmly.

Skinny and Piggy were indulging in a smoke break in their favorite hiding place. A small asphalt plaza, originally intended for waste containers, was located on a slope below one of the large buildings of the sanatorium.

On one side it was covered with thuyas so overgrown that it looked like a triffid attack was impending. On the other, a slope covered with a tangle of unkempt scrub. There were two waist-high massive concrete planters in front of the prickly wall, but there was still enough room for them.

"So the plan is clear," summed up Skinny. "We'll up the meds a little, she's already off enough, and then we'll do whatever we want with her for the night."

Piggy blinked with an absent look and a cigarette in the corner of his mouth.

"I don't know. Last time I was scared for three months that someone would figure it out."

Skinny put his hands on his hips.

"It'll be all right. Just use a rubber, and no biting. Hey, are you even listening to me?"

High soles of raw rubber squeaked on the asphalt. They both twitched. They looked up to see the soldier who had surprised them in the hallway earlier approaching. They immediately became nervous.

"Could I have a cigarette with you? Always better with company," he asked with a smile.

They looked at each other and then back at the soldier. Skinny shrugged his shoulders.

"Why don't you have one with your sister? She's a lot prettier than us."

"She doesn't really smoke. That lighter's just kind of a bad habit."

"Well, yeah."

The soldier smiled again.

"Now, gentlemen, do you have a smoke to spare too? I'm kind of out of them."

Piggy held up the box, indicating that he can have some.

"Very well. Now, a lighter, I suppose you'll have one too?"

The orderlies frowned in unison.

"What, that's some bullshit . . . You don't smoke!"

The soldier looked around quickly. Then he smiled. Really ugly this time.

"A brilliant deduction. Guess it's time I confessed. You see, I just don't like orderlies who abuse patients."

The head nurse found those two more than an hour later. They were both unconscious and naked. Skinny was draped over one of the concrete planters with his ass thrust skyward. On top of him, in a copulatory position, lay Piggy.

The head nurse had seen a lot in her career, but the sight of Piggy's hairy cheeks was forever burned into her memory.

She only set out to look for them so late, because an event had occurred in the sanatorium that completely overshadowed this episode. Two cars had suddenly caught fire in the staff parking lot. They were burning with a bright white flame and the firefighters called in were unable to extinguish them for a long time. Coincidentally, they belonged to the beaten orderlies.

✦ ✦ ✦

Lydie and Gunny headed towards the car where the boss was waiting. They both looked like cats who had just licked clean an unguarded bowl of cream.

"Please, Lydie," the soldier began. "You've worked with the boss before, but I haven't. I can't get through to him. I don't know what to expect. And it's gnawing at me. I've only heard some rumors about him, but...I don't know what to believe."

The girl looked up at him.

"He doesn't talk much about himself, and certainly not about the war in the Balkans. Only once, at a celebration after a successful mission. In Yugoslavia, he was getting orders directly from Ratko Mladić."

Gunny swallowed.

"Well, shit. Was he there? In Srebrenica?"

"No, he had another mission. To find and kill Hashim Thaçi."

"Yeah, I heard about that. A real bastard. He made a lucrative business out of the war. He dealt in drugs and prisoner organs."

Lydie nodded.

"When Thaçi became the Prime Minister of Kosovo after the war, the boss couldn't accept it. He left the army and Serbia and started working for the Balkan mafia as a hitman. Maybe he was hoping someone from the competition would put a bounty on Thaçi's head."

"That's some resume," Gunny nodded his head grimly.

"What about you and the war?"

He grinned bitterly.

"When I encountered something unnatural in the war and was the only one of my unit to survive, they put me in an asylum."

"Would you go back to the army if you could?"

"No," he shook his head decisively.

He paused. Lydie walked a few more steps before she, too, stopped. She looked at him. He wasn't looking at her, but in the empty space. It was as if he was looking hundreds of miles away.

"I've seen too much hypocrisy. Too many lies. I've held lists of terrorists and war criminals, and then I've seen pictures of them shaking hands with American congressmen. I've seen Raqqa. There was an IS base in that city, but also a lot of civilians. I saw what was left of that city. Just a few skeletal buildings and rubble. No one could count the dead. I saw villagers killed by drone strikes. Just a small mistake. One raghead like another. Too much hypocrisy. Too many lies."

She tried to smile at him, startled.

"You and the boss are more alike than you'd think. There's one thing you should know. The boss comes across as cold and unapproachable, but you can count on him."

"Good to know," the soldier nodded. "That was the longest conversation we've ever had."

"And probably ever will," she said quietly, digging her hand into her pocket.

By the time they reached the car, she had the lighter back in her hand.

Gunny walked around the car and sat in the passenger seat. Lydie sat in the back, next to the bag, from which a snoozing sound came.

Petar turned to them.

"Done?"

"To the complete satisfaction of all concerned," the soldier confirmed.

The girl just nodded and flicked her lighter.

At that moment, fire sirens sounded.

"I guess we'd better get going," Petar stated and started the engine.

They stopped in front of the house where the godfather of the local (modest) branch of the mafia lost his life. They got out of the car and looked at the property in front of them. The broken and twisted gate was wrapped in police tape. Seals were visible on the door to the house, even from a distance.

"What are we looking for here, boss?" Gunny asked, leaning comfortably against the hood.

"Something the cops missed. It doesn't fit. If the monster is the guardian of the castle, why did it make its way to town?"

The sound of a zipper opening came from the car.

"Because they took something from the place that our monster wanted back," a voice squeaked from the back seat. "He's gonna be one greedy son of a bitch."

Gunny sighed and peeled himself away from the car.

"You want me to go in there alone? It'll probably be faster."

"You may," Petar nodded.

"Not that I mind, but do you really believe I won't miss something?"

The gray-haired man looked him squarely in the eye.

"Yes. I'm well aware that you are smart, even though you like to pretend otherwise. And the fact that you used to be an MP. You're no stranger to investigation."

The soldier grinned.

"What the hell, boss, I might start blushing. So take it easy for now."

With that, he left. A moment later he could be seen swinging easily over the wall on the side of the property that was farther away from the surrounding houses.

He walked across the lawn to the front of the garage. Halfway through his stride he stopped and looked underfoot. He knelt down and picked up something small from the ground. With his other hand he picked up something else. He examined both objects carefully.

Finally, he straightened up and walked to the door. After tearing open the seals without much interest, he continued inside. The door swung on one hinge behind him and remained hanging askew.

After nearly a quarter of an hour he came out. He put the door back in place. He looked around, then walked around the building and out of their sight. Ten minutes passed before he walked along the outside of the fence back to their car. He pulled the surgical gloves off his hands. He crumpled them up and stuck them in his pocket.

"Well?" the boss asked.

"The godfather was killed upstairs. It was a real massacre again. There was the smell of spilled booze and shards on the floor. So I'd say the local godfather was there when that thing massacred his people in the castle, and needed to calm his nerves a bit. The place was trashed, but I did find something. There was a dent in the furniture and the floor he butchered him. A heavy weapon with a long blade. A machete or a sword. Something like that. Not an axe. It had a thinner and longer blade."

Petar stroked his chin.

"Interesting. What else?"

"I found two cigarette butts outside in the cracks of the pavement. Only one had traces of lipstick. There's a gate in the back garden. It doesn't make sense for the capo to run upstairs. That would put him at a dead end. There was someone else here. Someone who survived."

"I agree," the grey-haired man confirmed. "Good work."

"What now?" Lydia, who had been silent until now, asked.

"Now we're going to grab something to eat," came from the car.

"Actually, that's not a bad idea," Petar raised an eyebrow. "We'll have a late lunch. I heard about a small pub in the village of Kostelec where the meals are excellent. Besides, I think we have a decent idea of what kind of monster it is, but we need to be sure."

They got in the car.

"In the meantime, I'll call the mayor. I'm sure he'll be glad to lend us a helping hand again. Or rather both."

Gunny chuckled, but it was nothing compared to the unrestrained laugh that came from the bag.

The asphalt snake of a road twisted through the forest in serpentine curves. The Defender crossed the creek on a not-so-trustworthy bridge and parked in front of a dilapidated and apparently long-abandoned garage.

They got out and crossed back over the bridge, where a city police car was waiting at the curb. Clumps of ferns grew on the banks of the creek. Rainbow trout darted in the clear water. Gunny' hands twitched as if he was holding a fishing rod. It was a very nice place.

The cops who had stopped on the side of the road didn't even bother to get out of the car, only rolled down the window.

"So that was it?" Petar asked. "The old sawmill two turns back?"

"Yeah. It belongs to one of the old bugger's known cronies. Not a soul on the addresses in town. They must be holed up there."

The gray-haired man nodded.

"That would fit. There was smoke coming from the chimney. How many are there?"

"How should I know? Three to five. And to be clear, we're leaving."

"We were never here at all," added the older cop behind the wheel. "And watch out, they're really nasty bastards."

"All right. We'll work something out with them," Petar shrugged.

"Sure, birds of a feather flock together," grinned Gunny.

The cops scowled at them for their insolence out of habit, and when they found that no one, including Lydie, was impressed, they hastily left.

The Hunters returned to the car. On the bridge, the soldier paused for a moment, watching the fish in the water.

"Damn, this would be great fishing spot. Except for the mosquitoes," he added as he swatted one of them off his neck with a slap.

He sighed and continued past the bridge.

Petar was just talking through the open door with his bag.

"I need recon, and as soon as possible. Will you do that for me, Drinkin'?"

"Aye, o mighty satrap," came from within.

Then the door on the other side of the car opened, closed again with a slam, and the ferns on the bank of the stream moved.

"Drinkin'? How did he get such a name?" Gunny turned up his nose.

"You'll have to ask him," Petar replied dryly.

Lydie was throwing pebbles in the water under the bridge, while Gunny frowned at her for unnecessarily scaring the fish. Just then, as if a completely localized gust of wind swept through the greenery, the car door slammed.

"Report," Petar ordered through the open car door on his side.

"Did I join the army?" Drinkin' complained.

"Please."

"That's better. There are three guys in that shack. They're armed with pistols. I saw a hunting rifle propped up in the corner. They mostly hang out in the kitchen downstairs. One of them's cooking goulash. Not bad. Anyway, you can see they're as nervous as ferrets in a milk can."

"If there are three of them, it's evenly matched," Gunny scratched his chin.

"Count again," came from the car. "There's four of us and they are heavily outnumbered."

"Let's not be too hasty," Petar restrained him. "Remember, we need them alive. All of them. Apparently only one of them was a witness, and we don't know which one."

"Well, I suppose you have a plan," the soldier suggested.

"As a matter of fact, I do. Drinkin', how long before you can get us there without being spotted right away?"

"About a quarter of an hour."

"Good."

Petar paused in thought.

"Can I ask you a question, Drinkin'?" Gunny said.

"Yeah, they say we live in a free country. Haha."

"Why is your name Drinkin'?"

"I got it because I like to drink. Often and a lot."

The announcement was followed by a short burst of laughter.

"And while we're at it, I'd like a Russian squid. That mission made me thirsty."

"Maybe later, you'll have to make do with this for now," Petar replied, shoving a bottle of ink in his hand in the car. "And don't spill," the gray-haired man added, but by then guttural sounds were coming from inside the car.

"Can someone tell me what a Russian squid is?" Gunny asked with a slightly confused expression.

"Two ounces of vodka and one small bottle of black ink," Lydie said quietly.

"Ugh, that sounds disgusting."

"Don't criticize until you've tried it," the thin little voice squeaked.

Gunny pulled up his pants.

"The wise person recognizes that some experiences are less embraceable than others."

A chuckle came from the car.

"That's what Master Splinter of the Ninja Turtles said."

"Yeah, but that doesn't mean it's not true."

Petar sighed.

"If you're done, it's time to discuss strategy."

"Yes, boss!" came the chorus.

"That's better."

The stew on the stove in the corner of the kitchen smelled so good that Chauffer's salivary glands spontaneously went to work, even though he had no thought of eating. How on earth could it all have gone so terribly wrong? He had only managed to escape because he had took off in time and knew exactly which way to run.

He reached out his hand to take a card from the deck. His hand was shaking so badly that he was only able to take it between his fingers on the third try.

His companions, with faces so hard one could sharpen knives on it, looked at each other. The looks did not bode well, but he did not care.

He had encountered something beyond anything he could imagine. Just like the darkness he was met with. He had killed, tortured, or at least stood by and watched the torture, but now he faced true evil. And he was afraid. He was terrified that the monster would come for him too.

So now he sat in an old two-story sawmill built on the bank of a stream. The white paint inside was slowly peeling off, as was the yellow one outside. He didn't smell the mildew only because the bubbling stew was currently overshadowing it.

He placed his cards on the rickety table. He was giving up. This wasn't worth it.

"How about you finally tell us what's going on? The old man's been taken down. Okay. But by who?" one of the guys demanded.

"Was it the Popovice crew? I never trusted those swine," the other added.

The only difference between him and his partner was that he had blond hair instead of brown.

"I told you I don't know who they were!"

He wasn't stupid enough to tell them what he'd actually seen that night.

"Well, it's obvious it must have been rough. That girl broke down. But you're no ordinary whore. Get a grip, man!" Blondie scowled at him.

"If we don't find out who's trying to break up our crew, we're dead. We have to take the initiative," growled Brown.

"Screw you!" Chauffeur growled between his teeth.

"Hey, you..."

"And you too! You weren't there. You didn't see it."

"We didn't see what? Just spit it out already," Blondie said with a clear threat of violence in his voice.

"Shut up!"

Brown leaned across the table.

"You piece of shit..."

"Shut up, both of you! Can't you hear that?"

They fell silent. From the outside they heard the sound of a car engine running and wheels clanking on the bridge over the creek. Then the gravel on the road in front of the sawmill rattled. The engine stopped.

By this time all three of them were at the kitchen window, looking out.

Ten yards in front of the sawmill, a luxury green Defender pulled up. The driver's door opened and a gray-haired man dressed in a long coat stepped out of the car. He walked calmly about two yards away from the car. He looked the sawmill over thoughtfully. To the mobsters inside, he seemed to be looking right into their faces through the dusty glass.

Gun slides clicked, fingers turned off the safeties. Too late.

From under his coat, the man produced a matt semi-automatic shotgun. In one motion, he shouldered it and fired.

The first shot ripped long splinters from the front door.

The man took aim at their window.

"Shit!" Brown yelled.

At the last second, they managed to take cover behind the stone walls.

A second shot blasted a large circular hole in the glass of the window. The rest of the glass immediately began to crumble. The shattering of glass on the floor seemed louder than the shots.

Another shot. A shower of buckshot flew through the kitchen, ending the suffering of a Jesus on the cross.

The gunfire, which continued to devastate the kitchen and split the window frames into splinters, quickly erased any thoughts of returning fire from their minds.

However, it had a rejuvenating effect on Chauffeur.

"Take the rifle and get up in the attic. Get him from the dormer!" he ordered Blondie.

The latter merely nodded, and on all fours went to do as ordered.

"You take the back door! Go around the timber! I'll try to pin him down."

He didn't watch to see if Brown was following his order. He stayed safely crouched behind the wall. That bastard was firing shot after shot. He couldn't even stick the tip of his nose out.

He heard the stamp of feet on the rickety wooden stairs leading from the hall to the attic. Then came the creak of the back door. The room reeked of scorch as stew oozed from the perforated pot onto the stove.

They'll get the bastard. He's got to run out of ammo at some point.

The firing ceased as suddenly as it had begun.

All right, Chauffeur thought. The shots came from the same place and distance. So he knew exactly where to shoot.

With the gun pointed in front of him, he peeked out the lower right corner of the window.

Something with the force of a vice gripped his gun hand and pulled him out like a blackbird pulls an earthworm from the dirt. He felt a stab of pain as one of the shards in the frame cut into his side.

Then he was lying outside under the window, gasping for air.

"I'd leave the trigger alone if I were you," a voice as warm as an iceberg said behind him.

When he finally managed to focus, he found that the gun was still in his hand, but the grip that was breaking his wrist kept it pointed at his own chest.

"Why don't you give me the gun before you harm yourself?"

He nodded dazedly and loosened his grip. Good thing his finger wasn't directly on the trigger guard. The shooting course had paid off.

But how had it happened? He was at least ten yards away. The guy couldn't have gotten to the house that fast.

As he turned his head toward the car, understanding began to creep into his shaken brain.

A girl in a flowered dress stood by the car. She had a slight smile on her face and was holding the exact same shotgun as the man who had opened fire.

"Let's talk," the gray-haired man announced, then pulled Chauffeur to his feet with no apparent effort.

The girl took a dancing step toward them.

Still shaken, Chauffeur could only manage another nod.

In the entrance hall of the house, they met a bearded, army-style man who was carrying a limp Brown over his shoulder.

Chauffeur's vanquisher took a cursory glance at the kitchen. In a second, he assessed the extent of the devastation and directed his captive to the room across the hall that served as the living room. There, he made him sit down on one of the chairs, to which he secured him with plastic handcuffs.

Brown ended up the same way. He was then brought to consciousness by routine slapping.

Chauffeur watched it all in a kind of a haze, as if was only holding consciousness between his fingertips. Still, he couldn't help wondering where Blondie was. It was slowly working its way through his brain. Maybe he could still get them all out of this. If he seized the opportunity...

Just as his train of thought reached the home station, heavy footsteps sounded on the wooden stairs.

Why so loud?! He can't surprise them like that!

Soon, Blondie entered through the massive wooden door frame. His hands were empty and his face was twisted with sheer terror. He moved awkwardly and with extreme caution.

The reason was obvious. Drunks have monkeys sitting around their necks. He had something else there.

The creature looked like a little man about one foot tall. It had long bat ears, a massive hooked nose and big eyes with yellow irises. They were currently squinting in an expression that could be described as darkly insidious. It was wearing a tiny dark blue jumpsuit with black stripes and *Adidas* written on it. A Barbie doll had probably found a naked, bound and very traumatized Ken in her pink sports car one fine day.

The creature had its legs wrapped around Blondie's neck. Its right hand held tightly on the earlobe of its vehicle, while its left hand held a shiny razor, pressed under Blondie's jaw.

"Sit down, shithead!" the tiny mahout instructed Blondie.

Blondie obediently sat down on the vacant chair. The soldier tied his hands to it.

A blur flashed through the room. The tiny man reappeared, perched on the edge of the tabletop, where he was happily tapping his feet.

"What the hell is that?!" Blondie groaned, unable to take his eyes off the little man. His voice was hysterically breaking.

The remaining mobsters watched the gremlin silently, but with wide eyes.

"Something that's probably going to play the clumsy barber soon if you don't stop asking stupid questions," the little man squeaked, stroking his razor menacingly.

"Oh come on, Drinkin', we don't do that anymore," Petar said with slight reproach in his voice.

"If he pisses me off any longer, we'll take a little excursion back to the old days together."

Petar gave the mobsters a serious look.

"Now, youngsters, I'll ask the questions and you'll answer. Or I'll leave you alone with Mr. Drinkin' here."

The captives swallowed drily in unison.

"So, one of you witnessed the attack on your boss and probably also the one in the castle. Which one of you was it?"

"Me," Chauffeur sputtered.

"Okay. I'm interested in what attacked you."

"I ... Look ... ," he began. "Couldn't you treat my side first? It's still bleeding."

Gunny walked over to his chair, squatted down, and squinted critically at his blood-soaked clothes. With a swift movement, he ripped the fabric open, revealing the shard wound.

"It's already closing. You'll be fine. You should get it stitched up, but that's not on the agenda right now."

He paused, as if something had just occurred to him.

"Excuse me for a moment," he blurted out and hurriedly left the room.

He returned a moment later with a mess tin. He scooped up a spoonful of stew and stuck it in his mouth. He chewed, swallowed, and licked his lips.

"It's really good. You weren't kidding," he nodded approvingly at the little man.

Drinkin' gave him a thumbs-up—followed by his middle finger.

"I thought you said you were full at lunch," Lydie frowned slightly.

"I was," Gunny shrugged. "But that doesn't mean I am going to refuse more food, when there's an opportunity."

"Ahem," Petar cleared his throat ostentatiously. "How about we get back to the subject of our conversation? What did you see? And you may notice I'm asking what, not who."

Chauffeur glanced briefly at his two companions.

"You won't believe me. No one will believe me!" He groaned.

Drinkin' chuckled.

"What are you talking about, idiot? Look at me. I'm pretty incredible myself. The Incredible Drinkin', that sounds good. I'm just not muscular and green enough."

Chauffeur's jaw quivered as if he was fighting with himself.

"It was a goddamn headless knight!" he finally blurted out.

Blondie shook his head. Brown rolled his eyes.

"Are you sure?" Petar jerked his chin.

"Fuck no! Seeing a huge guy wearing armor, with a huge sword and no head, I guess I have plenty of opportunities to be wrong!"

Petar shot a glance toward the little man.

"Yeah, we guess it right," Drinkin' nodded.

With his nose and ears, it was a fairly obvious gesture.

"Do you know why he was after you?" the gray-haired man asked.

Chauffeur averted his eyes.

"No," he said quietly.

"But you do know," Drinkin' shouted. "You do know, you're just trying to screw us."

"No."

"Yes, you are, you're trying to screw us. Come on, be a man. Admit it."

"No."

The man twirled the razor in his fingers.

"You know how many liars I've had under this razor? What's the price of getting you to talk? An ear? A nose? Or something situated much lower?"

Chauffeur seemed to sink into himself in his chair.

"Well, all right! All right! There's treasure hidden in the castle dungeon. When we ran away, the boss still had a gold ring with a big stone."

"See?" Petar remarked good-naturedly. "You must be relieved now. You might as well have said so. You're not stupid enough to want to get the cursed treasure for yourself, are you? You'd end up just like your boss."

Chauffeur shook his head slowly. But his expression clearly indicated that he was only now beginning to realize the possible consequences of stealing the treasure.

"What are you going to do with us?" Brown said with an effort.

Lydie tugged on the grey-haired man's sleeve. Brown froze. For some reason, the frail girl frightened him, perhaps even more than the gremlin with a razor.

"Burn?" she asked timidly.

She wore the exact same expression as a child begging for a toy she'd just seen on a store shelf.

"I hope that won't be necessary," the gray-haired one replied.

She lowered her head in disappointment and stepped aside.

The mobsters began to breathe again.

"Him," Petar nodded his head to Chauffeur sitting in the middle.

The soldier drew his knife.

With a serious expression, he walked up to the prisoner, but then quickly walked around his chair and cut his cuffs.

With a hiss of pain, Chauffeur slowly straightened up, rubbing his bruised wrists as he did so.

"Come on, boy," the gray-haired man patted him on the shoulder.

They walked slowly to the car.

"What happens now?" Chauffeur asked uncertainly.

"That will be up to you," Petar looked at him seriously.

"Are you just going to let me go?"

The soldier behind him chuckled.

"And what did you expect? That we'd hire you?"

"We don't hire losers like you," Drinkin' squeaked by his right leg.

The gray-haired man raised a disapproving eyebrow.

"Enough jokes, I've got a few words for the young man."

They stopped beside the car. Lydie sat in the back. Gunny walked around the car and opened the passenger door. But he continued to watch Chauffeur over the hood. By this time, Drinkin' was in his bag in the back seat.

"We're going to leave now. And I'm sure I'll never see you again. If I do, you know what will happen," Petar said.

He opened the car door and got in the driver's seat. He was about to close the door, but paused with his hand on the handle.

"Like I said, it's entirely up to you. But don't ever talk about this. Ever. If I were you, I'd quickly change town, name, and maybe even your occupation. As I see it, there's not much prospect for you in the present one. It's also up to you how you arrange things with your associates. Frankly, they don't strike me as people with much understanding."

He closed the door and started the car. Gunny grinned mockingly at Chauffeur some more and then disappeared inside the car as well.

Chauffeur watched the departing car thoughtfully. He remembered that in the kitchen, in one of the cupboard drawers, there were a lot of sharp knives. He can do away with those two quickly.

They stayed in a guesthouse on the outskirts of Týnec. They ordered dinner to be brought up to their rooms and met for the meal in Petar's suite. The advantage was that they were able to strengthen their relationships through teambuilding. The downside was that they were having dinner with Drinkin'.

When he finished the announced Russian squid after an ink-stained pork tomahawk, Gunny couldn't take it anymore.

"Why do you keep drinking all that ink?"

The little man scratched his back and focused on him, slightly tipsy.

"You figured out I'm a gremlin, didn't you?"

"Yeah."

"Well, I'm a print gremlin. In the service since the invention of the printing press."

"Somehow I don't think you're haunting a printing press right now," remarked Gunny dryly.

Drinkin' took a sip, burped, and replied.

"In the year two thousand and two, I met Petar here in a print shop. He was there on business, because besides books they also printed counterfeit bills. I was teasing him a bit, as was in my job description, and he caught me. Nobody had done it before him. But we quickly found common ground . . . I've been working with him ever since. I was sick of the gremlin job anyway."

"Holy shit," was all Gunny could muster.

Lydie, sitting on the rug by the bed, smiled brightly like the sun. The story amused her.

"Let's cut to the chase," the boss ordered.

"Sure," nodded Drinkin'. "The Kostelec nad Sázavou castle was founded as a royal castle, but I'll be damned if I know which monarch was responsible. What matters to us is that in the year fourteen hundred and fifty it belong to the bandit knight Kuneš Rozkoš of Dubé. He robbed everyone on one of the important trade routes so vehemently that King Wenceslas sent one of his most reliable noblemen, Zdeněk Konopištský of Šternberk, to deal with him. He besieged and eventually conquered the castle. Kuneš and his sons tried to break the siege, but they were captured and Konopištský had Kuneš and his sons executed in the castle courtyard. They were beheaded. But only after Kuneš had to watch the deaths of the surviving castle staff and the rest of his family. Pretty cruel even by medieval standards.

"What's interesting: even though Konopištský claimed the castle for himself, the treasures found were less than anyone would have expected from a bandit like Kuneš. Just seventeen years later, Kostelec was besieged and conquered by the armies of King George of Poděbrady. And that was the end for the castle."

Gunny stared at the gremlin, mouth wide open. Drinkin' grinned.

"What are you looking at? I'm a print gremlin. You'd never believe how much I've read in hundreds of years. Plus, I have a photographic memory when it comes to texts."

Petar sighed.

"Drinkin'..."

"Oh, well," the gremlin rolled his eyes. "I also have a tablet in my bag and the internet is like my second home. But all I said was true."

The soldier just shook his head.

"But still...a headless knight? Really? I thought that here in Czechia we only had that Templar in Prague," the soldier mused.

"Bollocks!" grinned the gremlin. "In Zlín, for example, there was a headless knight named Miloš, who rode in a fiery chariot and chopped off the heads of passers-by with a falchion."

"Was?"

Petar cleared his throat before speaking.

"Exactly. They tried all sorts of things on him, and finally they hit him with anti-tank missiles three nights in a row. Devil knows if it wiped him out for good, but he hasn't shown up for a couple of years. Anyway, they're pretty tough bastards."

The soldier mused.

"From what I remember, with that Templar, all you supposedly have to do is stab him through the heart with his own sword, right?"

Drinkin' giggled until he fell off the dresser.

Petar smiled slightly.

"Have you ever tried stabbing someone in armor? That Templar wears a cuirass. Two millimeters of hardened steel between two layers of rawhide. Not to mention the ringmail and quilting underneath. Besides, they're superhumanly strong, so try taking his sword," he added.

"Okay, so what do we do about this one?"

"There may be a grain of truth in that rumor," squeaked Drinkin', who had recovered in the meantime. "I think there's a power that resides in the heart area that brings him to life. When I get near it, I shall know for certain."

"That's going to be a close call," remarked Gunny.

Petar shrugged.

"Gremlins can move unseen and they're fast. But yes, it's risky. The knight could still sense him, the way one magical being can sense another."

He tapped his fingers on the tabletop.

"We can't underestimate this. We have all day tomorrow to prepare and we'll take him out at night."

"Burn?" Lydie suggested.

Petar smiled for real for the first time.

"What do you think?"

Petar and Gunny looked across the moat at the ruins of the castle. They'd been crawling through it for almost two hours before that. Except for the dungeons; no one wanted to go there. Only Drinkin' had been bribed with two bottles of ink, and after less than two minutes underground he could confirm the existence of the treasure. But he took nothing from it.

Gunny scratched his beard and grinned unhappily.

"It's a shitty place for a cover fire. Theoretically, I could climb the opposite hill, but it's too overgrown, not to mention the rest of the castle tower would cover almost the entire courtyard anyway. The only reasonable firing position is right here."

He kicked the wall that was the base of the bridge with his foot. Lydie swept past and began scattering gray powder from her sack across the bridge.

"We need to draw him out to over there," Gunny pointed across the bridge, to the plaza below the castle palace. "I'll get him there. I'll take Dragunov, and I'll shoot through the steel plate with it. Just get him there."

"We'll need a decoy, and that'll be me. If it goes well, maybe I can take him down myself," Petar said.

"Really? What do you want to use?"

"This."

Petar showed him a small Israeli Uzi submachine gun.

"A fine toy for close-range live fire," the soldier acknowledged. "But against an armored and superhumanly durable target, no chance."

"I have special ammo. A Czech specialty. There's a hardened steel needle embedded in the soft core of the bullet. The core itself splashes against the armor, but the needle continues on. It goes through bulletproof glass like nothing."

"Okay, that's cool."

"Besides, the ammo was blessed by one of the last priests of the Lord of pure faith."

"You mean that bum from Rytířská Street in Prague?"

"That's the one."

"Good choice," Gunny nodded.

They both watched Lydie setting something up at the foot of the bridge, chanting merrily as she did so.

"I like watching her when she's happy," the soldier said thoughtfully.

"So do I," admitted Petar. "And if something goes wrong, she may be our last hope."

The sun had set half an hour ago, the shadows in the castle courtyard began to merge into a solid darkness. They were disturbed only by the warm light of a campfire in the middle of the courtyard.

Petar, wearing more practical outdoor clothes for once, was sitting on a shiny log. He seemed lost in thought. He tapped the communicator in his ear twice, turning it off.

"Drinkin'?" he said quietly.

"I'm here, boss," a voice from the bushes to his right assured him.

"Sometimes I wonder... I'm not sure if I'm not getting too old for this. I wonder if I should have one last blast and then end it."

"No, mate," the gremlin appeared right in front of him and looked him seriously in the eye. "What kind of stupid bullcrap is that? What would you like to do? Go take out Thaçi regardless of getting killed afterwards? No way, my brother. You've got a lot to repay. For everything you've done. Rest assured, I'll see to it that your accounts are in order before you have to answer for your sins."

Petar sighed.

"My biggest regret of all is dragging you into this mess."

Drinkin' gave a short laugh. A sad one.

"I wouldn't get dragged into anything I didn't want to get into myself. You're still a kid compared to me, mate."

This time Petar laughed. A few pounds of the weight on his shoulders disappeared.

"The old man here is philosophizing about the perspective of someone who is immortal."

"Nobody is immortal. Not even me." The gremlin shook his head. "Once people stop printing on paper, I'll cease to exist."

"That won't happen for a long time, I hope."

Drinkin' scratched himself behind his ear.

"I'd toast to that if I had something to drink. But I'll tell you anyway; they're starting to piss me off with those e-books."

With that, the gremlin disappeared from sight.

Petar switched the radio back on.

"Finally," came Gunny in his ear, sourly. "I just wanted to make sure you two noticed it's getting colder. Yeah, and the fog has started creeping in the moat, too. The artillery is over and out."

"Thank you," Petar replied, looking around.

The advantage of good outdoor clothing was that it could insulate him from even light frost. At the same time, however, it limited his perception of changes in ambient temperature. In any case, he could already feel the cold on the tip of his nose. A tendril of mist slithered over his boot like a snake. Fog and frost localized in a small area. A physical nonsense, impossible without a good dose of reality-warping magic.

He stood up and dusted off his pants. He put his hand on the stock of his gun.

"Well, come on! Let's get started," he said into the darkness.

As if on cue, heavy footsteps sounded through the courtyard.

The figure entering the warm firelight was clad in full plate armor. Though the light of the dancing flames tinted everything around it orange, the glint of steel dyed the figure blue, a shade similar to ice inside a glacier. Steam rose from the joints of the armor.

There was nothing above the broad shoulders, covered in steel plates, and the top of the cuirass. Yet Petar felt as if he could see a face clearly before him. Stark, as if cut from stone, with a moustache with drooping ends. Eyes filled with cruelty.

Petar had seen much in war and his later life, but there was never such concentrated rage.

He spat. Kuneš paused. Perhaps he wanted to let the fear work. Perhaps he was not used to such a reaction.

"Yeah, you are a big asshole," Petar smirked. "Let's see if you have a heart."

The hand with the Uzi flew up. His index finger squeezed the trigger and held it. In the sound of gunfire refracted off the crumbling walls, everything else faded away.

The chest plate sparked. The gunshots were joined by a sound similar to that of hammering nails into a full can.

The shots stopped.

The steel needles had gouged a hole in Kuneš's heart area that a man's fist could fit through. Thick, black blood flowed from the hole. The spine glistened white in the depths.

"Oh shit!" came the uncharacteristically clipped voice of the gremlin. "I never would have believed he could be so imbued with power."

Flesh wriggled in the hole like worms. It was beginning to patch itself up. Slowly, the hole in the armor was also disappearing.

"Looks like it," Petar muttered between his teeth. "We'll have to toughen up."

"Copy," confirmed Gunny over the radio.

He hastily put down the sniper rifle and fumbled for the incomparably larger weapon he had ready next to him. The end of the barrel of the anti-material rifle was fitted with a muzzle brake, making it resemble the end of a cannon.

He grunted slightly as he placed the weapon in firing position. After all, thirty five pounds are thirty five pounds.

"That'll be expensive. I wonder if they'll compensate us for the ammo," he muttered under his beard.

Lydie, standing a few feet away, was opening and closing the lighter in rapid succession.

Kuneš stepped forward. His armored boot stomped out the campfire. The flames were extinguished.

Petar raised his eyebrows slightly.

"Lights!" he ordered.

With a soft click, the spotlights they had mounted at strategic points during the day flared to life.

The headless knight turned his torso as if looking around in surprise. Then, however, he turned back to Petar. He twisted the broad blade of the sword in his lowered hand so that it flashed.

"Now what?" Petar asked, uninterested. "Will it be like the story of Sir Gawain and the Green Knight?"

The sword flashed in a luminous arc at exactly neck height. But Petar was no longer there. He crouched down and rolled under the blade. This brought him to the knight's left side. From his kneeling position, he planted a long shot into Kuneš's knee.

Not that the knight particularly minded., Petar jumped away at the last moment before an upward swing could cut him in two.

Kuneš stepped forward and his leg almost buckled under him. The tangle of metal and black flesh had not yet had time to regenerate.

Petar took off along the wall of the main building. This was going to require a bigger caliber. The 12.7 of the Gunny's Zastava M93 Black Arrow anti-material rifle seemed sufficient to him.

Drinkin' suddenly appeared on the wall to his right. He grabbed Petar's sleeve and, while holding onto the wall with his other hand with all his strength, yanked him back.

It was at the last moment. Another figure in armor, who had just emerged from around the corner, swung his arm. The barbed ball of a flail flew through the place where Petar would have run if Drinkin' hadn't stopped him. It practically crushed one of the stones in the wall. Fragments flew around like shrapnel. One of them grazed Petar's face.

"Boss, we are in deep shit!" yelled the gremlin. "That's one of Kuneš' sons they executed with him!"

From the other side, Kuneš himself came within blade range. The sword blade whistled again.

Petar rushed through the nearest hole into the castle building. He needed to buy them time. Drinkin', who was anxiously watching the progress of the other headless knight, could not dodge in time.

"Ouch!" the gremlin yelled and disappeared.

A bloody tip of his long ear hit the ground.

✧ ✧ ✧

"What the fuck is going on?!" growled Gunny, who was lying down, watching the ruin from the foot of the bridge through the sights of his rifle.

He almost fired at a figure that had squeezed through a narrow hole at the base of one of the outer walls of the palace. It was Petar, hurrying into the open space in front of the bridge.

"Oh, hello," the soldier muttered as he took aim at the knight with the flail, who had come around the side of the building and was just entering his field of vision.

"Where did you come from all of a sudden? Whatever, it's time to say goodbye."

The gunshot was so loud that it deafened Lydie standing nearby. The rifle twitched as if trying to tear off Gunny's shoulder, but he was used to that.

Kuneš's son ended up much worse. The bullet had actually ripped *his* shoulder off, along with a quarter of his rib cage. The arm came crashing to the ground with a muffled thud and a splash of black tissue. Or rather, the rest of the arm had.

The headless knight walked on. Without hesitation, he headed towards Petar, who raised his Uzi defiantly.

"Just a scratch?" Gunny grinned.

He planted the second blow in the knight's pelvis. The knight's legs flew sideways like bowling pins, his torso and remaining arm falling with a sickening splash to the root-ridden ground.

The legs were wriggling like snakes. A fragment of the blown-off arm struggled to reach the torso. To no use.

"Wait a minute," Gunny twisted his lip thoughtfully. "Didn't Kuneš have more sons?"

"Behind you!" Lydie yelled.

The soldier immediately rose to his knees and turned. A flash of steel flew toward him.

Instinctively he raised his rifle in front of him.

The impact shook his entire skeleton, which tried to jump out of his body. The heavy rifle flew out of his hands.

He staggered backwards, and a rock on the edge of the moat loosened under his foot. Then he just rolled down. All he could do was protect his head.

At the bottom of the moat, he scrambled shakily to his feet. He heard a stamping sound, and looking up at the bridge, he saw Lydie running halfway across. She leaned against the railing and looked down at him.

"Watch out, he's coming for you!" he shouted at her.

Kuneš's son number two had just reached the bridge. His armor gleamed and he was swinging his sword in anticipation.

"That one is mine. You go help the boss!" she told him in a voice that didn't allow any objections.

Gunny turned toward the inner slope of the moat and began to climb up the jutting tree roots.

"I just hope the whole Kuneš family and their matron and little brats don't arrive too," he grumbled.

Lydie stood motionless in the middle of the bridge. A massive, headless knight was approaching. His feet raked the grey powder that covered the bridge.

Finally, he stopped about seven feet in front of her and bent his torso as if to see what was crunching under his feet. Then he straightened up again and refocused on the girl. In the face of her determination, he suddenly looked somewhat uncertain.

"You shall not pass!" she shouted, flicking her lighter at him.

This time a flame actually shot out of it. And fire erupted all around.

The magnesium powder ignited under the knight's feet. The white flame, at five and a half thousand degrees, rose a good eight feet high. It melted both flesh and the metal of the armor.

The headless knight, though staggering, clumsily advanced a step. The girl furrowed her brows in concentration. The flames shot higher, igniting another pile of magnesium directly beneath the knight.

Orange tongues of fire from the burning wood began to crawl under the bridge. Still, the headless knight raised his sword arm.

The girl swung her left arm violently. The tongue of fire cracked like a whip and wrapped itself around the knight's arm. In one heartbeat, it burned through the elbow of the sword-holding arm. The burnt sword arm twisted and disappeared under the bridge.

The figure in front of the girl dropped to all fours. Within three seconds, all that was left of him was a melted puddle.

Lydie turned and walked unhurriedly to the end of the bridge and then between the remaining walls of the bridge gate.

The fire spread rapidly behind her. Unchecked, the flames whipped to such a height that they threatened to burn the treetops. Leaves twisted by the heat fell around like rain.

The girl turned around. She stretched out her hand. The bridge crackled and collapsed into the moat.

Meanwhile, Kuneš pushed Petar up against the wall of the building. The old hitman needed all his speed and experience to dodge the slashes of the knight's sword. His shots only slowed the monster down.

He misjudged the distance and slammed his back into the wall.

Kuneš readied himself for an angled slash. He swung his arm down. Petar could only crouch.

But the sword didn't land. Surprised, Kuneš raised his hand. Someone had cut a tendon on the inside of his plate glove, just above the cuff.

Above him, in the niche of the wall, Drinkin' grinned. In one hand he held his razor, in the other the sword of the headless knight.

"That's for my ear, you bastard!" he bellowed at Kuneš.

Up the gentle slope ran Gunny.

"The sword—throw it to me!"

The gremlin huffed, and with noticeable effort, threw the sword in an arc towards the approaching soldier. Gunny ducked with a curse. The spinning sword slammed into the ground where it remained stuck.

"Why didn't you catch it?" Drinkin' chuckled.

"Because I'm not completely stupid and I'm not going to get my fingers chopped off!" Gunny said, grabbing the hilt.

Petar seized the opportunity, squeezed past Kuneš and shot through his legs with a long shot. The headless knight sank to his knees.

"Just like an execution," gasped the approaching soldier.

At that moment, something occurred to him. Maybe it was stupid, but he trusted his intuition.

He waved the sword just above the armor. In the place where Kuneš used to have his neck when he had been alive.

The headless knight fell lifeless to the ground. Steam stopped rising from the armor's joints. The unnatural chill that had radiated from his body vanished.

The Hunters gathered around the motionless body.

"How did you know where to hit him?" Petar asked.

His almost unnatural calm was gone. His expression was stunned.

"I don't even know." Gunny looked thoughtful. "I thought I could almost see his head. And the way he was kneeling, it seemed like a good idea."

"And it was," Drinkin' nodded.

He was seeing the former soldier in a very different light now.

"What next?" Lydie asked.

"We'll take good pictures and collect samples so the SRS won't give us a hard time about the bounty. Then we'll throw them in the fire and you burn them to ashes. Just in case," Petar decided.

"Have fun. But without me," growled Drinkin', rubbing his cut ear. "I've had enough for today."

As they said, so they did. Finally, they stood on the outside of the moat, looking down at the burning remnants of the bridge.

"Have you completely lost your minds!?" a desperate cry cut through the night.

The mayor was crawling up the slope on all fours to join them, leaves stuck to his hands, his glasses sliding off his nose.

When he scrambled up to them, he finally straightened up. His face was as red as a scalded slaughterhouse pig.

"You call this discreet!?!?" he yelled. "Do you have any idea what the heritage commissioner will do to me? All the work they've done over the years is gone!"

He stared in horror at the burning ruins of the wooden bridge at the bottom of the moat.

"Did you have to destroy that damned bridge too!?"

"That's the best way to burn them," Lydie replied quietly.

"Well, it'll be better if there aren't too many tourists around anyway," the soldier replied.

"I'd still recommend planting a grate at the entrance to the underground. So it doesn't happen again," Petar added.

The mayor stared at them in mute shock for a moment, then raised his hands to the heavens and roared inarticulately.

That seemed to calm him down a little. He began to pace back and forth, measuring them menacingly. Finally he stopped in front of them, hands on his hips.

"Now listen to me very carefully! The heritage authority, the civic associations, the forest service, the fire department. These will all be interested in what happened. And do you know that there is a military base not far from here in Lešany? So the army will take notice too! "

He took a deep breath and then let the air out slowly, like his therapist had taught him.

"You'll work out some agreement with the SRS," Petar remarked calmly.

"If you think you're going to pin this colossal mess on me, forget it! I'm not just going to take the blame."

"Yeah? How much would you bet on that, mate?" a voice said beside his knee.

The mayor's eyes dimmed for a moment, the corner of his mouth twitching on its own accord. When he finally dared to lower his gaze, he saw Drinkin' with a bandaged ear, who had just begun to piss on his leg. Then his consciousness finally gave up and he collapsed to the ground.

"Do you think he'll try to dig up the treasure?" Lydie wondered.

"Only if he's totally stupid. Which, of course, is possible. He's a politician," added Drinkin', unusually serious.

"I suppose it's a question of greed and death," Petar shrugged.

The soldier eyed the prone man with interest.

"To be honest, I don't like politicians either," he said thoughtfully.

Drinkin', sitting behind his desk, leaned back comfortably in his custom-made office chair. He folded the newspaper and carefully placed it next to a large glass filled with dark blue liquid, from which a straw and a colorful cocktail umbrella protruded.

The newspaper was the *Týnec věstník*, and there was a big headline on the front page: THE MAYOR WAS RUNNING NAKED IN THE WOODS! IS HE AN EXHIBITIONIST? IS HE THE ARSONIST WHO SET THE CASTLE BRIDGE ON FIRE?

The gremlin looked delightfully at the stack of forms that loomed before him like a true mountain of bureaucracy. Alexandra from Fantom's office claimed that the new SRS forms were more complicated than ever. He was looking forward to taking a closer look at them. Life is like a box of chocolates and he's picking out the best bits.

JAKUB HOZA (* 1978)

A martial arts expert and fencing enthusiast who has been involved in these hobbies for more than thirty years; he applies his knowledge and experience not only to improving his physical appearance of a tough guy who is not to be trifled with, but also to writing fight scenes. Interestingly enough, Jakub's real-world job is in the IT industry, which is not exactly brimming with physical, adrenaline-pumping action. Given that, he enjoys it all the more in his vivid imagination.

Jakub's beginnings as a writer are also linked to literary competitions; in 2011, his short story "The Hell Hole" ("Díra do pekel") caught the attention of publisher Egon Čierny so much that three years later Hoza was able to debut with his fantasy novel *Theatre Macabre* (*Theatre macabre*, Klub Julese Vernea, 2014). The gritty action story featured his favorite Nathaniel Darnsworn for the first time. A loose sequel, *Shackles of Destiny* (*Okovy osudu*, Klub Julese Vernea, 2017), was published three years later, and he returned to Nathaniel for the last time with the aptly named book *Like Death Itself* (*Jako sama smrt*, Mystery Press, 2022). In the interim, the author has focused on a new hero—Scarecrow, a former state assassin who is not to be provoked (like Hoza himself). Scarecrow's first novel, *Through the Fire* (*Projít ohněm*, Klub Julese Vernea, 2020), is a gritty splatterpunk action novel set in the near future, which the author enhanced with a prequel called *To Hell and Back* (*Do pekla a zpět*, Mystery Press, 2021). The last book so far with Scarecrow is called *Scorched Earth* (*Spálená zem*, Mystery Press, 2023) and he's certainly not done with this hero yet. And it's Scarecrow who brought his creator to the *MHF* project in a way that just couldn't be ignored.

A Walk in the Park
Jiří Pavlovský

It was a park. But in Prague, any piece of green that's bigger than a postage stamp is considered a park. Anything that can serve as a dog toilet, or in case of an emergency, as a human one. This park was on Charles Square and a road cut it in two parts. In one part was something between a fountain and a swimming pool, in the other a slightly larger grass area. We're talking about the part on the left side of Charles Square, if you were looking from above, from Ječná Street... and of course on the right, if you were looking from Resslova Street, where the paratroopers found it was unwise to hide in a church during WWII.

That park contained a playground, some of the necessary statues of the greats of the past and, of course, a modest grassy area with a trampled cross path, and a small, lonely group of trees that crouched off to the side, brooding about suicide.

The park, as usual, was circled by a path lined with garbage bins and benches on which sat mothers (waiting when their children playing in the sandpit will start crying), tired pensioners, lovers, and homeless people.

It was September, so the days were still quite warm, and although the homeless mostly occupied the opposite side of the park, quite a few of them spilled over here as well. They slept in the fading sun, surrounded by bags with their belongings and plastic bottles. Not all of them, of course. Some chatted, smoked and drank, some tried to

215

get a few coins from passing people, and some skipped that futile part and went straight to swearing at anyone around them.

Fry was one of the homeless, but the guy he was looking at wasn't—though he tried his best to look like one of them. At first glance, everything seemed fine. The strange homeless guy was sitting on a bench, leg over leg, arms draped over the back of the chair, wearing several layers of clothing (too much branded stuff), bags laid next to his shoes (too new). Even sitting up, it was obvious he was tall. With his long, bent legs and his arms outstretched (no dirt behind his fingernails), he gave the impression of a spider. The only thing that kept him from looking like someone from a horror movie (hell, he had those layers of clothing perfectly matched and adjusted) was a face (too clean) with a friendly smile (with too many and too white teeth) and the satisfied expression of a man who is exactly where he should be.

Fry (he didn't get his nickname because of a drug addiction, but because he occasionally helped out at the nearby fast-food stand) saw all of this from the neighboring bench. Fry didn't like that guy. He didn't belong here. He looked like he'd dressed up as a hobo for a fancy-dress party and forgot to change back. Fry was triggered. It was worse than wearing a blackface.

Fry fished in his plastic bag, pulled out a plastic bottle, took a sip for encouragement, closed the bottle, stuffed it in his bag, stood up, and walked determinedly over to the bench with Lanky. Even the stains on his clothes looked orderly, almost geometrical, more like the result of an artistic intent than hygiene issues.

But who would give a homeless man a second look.

"This bench is mine," Fry said aggressively to start the conversation.

"Congratulations," Lanky said calmly. "It's a very nice bench."

"I want you to beat it."

"Me too, believe me," sighed Lanky. But he didn't move. He just continued to smile contentedly.

"Then get the hell out," Fry snapped. "And presto. And be grateful." He leaned closer to Lanky. "I've been in prison before. And I have no problem going back there."

Lanky looked him in the eye. "Trust me, I respect a man with ambition and plans. It's just that, unfortunately, I'm stuck here. Frankly, I'd hate to fight you over this bench; neither of us would like that. So I suggest you tolerate my presence for a while. Then you won't have to spend several days in the hospital and me in the shower."

"Are you a cop?" Fry guessed. That would explain a lot.

"Me?" Lanky laughed. "Do I look like ... ?" He ran his eyes over his dirty clothes, "Well, you're right, I do look a bit like a cop when I think about it. But I'm not. I am," he lowered his voice, "a member of a top-secret group of Hunters who are seeking out and killing monsters in our country."

"Monsters."

"Yes. One of those guys who does all the essential work of researching and finding out vital information so that some steroid muscles can come in, do what we tell them, and get all the glory and money for it."

"I've never seen a monster before."

"We're very good at our jobs," Lanky said.

"You're not a cop," Fry decided. "You're nuts."

"I'm afraid you're right on both counts. Can I get back to looking for monsters?"

Fry wondered if he shouldn't pull him up after all, but you never know with crazies. He still remembered that dude who had bitten everyone around him. The bites themselves hadn't been so bad, but then they'd all had to go to the doctor. But again, he couldn't back down. Then he'd look like a pussy. He had some prestige. "Go look for them in your shithole! Get off my bench! Get the fuck off, you and your Hunters!"

Lanky put a finger over his narrow lips. "Shh. You can't talk about Hunters."

"Yeah? And what are you going to do to me if I talk about them, huh? You gonna send some boogeymen after me?"

Lanky revealed a cloak, then another, pulled up his sweater and showed the butt of his pistol. "I'll kill you."

Fry froze. Something told him this was no toy.

"We're a secret organization," Lanky continued. "So if anyone finds out about us, it would be really bad for them."

"I...," Fry began, but somehow he ran out of words.

"We usually do this more subtly, but...," Lanky shrugged. "You won't be the first to disappear here in the park."

"I...I won't say anything," Fry finally stuttered.

Lanky patted the seat next to him. "Sit here ... or rather," he patted it a little farther away, "sit here."

"I..."

Lanky just patted the bench again, and Fry sat down. Lanky's resemblance to a spider was growing. The way he looked at him ... that must be the way a spider must look when it's going to eat a pretty fat fly.

"You are very lucky," Lanky said. "I haven't told you anything important. Not the name of our organization, not who's our leader, where is our headquarters, not even our favorite ice cream flavor. And if you cooperate, I won't tell you anything else. But if I get the feeling that you're lying to me, or that you don't want to cooperate..."

Fry needed a drink. "Can I have a drink?" he asked.

"Help yourself," Lanky said. "To come clean ... cleanish, considering our outfits ... I was sent here to blend in with the crowd, so to speak, and observe the situation. It's probably unnecessary for me to be here, except that everyone has to spend some time in the field, even though I would be much, much more useful in the office. But who am I to complain? No one important," he sighed. "I'm quite envious of you sometimes. No bosses, no assignments..." He watched Fry trying to pour the entire contents of the bottle into his stomach. "No liver..." He sighed. "I won't beat around the bush. I hate this blending in the crowd and I'm bored by observing. So I figured I'd speed things up and delegate to people who are already present."

It took Fry a moment to realize that meant him. "But I ... I don't know anything about anything."

"That's what I hope you're wrong about. Or at least you can get someone who is better informed. One of the, shall we say, regulars."

"I don't even fucking know what's going on!"

Lanky raised his eyebrows like a conductor taking baton. "About a dozen people have disappeared here in this park in the last year. Eleven that we know of."

"Here?" Fry asked. "Are you kidding me?"

"And that's the point. I'm not. Last time the cameras picked them up, they were heading for the park, and then nothing showed on the other side."

"So they came out the other way. People go as they please."

"Anything's possible. The bottom line is we have unexplained disappearances and the only thing those people have in common is this park. It could be a coincidence, it could just be some freak that is lurking here, lures people out somewhere and then takes them away... but it's always happened during daytime. And there's no place around here where you can do that without being noticed."

"During the day?"

"Always in the daytime. Usually sometime in the afternoon, around two or three o'clock. That's not a time you'd want to kidnap someone."

Fry was, against his will, intrigued. "Monsters walk at night," he stated confidently. "And if there was a monster here, someone would notice."

"I'm not so sure," Lanky countered. "It could have been camouflaged somehow. Or just extremely fast."

"The worst thing that happens here are fist fights. Yeah, someone got shanked here once, but that was a really long time ago. And it was on the other side."

"We've been looking into that, too, of course. Local history is always important. But nothing substantial came out of it. It's just... we still have eleven missing people who were last seen heading towards this park."

"So they were abducted by aliens," Fry waved his hand.

"We don't know anything about aliens," Lanky acknowledged. "But the witnesses didn't notice any flying saucers."

"The witnesses? Who?"

"One witness, actually. He saw Adriana... that's one of the last missing people... walking down this path." Lanky pointed to the path that led diagonally across the lawn. "Then he looked for his dog, and when he turned around, the lawn was empty."

"Oh, shit," Fry said. "That has to be aliens."

"Or an accidental teleportation. Or an ascension. Or they became invisible. Or they just suddenly got tired of existing." Lanky shrugged and leaned back on the bench. "No one knows anything."

Fry looked at the small patch of grass with new respect. How long would it take him to go to the other side? Twenty steps? What could happen in twenty steps?

"And this is where you—Mr. Miroslav Jíška—come into play," Lanky said.

Fry twitched. He hadn't heard that name in a long time.

"I don't enjoy observing and tracking, but I know a lot of people and I'm really, really good at my job. So I checked you out. Just in case you thought that if you disappeared from this park, you'd disappear from me too. Not only you won't, but you will probably have a nasty accident later. Why can't I just watch my mouth..."

"But you didn't actually tell me anything! You said it yourself!"

"But only you and I know that. Calm down, I don't want you to do anything sick. I just want you to stand up, check on all of your alcoholic acquaintances and see if they've noticed anything."

"Ha!" Fry blurted out. "If they've noticed anything? Most of them wouldn't have noticed if a herd of elephants were trampling around. They're already out of reality."

"I don't think so," said Lanky.

"I know them, I..."

Lanky stopped him by raising his hand and pointing a finger in front of him. On the other side, a homeless man had just gotten up from the bench, stood up, held onto the back of the bench, looked around, and spotted Fry. He waved at him and started walking toward him, heading toward the path across the lawn...but then he turned right and followed the sidewalk. He took the longer way.

He didn't set foot on the lawn.

"Something tells me," said Lanky, "that they noticed something after all."

They noticed, but they didn't know about it, or they couldn't describe it anymore. There was only a feeling, a hunch, an unpleasant aftertaste in the air. Some of them left, moved to the already crowded other half of the park, or somewhere else, but for some there was nothing else left. The park was their home now, during the day and sometimes at night when there was nowhere else to go. And after all, for most of them, fear was already a constant friend. A little more, a little less, it didn't matter so much.

And better an enemy that you can't see, that doesn't really threaten you in any way, than one that will beat you up and steal what little you have.

So they stayed here.

"So just a feeling, huh?" Lanky said, dissatisfied. "That's it?"

Fry watched him shift in his seat, hunching over as he stretched his long arms. He wanted to ask if everything was all right, if that was enough, if he had accomplished his task, if he could go now, but he was afraid that any word would alert Lanky about his presence and he would be killed. So he'd rather remain silent, hoping that Lanky might forget about him, that he would get up and leave and everything would be all right again.

Lanky looked at him, extinguishing Fry's dreams. "I expected more."

"I . . . it's not my fault."

"No one saw anything, no one heard anything, this place just doesn't have good vibes." Lanky shook his head. "I don't believe it. And not just because I don't like the word 'vibe.'"

"Can I go?"

"To where?"

". . . home?"

Lanky paused in thought. "One of us here seems to be misunderstanding the term 'homeless.'"

"The shelter . . . that's where I have . . ."

Lanky waved his hand. "It doesn't matter. You still have time and this place needs to be monitored. Not all the time, of course. Only in the afternoon. Get me a couple of people, we'll give them paper and a pencil—Can you write?—okay, paper and a pencil it is. And you'll write down," he jabbed his finger to the left, "who entered this lawn, at what time, and . . . ," he jabbed to the right, "who came off."

"Also at what time?"

Lanky paused. "Points for effort, but no, that's unnecessary." He looked at the path through the grass. An elderly lady entered it with a shopping bag and left it at the far end. A group of women stepped onto it, fighting their advancing age with luxurious clothing. They crossed the lawn and stepped out onto the sidewalk. Then a couple of men who were arguing about something important, a group of youngsters who were showing their friendship by punching each other in the shoulder with their fists, a guy in a metal t-shirt, a guy in a tank top pulled up over his bulging belly—he could disappear if there was any justice—stepped on the grass and they all made it to the safety of the pavement.

"I guess someone should write the people who go from here to there . . . and someone else the ones who go from there to here. And it should be two people doing both, for control. Someone who won't write about flying octopuses."

"And...what do I tell them?" Fry asked after a long moment. "What's the payoff?"

Lanky didn't understand at first, then automatically ran his hand down to where his gun was, but paused. "You're right. They deserve some reward. We can throw it in the cost. A hundred an hour? Is that okay?"

Fry bulged his eyes. A hundred crowns for lying on a bench and taking notes?

"Okay," said Lanky, who misinterpreted his look. "A hundred and fifty. But no more." He handed him a business card with his phone number. "Call it when someone disappears. Don't lose it. I'm gonna want it back."

The homeless man's head nodded like a bobblehead behind the car window. "We'll do it."

"Great," Lanky said. He leaned back against the bench again and stopped noticing Fry. Eventually, the whole thing took a turn for the better.

He was free. He'd have to come in for a check-up, but he wouldn't have to sit around in this humiliating costume.

He moved to leave the park, to wash up, change into something cleaner, have a latte.

Unfortunately, he went across the lawn.

The walk was really about 20 to 30 steps long. Less if you had long legs, and Theodor Kristián (a name he got from his parents...and with that name came a constant sense of injustice) did. He crossed that line easily, in no time. He crossed it two or three times before he realized something was wrong. He looked under his feet. Then forward and back. The beaten path twisted and turned around him and connected back behind his back, forming one big circle. He looked up. Birds in the sky were stuck in a blurred photograph. The wind wasn't blowing, and the people around the lawn remained stuck in the middle of started motions.

Damn, he thought. And I hadn't given Fry a paper and a pencil.

He stopped. There it was. He would become a part of the statistics. A joke in the Fantom office. No way.

He looked around. The small patch of forest in the corner of the lawn suddenly seemed much denser, the trees towering higher, pulling apart as if it were a forest explosion stopped just at its beginning. Just a few moments and they would...

They were everywhere.

Theodor stood in the middle of the forest, plastic bags in hand. He could smell it, smell the moss, the pine cones, the soil beneath his feet. That small forest was like a land trap, waiting for people to spring up at the right moment, to draw them into its universe, to enclose them in itself. Theodor looked at his cell phone. It was dead. Not only did it not pick up any signal in this world, he had no use for it. It was a strange artifact serving a mysterious mystical purpose. Even Theodor himself suddenly couldn't remember what it was used for or how. It fell from his hand into the fallen pine needles.

The forest stretched into the distance and Theodor started to run.

He ran, dodging trees, ducking from under branches that reached for him—until he came upon his lying cell phone.

He was running in circles. He hung the plastic bag with his belongings on one of the branches. He took a step away from it—and saw it in the distance in front of him. He turned to his right, took a step forward—and there it was again. Of course it was behind him too. He sat down under a tree. He must not panic. Panic means death. If he could keep his cool, he would surely pull through. He's smarter than some stupid forest.

But he knew that these things didn't necessarily have a failsafe or some hidden maintenance exit.

He's got an advantage, though. His disappearance was witnessed by Fry, so...

So Fry would run away, hoping he would never see Theodor again in his life. He hasn't even done any work yet, so there's no reason for him to save him. And even if he decided to do it, then what? He doesn't know who to call, and the police would laugh at him.

So what about the others? The rest of Fantom? How long will it take for them to figure out he's missing? This assignment was, he had to admit, pretty low on their priority list. He didn't even have a backup; he was just going to make a call tonight. If he didn't call, then what? Someone would probably check it out, find out what was going on, investigate and rescue him.

Just hold on till tomorrow.

But . . . is there a tomorrow? The sky above him hasn't moved.

He didn't take any watch because of his disguise, his cell phone froze . . . maybe he could make some sundial? Just to know how time passes around here.

He looked in his bag for something he could use. Quality wine in poor quality packaging. Gloves in case he had to touch some real homeless people. A spare pair of socks and then a bunch of rags to blend in. He still had his wallet with his ID in a pocket, but he doubted anyone would legitimize him here.

And of course, he had a gun. What if he fired a shot here? Here, in this closed universe? Would a bullet come back and hit him in the back?

Thinking of timekeeping, he broke off a twig from one tree (somehow subconsciously expecting a roar, gushing blood, or a brutal counterattack, but all he got was a twig), stripped the bark from one side with his teeth—and drove it into the ground. It stopped a few inches below the surface, not even managing to catch itself. Theodor pressed on. It wouldn't move. Stupid place. He pulled it out . . .

The twig was covered in blood.

Theodor took a breath. Breathe in, breathe out, breathe in. A twig covered in blood. It doesn't have to be human blood. It could be some red clay. Or he just killed a mole.

Or something else. Something bigger that's gonna come out, screaming, any minute. Theodor backed off. Then he put his hand palm down. The earth was still, like any good soil.

How deep had he driven it in? A few inches?

He began to dig. The dirt was denser than it looked, staying behind his fingernails, the pebbles grazing his fingers. He ignored it. He had to find out what was down there. He already found something there, something soft, something pale . . .

A human hand.

There was a human hand buried in the dirt.

He didn't yell. After all, he'd seen some corpses before. Just not usually this close up. And usually only in photos.

The hand was pale, only the back was bloody . . .

If they're bleeding, they must still be alive! Dead men don't bleed!

No, they can't be alive, they're buried under a pile of dirt.

What if there's no time here? What if it's impossible to die here? Am I breathing?

He was breathing. Quite loudly and frantically. He stopped breathing. Do I need to breathe?

He did. But . . . can he die?

No, his desire for experimentation didn't go that far.

He had to dig up the body. So he started digging. Someone had buried the body standing up, hand held up as if to grasp something. He dug like a madman, haunted by the crazy vision of a man covered in dirt, with it in his eyes, in his mouth, in his throat, but still alive, being trapped in eternal darkness. He was . . .

Theodor stopped. A zombie? No, zombies don't bleed.

How does he know that?

He didn't know. All he knew was that he was frantically trying to dig up something that might not be human at all. Maybe it's not human anymore, maybe it never was. Maybe it's just a hand reaching somewhere deep into the earth, and if you get close to it, if you uncover it, it grabs you and pulls you down.

But what if it doesn't? What if it's a human and they are dying?

Theodor sat down next to the hole he'd dug. It wasn't very deep yet. The truth was, if they hadn't died by now, they'd stay alive for a while. If they hadn't died . . .

Theodor started poking that exposed palm with a twig. If the one down there is alive, they can feel it. If the one down there is alive, they'll move their hand, make a sign. If the one down there is alive . . .

The hand didn't move.

Maybe the one down there is a quadriplegic, Theodor thought. Or maybe it's some kind of magical immobilization spell.

Or maybe dead people are bleeding here. Is the answer buried down there, or is it a trap?

He didn't have much choice anyway, so he bent over the hole again and keep digging.

Yeah. He was definitely dead. Theodor could tell, even if he couldn't try to check his breath with a mirror. The dead man's gaping mouth was full of dirt, as if he were testing how much he could eat in one swallow. And Theodor didn't have a mirror anyway. Maybe some movement of his eyes . . . what eyes? Two holes full of bloody dirt.

Theodor stepped back and tried to imagine the dead man without all the dirt and grime around him, still alive. Yeah, it was one of those missing people. Homeless? Hapless? Definitely lifeless.

Theodor Kristián was looking at his future. This is what awaits me. I'll end up in the dirt. But how will that happen to me? Will something pull me in? Will I fall in it? Will I be killed and buried? No, by the look on his face, or what's left of it, he made it into the ground alive. Great, there's a lot to look forward to.

There are many teams fighting the supernatural and the unnatural. Some rely on magic, others on ammo. Some, like Jonáš's team, rely on magic, chaos, and improvisation, while people from Fantom rely more on weapons, planning, teamwork, and gathering detailed information on the enemy. He had the weapon, though Theodor would gladly trade it for a working pentagram. The team consisted of him and the corpse. And he doesn't know shit about the enemy.

Think, think!

This couldn't happen on its own. Someone had to start this.

Could this be a consequence? Cursed places do occur from time to time, they are not all that exceptional. But nothing major has happened here in the recent years. Nothing that would have the power to make this happen. Even that murder happened in the other part of the park.

Was it created on purpose? Why? Why would someone set a death trap in the middle of Charles Square? It's not destructive enough to make a bigger impact. Sure, it could have targeted a specific person who walked by, but if someone had that kind of power, why make it so complicated? And why would it still work?

Maybe it hasn't gotten its victim yet. Or it can't be shut down.

Could it be a side effect? One of those things that show up in places where wizards have fought each other, where monsters have been summoned; or it was just the revenge of nature, fed up with being pissed on by dogs.

"I don't have a dog," he said out loud, just in case. "And I promise not to walk across the lawn again!"

MO, think of a modus operandi. You're the know-it-all, the one who's smarter than everyone else, the one everyone goes to for advice—if they have no one else to go to because you usually give them a hard time.

"And I promise I'll become a better person," he lied, just to be sure.

Nothing happened. He leaned against a tree. What now? Just wait to die? He wasn't hungry. He wasn't thirsty. He just had his own little, tiny piece of a forest to himself.

He screamed and started running. He ran and he didn't know where to, just forward; he jumped over the hole with the dead man once, twice, three times... If he runs for long enough, he'll break it; he'll break this vicious circle, it's like banging on a door, banging on it over and over again, and you don't care about the blood, or the broken finger bones, you are banging with your hands, with your feet, with your head, until you break the door down.

Or until you collapse, half unconscious, on the floor.

He fell and rolled over, gasping for breath. Nothing changed. He was still in the same place, just exhausted. Maybe he should lie down for a while and wait; surely Fantom had been alerted and everyone was looking for a way to get him out of here. They can do it. All he has to do is wait.

He should start thinking about how to set up camp here. Even if he didn't finish a sundial, night should have fallen by now. He was in the park around 3 p.m., he could have been here for what... four, five hours? At the very least, it should be starting to get dark. But not here, where timelessness still reigned above his head.

At least it wouldn't get cold. Still, he'd have to camp somewhere. He had something to drink, some food too (would the food spoil here?), but that would last him until tomorrow, the day after at most, if he rationed it a lot. He's not hungry, he's not thirsty, but no one has guaranteed that he will be that way forever.

Don't give up, pussy, he ordered himself. Go! You can break it.

He was exhausted; he'd rather have rolled over and fallen asleep, and deep down he knew it was hopeless, but he also knew there was nothing else he could do. And that if he stopped going, if he stopped doing the one thing he could do, he'd give up everything and then it would be his end.

He took the next step.

And then...

Something changed. Something was different, he felt it on his tongue, he felt it at the back of his neck, he felt it in his hair.

Wind was blowing. Just slightly, but it was there. He licked his finger and tried to guess where it was blowing from. Over there! There's...

In the distance, almost obscured by the trees, was an opening to another world. A world without trees and without needles. He could have sworn a dog had just run there. That's it! That's it, it's timed! The gate opens and closes at a certain time, and whoever's around...

Don't think! Go!

He ran, hoping it wouldn't close right in front of him, that he would make it. Was it getting bigger? Yes, it was getting bigger, it was getting closer...

And then his feet hit the mud. Suddenly he had nothing solid under him; he slipped, he swung, the mud covered him, clogged his eyes, his mouth, his nose. He tried to grasp at something, but there was only slick, deep mud all around him.

No, not just mud. A swamp.

Now he knew how the others had died. And he knew what killed them.

But it was as good as a dead horse to him now.

Fry sat on the bench and stared at the empty space in the middle of the lawn. He must have blinked ... or rather fallen asleep. Lanky was there, and then suddenly he wasn't. But it wasn't a sudden disappearance, just a blink and he was gone. It was as if he'd slowly walked away in a hundredth of a second, which was impossible, Fry knew that. He looked around. No one reacted, not even the people with the dog, the drunks around on the benches, the group of fancily dressed women ..., no one noticed anything was wrong.

Just him.

What now? Should he do something?

Call the police? Yeah, he could imagine how that would turn out. So you saw a man disappear? And he couldn't have just taken off on those pink mice that were running around?

He was holding a business card with Lanky's phone number in his hand. Well, it was probably his phone number, the name didn't seem the least bit plausible. What now? Should he try calling him?

He tried it on his old Nokia, holding it away from his ear, because you never knew what would happen if you called ... somewhere else. Nothing happened. There wasn't even a dial tone; the phone wasn't going to acknowledge this number as worthy of its concern. On the other side of the business card was a printed capital F in front of nine digits. He should call the people from that secret organization that would probably kill him.

Or they'll give him a fortune for the information.

Or give him a fortune and then kill him.

He threw the phone back in the bag. This really wasn't worth his nerves.

But what if Lanky gets out and comes after him? What if he wants revenge?

Fry hesitated, thought for a moment, then got up and got out of the park, out of Prague, and out of this story.

Theodor lay sprawled in the swamp to distribute his weight and slow down the dive. He had no idea if it was working; he thought the swamp was more likely savoring him, swallowing him in small pieces, like a particularly tasty piece of cake. He lay on his stomach, arms outstretched, and moved his legs carefully, as if he was swimming in slow motion, to slowly try to kick himself out of the muddy grip. So as not to create air pockets pulling him back down. Slowly... slowly... slowly... just don't lose your nerve and don't panic.

His eyes darted around frantically, looking for something to grab onto. A sward that would indicate that there was a patch of earth... or a stump...

There was one, out of his reach. He moved his arms in a breaststroke, but the mud held him firmly. He didn't give up, paddling his arms smoothly, not speeding up, moving, not stopping. He didn't know how long it took; time didn't play the slightest role here. He hadn't moved an inch in the swamp... unless you count the downward direction. He was doing great at that.

Not far from his right hand, his plastic bag was lying in the mud. He reached for it, moved awkwardly, the mud bubbled beneath him, and only the top half of his body stayed above the surface.

Don't panic! Don't panic! DON'T PANIC! Regular movements with his legs, arms outstretched, keeping afloat, taking a look in the bag.

Hope is a bitch. He knew he wasn't going to find anything useful in the bag, but the voice in his head began to convince him even so that maybe a rope had gotten in there, a rope with an anchor..., and it was putting together an absolutely convincing argument as to how it could have happened.

No rope inside. All that was in the bag were his clothes, a bottle, a pack of cigarettes, matches ... Nothing that would get him out of the swamp.

Although ...

He absolutely mustn't screw up now. No sudden movements. He tied the leg of his trousers together with the sleeve of his sweater. It was hard as he tried to move his arms as carefully as he could; by the time he managed it, he had the mud up to his belly. He didn't give a damn about safety, he was already upright in the swamp, tying the sleeve of his sweatshirt to a plastic bottle filled with mud so tightly it was squeezed in the middle. It wasn't exactly an anchor rope, but it might do the trick. He tossed the bottle toward the stump. It didn't fly far enough; it disappeared beneath the surface with a splash. He pulled at his bound clothes quickly, in panicked terror of losing the bottle, but it reappeared, skimming along the surface towards Theodor, who was already chest-deep in the swamp, leaving a small and rapidly filling furrow behind it.

He didn't have many more tries left. Was there anything closer?

The head! That half-excavated corpse. It was a little closer. He took a breath, spun the bottle over his head like a lasso and threw it. The bottle traced an arc in the air, dragged his clothes behind it, flew past the dead man's outstretched hand; Theodor tugged at his trousers, the bottle rolled back and encircled the protruding hand. Once, twice ... and that was enough. It landed on the ground. Theodor ignored the mud already clinging to his neck and pulled carefully. Slowly, so the grip tightened and the bottle wouldn't loosen. And only then did he begin to pull himself closer. Carefully, as if he had all the time in the world, which was probably true. The muscles in his arms ached, reminding him of the old days where they'd tried to teach him how to climb a rope at school. This was the same, only he had a ton of extra mud on him. And he was fighting for his life.

Slowly ...

It seemed nothing was happening at all, just the searing pain in his arms was getting worse. His eyes were fixed on that increasingly bent arm and the bottle that trembled at its side. At any moment, something might come loose.

But it was the mud that gave way and let go of his legs. Theodor felt a surge of energy, pulling himself up, slowly rising above the surface and following it to the coveted piece of solid ground. By then, he was using his legs to help—

The arm broke at the elbow and the rope came loose.

Theodor began to dive into the depths again. But he so was close, he could almost reach the hand, so he grabbed both ends of his improvised rope as if he were going to jump rope, and threw it over the hand. He pulled. The rope didn't slip. He was sure of it now, he could do this, he could do this . . .

He did it! He landed on solid ground, covered in mud, but happy. He's the man, the king of the world!

Well, except for the small problem of getting out of here.

He was looking at a window into his normal world, just out of reach, in the middle of the swamp.

"And . . . ," Karla asked.

"And?" Theodor Kristián answered, already scrubbed clean and shaved, in new clothes, with a massive watch on his wrist. Karla would have bet he'd also managed to get a manicure done, because nothing was more important than perfectly manicured nails.

"How did you get out of there?"

Theodor shrugged with the expression of a ruler talking to rabble trying to bask in the rays of his glory. "Simply. If you know who's behind it, you know how to get out."

"And?" Karla asked again. "Who's behind it?"

Theodor Kristián smirked. "But that should be obvious by now, shouldn't it?"

"Would you like to order?"

They met in one of the cafes around Charles Square. Of course, Theodor had no intention of going to Fantom's headquarters, as it was located in one of those bizarre cities that weren't Prague, and thus it was a wonder anyone bothered to plot them on a map at all. And in the Prague office . . . The truth was that everyone there was so glad that Kristián had dropped out for a while that Karla didn't want to spoil their brief moment of happiness and comfort. So they met in a café that was so hipster that the menu said Coffee, Coffee with milk or Coffee with frothed milk.

"Grande latte," Theodor said.

"You mean 'lots of milk with a little coffee,'" the waiter corrected him.

"Black coffee," Karla added her order. "Large."

The waiter nodded and walked over to the man operating the levers of the space machine. "One large normal, one girly."

"What on Earth kind of a place is this?" Theodor asked.

Karla looked around. "A café. They make coffee here."

"The hell they..." Theodor sighed. No, he mustn't get distracted. He had just been born again. He must enjoy life to the fullest.

Karla unbuttoned her jacket. She was rather petite in stature, looking frail and vulnerable, which was usually the last mistake a lot of people made. She walked around dressed strictly for business, her brown hair pulled back into a bun. She looked more like a teenage municipal clerk than the head of Fantom's Prague research department.

"So who's behind this?" she asked again.

"Behind the coffee?"

Karla refused to comment on that.

"Who is behind this? Think about it. The forest, the swamp, the inability to find the right direction, the lure...," he looked at Karla. "Bludiczkas."

Karla sputtered. "You're out of your mind, aren't you? Bludiczkas? And in a park in Prague?"

"It's strange, yes, but there *is* a forest."

"Have you seen that forest? It's six trees! It's not a forest, it's a rock garden!"

"As you can see, that's enough. There's no telling how big a space..."

"And these bludiczkas," Karla started, "did they do it themselves? Or did they team up with Little Red Riding Hood? Or with Cinderella?"

Theodor raised his eyebrows. "Those are fairy tale characters."

"Exactly."

"The existence of bludiczkas has been documented. In 1815..."

"In 1815, they were still burning witches! Those are not exactly reliable sources!"

"Your coffee," said the waiter. He placed it in front of them. "Would you like a straw with it?" he asked.

Theodor snorted and the waiter floated a little further away.

"First of all," Theodor said after a moment, "they didn't burn witches anymore in 1815. As you would know if you were even a little interested in history and didn't get all your information from TikTok alone. Bludiczkas were a documented fact. In 1815, they even caught one and studied her. The fact that they could change into dancing lights may be superstition, but they could affect one's perception of the environment. But mostly they worked with their sexual energy."

"Sexual energy. That explains a lot."

Theodor ignored her. "They were basically the Czech equivalent of sirens. They just didn't use singing...at least, that's what the records say. It's quite logical, given the environment."

"Or maybe they just didn't have a musical ear."

"The last death probably caused by the bludiczkas dates back to 1875. They haven't been seen since, and it's assumed that they disappeared sometime around the time of forest cultivation and the placement of hiking signs."

"Right. Let's get serious." Karla waved away his attempt to object. "Let's talk seriously. The irrefutable fact is that monsters are connected to their environment. If they don't have a suitable environment, they die or they are fundamentally weakened. It's like viruses. What was once a deadly threat is now a minor inconvenience. You used to die of it, now aspirin will fix it. Am I right?"

"You're right."

"Even if we accept the existence of bludiczkas and accept that this is their modus operandi, this is well beyond their capabilities. It was beyond their capabilities even in the days of their greatest power. Which are now, with the state of the forests and all, really long gone. Or do you have any proof that they were capable of this sort of thing?"

"I don't have proof that they weren't either. And they could...they could have allied with someone."

"Yeah. With the Snow Queen...I know, I know, I'm not going to completely dismiss it. But...isn't it likely that you just latched onto the first possible explanation? That it could be something else?" Karla leaned across the table. "Listen, you did great. No matter how you did it—and you bet I'm going to want it detailed in the report—you did it. You got away. But this...you grabbed one aspect of all the symptoms and built your theory on that. You are ignoring everything else."

Theodor took a sip of coffee. And then another. "This coffee is good." He took another sip. "But on second thought, I lived in the wilderness for a while. It leaves a mark on you."

"All right, Tarzan. Write it down and we'll take a look. The pros will take over. I mean . . . people from the action team."

Theodor snorted. "Action team . . . Why action team?"

"Because that's their job. You supply them with the information, they handle monsters."

"Why not me? What's the difference between me and the action team people?"

"Muscles? Combat experience? Charisma? Being sexually attractive?"

"Ouch," Theodor said.

"Teamwork, reliability, commitment . . ."

"No. The main difference is money," Theodor cut her off.

"Money?"

"We do most of the work, and what do we get out of it? Just a base salary. Who gets most of the money from TEFLON? Them."

"They risk their lives. They're eliminating monsters."

"Based on the information they got from us. If they know what it is and how to do it, it's easy enough to hit it on the head and kill it."

"You've got to be kidding me."

"In the end, it's always about information."

"They have years of training and experience."

"So do I—and what do I get out of it? A few cents and social security."

Karla leaned back in her chair and eyed Theodor inquiringly. "What're you trying to say?"

"I want to finish the job. I have the right to do it. I almost died already."

"And do you want to finish the case, or the dying?"

"I know how to deal with bludiczkas."

"If they're bludiczkas."

"They *are* bludiczkas."

"To be clear," Karla said. "We sent you into the field because you've been successfully avoiding it for five years. And since you're getting on everyone's nerves at the office, we gave you this mission. I figured if you had to sit with the homeless for a couple of weeks, it'd cut you down to size. And of course, you immediately tried to wriggle out of it, then walked right into a death trap like a total idiot ... but then you somehow managed to get out of it, and apparently achieved some kind of goddamn enlightenment in the process, and now you're going to dedicate your life to finding a group of all-powerful bludiczkas who prey on people in Prague parks?"

"Sort of. I was enlightened by the fact that I was risking my life for some thirty grand."

"Plus the bonuses."

"Plus, it'll help the company. How long has it been since we scored in Prague? A couple of years, huh? And if we hand this over to the action team, all the glory ..."

"And the money ..."

"... and the money will be swallowed by them. Don't tell me it won't help you if you score some serious points."

Karla didn't answer. It was the truth. The Prague department was more on the edge. There were few monsters and a lot of competition. The freaks around Jonáš ... most of the big events were solved up by them these days. Yeah, this was just ... bludiczkas or something ... but it still might have helped.

Karla was ambitious, and Theodor knew it. So she just sighed. "How do you plan on finding your bludiczkas?"

"Easily enough. I know what they look like."

"Would you like to order anything else?" The waiter broke into their discussion.

"Evian," Theodor said.

"We don't have Evian. But I could bring tap water from the faucet for you? That's about the same."

"Something sparkling then. And no, I don't mean your sense of humor."

"Twice," Karla said.

"I'll do my best."

"How do they even make a living with that kind of behavior?" Theodor wondered.

"Sometimes I feel like it's part of the style these days. It creates an atmosphere."

"Bullshit."

"So you've seen them?"

"Just before I went in there. Three women. Fifty-something, well-groomed, fancy clothes..."

"Aren't you a bit of a misogynist? Why would they be bludiczkas?"

"They were the most likely suspects."

"You know what they say about having a hammer in your hand?"

"That you're supposed to watch your fingers?"

"No. That the whole world looks like a nail."

"All the more reason to watch your fingers."

"You've decided that bludiczkas are behind this, so of course it fits your formula. And you don't see anything else. Were they running around a meadow?"

"No."

"Were they glowing? Were they trying to charm you? Cast spells on you? Did they try to dance with you till you fell asleep?"

"Not that I noticed."

"Your water. Don't drown."

Karla threw up her hands. "So what if they were, and I'm just guessing here, just some clerks who happened to be walking to work?"

"For one thing, they went by just before I disappeared. And then there's another thing. Something about them didn't sit right with me, but I didn't realize it until it was too late. It wasn't until I realized that this was the work of bludiczkas."

"And what was that?"

"They were wearing high-heeled shoes. Elegant shoes. Really high heels."

"And... oh."

"Yeah. You don't walk across grass in those."

"Hm. And usually not to work either."

"Unless you walk with such light steps that not a blade of grass will bend under you. They were bludiczkas."

"I'm not saying you're right, but it's definitely weird." Karla took a sip of water. "I'm not saying you're right... but maybe we should talk to him. This stuff is his turf."

"Talk to whom?"

"The big boss."

"Ours?" Theodor didn't understand.

"Theirs. If there are bludiczkas in Prague, he'll know."

"You mean..." Theodor's eyes lit up. "Great. When should I leave?"

"I haven't decided if we're going to do it yet. And even if we were going to ask him, we're certainly not going to send you. Your negotiating skills are...are...actually, they more like *aren't*. Remember that time you were supposed to be talking to those rarachs?"

"In the end, we defeated them."

"Yeah, but they originally came to Earth just to arrange a wifi connection. So no, you're really not going to negotiate."

"This is my case."

"This isn't a toy for you to usurp for yourself. I assign the contracts."

"Then assign it to me," Theodor Kristián said. "I'm the furthest along in this."

"I'll think about it," Karla said.

Theodor thought about it too. "I'm offering you a deal."

"We hunt monsters. We don't trade stocks."

"I'll keep the case. I'll go to the boss. And in return, I'll tell you where the bodies of those who disappeared are. You can give them to the bereaved. At least that's the way I think it's done. And most importantly, you won't run the risk of someone discovering them by accident and starting a panic."

Karla muttered a few curses into her glass of water. "Someone? By sheer chance? Like after they get an anonymous phone call?"

"Anything's possible," Theodor shrugged.

"Are you blackmailing me?"

"We all have our hobbies."

The waiter returned to their table again. "Anything else you would like to order?"

"Yes. Can you kill this man? How you do it is entirely up to you. You can poison his coffee. You can beat him to death with a coffee machine. You can chop him up and put him in a stew. I'll leave that entirely to your discretion."

The waiter nodded his head sagely. "I'll be back in a minute."

"This is my suggestion," Theodor continued in a conciliatory tone. "I'll tell you where the bodies are. You dig them up. You check them out. If their cause of death matches what I say—you give me a chance. I just want to be there, that's all. I don't even have to talk."

Karla really wasn't buying this. Theodor was physically incapable of not talking. "And if there's not a match?"

"I'll obediently go back to the office and keep gathering information for the less intelligent but more muscular ones."

"Hmm. That sounds tempting."

"Would you like anything else?"

"The check."

The lawn in Charles Square was surrounded by a high wall. It was covered with apologies, saying that everyone was sorry for making your life difficult, but it was to improve the quality of life, so it was fine. Maybe not quite in those words, but the meaning fit.

At the edge of the lawn, safely surrounded by a wall, stood Theodor Kristián, watching two guys digging shovels into the ground. Even though he wasn't working, he was sweating. For the first time in his life he was seized with the fear that he had made a mistake. That he might not be in the right for once. They'd already had two holes, and apart from the absence of soil, there was nothing in them. Time stretched on forever, and even further, and every dig of the shovel into the ground felt like a kick in the balls.

"Are you sure?" One of the diggers asked as he began to dig a third hole.

"You should have brought an excavator," Theodor sighed.

"Sure," the digger grinned. "An excavator." He chuckled, as if Theodor had made a joke that could have been featured in a New Year's Eve skit at the very least. "An excavator."

"There's nothing here," the other said. "Should I dig deeper?"

Karla had a blanket spread out on the lawn, her glasses on her nose, a glass in one hand, a book in the other, and she looked as if summer wasn't over yet. She looked up from her book. "Should they dig deeper?"

"No," said Theodor reluctantly. "Don't you have some gadget to show where the bodies are?"

"I thought you knew where the bodies are. At least, that's what you claimed."

"I didn't claim to know their exact location to an inch!"

Karla shrugged. Right. She didn't want to embarrass herself by perpetuating her confidence in his theories by signing off on a request for some heavy machinery. Two guys with a shovel, that's about all he could expect.

He returned to the path. Where'd he show up? Somewhere...
somewhere around here. How the hell was he supposed to know? So,
if the exit was here, then...

He took three steps back. "Try it here."

"Are you sure?"

No, he wasn't sure. He wasn't sure at all.

"I'm sure."

"It's your money," the man shrugged. Karla looked at her watch.

Theodor thought hard. His whole theory rested on an assumption
that he hadn't been teleported anywhere, that he had been in the same
place the whole time, just in a different space. The dimensions of the
location would fit, the circle he was in in the forest was roughly the
size of a lawn. He must have been here the whole time.

Of course, it was also possible that he had been transported to
somewhere outside of Prague, that the whole circle wasn't just a
different face of this park, but the normal face of a different place. But
then...

...they couldn't have been bludiczkas.

"I found something," the digger exclaimed, and Karla reluctantly
looked up again from the book with the half-naked vampire on the
cover. This was it!

The man reached into the hole and pulled out a ball. He squeezed
it and the ball squeaked lightly. "Is this what you were looking for?"

Karla smiled.

"No," Theodor said.

"Too bad. There's still...wait a minute..." The man bent over the
dug hole.

"What?"

There was silence for a moment. "I think we found a hand."

Theodor walked over to the dig site. A few fingers waved from the
dirt, together with the back of a hand, where someone had recently
stuck a twig.

"Hey," Theodor said to his old familiar hand. "You have no idea
how glad I am to see you." He turned to Karla. "So now can we get
some heavy machinery?"

In the end, they found fifteen bodies there. Fifteen corpses, all
hidden under the grass, standing up, with their arms stretched

upwards, towards where the dogs were running around. In their mouths, lungs, stomachs... was dirt. They were buried from the inside.

And Theodor got what he wanted.

The car leaving Prague was silent.

Karla was thinking about the bodies, pulled silently out of the dirt, wrapped in green plastic bags and discreetly taken away. That was probably the worst part of it for her. Bodies crammed into carts marked "Woods and Gardening," thrown on top of each other, pretending they were just a batch of dirt and cut branches. She knew she should have resigned herself to the fact that death was random, brutal and cruel, but this lack of posthumous dignity hit her more than it should have. Probably also because it was her decision to make. Some bodies of the deceased, with family and acquaintances, would eventually be found somewhere and delivered back, with a tale of accident packed in, of a crime explained, of suicide... tailored to each body. They'll be released one by one, found in various places around Prague and the country. No one wanted it to look like a mysterious mass murder.

The SRS had an extra department for that, of course; poorly paid, as was the custom. People with circles under their eyes studied the biographies of the dead and devised convincing ways they could go off the grid so as not to raise unnecessary questions. It didn't always work, and sometimes they had to come up with additional justifications for why a blind grandmother died in a motocross event, but it more or less worked.

Karla didn't even ask what would happen to those who had no relatives or loved ones.

She cast a glance at Theodor. What would happen to him when he died? Would he end up in the stomach of some creature living in the basement of the SRS headquarters? Or will a group of endgame creators prescribe him death by autoerotic asphyxiation?

"What?" asked Theodor from behind the steering wheel.

"Nothing," Karla said. And there was silence from then on.

The car was silent. They tried to talk, but there weren't many available topics. They tried to play music, but one side was pushing for classical music and the other side was pushing for K-pop. Which didn't really go together, so it ended up being quiet again.

It was a really long ride.

The car was silent.

They crossed the Polish border. It was the beginning of autumn, so Szklarska Poręba was not as crowded with visitors as in winter, when people come here to ski, or during the holidays, when people come here for God knows what reasons. But they still had a problem finding a suitable place to leave their car. Karla was nervous like railway barriers when train tracks are rumbling in the distance. They got out of the car and walked down a path, Theodor with the firm stride of a robot. After what he'd been through, it was no wonder he was afraid of nature.

"Here," Karla said.

It was nothing fancy. There was a stone slab in the ground that said Rübezahls Grab. And upside down, misspelled, was the name of the person they were looking for.

"Why here?" sighed Karla.

"For the irony? Maybe he wants to dance on his grave?"

"He won't be dancing, I hope."

"In my opinion? It's far away. He wants to see how high we can jump, just to meet him."

"You don't like him much, do you?"

Theodor just shrugged. "Should I?"

He was right. Although he was portrayed in fairy tales as a sort of beardier Karl Marx, the truth was that he was more of a monster. No, not a monster. A deity. A small, but destructive one. Storms, avalanches... and of course, as deities go, with penchant for kidnapping and raping women. Someone estimated that up to half the current population in and around the Giant Mountains has his genes.

Theodor nudged Karla and pointed to a tree.

"What?"

"A jay."

She measured him with her gaze. "You can't believe everything you see on TV."

"I bet he's watching us." He waved to the jay and it flew away.

"Message received."

"It was just a jay," Karla said. "And if he's coming, it's because our boss called him and explained that it would be really nice of him to come. That they'd have his back if there was a problem again. When they find some girl in the woods who's been raped."

"I thought..."

"What? That he'd quit that? That his little buddy became soft in his old age? No, we're not that lucky."

"Another reason we meet here," Theodor said, looking around cautiously. "We have no jurisdiction here."

"Not that it would do us any good. A human would have ended up in jail long ago. A monster...a monster we would kill. But he...we need him. It's better to get along with him." Only when Karla said that out loud, it dawned on her how much it pissed her off.

They sat down by a wooden table where the tourists could eat their snacks, right next to a map and an information board. The sun was already setting behind the mountains when he appeared. He was much smaller than they had expected, no crossing mountains with a single stride, not even paper ones like in a TV show. His beard was trimmed short and greying. He wore a windbreaker and comfortable hiking pants and boots. In his hand, the Lord of the Woods held a staff.

He sat down opposite of Karla and Theodor, left his staff on the bench to his left and put his hands on the table, stroking the wood with his palms.

He wasn't big, he was old, but he still exuded power. He looked like an aging mob boss, a guy who could sentence you to death with a snap of his fingers...and who really fucking loved snapping his fingers.

"So?" he said without much ado. He didn't bother with introductions.

"First of all," Karla began, "we're really grateful you gave us some of your time. We appreciate it."

He said nothing, just ran his expressionless eyes over her. Then his eyes slid to Theodor. "Go on."

"We have a problem," Karla said. "Something's killing people, and..."

"What a tragedy," the man said coldly. "An unimaginable misfortune."

"And...yes."

"Everyone's death is a tragedy." He spoke as stones rolled down the hillside. "But there are so few of you. You are almost on the verge of extinction."

"Not exactly..."

"How many have died so far that you had to visit me? Hundreds? Thousands? Hundreds of thousands?"

"Fifteen."

"Fifteen?" The Lord of the Woods shook his head. "A terrible tragedy. At this rate, no man will remain."

"Every human life is . . ."

"Sacred? Important? Everyone could be the next Mozart, Einstein? Why is it that the dead are always this ambitious, that with every death one gets wiser and becomes a genius?"

"It's a matter of principle," Theodor said.

"Your principle. It does not concern me. I have my own. Or shall I come and report to you how many hares died just yesterday? How many deer have people shot? How many foxes have been run over by cars, asking what are you going to do about it?"

"I'm sorry, but that's not the same thing," Karla objected.

"Why? In what way is such a person better than, for example, a beaver?"

"Brain? Self-awareness? Art?" Karla suggested. Damn. She knew better than to get into such a debate. She was only playing his game with this, but she couldn't help it.

The man just lifted his hands slightly and clapped them on the table. The surroundings shook. "Art. You like something, so you declare that it's something special, that it's the thing that makes you better than everyone else. Why do you think other creatures don't have their own art, equally valuable and essential to them? You just can't perceive it, just like squirrels can't perceive *Fast & Furious.*"

"Porn," Theodor said, and silence fell around the table.

"What?" the Lord of the Woods thundered softly.

"Porn. We can talk all we want, but it's definitely more fun to watch two banging people than two banging rabbits. I'm guessing you feel the same way. Besides, talk to a rabbit as long as you want, it still won't blow you."

Karla closed her eyes. This was exactly what she was afraid of.

"Porn is for losers," the Lord of the Woods stated firmly.

"Excuse me?"

"For those who have no other choice but to watch," said the Lord of the Woods contemptuously.

Theodor grimaced. "I'll try not to take that personally."

"Feel free to take it personally."

"I'll overlook your absolute lack of taste. The point is," Theodore didn't budge, "that even if you can change into whatever you want...," he continued, "I'm still convinced that sex with human beings is the most fun."

"That's your defense of humanity?" the Lord of the Woods asked. "I'm supposed to assist you in saving insignificant individuals... because you're good for sex?"

"It may not be the ultimate reason, but at least it's true. Good for sex and good at it. And then there's this other reason."

"What's that?"

"It's a mystery."

"And?"

"Mysteries are great."

"Mysteries are. Solutions aren't."

"People started disappearing in the middle of a park in downtown Prague," Karla said. "They find themselves in a forest there's no escape from, where all the roads lead back until there's a way out. When they try to escape, they fall into a swamp and drown. After death, they reappear back in the park. Or rather, under the park."

"It was a forest, and you are the Lord of the Woods," Theodor added. "We need information."

"And what do I need?"

Karla took the floor. "What can we give to the one who can have everything he can think of?"

"How about you?" said Lord of the Woods.

"Okay," Theodor said.

"No," said Karla. "That is off limits."

"Him, then," said Lord of the Woods.

"Okay," said Karla.

"Okay," said Theodor.

"Really?" Karla asked.

"I can sacrifice myself for the team." He turned to Lord of the Woods. "They tried to kill me. I'll do anything to get them."

"A revenge?" Forest Lord said. "Is that what you want?"

"Another thing that's great about us humans. We're incredibly vengeful," Theodor said, his eyes fixed on the Lord of Woods. "And the fact that we invented matches."

It took Karla a second to realize what Theodor had just said.

"Are you threatening me?"

"I have no reason to," Theodor said calmly. "But surely you understand that there are some things one can't let go of."

"I can crush you like a bug."

"That would be an answer too."

Somewhere nearby, there was a roar and the wind picked up.

Karla stood up abruptly. "I apologize for my colleague, he doesn't know how to behave. He's an idiot, but if we want to . . ."

"They're bludiczkas," Theodor interrupted Karla.

"That's not certain," Karla objected. "But it's one possibility."

"Bludiczkas." Theodor repeated. "And that's your thing."

The Lord of Woods watched them for a moment, then relaxed his clenched fists. The wind died and the hungry eyes that had been watching them from behind the trees disappeared.

"All right. I won't even ask for anything for this," he said. "Because bludiczkas are dead. They're dead or gone. That's the same thing. They died with their natural environment. Like bisons or aurochs. They've been weakened by tourist signs and killed by cell phone maps."

How many supernatural beings could have become extinct like that? How many have disappeared without us even knowing, Karla thought. And then she thought of something much worse.

And how many could have been born this way?

Theodor opened his bag and fished out several photos. "It's from a street camera, but you can see the faces."

The Lord of the Woods looked at the photos. The wind blew, the treetops began to bend, and Theodor held his bag to keep it from falling to the ground. Two things were clear to him. One, that the Lord of the Woods recognized these women . . . and two, that he should never play poker.

The Lord of the Woods realized it, too. He pushed the photos back. "Bludiczkas."

Theodor tried his best not to say, "I told you so!"

"I told you so!"

Unsuccessfully.

"I hardly recognized them, they've changed a lot. And the clothes . . . they always only wore light robes, almost translucent . . . and they were much thinner. And younger. I thought they were dead. One day they just disappeared. I can feel it. I can feel something different, I can feel every single thing that's happening here. And I feel everything disappearing, everything dying." He sighed. "When you live too long, all you see is the dying."

"They didn't tell you anything?" Karla asked.

"No."

"Do you have any idea why they moved to Prague?"

"I have no idea why anyone would move to Prague."

Theodor snorted.

"Any idea how they can suddenly make people disappear?"

"In their last years, they haven't been able to make a snowflake disappear in the middle of a blizzard. So no, I have no idea."

"How can we find them?"

The Lord of the Woods didn't laugh. His face had been serious throughout the conversation, with emotion only occasionally crossing it like the light of a dying flashlight, but now he was pretty close to it. "They're bludiczkas."

"Which means?"

"That you won't find them unless they want you to."

The car was silent.

They drove along the highway in the dark, and Karla wondered how she was going to describe the whole thing in her report. The relationship between humans and the Lord of the Woods had certainly not improved with this visit. Shit, she knew it was a mistake to bring Theodor along. Plus, it turned out he was right, which was maybe even worse than a pissed off . . .

"I was thinking about the art," Theodor jumped into her thoughts. "Was he right?"

"About the porn?"

"What? No, he was bullshitting. Asshole. About the art."

"That beavers have their Beethoven?"

"That it doesn't count. It's like when kids scrawl something and their parents say how wonderful it is and that it should be hung on a wall. We lack an unbiased critic."

"Someone who's not human?"

"An alien."

"When we find one, we can promote them to a film critic."

"In every sci-fi film, the aliens are excited about Mozart, operas, our greatest art. They work as confirmation of our opinion. But what if we meet aliens and it turns out that in their opinion, the best thing mankind has ever created is the song *Yeah, you got that yummy-yum?* And not ironically? What if they worship Uwe Boll's movies?"

"Then it will be necessary to exterminate them. Declare a cultural galactic war," Karla admitted.

"And what if they're right and we're wrong? What if we all have the wrong receptors?"

"If we've all got it wrong... then that's a good thing, right? Voice of the people and all that."

"The voice of the people is an idiot."

"So actually, the aliens would have the same taste as us. They just wouldn't be faking it."

Theodor shot her a startled look. "Oh, my God. That's an even scarier thought."

Karla reached for the radio button and started looking for any station playing old Czech hits. "But aliens aren't exactly our problem right now. Right now, our problem are the bludiczkas."

"Bludiczkas," Theodor rolled his victory over his tongue.

"What are they doing in Prague? How did they get that power? Why are they killing people?"

Slovakian pop blared from the radio, and they both tried to remember the singer's name at the same time. Habera? Ráž? It wasn't Žbirka, they would have recognized him... Müller? Were there any other Slovak singers?

The car was silent for a while, then Theodor leaned over and turned off the radio.

"There is one more question. Perhaps the most important one."

"More fundamental than how they got the power?"

"Yes. You've seen the pictures. These are all brand clothes. Expensive brand clothes... or really, really good fakes. Where did they get the money for that?"

Karla almost drove her car into a ditch. "You're just saying that now?"

"I thought you'd have noticed that, too. You're a woman."

"Excuse me?"

"The clothes, the purses, the shoes... the shoes weren't visible in the picture, sure, but still."

"I'm not that kind of a woman."

Theodor, shrewdly, didn't comment on that.

Karla wondered. "But ... if they bought it here ... are there many stores that sell this stuff? Well, I'm sure there are, but not as many as normal clothing stores."

Theodor was starting to see the picture, too. "And we can start by asking around. If they're living near Charles Square, there's a good chance they'll be shopping in the center of Prague."

Karla grabbed the phone.

"It's four in the morning," Theodor informed her.

"All the better. Have them start as soon as they get to work. They have the photos. They'll find out where they can get them. By the time we get home and get some sleep, we'll know."

He didn't arrive at the office until about 4 p.m. Fortunately, there were no fixed working hours. Some days there was just a security guard, but if there was an "event," folding chairs were brought out and slept on. Of course, this didn't concern Theodor. Since childhood he had disliked sleeping around anyone else, which had interfered irritatingly with any attempts at any relationship that had a chance to become if not serious, then at least not entirely comedic.

In short, he had been told to arrive at four, so there he was at four twenty-five. He rode the paternoster up to the third floor, jumped out and walked down a long corridor where the walls were covered in magical ornaments and other security spells. He wasn't a dark mage, he wasn't going to slaughter everyone, but he still felt slightly nauseous. Maybe that was why a lot of people preferred to sleep in the office.

It was only when he slammed the door behind him that his stomach stopped churning and his brain finished convincing him that he should commit suicide immediately. Hey, everything was wonderful again.

He was about to make coffee when Karla hissed at him and dragged him by the arm to her office. "We got 'em!"

"So fast?"

"Yeah! We found the shop they used to go! On the most expensive boulevard, what else. What's more, one of them left her phone number there in case new merchandise came in." Karla looked at her notes. "That led us to her name, Veronika Míšková, and from that to where she works! Konxept. Computer marketing. We checked her colleagues and two of them match the photo! We got them!"

Theodor sat down in a chair. Obviously, even bludiczkas aren't immune to a shopping spree. "What now?"

"We need to get them as soon as possible. You disappeared just two days after the last victim. The intervals are getting shorter. They're steadily getting stronger. We'll pick them up in their office." Karla raised her thumb. "First, they'll all be there together." Forefinger. "Second, they won't expect it. They'll feel safe." Middle finger. "And there won't be any nature except maybe a potted ficus. No park. No forest."

"They'll be more dangerous together."

"They could be. But we have to take our chances. They might find out you escaped." She lowered her thumb down. "And I'm sure they noticed the park being dug up and could have put two and two together." Pointer finger. "We're putting a unit together. Do you want to join it?"

The remaining raised middle finger didn't exactly look like a warm invitation.

But Theodor was suspicious. "How will the bounty be divided? Still the same?"

Karla shrugged indifferently. "Nothing has changed. Those who kill the monster get the most. The bounty here will be divided among the entire action team. Which still isn't a huge deal, but it's at least something."

"I'm going," Theodor said. "Maybe someone will die and there'll be more left."

Karla gave him a questioning look.

"What? I'm joking."

"You don't joke about that."

"Okay, okay," Theodor growled. "I'm prepared to accept a share."

"Fine," Karla sighed. "Then go get your gun. We'll be on our way in a minute."

The gun was handed to him by a guy with a shaved head in a room full of guns and provocatively stacked boxes of explosives. He only came up to Theodor's chest, but he made up for it with the width of his shoulders. He was just showing Theodor a gun and saying a lot of strange and uninteresting terms. Type, ammo, sighting, rate of fire . . . blah, blah, blah.

"Or then there's this," he pointed to an almost identical large model. "It's blah, blah, it's got blah, blah, blah, and with that blah, blah, blah . . ."

Theodor stopped him with a raise of his hand. "I'm sorry," he uttered, unexpectedly polite, "but I just have one fundamental question. If I press down here, will something fly out of this hole and kill whatever it is I'm aiming at? If so, that's all I really need to know. Give me, like, this nice little thing and this nice big thing. And a plastic bag to go with it, so I don't run around Prague with it in hand."

The weapons expert looked at him incredulously. "What I'm telling you is absolutely vital information."

"Maybe to you," Theodor objected. "I'm not taking it away from you, everyone has something. I, for one, collected stamps as a kid."

"I can't let a man who doesn't know how to use a gun into action."

"I didn't say I didn't know how to use a gun."

The expert slid the gun over to him. "Let's see it then. There's the target. Try . . ."

Theodor reached for the gun, cocked it, aimed, and fired three times.

In the center of the target, three bullet holes coalesced into the shape of the Mickey Mouse logo.

The expert looked closely at the target, then at Theodor.

"Just because I'm not interested in guns doesn't mean I can't shoot. It's one of the many things I have a knack for," Theodor said.

"If you're good with guns . . . why aren't you in an action group? Why aren't you in the field?"

"I can use a shovel," Theodor explained amiably. "And I didn't become a digger either."

The weapons expert looked at him for a moment. "This is the first time I'm not sure which side of a gunfight to support."

"I hear that a lot. You got that bag?"

They eventually gave him holsters for both guns, and Theodor tucked them in, hoping he wouldn't have to take them out. He didn't like guns. They made noise and a mess. He got into the car where the rest of the team and Karla were already sitting, looking at him like he had an itchy rash in his crotch.

"Let's go!" Theodor instructed. After another clash of gazes with the team leader and a brief explanation of who was in charge, the same command was given, but this time it was official, and the car was off.

In Prague, the big black car looked about as inconspicuous as a hippo in a swimming pool. They drove through the busy traffic to somewhere near Jungmannova Street, where the Konxept company was located. It was not a place where one could park easily, especially with a car that was the size of a tank, so it squeezed in front of a garage entrance. Six guys jumped out and ran down the street in a slight crouch. Behind them, already in a less professional position, walked Theodor. He was wearing a bulletproof vest, but otherwise didn't appear to be preparing for a fight, more like for an afternoon meeting in a café. Karla, meanwhile, explained to the guard who angrily ran out of the garage entrance to mind his own business, and walked behind the team.

Hidden behind a moving truck, the soldiers ran through an arched entryway into the building, sideways to the stairwell, and without a stop ran up the stairs to the third floor, to a heavy door with a Konxept Ltd. sign.

From within came a quiet growl. Soldiers lined up on either side of the door, while Theodor ran hard after them. The commander turned to him. "Stay behind us, all right? Get inside when we give the all clear, okay?"

Theodor didn't listen to him. He was focusing on the sounds from inside.

"Cancel it. Cancel it now."

"Are you crazy?"

"The sounds . . . that's a shredder. Someone's in there destroying files. And outside . . . the moving truck? That must have been for them. They know we're coming."

What did the Lord of the Woods say? That if the bludiczkas don't want it, they'll never find them?

What if they wanted to be found?

By then, Karla had arrived.

"It's a trap," Theodor said.

The commander turned to his men. "You heard him. Be prepared for resistance. We're going in."

"So I don't...," Theodor managed to say, but by then the door had burst open, the men had rushed in—and stopped. Theodor peered inside. A long corridor stretched out before him, going on forever, with more and more corridors branching off from it like branches.

At least it wasn't a forest.

The soldiers took another step, and suddenly the whole unit was gone, except one surprised man who looked not at all military and professional, but like a frightened boy. He looked around, took a step forward—and screamed in pain. His arm wrenched back, his back arched, his legs crossed, as if every part of him wanted to go in a different direction.

"Stay still!" Karla shouted. "Help him somehow!"

His scream was drowned out by a drawn-out roar, strengthening and closing in. They didn't even have the time to see how it happened, but a second soldier flew through the ceiling, hit the floor, and splattered. The bulletproof vest remained intact, but what was inside it went flying all over the place, like he was a tube of toothpaste someone stomped on. Blood and chunks of flesh hit the walls, the ceiling, the screaming soldier, who moved back violently—and hit the floor in a dead heap of broken and dislocated bones.

The heavy door next to Theodor shuddered as bullets slammed into it. A soldier rushed sideways along the wall, firing blindly forward.

"Hey, stop it!" Theodor yelled, but the soldier didn't hear him. So he and Karla backed up to the stairwell and drew their weapons.

"They're ours," Karla said.

"Not anymore," Theodor said... but he didn't want to peek out and return fire either. And not just because he was afraid that a soldier might hit him.

The shooting stopped.

Theodor slowly approached the door and looked inside.

The man was lying sideways on the wall, with a hole in his chest from which blood was pouring out onto the opposite wall. It crossed the corridor like a red ribbon destined to be cut. And then there was a thud, and the wall swallowed him.

Karla shoved him from behind. "We have to help them somehow."

"They're dead," Theodor said, sliding down the door into a crouch.

Suddenly he laughed. "The supporting team of supporting characters has been slaughtered, and it's up to the main character and his girl to stop the evil."

"This isn't a movie."

"Think of it as a movie. It helps you to keep your distance."

Karla sat down next to him and breathed deeply for a moment with her eyes closed. "This isn't a movie. And if it was, I'd be the heroine and you'd be the comic male side character."

"Oh yeah, I forget what times we live in. Wouldn't you rather be a superior?"

"Superiors in movies don't end well."

Theodor stood up. "Okay. Shall we go in?"

"Are you crazy?"

"Yeah. One hundred percent. Absolutely and undeniably." He opened his bag. "I'm mad, but I'm ready. Remember how you asked how I got out of the woods?"

"Yes."

"The bludiczkas work with your senses. They confuse you. You think you're doing something, but you're actually doing something else. And worst of all, if your senses believe it, your body believes it." He showed Karla two objects. "I was hoping I wouldn't need these. Earplugs." He stuffed one in his ear. Then he put a clip on his nose. "It was worse in the woods, I had to stuff my nose with moss."

"What about me?"

"I need someone to cover me. I'll be completely defenseless." He pulled a thin rope from his bag. "It should hold. Tie yourself to me."

"You're really out of your mind. We'll go back and call for backup. We underestimated . . . I underestimated them. We're going to get them hard way. We'll take them out from a distance with drones, no one can fool those."

"They'll all be gone by then. They'll get away."

"So they'll get away!"

Theodor shot her an angry look. "They almost killed me. And now they must think how much smarter they are. They're not smarter. I'm not going to let some old matrons beat me."

"You want to get yourself killed just because of your bigoted misogyny?"

"And for the money it's worth. It'll be the best-paid misogyny in history!" He tied a scarf around his eyes and stuck the other plug in his ear. "I can't see or hear anything now. Are you tied up?"

"Yes," Karla said, but then realized he couldn't hear her, so she just patted him on the shoulder.

"Good," Theodor breathed through his mouth. He was talking very loudly, more like shouting in fact. "Now comes the worse part. Because that alone isn't enough, you still have some internal control in your head, something that keeps you walking straight, keeps you balanced." He walked over to the wall, ducked his head—and hit the wall with it. He staggered, blood dripping from his bruised forehead onto his scarf, almost falling to the floor. "It's okay, it's okay," he waved his hand, the opposite way Karla was. "Just...if I pass out, wake me up."

"Stop it," Karla yelled, but of course, he didn't hear her.

The second headbutt to the wall left a large bloody smear on the plaster. "I...should...have...taken...the...ham...hammer..."

Thud.

Karla screamed.

"I...came...upon it by ashident," Theodor continued with an effort. "When yoo are roonning blindly throogh the woots, shometimesh you hit yoorshelf." Thud.

Karla grabbed him and ripped off his scarf. His eyes were bloodshot under it. "It's ookay," he said with an effort. "Here wee go." He dropped to his knees. "Good," he said. "Good." He straightened his scarf, leaned against the wall, and started forward, stumbling. At first Karla was afraid he was going to fall down the stairs, but instead he just bumped sideways into the doorframe and rolled in, dragging Karla with him. "Better...lose...yoor eyesh. Not...alwash. Better."

"How do you know where you're going?"

He tried to point to his head, but missed. "I...shaw...the mop."

That was scary rather than comforting.

They walked through the door, the world swirled around her, Theodor disappeared, and the roar of the shredder echoed in all directions. The floor rattled beneath her feet. The rope reached out and jerked her forward. She closed her eyes and let herself be pulled. When she opened them, Theodor was in front of her again, staggering from side to side like a drunken sailor in the middle of a storm. She closed her eyes.

When she opened her eyes again, Theodor was heading for the

wall. She closed her eyes again. He kept pulling her forward, not stopping. She gritted her teeth, waiting for the impact—no, she mustn't do that; that would be playing their game.

They kept going forward.

When she opened her eyes, they were walking crookedly down a corridor, inches off the ground. She closed her eyes.

When her eyes opened, they were spinning in a circle, and Theodor's body was bent at a right angle. She closed her eyes and covered her ears.

When she opened her eyes, the world was rushing forward around them, spinning... She pressed her eyelids tightly together.

When she opened her eyes, they were standing in front of a door marked Konxept, Head Office.

They reached their destination.

Theodor hit his head on the door and the impact threw him into Karla's arms. "We're here!" She said, then remembered he couldn't hear her. She gripped his shoulders and pulled the blindfold from his eyes. Oh my God. His pupils were barely visible in the red whites. He tried to focus on her. She pointed to the door. "We're here!"

He didn't understand. He closed his eyes, leaned against the wall, opened his mouth, grunted something, paused in surprise, pulled his earplugs out of his ears, and sprayed the floor with yellow vomit.

He wiped his mouth. "We're...here..."

"How are you?"

"I think I have a... concussion," Theodor said slowly. "And... maybe... the flu."

"I'm on my period and I'm not complaining," Karla encouraged him. "Pull yourself together. We have to finish this."

Theodor nodded and consequently vomited again. "It's... it's better now."

"And thank you," Karla said.

"We haven't...won...yet..."

Karla pulled out her gun. Kick the door in, or open it carefully? She pushed the handle. It was unlocked. She pushed the door open and stepped aside.

The only sound she heard was Theodor gagging.

There was no one inside... and no, it certainly didn't look like the head office. Behind the door was a long room with two rows of desks lined up behind it. A computer sat on each desk... and the only other decorations were a coffee machine and a white board in the front, which was currently covered by colorful smudges.

She stepped inside, the barrel of her gun following her gaze. Right, left... Only the hum of a shredder could be heard somewhere in the distance. And then it stopped. The room was quiet and empty, but someone could have been hiding behind every desk, could have jumped out and blasted them to pieces. She crouched behind a desk.

Theodor staggered into the room, wiping his mouth and slumping into one of the office chairs with a sigh of relief. "Hey, computer."

"Shh!"

"Shhh," Theodor said to the computer and turned it on.

Karla ran through the rest of the room. "No one's here! Where is everyone?"

Theodor shrugged. "Maybe... they're on... company leave."

"After what happened out there? They massacred our entire team!"

"Could have..." Theodor's head spun. "It could have been an auto... automatic defense. Like ours. A magical trap. An echo."

"Echo?"

While the computer was booting up, Theodor searched the drawers. He found a half-empty bottle of soda and drunk it. He didn't offer it to Karla.

"If... if they're doing... any magical... rituals... summoning demons..."

"Then it'll affect the surroundings. Right."

The melody of Windows booting up echoed through the room. "Think you can get in?" Karla asked. "You think they don't have it locked?" She began scanning the surrounding tables.

Theodor gave her an uncomprehending look, then turned to the monitor. "They have it... locked. Shit. I'll have to... kill... call our..."

"IT department? Yeah, they could log in remotely. Or..." Karla reached over to an archaic monitor, peeled off a yellow post-it note with a password marked on it, and showed it to Theodor. "... we can use this."

"Also... a solution," Theodor admitted reluctantly.

Entering the password took him a few tries, and Karla was about to ask him to stop, but he finally managed to get all the letters right and the computer let him in. Karla, meanwhile, listened to the silence, to see if she could hear the thud of feet, the click of a doorknob or a slide. Slowly she moved from desk to desk, ready at any moment to sink behind it and return fire.

"Oh, look at this," Theodor said after a moment, satisfied, if a little hoarsely. And then, "And look at this."

"What?"

"Well . . . I know what they were doing here. And I even know how they . . . managed to strengthen their . . . abilities so much."

"Magic?"

"No. Something much, much worse." He looked at Karla. "Discussion forums."

The computer was full of it. Each click on the top bar threw them to a different page describing what terrible things will happen to you if you get a COVID vaccination, secrets the government doesn't want you to know and you're supposed to share before they delete it, all the things that are a hologram or just manipulation of the rest of the public, and the constant calls not to be the sheep. And on top of that, elaborate texts on several websites describing the atrocities the Ukrainian army is carrying out on its own people so it can frame innocent Russian visitors who just happened to be passing by.

All guaranteed to be true.

If Theodor's head wasn't spinning before, it would be spinning now.

"What's that supposed to mean? What the hell is that?" Karla didn't understand. "Is that what they read here?"

Theodor looked at her. "I am the one who hits walls with his head, not you. I have a right to be stupid. Of course they don't read it here. They write it."

"You mean we risked our lives and six people died . . . just to find an office where a disinformation website is being created? Do you know how many there must be everywhere?"

"You don't get it, do you?"

"Get what?"

"This isn't about the site. All this . . . is just a tool for them."

"For . . ." Karla was starting to get it. "For the bludiczkas."

"This is a godsend for the bludiczkas. In the past, they could fool one person in a year, now they can do it by the hundreds! And since there was COVID . . . do you know how many people they could have killed by fooling them into doing something stupid?"

"So that's how . . ."

"Yeah. They leveled up through the roof. They were like vampires working in a blood bank. Necrophiliacs in a morgue. This . . . this must have been their dream come true."

"But why were they killing people in the park?"

"Maybe as a reminder of old times. Or maybe their excess energy just had to go somewhere. They walked through the park a lot, so they just . . . contaminated it." Theodor shrugged. "Whatever. They're gone." He looked out the window at the street, resting his forehead against the glass and leaving a bloody smear. "Think the fire department can come get us? Or a helicopter? I'm not going down that hall again."

At that moment, the door to the hallway flew open. Karla dropped to her knees and aimed her gun. Theodor just turned his head.

One of the team members burst into the room and fired at him. Theodor rolled rather than jumped, but the result was the same. The shot missed him. The soldier took two steps forward and a stream of mud came out of his mouth. It flowed down his uniform, his bulletproof vest, even started to flow from his nose, and a brown stain appeared in his crotch. Karla's trigger finger hesitated.

"Shoot!" Theodor yelled, forgetting that he himself was armed.

Karla fired, the soldier moved, and the white board behind him shattered into pieces. He took off towards Karla, following a path that only he could see, a path that twisted through the air. It's quite confusing when you have to shoot at an attacker running upside down towards you.

He ran past Theodor, who was struggling with his pistol holster. The soldier's mouth was still oozing mud, and only a little way from his mouth it remembered gravity and started to collapse in the right direction, splashing across the floor.

Karla jumped behind a table.

The soldier pulled the trigger, and splinters from the parquet floor flew into the air. Karla, thanks to old shooting lessons and current aerobics classes, managed to roll aside and empty her gun into the soldier.

He paused, his eyes bulging and bulging until finally they popped out of their sockets and mud began to ooze from his skull like champagne from a bottle.

He slumped to the ground.

The door's lids shattered and a giant boar crashed in, smashing into the opposite wall. It shook its head and glared at Theodor.

"You've got to be kidding me," Theodor said, shooting at the boar. The bullet pierced its forehead, the recoil threw Theodor's unprepared arm upward, and the second shot hit the ceiling. Both shots had roughly the same impact on the boar.

"You've got to be kidding me," Theodor repeated, leaping over a table as the boar destroyed the chair he'd been sitting in moments before. He landed hard on his knees.

He fired again, but unlike the soldier, the ammo didn't work on the boar. The soldier was, after all, a borrowed tool. The boar was . . . what exactly? A symbol of the forest?

It was definitely pissed.

Theodor was zigzagging desperately in front of it. He had the advantage of greater momentum, but the boar had the advantage of immortality and unstoppability. Theodor would have traded with it in a heartbeat.

Karla fired several shots at the boar, the only achievement being that it noticed her as well.

A heavy thud of hooves came from the hallway and another boar burst through the doorway of the room. No, not a boar. The nightmare of a hunter who dreams of boars. Huge, with an elongated snout resembling a crocodile. The tusk has carved a furrow in the doorframe.

Theodor looked around for somewhere to climb, but the room did not offer many choices. Only desks with computers, and those weren't hard to knock over.

"How can they be killed?" Karla yelled at him.

And Theodor was forced to say the sentence he hated most of all. "I don't know!"

He jumped aside. The smaller boar missed him by only a few millimeters, while the other stood near the door, watching Karla. There had to be a solution to this. If they were summoned by bludiczkas, just kill them. But there were no bludiczkas here. There was no way to weaken their powers. There was no way to . . .

Theodor had a crazy idea.

"Call tech support!" he yelled at Karla.

Karla shot him a look even more terrified than when she looked at boars.

"They need to crash their servers! If their network goes down..."

"...it will weaken their power," Karla finished. It might work. If they were drawing power from disinformation, crashing the site might weaken them at least a little.

And besides, they could send reinforcements while they're at it.

The boar in the front opened its muzzle. Wider than any animal should be able to. A giant maw with several rows of needle teeth.

Karla, her gaze flickering from her cell phone to the boar, began to dial.

Theodor was too slow. There was too much to keep track of—the result was that the smaller boar dug a tusk into his leg and knocked him to the ground. It ducked its head, ready to rip open his stomach. Theodor managed to kick it in the side of the head with his uninjured leg; the boar staggered and drove the tusk into the wall instead of into Theodor.

The wall shook and a painting of flowers fell from it.

The other boar slowly made its way to the Karla, who was on the phone. Theodor had to restrain it—but he couldn't handle two boars at once. Hell, he couldn't even handle one. If he could just get rid of it...

He grabbed a sturdy computer monitor and smashed it over his boar's head. The beast may have been immortal, but blows to its head were not pleasant. It staggered, its legs buckling, giving Theodor just enough time to get away. He limped to the other side of the room, dragging a slab of the broken table behind him.

He looked around for Karla. She was shouting something in her phone, backing away from the big boar, which walked toward her with the deliberate stride of a movie serial killer. No, he didn't have time to deal with her now. His boar lunged forward, slamming into the board Theodor had set up for it, pinning him to the wall between the windows along with it. It roared, its hooves slipping on the parquet floor, and the board began to splinter.

Damn, this sucks. Theodor looked around, but found nothing he could use. If the boar doesn't stop...

The boar stopped.

It pulled its tusks out of the wood and took a step, a second step, a third, ducked its head, and prepared to run. Theodor moved half a meter away. The boar followed him with its gaze. Theodor dropped the board by his feet.

"Come on, piggy," he said.

The boar took off.

Theodor kicked one edge of the board up, sat on his butt, lifted it above his head, and braced it against the windowsill. The other edge of the board was still propped up against the parquet floor, and the whole board formed an improvised platform suitable for wheelchairs and boars. At that moment the boar's hooves struck it. The board vibrated in Theodor's hands, the wood cracking painfully—but it held. The boar ran up it like a ramp, tried to brake but didn't make it, shattering the window and flying out into the street.

Theodor didn't even look after it, so he had no idea if it had splattered on the pavement below, much to the surprise of the pedestrians, or if it had vanished into thin air. He ran after the big one headed for Karla, and thought of nothing better than to punch it from behind—with all the force of his fist—in the balls.

The boar's hind leg just missed Theodor's head by a few millimeters, and then the boar's roar filled the room.

And then came Karla's quiet voice on the phone. "Yeah. This is exactly why I need it. So hurry the fuck up."

The boar began to turn. It stomped its feet angrily, and tables flew aside on contact with its body. It looked like it was getting bigger and bigger by the moment. It surged forward.

Theodor had nowhere to go. There was only one way left—up. He pushed off the table and caught his fingers on the overhead light, the cover of a fluorescent lamp that stretched across half the room. He had no idea how he'd come up with the idea that it might work. He'd never done rock climbing, and he certainly wasn't the type to hold onto a perpendicular rock with his pinky and still be able to do a crossword puzzle at the same time. And he had no idea why he thought a fluorescent light would hold up. It was just plastic.

Both gave in at the same time. But even the few seconds the lighting and his fingers lasted slowed his fall, and it was enough to make the boar choke and crash into the wall below him. The room shook and a cloud of plaster rose into the air. Theodor fell to the floor, and before he could scramble to his feet in pain, he could smell the stench from the boar's maw again.

The room was in pieces, parts of broken computers, monitors and desks were lying everywhere, there was nowhere to hide. Theodor limped backwards, blood dripping from his leg on the floor, and reloaded his gun. Not that he thought it would do him any good. It was more like his lucky rabbit's foot.

The boar bared its shark rows of teeth at him. You could see all the way down its throat, where something red was bubbling and overflowing. Theodor had a nagging suspicion that he would be soon getting a closer look.

At that moment Karla came up to the boar from the side and stabbed a pair of scissors in the boar's side.

So stupid, Theodor thought, but maybe it'll pay attention to her for a while. After all, women come first.

And then he took a good look at the scissors. There were wires tied to them that led to an electric extension cord. The boar just turned its head slightly. Karla, with the plug in one hand, ran to a socket in the wall and stuck it in.

A gleam flashed in the boar's eyes. It opened its maw and sparks skipped between its fangs. Theodor smelled the stench of burnt bristles. The boar's eyes exploded in their sockets. It roared, and bubbling red liquid spewed from its maw and with a hiss began to burn its way through the floor.

It certainly wasn't pleasant. This had to . . .

The boar slumped to the ground, jammed the scissors deep into its side, rolled over, ripped out the wires, and severed the connection. It stood up again. It reeked of burns, oily matter oozing from its eyes, red goo pouring from its maw, but it was still alive. It sniffed. It looked confused; the smell of its own burning bristles overpowered everything else. Theodor carefully backed out of its reach.

"Well?" he hissed to Karla. She just shrugged.

How long could it take to take the servers down? Minutes? Hours? They didn't even know if it would work, that was just wishful thinking. They just hoped it would work like breaking a pentagram in a magical ceremony, like chanting an incantation . . .

The boar picked up their scent.

"We must escape into the corridor," said Theodor.

"We won't survive there."

"Better there than staying here."

The boar took the first step towards them. Keyboards and fragments of desks crunched under its feet. Theodor threw a chair at it. It hit the boar in the snout and the beast jerked in surprise. Karla pointed a finger. There was blood coming from the side where she had stuck the scissors in. Just a light trickle, but it was blood.

The boar gave them a blank-eyed look. It opened its maw . . . and Theodor wasn't sure, but it seemed to him that the mouth had opened a little less, and there weren't as many rows of teeth either.

He and Karla looked at each other, then they both pulled out their pistols and started shooting. Bullets bit into the animal's flesh, chunks of fur, flesh and bone flying off the boar. It exploded in mud and blood, screaming, thrashing . . . dying.

Theodor was overcome with fatigue. He sank to the ground. "Behold," he said. "The power of the internet." Then he pondered that. "But we won't tell them. I'm sure the IT people would want a cut then, too."

He was exhausted. Okay, he had to admit that field work was a bit of a chore, too. Although, as he proved, if you're a little handy, it's no problem to get it done. A little intelligence, a little insight, and it's all handled almost seamlessly. He should probably bandage that leg before he bleeds out.

And then slow footsteps came from the hallway.

Karla listened to the approaching footsteps and tried to count. How many soldiers had she seen die? Could there be anyone else alive out there? Could they save anyone?

No, those footsteps didn't belong to any soldiers. None of the soldiers wore high-heeled shoes.

Blades of grass grew up between the parquet floors, the debris of the tables was covered in moss, and the air was suddenly fresh and oxygenated.

Karla could smell the scent of pine needles.

The footsteps tapped out their elegant rhythm on the floor of the corridor, never changing pace, already outside of the room, already . . .

The most beautiful woman in the galaxy entered the room and carefully stepped around the corpse and the mud puddle. She smiled, and that smile made Karla's heart explode. She had never believed in love at first sight, she had never even been into girls much—those few attempts in college didn't count, you try all sorts of things there—but now she understood she had been making a huge mistake.

The gun had fallen out of her hand. She would need her hands when she touched her, when she kissed her, when they were together...

The face of the most beautiful woman in the galaxy collapsed inward and blood spattered the wall behind her. Karla screamed.

"What?" said Theodor, gun in hand. "I thought we were supposed to kill them?"

"You... you..." Karla wanted to reach for the gun and shoot him, to get revenge for killing her love, but before she could bend over, the feeling faded and only confusion remained.

"Is something wrong?" Theodor asked in confusion.

"You... you didn't... you didn't see her?"

"Of course I saw her. If I didn't see her, I couldn't have shot her, could I? What were you doing?"

Karla took several breaths. She didn't understand. She didn't understand it at all. Unless... she looked at Theodor. "You... sorry, but... you're not all that interested in girls, are you?"

Theodor was offended. "What are you talking about?"

"It's not a big deal these days, you know that... and the company has no problem with it, no need to..."

"Hey, you start acting like a madwoman, and I'm suddenly gay? I could tell by the look on your face which one of us was the gay one here. So don't blame it on me, please."

"That was just... yeah, well." Karla leaned back against the table. "We should have interrogated her."

"I'm sure you'd want to squeeze her out." Theodor was still pouting. "Thoroughly. Nothing beats a good oral intercourse."

Karla bent over the woman. She already looked normal, like an aging football player's ex-wife, in expensive and tight clothes. She didn't understand what could have been so attractive about her. "We need to search her."

"Oh, I'm sure you need to..."

"Stop it, will you? Please stop." Karla looked out through the open door into the hallway. It was completely normal, with a kitchen across the hall. "I don't think there's another one here. They must have escaped. Everything's fine again."

Theodor wondered for a moment if he could milk some insult out of that speech after all, but found nothing there. "You mean we're only going to get paid for one?"

"You'll get paid," Karla said. "You got her. It was your kill."

Theodor shrugged modestly. "Actually, that's true. How much for her?"

"You don't know?"

"I never had any need to find out. I'm above that sort of thing. How much?" Karla told him, and Theodor's eyes bugged out. "What?"

"I double-checked it."

"If I . . . if I got a part-time job for the day, I'd have made more! If I took my old magazines to the recycling center, I'd have made more! Has everyone gone mad?"

"The bludiczkas are seen as weak and harmless creatures. They're at the bottom of the list."

"This was not a weak and harmless creature! She killed an entire unit! She sent a boar after us! Two boars!"

"I know. I know, but that's just the way it is. Maybe it will be adjusted in the future."

"For this kind of money . . . the bosses really can suck my dick."

There was silence for a while.

"I'm sure they'll—"

Autumn was slowly ending and the trees had leaves in shades of yellow and brown. It happened every year, and yet every year photographers saw it as the hottest trend, flooding the internet with more and more photos of leaves. Theodor waded through the leaves and didn't give a shit about them. Yes, he had changed. He had become a tough guy. A dangerous guy. A monster killer. Okay, so far the score wasn't the highest, but it was just the beginning.

It was cold, but the man waiting for him on the bench in the middle of the forest didn't seem to feel it. He was dressed lightly, with a leg slung over a leg, pipe in hand.

"No smoking in the woods," Theodor admonished him.

The man ignored it. "Why did you want to see me again? And where's that chick that was with you last time?"

"It's just me. Just the poor and lonely me."

"Hmm."

"I just wanted to ask...haven't you heard from them? The bludiczkas?"

"No."

"I don't know if you get the latest news, but we only got one. She stayed on site, maybe to dispose of evidence, maybe to deal with us. Growing power blinds you. I believe she wanted to see what she could do. And she was able to get her head blown off."

"Which one was it?"

"The one with the hole in her head," Theodor clarified. "But what I wondered was how they knew about us. How they managed to set that trap for us."

"Who knows? They're bludiczkas. I never truly understood them either."

"But it didn't bother me for long. There weren't too many suspects."

The man took a drag from his pipe. It was quiet for a moment, the forest itself quieting around them, as if it was wondering what to do next. "I left them a message. I had no idea they were going to kill anyone. I wanted them to escape. After all, I am the Lord of the Woods, and they used to be a part of the woods."

"When we find them, they'll be a part of it in the form of fertilizer. Do you have a hand in those disinformation sites?"

"I have no idea what you're talking about."

"Maybe. On the other hand, if people harm and destroy each other, it won't exactly be a bad thing, will it?"

"You manage that even without me."

"We want to know where the remaining bludiczkas are."

"I don't know."

"Strange."

"What?"

"I got lost three times on the way here. And in the last month, three tourists have gone missing in these parts."

"Tourists get lost all the time. And don't blame your poor sense of direction on the bludiczkas."

"It's been two months since six of our people died. And fifteen more civilians before that. And me too, almost. I knew all along that you had warned them and that they would flee here. Where else would they have gone?"

"If you're accusing me of something..."

The trees around them began to bend in the gusts of wind. Theodor had to raise his voice.

"It's been two months... more than two months. Do you know why I waited so long to come back in the woods here?"

"Why?"

"Because it took this long for the bounties on bludiczkas to be raised. And it also took a while for explosives to be placed inconspicuously around this forest." He pulled a detonator from his pocket. "We'll make a little fire. A few dozen hectares, nothing big. But it's enough to make a man connected with the woods a bit cuckoo."

"You... you can't do this," said the Lord of the Woods. "They won't let you do this!"

"They did. Protection of nature is a nice thing, but your dating methods?" Theodor shook his head. "That won't do these days. Just mention it and no one dares say no. No one wants to stand up for a sexual predator." He raised his hand holding the detonator.

"No!" the Lord of the Woods shouted.

"I'll have to share with the others, but that's the way it is. It's good money for the bludiczkas, but for the Lord of the Woods?" Theodor smirked, pressed the button, and the forest around him began to shake. Explosions echoed in the distance and fiery flames flickered above treetops.

Theodor smiled, content.

"That's what you get for badmouthing porn, asshole."

JIŘÍ PAVLOVSKÝ (* 1968)

A personality of almost renaissance range—a film and literary critic, a searing glossator, an author of witty bon mots, a comics enthusiast and a peculiar writer, a creator of strange worlds, a co-director of the comics publishing house CREW and an owner of a distribution company—the main character of this essay is all this and much more.

Jiří Pavlovský's early literary career is connected with the now legendary literary group Rigor Mortis, where he attracted attention with his humorous fantasy short story "Visit Me Tonight, Said Death, and Hit a Golf Ball into the Eighteenth Hole" in the anthology *Mlok 1994* (Klub Julese Vernea, 1994) and other hilarious texts, on which he collaborated with similarly inclined Štěpán Kopřiva. At the turn of the millennium, he was behind another memorable collection with Marek Dobeš titled *It's Good to be Dead* (*Je dobré být mrtvý*, Klub Julese Vernea, 2000). As an author, he does not hesitate to venture into a variety of themes ranging from erotic to cyberpunk to classic science fiction and fantasy, but he always treats them in a specific way, full of black humor, sarcasm, irony, unexpected connections, and strange aesthetics, so it is no wonder that he has become a welcome visitor to various anthologies such as *Orbital Sherlocks* (*Orbitální Šerloci*, Mladá fronta, 2006), *Shines of Swords, Flashes of Lasers* (*Třpyt mečů, záblesky laserů*, Straky na vrbě, 2008), *Legends: Cursed Libraries* (*Legendy: Prokleté knihovny*, Straky na vrbě, 2013), *12 Immortals* (*12 nesmrtelných*, Argo, 2015) or *Legends: Praga Mater Urbium* (*Legendy: Praga Mater Urbium*, Straky na vrbě, 2020).

However, all this was not enough to satisfy him, so he came up with his own project, Hammer of Wizards, a series of urban fantasy novels set in his home city Prague with a quite bizarre set of heroes, where he is involved not only as an author, but also as a coordinator of other writers' stories, whom he allows to play on his turf. The series about a former Inquisition agent, Felix Jonáš, and his team of misfits is one of the most original domestic series, which he plans to follow up with a new season in a few years.

Moreover, Jiří Pavlovský is a fan of the Monster Hunter series; hence his participation in the *MHF* project, which was as inevitable as it is welcome.

A House Worth Every Cent
Michaela Merglová

Old Bulíčková had a stroke at the blessed age of ninety-eight. While the stray cats found her body right away, it took nine days for the home nurse. The young nurse who went into the house on the hill also nearly had a stroke when she discovered Norman Bates' mother in the rocking chair. In her first panic attack she dialed the wrong number, and so an exterminator, a local psychic, an ambulance, the police and finally the coroner took turns at the country house at the end of Zvědavá Lane. The old lady had no friends or relatives, so she was promptly sent to the cemetery, which was literally a stone's throw away from her home.

A flashy car pulled up at the house and a chipper lady in a tube skirt jumped out. The broker hammered a large "For Sale" sign with her retouched photo and phone number by the entrance and less than a week later put it away again, its place taken by a beat-up Škoda belonging to a laughing couple. The young couple had brought tools and buckets of paint, but that night a roar sounded through Jilemnice as they ran through the cemetery like two frightened rabbits.

So the sign reappeared, this time a little smaller and without the broker's photo.

Next came a Toyota, which brought a new couple and their three children, but at the stroke of midnight that Toyota was started loudly and drove off into the darkness with the whole screaming family.

In the following months, a Ford, a Citroën and a Velorex took turns at the mansion. The advertising banner was replaced by ever-shrinking leaflets, until finally all that was left was a hand-scrawled sticker with a phone number on the front door. When a Volkswagen parked outside the mansion with a marijuana-scented foursome, more suited to Woodstock than a haunted house, judging by their clothes, the considerably distracted broker just handed them the keys and muttered something about luck.

Surprisingly, no screams carried through Zvědavá Lane that night, but the broker quickly realized that her nightmare had reached a new phase. The hippies in black body bags headed to the same cemetery where old Bulíčková was buried.

The sticker disappeared and the door was taped shut with police tape.

The house on the hill above the Jilemnice cemetery was officially haunted.

"No shit, dude, that's bullshit."

"Then why are you coming here with me, smart-ass, huh?"

"Well, if it *is* true, I could buy a Playstation..."

The dried rosehip bush crackled as Anka pushed through it, sliding harmlessly down her sports jacket. Her cousins continued to bicker behind her back, and she was almost certain that if someone knocked their heads together, they would thud hollowly. Marek and Pepin weren't the sharpest tools in the box; it was just that none of her classmates were talking to her.

Kids could act like real bitches sometimes.

The boys decided to spend today's afternoon snooping around the haunted house on the hill. There were all kinds of rumors about it, from vampires to mummies, and Anka found a reference to Nazi gold bars in old letters in the library. And since Marek's single mother turned every penny three times, Pepin as a part-time letter carrier didn't exactly make a fortune, and Anka wanted to get out of Jilemnice, the three of them came to a consensus that the gold bars were worth checking out.

They had to be stealthy—after all, the lane wasn't called Zvědavá[6] for nothing—and had already spent nearly an hour combing the garden, because Marek had quite cleverly pointed out that Nazi gold

---

[6] "Zvědavá" meaning "curious."

bars were almost always hidden in the ground. They were trying to find anything that screamed *secret stash*. They crawled through the filthy shed that was practically falling apart, peered into the moldy beehives and the rabbit hutch overgrown with rose hips, and inspected the roots of the old lime tree.

Pepin was now digging up clump after clump of brambles with a rusty spade, while Marek was helpfully advising him how to do it properly.

Anka climbed up the wall. The wind caressed her cheek, the sun slanting towards the horizon, bathing everything in a warm amber glow. No one tugged at her red braids or mocked her for her big glasses and baggy old clothes. Today was a good day.

"Screw it, let's go check the house," Marek decided, probably because their search party seemed to be losing their resolve. Anka jumped back down on the grass.

Old police tape with the words DO NOT ENTER stretched across the door and windows, and the boys tried to peel it off discreetly. Meanwhile, Anka squatted on the porch and poked her finger in the crack between the tiles. There were daisies and thick, richly blooming bluebells growing through. She plucked a few blossoms and twirled them in her fingers. If she could find more, they'd make a nice wreath for her hair . . .

"Ready!" Marek announced.

She looked up. The boys had finally simply torn the tape and were pushing their way through the crack in the door into the house. She quickly got up and followed them.

The smell of rot and cat urine hit them. All three of them slapped a hand to their mouths and noses. "Dude, this place smells like my mom," Pepin grinned.

Anka punched him in the shoulder.

"Ow! What was that for?"

"For my aunt," she replied.

Marek laughed, but suddenly fell silent and turned to the entrance. "What?" Anka asked. But then she heard it too.

A car pulled up in front of the house.

The old Chevy had a lot of work to do to wiggle its way up the narrow cobblestoned road to the house. The car sputtered and twitched with every turn, as if its engine was powered by a hamster in a wheel. The tires finally squealed on the gravel road; a skinny blonde turned the keys in the ignition, and the car stopped with a hiccup in front of the house.

Jolana leaned back in the middle seat to get a better view of their destination. But before she could get a good look at the mansion, the blonde had already opened the door and turned to the trio crammed in the back. "Let's move, sloths, we don't have all day. Go, go, go," she urged them, stepping out herself.

The young man in the passenger seat, whose profile looked like a pale version of James Dean, sighed dramatically, lifted the collar of his black polo shirt and followed her.

"You can go this way," said the thin man on Jolana's right, whose appearance most closely resembled that of a mad scientist. He pushed glasses as big as ashtrays up his nose, raked his thinning hair, and after a brief struggle, managed to open the jammed door.

When the five Hunters scrambled out of the car, the body lifted considerably off the ground.

The blonde was already fishing for something in the trunk, James Dean lit a cigarette, and the mad scientist pulled a stack of papers from his leather satchel. The last of the group looked the oldest and also the most serious. He had wild dark curls, bushy eyebrows, a bit old-fashioned sideburns, and a deranged look in his eyes, as if he'd seen too much.

She didn't know any of them properly yet, but Libor from Fantom had a lot of praise for them, and they worked around the Kokořín area, so they were willing to come here to help her with the haunted house.

She looked around and tried to recall the names of her new teammates. The wild-looking guy introduced himself to her as Larry, the scientist was Viktor, the dandy was Vladimir, and the fragile girl in latex...

"Vávra! Where the fuck are the feathers?"

Larry startled and turned to the blonde, who was buried in the trunk with only her legs and round leather-clad ass sticking out. "It's in the back in the backpack," he growled. "And I told you not to call me that," he added more softly.

The blonde poked her head out of the trunk, an implacable

expression appearing on lips lined with red lipstick. "I'm not calling you Larry," she refused firmly.

"Why not?"

"Because your name is Vavřinec."

Larry made a face. "In English, it's Larry and all our names start with a V," he muttered. "It could be confusing for her," he nodded his head toward Jolana.

"I hope she's not so stupid that she can't remember three names," the blonde snapped, her eyes like thorns staring right at Jolana. "Are you stupid?" she barked out.

Jolana felt herself blush. "No," she breathed, but it didn't sound convincing.

"No," the blonde repeated, pointing her index finger at the remaining pair. "That's Viktor, that's Vladimír."

"Vlad," the guy in black said in a melancholic tone, but the blonde wagged a warning finger.

"No one has ever called you Vlad and no one ever will, and if you try to add Impaler to it, I'll impale a stake right up your ass, got it?"

Deciding not to fight a losing battle, Vladimír just let out a long sigh, took a drag from his cigarette and walked away.

The blonde looked around. "What's wrong with you idiots today, seriously? A new girl shows up and suddenly you all have to act macho and make up some shitty nicknames?"

"I'd just like to point out that I didn't make up any shitty nickname," Viktor objected, smoothing back the unruly tuft of hair sticking out.

"That's because it wouldn't help you with any girl anyway, honey," the blonde retorted, turning back to Vavřinec. "Anyone else has any comments? No? Great. So now can someone finally tell me where the fuck those feathers are?"

Vavřinec aka Larry met Jolana's gaze and lowered his eyes in shame. "I told you it's in the backpack in the back of the trunk. In the yellow one."

"There is no yellow one."

"Of course there is!" Vavřinec dove into the trunk next to the blonde and started pulling things out of it.

Jolana walked slowly over to Viktor. "What are these feathers for?" she asked in a whisper.

"It repels evil forces, especially chorts," he explained.

"And won't holy water do the trick?"

"Yeah, but feathers are more localized. It's more potent, plus we're using kingfisher feathers, and they're hard to find." He flinched as a notebook slipped out of the papers in his hand, and another one flew away in his attempt to catch it.

Jolana bent down to help him. "Is this all related to the house?" she asked curiously as she handed him back the thickly labeled papers.

He nodded. "The information you sent me, plus my own research. I asked around a lot in the community, I know a few elves in Háj, and they recommended a local informant who got me a lot of additional data."

"And who is our most likely suspect?" she asked as the argument over the yellow backpack grew louder behind her back.

Viktor licked his lips. "It's a little convoluted," he admitted. "People's testimonies vary a lot. The first tenants swore that a headless horseman chased them through the cemetery. Others said it started with noises in the old barn, which would point to a *stodolnik*. So far, the most likely conclusion I've come up with is a black lady, a rampaging *melusine*, or a *bosorka* who cursed this place. But everyone agreed that the house began to echo with screaming, screeching and banging just after dark, lights and appliances switching on, and according to the autopsy reports..."

"You got the autopsy reports?" she interrupted him in surprise.

"Sure. But they don't say anything that would..."

"So, boys!" The blonde interrupted his explanation, putting her hands akimbo like an angry dominatrix. "And lady," she added, looking at Jolana. "*Larry* here," she drawled his nickname mockingly, "made things a little difficult for us when he left one of our bags at the hostel. Fortunately, the SRS warehouse of paranormal junk in Stará Paka is not far from here, and I have a great relationship with the manager."

"Is that the guy who tried to pick you up by giving you a beer with Rohypnol?" Viktor said.

"No, this is the guy who tried to pick me up by telling me stories about the Lord of the Woods."

"No difference," Larry muttered quietly.

"Look, I know him so I'm going to go over and plunder that place a little. I'll be back as soon as I can, but I probably won't make it before dark. Can you manage not to screw up the first tour of the house at least?"

Vlad took a drag from his cigarette. "This line of discussion seems rather unfortunate," he remarked dramatically.

Before the blonde could take a breath and start another tirade, Larry interrupted. "Look, Len, don't make idiots of us. Or do I have to remind you who fought that *navka* at Pšovka while *some* of us slept at the Kanín train station because they got drunk on box wine?"

The blonde deflated. She obviously didn't like that story, so she just raised her head haughtily. "Vávra pulled out the bags, so go dig through it. I'll be here soon, kittens. Behave yourselves." Her leather pants creaked as she reached the driver's door.

While Jolana didn't like the fact that they were splitting up, she was actually a little relieved that the prickly woman wasn't going to boss them around. She realized one thing, though.

"The two of us weren't actually introduced," she said. "I'm Jolana." The blonde frowned. "I know."

"Great, but I don't know your name. Larry called you Len, so I'm guessing it's Lenka?" she tried.

The blonde glanced at Viktor, who quickly hid behind his papers. He was the one in charge of communicating with Jolana, and obviously this minor oversight in introducing the team fell on his head. "No," she retorted sharply, slamming the door.

Jolana blinked in surprise.

The car started. The blonde rolled down the window and leaned her elbow on it. "It's Lenora," she snapped, her eyes fixed on the rearview mirror as she backed away from the house.

"Oh. Like that village in the Bohemian Forest?" Jolana guessed.

She got no answer; the American veteran rattled back up the driveway before Lenora backed out, then shot down Zvědavá Lane with a screech of tires.

All that remained by the house was the smell of burnt rubber, dust swirling in the dusk, and a pile of backpacks and bags dumped haphazardly on the ground.

And above all, peace.

Lenora's departure had a noticeable effect on the mood of the rest of the team.

Vlad flicked his cigarette butt into the bushes and straightened up with sloppy grace.

Viktor lowered the papers he had been instinctively hiding behind.

Larry knelt down by the backpacks and began to pull weapons from them.

Jolana stopped paying attention to them and finally looked at the reason for their arrival.

The house on the cemetery hill looked like most buildings in Jilemnice—picturesque. Thatched roof, half-timbered gable, a coat of green paint on the wood between the windows. But unlike the others, it impressed with its size. It had three floors and looked more like a mountain hotel than a family house.

But decay was everywhere. The paint was peeling, the window frames were rotting and the grounds were overgrown with uncut grass and rose bushes. Lids of the beehives at the back of the garden had caved in and the shed looked like something a wolf would blow into and the whole thing would collapse to the ground, with all three little pigs inside.

"Hey, Jolana. Come get your stuff," came Larry's gruff voice.

Vlad was standing astride, wearing a black patterned coat combining the aesthetic of a Nazi officer with a modern dandy, and he was in the process of sliding a trio of stakes with art nouveau silver tips into a leather chest rack.

In contrast to that, Viktor was balancing two large leather satchels on top of his body, and clutching a third in his hands, glass softly clinking in it. A tug on the zipper, a rustle in the bag, and Larry spread three boxes of clinking ammo in the grass. "Hollow point, lead with silver tip, normal," he tapped them one by one with his finger and looked up. "What kind of a gun do you have?"

"A knife," Jolana replied, squatting down beside him.

Larry frowned. "Don't you have a gun?"

"We're in Jilemnice, not in Texas."

A match struck above her head as Vlad lit another cigarette. She turned her head to see the dandy smiling crookedly as he nonchalantly rested a shotgun on his shoulder. "We live everything as it comes, without warning," he said.

She wrinkled her brow in puzzlement. "Excuse me?"

"Kundera," Vlad smiled, exhaling cigarette smoke.

"Kundera?"

"Milan Kundera," he clarified.

"Don't mind him," Larry waved a hand. "Mr. Intellectual likes to talk in quotes."

"Why use your own words when everything important has been said with much more feeling in times past?" Vlad shrugged.

"And who said this?" Jolana wondered.

Vlad bared his perfectly white teeth. "Me." Then he reached under his coat and pulled out a shiny Beretta. "You know how to use this?" he asked.

She nodded.

He handed her the weapon and smiled with satisfaction. "Well, as the classics said, truth and love will overcome lies and hatred. Take the gun and come on. It's time to find out the truth about this damn place."

Anka stood as still as a living statue and heard the nervous Marek and Pepin breathing loudly behind her.

They watched the strangers through the lobby window. One of the women and her car left, and the four who remained armed themselves to the teeth and spread out across the grounds—two were headed for the cemetery wall, two for the shed.

"Clear," Marek hissed. "Let's go."

Anka started to back toward the door, but her cousin caught her by the sleeve.

"Not there!" he growled.

"Where do you want to go then?" she didn't understand.

"Well, further into the house, of course," he replied calmly.

Anka blinked. "There are four strange armed people here—we'd better get out of here while they're loitering in the garden."

Marek stepped over and looked at Pepin. "Look," he began cautiously, "they don't seem to be rushing in, and we've already been through the garden. Let's take a look around the house and then we will get out."

"But they have guns!"

"And? They're outside."

"For now! But what if they come in here?"

Marek licked his lips and hesitated.

"Dude, they look like larpers who came here to do stupid things after they heard about the haunted house," Pepin took the initiative. "Just look at that vampire in black—a larper for sure! Nobody's stupid enough to walk around with a real shotgun on their shoulder at the end of Zvědavá Lane where all the Jilemnice gossipers lurk."

Marek snapped his fingers. "Yeah, larpers! That makes sense. I bet they're some Prague tourists who came here like it's a zoo visit. It'll be fine, you'll see. And if not, we can still jump out of the window."

The girl looked from one to the other. They both grinned proudly and were already rushing out of the lobby and on into the hallway.

She twirled the flowers in her fingers and sighed. "Okay, fine."

"YES!" Pepin signaled, punching his fist in the air. "Up for the gold!"

"But we have to scram in an hour," she added quickly. "I don't want to stay here after dark."

"Sure, no worries," Marek chimed in, pointing down the hallway. "After you, ma'am!"

Viktor walked to the cemetery wall and looked around carefully. The grey concrete wall was overgrown with ivy and lichen in several places. Viktor stopped at a large crack, beyond which grey marble crosses peeked out, ran his finger along its edges and frowned.

"Anything interesting?" Jolana turned to him when he stopped.

He squatted down, nearly overbalancing himself with the weight of the three satchels.

"Do you want me to carry anything?" she offered quickly, but he shook his head.

"Nah, it's okay, I'll handle it," he muttered, digging through one of the bags and pulling out a bottle of liquid. "See that white powder on the wall?"

"Huh?"

"Some monsters leave chemical traces behind." He rummaged in another bag and found a pipette.

"Like devil's brimstone?"

"That's right. But this isn't sulfur."

"What is it?"

"I'd say Chile saltpeter. Nitratin," he added when he saw her blank face.

"Okay, and what creature leaves it behind?"

"I have no idea," he breathed. Almost ceremonially, he drew the liquid into the pipette and dripped it on the white powder. When nothing happened, he cleared his throat. "Or maybe it's just peeled paint," he said in frustration, straightening up heavily and turning toward the house. "It would make sense, they painted the first day, and if they ran that way afterwards..."

"What exactly are we trying to find?" she interrupted him.

"Traces." Viktor raked through his sparrow's nest. "The first couple swore they were chased by a headless horseman from the house through the cemetery. And this is the only place low enough to get to the cemetery."

"The headless horseman is supposed to show up at midnight, and his horse leaves prints surrounded by hellfire, right?"

"Or brimstone, depending on whether he's coming out of his grave or through a portal from hell. In any case, yes, if a headless horseman rode through here, we'd see scorched grass, hoof prints in the dirt, the remnants of a strong electromagnetic field..."

"We could try an EMF detector!" she gasped excitedly, pointing to one of Viktor's bags. She had never tried an EMF detector before. Although she had downloaded an app on her phone, she strongly doubted its legitimacy. Her phone buzzed with supposedly heightened electromagnetic resonance in the least scary places, like the candy store by the town square or a corner of a bus station. The latter was indeed scary, but for entirely different reasons than the paranormal.

Viktor, however, smiled indulgently at her suggestion and pointed with his thumb at the row of crosses behind the wall. "I'm afraid that might not mean anything here, considering..."

"...that there's a graveyard, sure," she nodded, feeling a twinge of embarrassment.

Jilemnice was a quiet town, and so she had so far only dealt with smaller bounties—*rarachs* causing mischief in the crops of local gardeners, a curse or suspicious nightmares. But she'd never faced any of the things Viktor had found in his research. While headless horsemen, a stodolnik or a bosorka sounded like lesser evils than vampires and the undead, she still had considerable respect for them.

She looked around and her gaze fell on the marble crosses and moss-covered statues of angels. "You mentioned a bosorka and a black lady," she said slowly. "But shouldn't we also take into account the fact that the house is so close to the cemetery? After all, all the trouble started when they buried the original owner, and a lot of the phenomena sound like the ravings of a vengeful spirit. What if..."

"Cremated," Viktor interrupted. "Sorry to jump in, but that was the first thing I checked. Mrs. Bulíčková stayed in the morgue, where they determined a natural death with no external cause, and then she was taken to the crematorium, from where she went to the family vault in a cheap urn. If it's a ghost, it's not hers." He poked his finger in the lichen once more and smiled. "But it's probably not a headless horseman either. There's nothing here to suggest that."

"Too bad," she breathed as they made their way through the tall grass back to the house.

Viktor tried to untangle the tangled straps of the two satchels, but only succeeded in dropping the third one on his foot. He grunted, winced, and grabbed his leg, causing the tangled remaining bags to roll off his shoulder as well. Viktor fell on his ass in the grass. "Were you hoping for a headless demon?" he huffed as he picked himself up.

"I was hoping for a hot young Johnny Depp," she replied with a laugh, shaking her head. "But mostly I was hoping for answers."

"You will get them, you will." He ruffled his hair and rose to his feet. "The answers. I can't promise Depp."

"What a shame."

He reached for the large satchel, but Jolana snatched it from his hands. "I'll carry it," she said firmly.

"I can handle it," he protested lamely.

"I know, but if a headless horseman happens to show up, I'll need you to have functional legs, too."

"And what if that sexy Depp shows up?"

"Then I'll catch up to him even if I have to be festooned with all the bags we have, don't worry."

The house was shady, large and unkept. Long strips of plastic were lying on the tiles in the hall, probably dragged in by the first tenants in the naive hope of redecorating. A few steps away, they saw the tattered, tacky brown wallpaper and a huge white stain where they had probably knocked over a can of paint in panic.

"What's the plan?" Anka turned to the boys.

Marek scratched his neck. "Like . . . the gold will probably be in the attic or basement."

"Or inside the safe," Pepin added quickly.

"Or inside the safe," Marek nodded. "So I guess we should split up. I'll run out to check the attic, Pepin will look for the safe, and..."

"No," Anka retorted quickly. "We shouldn't split up."

"Come on, you're not worried, are you?" Marek teased.

"Of course I am," she blurted out. "It's about to get dark and the last people who slept in this house were carried out feet first, remember?"

"That's why we should split up though, so we can cover more ground," he countered.

"But..."

"I'll go with you to the basement, then," Marek breathed, as if he hadn't registered her words at all, and exchanged a knowing look with the freckled Pepin, as if to say, "Women, eh?"

Pepin saluted jokingly and stomped up the stairs.

Anka sighed. "We shouldn't have split up," she insisted, but Marek was already striding further into the house.

When Jolana and Viktor reached the house, she saw Vlad walking on the other side and Larry shaking some mess out of his hair.

"Anything in the shed?" Jolana asked.

"Lots of things, but not a stodolnik," Larry grunted.

"*The skeleton—*

thing is bad,

he'll come and

you're trapped," Vlad recited, and when Jolana looked at him with raised eyebrows, he flashed a bright smile, "Egon Bondy."

"Egon Bondy is hiding in the old lady's shed in Jilemnice? Wow, and I thought he is buried at the Smíchov cemetery."

"Irony is the weapon of the unfortunate," Vlad said, snapping his fingers. "Jaroslav Havlíček! A local native."

"And how is Egon Bondy connected to the shed?" Jolana wondered.

"There was a lot of crap in there, and as we moved some stuff, a nest of bird bones fell on me," Larry said, ruffling his curls again. "There were lots of skeletons of mice and shrews and other vermin, probably some kind of poison. But otherwise, no sign of anything else. Definitely no monsters."

"We found no trace of a headless horseman," Vikor reported.

"So if it's neither a headless horseman nor a stodolnik...," Jolana began, glancing from one to the other, her gaze finally falling on the large mansion, the facade of which cast a dark shadow over their heads.

"Time to go inside," Vlad added, stepping up onto the porch and pushing the torn police tape aside.

The corridor behind the lobby resembled a hotel. On the left and right were closed doors, of which Anka counted eight even in the darkness. The last one, directly opposite the entrance, was the only one open.

Marek flicked the switch, but the lights did not come on. "Hmm," he grunted.

"Maybe the fuses are blown?" she asked, but at that moment they heard huffing on the stairs and saw Pepin rushing down.

"Is something wrong?" turned Marek.

Pepin threw up his hands. "It's locked."

"Like, everything?"

"Like right above the stairs there's a locked grate."

"And there's no way to get past it?"

"Dude, I'm a mailman, not an Azkaban prisoner. What about you?"

"Nothing yet, we haven't even tried...," Anka started, but didn't finish the sentence. They all stared into the lobby, where footsteps and voices came from.

Marek grabbed the nearest doorknob and panicked when it didn't move.

"Oh shit, dude," Pepin gasped. Anka and Marek grabbed one arm each and pulled him briskly into the only open room at the very end of the hallway.

The front door opened.

The strangers entered the house.

Jolana remembered the map she'd scanned for Viktor when she'd contacted him—the mansion had three floors, plus an attic and a basement, for a total of nearly four hundred square feet of living space. So it was definitely not a tiny place.

"Bedroom, green lounge, red lounge and restroom," Larry listed, pointing to the various crosses on the map. "They found one body in each of those rooms. The two in the lounges died of sudden cardiac arrest; the woman in the restroom suffered acute poisoning and, according to the coroner, basically shat her guts out. The one in the bedroom had a fractured skull from an unfortunate accident including a fallen painting, so everyone is obliged to wear this," he added, raising his right hand.

"A helmet?" Vlad breathed in disgust, leaning casually against the old pendulum clock in the corner.

"Peltor brand protective helmet, there's no better on the market," Larry clarified.

"Maybe for workers."

"You're a paranormal worker, so just wear it and shut up," the older Hunter growled at him.

"I'm sure there were better colors on the market," Vlad muttered as he was handed a canary yellow helmet.

"We're going to a haunted house, not a fashion show."

Jolana and Viktor tightened the chin straps without protests while Vlad continued to twist the helmet in his fingers. "Vávra, this is really gross," he sighed in frustration.

"No, *Vladimír*, it'll be gross when your own brains come out of your ears," Larry assured him.

Vlad sighed dramatically.

"Didn't Paul of Tarsus say he rejoiced in his suffering?" Jolana tried, but Vlad gave her an annoyed look.

"Paul of Tarsus also said that the world should belong to the fools," he replied. He leaned the shotgun against the side of the clock and smashed the helmet on his head in resignation. "And apparently he got his wish."

"Tighten that strap," Viktor urged, but Vlad shot him a look sharper than the stakes he carried on his chest.

Larry cleared his throat. "Well, we've all got bulletproof protection and guns, and it's time to figure out where everyone's going," he continued in the voice of a Boy Scout camp leader. "We'll head out in pairs like we did just now, and look around for clues. Have your EMFs, garlic, salt, guns and just about everything else ready, and if things get rough, call the other group," he tapped the radio at his waist. "We don't know exactly what we're up against yet, so don't take any chances. There'll be time for a heroic rodeo." Then he pointed his thumb at the old flat staircase. "We'll take the top, you take the bottom, okay?"

Jolana nodded and looked at Vlad, who still looked stylish even with the yellow helmet on his head. "Any quotes for good luck?"

"Every true adventure begins with a collision of fantasy and reality," he obliged immediately.

"Ota Pavel?" Viktor guessed.

"Karel Čapek," Vlad replied, reaching for his shotgun. "Well, good luck, newts."

The room in which they hid was a long, dark corridor, and the only light came from a small, dusty skylight through which a doll, let alone a man, could hardly squeeze. It had probably served as a huge pantry, but age and Mrs. Buličková's limited mobility had turned it into a museum of dust, mold, and the remains of old food.

There were bags with lumpy grey matter spilling out of them. Cans with something that swelled beneath their puffy lids. Folded paper pastry bags forming little rotting pyramids and plastic margarine boxes lined up as neat towers of Babel. Water dripped from the ceiling into a large plastic laver balanced on pillars made of beer crates, and a maze of rusty shelves dominated everything, with old cans and oily jars full of compotes, purees and jellies.

Marek picked up the nearest one. "Znojmo pickled cucumbers, '92," he read from the yellowed label and frowned. The brownish-green jelly inside did not match the description in any way. He set it aside and reached for another one, perhaps hoping to discover preserved gold.

"Dude, how do we get out of here?" Pepin whispered in a panicked voice, measuring the skylight with his palms as if hoping to spread it open.

Anka shivered. Her heart was still beating wildly from being locked in a strange house with armed people who had probably come here to steal, yet she felt no fear, only anger that she had told the boys and they hadn't listened.

She realized she was still clutching the daisies and bellflowers she had picked outside the house. She could have just thrown them away, they would have been lost in all the mess and dirt, but just as she was about to let them go, guilt stabbed her—they had been growing quietly just a moment ago and she had picked them. She should at least let them live for a while, now that she had.

As if in a daze, she scrabbled for the nearest empty jar, reached the laver with drip water, and scooped it into her makeshift vase. Then she set the flowers on the shelf between pepper stew and faded ajvar.

At that moment Pepin waved his hands at them. "There's a door," he hissed, pushing aside moldy crates. Indeed, a keyhole-less door, apparently unused, appeared between the shelves.

Pepin took the handle cautiously.

"Where do we start?" Jolana asked.

Viktor flipped open the dusty lid on the fuse panel. "First things first, let's get the lights on," he said, flipping the switches up in an unexpected crackle of sparks.

The room beyond the door flickered. Something huge in the corner shook loudly and began to growl.

Pepin yelled and slammed the door back.

"Did you hear that?" gasped Jolana.

Viktor, who was blowing his tingling fingers, nodded. "I did."

"Like a cat getting electrocuted?" she guessed. "It smells like urine everywhere, maybe..."

"Maybe," he conceded, but his hand slipped to his waist. Like her, Viktor had a gun in a holster at his waist, but the small Ruger felt like a child's water gun in his palm.

He pushed at the door and stepped into the hallway.

Vlad watched Larry fumble with the lock of an old door with an ornate grille, tapping his foot.

"Good things come to those who wait," Larry looked up at him.

Vlad grinned. "And every waiting represents a shackled impatience. Otta Babler."

Larry twisted his lockpick. "Sometimes I really wonder what your brain looks like," he remarked. "Because every time you pull out a quote, I imagine you've got a giant filing cabinet with a cataloging system in your skull."

The lock clicked.

"I think you'd be disappointed," Vlad stretched, watching the grate swing open with a creak. "My brain will be as gray and disgusting as everyone else's. Besides, as Ivan Fontana would say, 'A man's absolute worth is in his brain. The real value is in the character.'"

Larry stood up and dusted off his knees. "You really are a freak, Vlad."

Vlad's teeth gleamed in a smile. "A freak with a shotgun, baby."

When Marek ventured out of the pantry a second time, this time armed with a huge bottle of chutney, they found that they were in no danger. The light came from a light bulb hanging lonely from the ceiling, and the shocks and thunder worthy of a rocket launch to Mars were provided by a refrigerator from the days when such devices could serve as fallout shelters.

They found themselves in the kitchen.

There was no window, and the stench of ammonia was more concentrated in the air here than in the hallway. It made Anka's head spin. Cats were obviously in their element here, because thick tufts of dark fur and feces covered the floor.

"This is disgusting," Pepin whispered.

Despite the huge space, the kitchen felt cramped. A large dining table was lost under a mass of cardboard boxes, the chairs were covered in plastic bags, glass bottles were standing on the floor and the worktop was drowning under bags, newspapers, magazines, empty cereal boxes and detergent bottles.

"Grandma didn't throw anything away, did she?" grumbled Marek, pushing aside a column of margarine tubs with his foot. They seemed to have found liquid gold, hidden in the jars, rather than Nazi gold bars.

Anka shuddered in disgust and glanced at her watch.

6:38 p.m.

Sunset was at seven.

There's still time, she reassured herself mentally. *We still have plenty of time.*

Now we just have to figure out a way to get out of this mess.

Viktor flicked the switch. Intense red light flooded the room from a dusty chandelier.

They both gasped in unison.

The Red Lounge didn't earn its name for nothing.

Red linocut faces grinned from the walls. Underneath, feather pillows and knotted ropes lay on velvet footstools. Above an Art Nouveau table with a mirror, a huge fan made of dyed peacock feathers and four leather whips arranged on hooks according to their size caught the eye.

From a painting, a larger-than-life Mrs. Bulíčková was looking down on them; her likeness was captured by the artist at a time when the one with the most interest in her body had been gravity. A huge metal cross with handcuffs and details in faded red leather stood against the wall on the right, a long plush sofa on the left, and above it was a display case with a majestic collection of...

"I was expecting to find a lot of things here, but I admit that I really didn't bet on a collection of dildos in the room of a brothel madam from the nineties," Jolana sighed.

Viktor cleared his throat. His cheeks were a thematic shade of purple, and he carefully avoided looking at the portrait of the naked former owner. "This is where they found one of the last tenants with cardiac arrest."

"Well, if he lit a UV lamp in here, I'm not too surprised." Jolana idly poked a finger at the oily plush handcuffs. "You want to explore this place?"

"I'm sure the other rooms will provide more clues," Viktor cleared his throat and backed out into the hallway.

Jolana laughed, but followed him. As she closed the door, she thought she heard the scurrying of rats behind her.

"It looks like the hotel from *The Shining*," Larry grumbled, running his fingers over the moldy geometric wallpaper in the hallway.

Vlad, who was clearly more interested in the ancient piano next to the staircase, gently tapped out a few notes. "Monsters are real. Ghosts are too. They live inside of us, and sometimes, they win."

"A little out of your usual range, to quote King, no?"

Vlad shrugged and closed the piano again. The piano shuddered at the click of the lid, as if it was one strong sneeze short of buckling under him. "Just because I prefer our people doesn't mean I'm an uncultured barbarian." He wrinkled his nose. "But the smell is really awful."

"What a wasted opportunity to quote Hamlet!" Larry laughed, raising his hand in a dramatic gesture. "Something is rotten in the state of Denmark! Come on, where's your literary soul?"

"Suffocated by the stench of cat piss," Vlad sighed, pushing open the first door with his shotgun.

The clock read 6:44 p.m., and there was not a single window in the kitchen, only the door back into the pantry and out into the hallway, where they could hear the chatter and footsteps of strangers with guns.

But Pepin and Marek were clearly not worried about ghosts or intruders. They scanned one locker after another as if their instinct for self-preservation had taken a vacation.

Pepin suddenly straightened abruptly. "Hey, look what I found!" He was grinning excitedly, clutching a paper box in one hand and waving a blue tube triumphantly in the other.

Marek squinted his eyes. "What is it?"

"Jesenka, dude! And it's not expired!" Pepin was already squeezing sweet condensed milk into his mouth, grinning happily.

Marek's eyes lit up. "No way!" He quickly grabbed the box.

"Guys, maybe we should..."

"Anka! Anka, here!" Marek hissed at her, thrusting a can with sweet condensed milk labeled Salko in her unresisting hands.

Anka slumped her shoulders and just watched as her cousins filled their mouths with the sweet Jesenka and chuckled softly. She stared blankly at the can in her hand. She didn't even spare a thought for the milk inside. But cat hair swirled around her legs as Pepin did a comical victory dance, and something occurred to the girl.

It took a moment before she saw a bowl on the floor among the mountains of clutter. It was lying next to a pile of scattered ice cream boxes, but it was quite unmistakably the cats'—it had a picture of a paw on the side.

Anka knelt down beside it and opened the can. When the thick, sweet milk stuck to her fingers, she wondered if cats could actually eat Salko. Dogs weren't allowed chocolate, so couldn't a can of sweet milk hurt the cats?

She looked around as if to make sure, but no matter how hard she looked, she couldn't see any cats anywhere—just hair, poop, and that ever-present smell.

Shaking her head, she set the can down beside the mess on the table and looked at her watch with growing anxiety.

The time jumped to 6:50 p.m.

"Hey! There's something here!" Marek hissed in a whisper, tapping his foot on the floor.

His stomping sounded hollow.

Even the green salon did honor to its name. There was a moss chandelier, a khaki carpet, spruce wallpaper, and furniture made of malachite-patterned plastic. Mrs. Bulíčková was obviously fond of eccentric furnishings in her home, as posters of Czech singers in the psychedelic style of Andy Warhol looking down from the walls. In shades of green, naturally.

"Do you think that the hippie here had a stroke after seeing this?" Jolana pointed to a framed picture with four portraits of Waldemar Matuška.

Viktor waved his pistol towards a pile of vinyl records, on top of which lay an LP record called *Uppers and Downers*—folklore songs by *Jan Slabák's Moravanka.*

"I'd guess it was because of the choice of music."

"This house is an awful mishmash," she shook her head.

"There's only two salons, we should be past the weirdest stuff by now," he comforted her, flipping through the vinyls.

"Anything interesting?" she asked.

"Surprisingly, yes," he nodded.

Jolana stepped closer, expecting Viktor to reveal a clue that would bring them closer to understanding what they were facing here. Instead, he pulled out one vinyl after another. "Bowie, Beatles, Jethro Tull . . . Maybe I'll take something when we're done here!"

"Isn't that stealing?"

"Not if no one knows."

They spread out around the room. Jolana peeked behind the furniture, ran her hand over the bottom edge of the chairs, bent over the carpet, but found nothing but cobwebs, old rodent skeletons, and a dried-up milk dish—no herbs, no chalked symbols, no wax or bloodstains. She flicked the dried flowers in the vase with her finger and shook her head.

Viktor put the pistol back in its holster and squatted on the ground. He ran his fingers over the soiled fibers of the carpet, keeping a close eye on the EMF detector display. "This is where the police photos say they found the guy," he said. "If there was an angry ghost here, there'd be energy left behind, but there's nothing here at all."

"But?" she pitched, sensing he wasn't finished.

"But it seems to me that there is something here after all, see? This little thing? And here?" he pointed.

She bent down. In the high-pile carpet she saw tiny paws at regular intervals. "That looks like the tracks of an animal. It smells like urine everywhere, probably a cat..."

"But this is much smaller."

"So maybe a mouse? I found quite a few skeletons of shrews."

"Maybe..." He shuffled his glasses thoughtfully up his nose and looked at her. "Did you find something?"

"Nothing that requires an exorcism besides that radio over there in the corner," she replied.

Viktor glanced at the large transistor radio with a cassette unit and chuckled. "I remember Grandpa used to have one of those," he said, his eyes twinkling dreamily. "He used to play Karel Gott's songs on it from morning till the night for the whole village to hear. Everybody hated him for it. Only his wasn't growing mold."

Jolana cast a skeptical glance at the furry layer covering the speakers in thematic green. "This is really a house worth every cent."

The upper floor held eight rooms, each with an entry from the corridor and each looking like a mausoleum—furniture covered with age-yellowed bedspreads, corners of the walls nibbled on by black mold wheels, dust dancing above the floor. The biggest surprise awaited them in an unused smoking lounge, where they found a framed official portrait of first Czechoslovakian communist president Klement Gottwald with a noose painted around his neck and two crosses for eyes.

"Viktor said the family had the place confiscated after the war, and in the 1970s the Socialist Youth Union used to hold conventions here. The owner only got it back in restitution in the nineties," Larry explained as the portrait was set aside.

"So maybe it's haunted by dead commies? Cool. I've always wanted to smash Comrade Gottwald's face," Vlad said.

Larry chuckled. "And are you going to do that before or after you quote Václav Havel to him?"

"After, naturally. I couldn't possibly deprive him of the Garden Party monologue. I'm no barbarian."

Larry squatted down and ran his fingers over the floor in the last of the rooms. A swirl of air made gray wisps dance around his feet.

"Anything interesting?" Vlad asked, his hand on the doorknob of the last room, when he saw Larry sniff his fingers and brush himself off.

Larry shook his head. "I'm not sure," he replied. "It smells like cat piss everywhere."

"You don't say; I didn't even notice," Vlad grinned.

"But I haven't seen a single cat yet."

"They probably escaped when there was no one to feed them." Vlad turned the doorknob and entered the last room.

Larry stood up. "But why is there not a single trace of them in all this decades-old dust?"

Anka stared at the dark hole in the ground framed by the rectangle of a trap door.

Marek picked up the phone and shone a light in the darkness.

"Dude, it's a basement!" Pepin squealed with the excitement of a child as they saw an outline of stairs.

"That's where we have to go," Marek gasped.

"You guys are crazy!" Anka hissed.

The boys exchanged glances, and Marek stepped provocatively on the first rung. "We're looking for gold."

"It's getting dark! We have to get out of here, not go deeper in the house!" she whispered urgently. She looked at her watch and swallowed.

At that moment, the sound of an ancient pendulum clock came from inside the house.

Diiiing.
The first blow startled Jolana so much she jumped a little.
Diiiing.
Viktor jerked as his EMF reader's display flashed red.
Diiiing.
Vlad crossed the threshold and stood stunned as his eyes reflected giant shelves full of books.

Diiiiing.

Larry heard Vlad's gasp.

Diiiiing.

Anka stared nervously at the large seven followed by a pair of zeros on her watch.

Diiiiing.

Marek, who was just about to descend the stairs, slipped and slid awkwardly down on his ass.

Diiiiing.

Pepin tried to shine his own phone's light at his cousin, but the device slipped through his sweaty hands and fell down after Marek.

There was a heavy silence.

Jolana straightened up. "Stupid clock," she forced a laugh to shake off her surprise. "I didn't even notice it."

"It was in the hallway," Viktor replied absently, but didn't take his eyes off the EMF detector.

"Is something wrong?" she asked, taking a quick step toward him.

Viktor tapped the display in puzzlement. "Something popped up for a second, but... There's a lot of appliances in here, the power's on, so it was probably just interference."

Jolana snapped to attention. "Something popped up when the clock started striking? Isn't that weird?"

"I..."

"FROM THE WALL IT STARES BLANKLY AT ME—A DARK HOLE WHERE THE SAFE USED TO BE..."

Jolana and Viktor shrieked in unison.

Solid wood bookcases stretched from ceiling to floor, with volumes squeezed side by side on the shelves.

"Finally, a stylish place in this dump," Vlad whistled, stepping forward. "Proust, Joyce, Turgenev..."

"Boring, boring, boring," Larry grinned from the doorway.

Vlad shot him a disapproving look. "There's Stoker and Shelly. Or would you prefer something simpler? Some pulp named *Tentacle monsters and alluring astronauts?*"

"I prefer *Revenge of the Surfboarding Killer Bikini Vampire Girls* like

Lister," Larry winked at him. "And unless you find *Necronomicon* here, we can ignore the library."

"You might."

Karl Gott's song shook the floor.

A double roar followed it.

Larry immediately stopped smiling. "Viktor? Jolana? Are you okay?!" he shouted into the radio.

Gott fell silent.

The shouting stopped.

"Viktor! Come in!" growled Larry again and turned to run down the hallway toward the stairwell.

The radio woke up. "We're all right," Viktor's voice answered. "We just got caught off guard by the radio."

Larry relaxed.

At that moment, Vlad yelled.

Pepin froze, but Anka did not. As soon as Marek disappeared into the darkness, she started for the staircase.

On her knees, she slid to the opening, grabbed the wooden frame and jumped down on the stairs. They were steep and wet and slick, making her sneakers slip. And that's exactly what happened on the second to last step and Anka fell on her back. She quickly shoved her hands under her, pain shooting through her right palm.

"Ouch," she heard from the side in the darkness.

She blinked.

Her eyes began to adjust to the darkness and take in the space around her. Marek was just picking himself up off the ground and examining the hole on his pants.

"Dude, are you okay?" came from upstairs.

Anka looked down at her palm. It glistened damply, and even in the dim light she could see that the skin under her pinky was torn—probably the work of a splinter or a nail sticking out. *I'll have to wash it out so I don't get tetanus,* she thought, yet she calmed Pepin softly. "Yeah, we're all right."

Marek had already found the phone and beams of white light ran through the basement. It seemed as if the things from upstairs had grown through the floor to here. Cables sprouted from the ceiling, stalagmites of crates, jerry cans and plastic barrels rose from the sides, where piles of slimy dirt glistened. Droplets of water glistened on cocoons of old cobwebs, and Anka could have sworn she heard scurrying somewhere in the corner.

"Wow, this is really disgusting...," Marek whispered, his eyes bulging. His resolve was obviously wavering. "Maybe we should..."

"I'm coming to you!" Pepin shouted, hurrying down.

Anka wiped the blood on her jacket. At that moment she heard a thud above.

They looked up and saw that the trapdoor had closed above their heads.

Then there was music.

And a roar.

And the scurrying again.

This time much closer.

Vlad ran his fingers over the spines of the books and lazily looked up to examine the titles on the top shelf. And there he saw it.

The Way of Blood. The Good Guy and *The Cynic*, both volumes of the unavailable Kulhánek[7] in perfect condition. And next to them...

He gasped.

Nightclub 1 and *2*.

The complete *Wild and Wicked.*

Even *The Lords of Fear.*

"Lull the enemy, then destroy him," he smiled broadly with the only Kulhánek quote he could think of, and clasped his hands together. "Vlad, you've earned your retirement!"

He pulled himself up on his tiptoes. His fingertips touched the book, but he hadn't reached it yet, his belly sliding down the spines. Just a little more, just a little more...

He braced himself against the shelf to get higher.

A rustling sound came from the room.

---

[7] Jiří Kulhánek is one of the most prominent figures of the modern Czech science fiction and fantasy scene. In the 1990s, he stood at the birth of a subgenre that is now called the Czech action school—a distinctive offshoot of splatterpunk with over-the-top action, indestructible heroes and politically incorrect black humor. However, Kulhánek is infamous for being dissatisfied with his published works and stubbornly refusing to reprint them, which is why his books have become unavailable and pricey collector's items.

Scurrying.

Vlad gripped the white spine with the publisher's logo between the tips of his fingers and pulled.

The bookcase tipped over with a thud.

Larry turned around just as Vlad came crashing down, followed by a giant, massive bookcase. The black-coated Hunter was still clutching the book when he landed on his back on the floor. The canary yellow unfastened helmet bounced off his head and swung like a spinning top against the wall. Heavy volumes drummed on the floor.

Vlad's scream was muffled by the combined power of *The Strontium* and *The Prospect of Eternity*.

The wood rumbled with a crunch.

"Vlad!" Larry yelled and run to him

Dust and torn pages swirled through the air. When they settled down a little, Larry realized Vlad had been right.

His brain really was as gray and disgusting as everyone else's.

The ceiling shook. The moss green chandelier swung, clanging, and a blizzard of dust and flakes from the old painting descended on Viktor's and Jolana's heads.

"What was that?" she yelped.

"Larry? Vlad? Are you all right?" Viktor called in the radio.

Silence.

White noise.

Muffled scurrying somewhere in the room.

"FROM THE WALL IT STARES BLANKLY AT ME—A DARK HOLE WHERE THE SAFE USED TO BE..."

Viktor and Jolana turned to the transistor. The radio roared at the top of its lungs despite the mold and the fact that it was switched off.

"Pepin, why did you close it?" Marek frowned and shone his light up to the trap door.

"I didn't close it!"

"Then who did?"

"I don't know!"

"You were the last one in, so who was it, huh?"

"David Copperfield, you idiot!"

Anka stepped decisively into the escalating argument. "It doesn't matter, guys, come on, cut it out!"

Marek took a breath to say his last word, but his gaze slid to her hand. "Jesus, what happened to you?" He shone his phone directly at her palm.

It was the first time Anka had seen it directly in the light, and she was almost frightened herself too. She hadn't felt the blood dripping down her fingers until now, but there was a deep gash in the muscle under her pinky.

"Holly shit, dude!" Pepin yelled, digging through his pockets for a handkerchief.

Together, the boys bandaged her arm with the thankfully unused handkerchief, spilling out one piece of advice after another.

"You have to disinfect it."

"Dude, my aunt's gonna be pissed..."

"And clean it up so you don't get anthrax."

"Tetanus, dude."

"It's the same thing!"

"It's not, dude!"

Pepin found his phone in the dark to demonstrate the difference between tetanus and anthrax, but realized that the screen was cracked and wouldn't pick up a signal.

From the floor above them came a scream and a thud that rang through the house.

And then something scratched in the darkness.

Larry cautiously touched the shoulder that stuck out from under the shelf, but the squashed Hunter didn't move. The radio at his hip was crackling.

He ignored it.

"Vlad?" he said softly. Then he noticed the puddle that was slowly widening where Vlad's head used to be.

Larry howled.

"Larry? Vlad? Are you okay?" Viktor's urgent voice echoed for the umpteenth time.

Larry stood up and angrily pressed the button. "No!" he barked. Then he threw the radio across the library.

He pried the shotgun from Vlad's motionless fingers and

pumped it. "Come out, you bastard, let's dance!" he yelled, stepping forward decisively.

Viktor pressed the radio button again. Karel Gott's voice faded, replaced by shouts from upstairs. "Come out, you bastard, let's dance!" Larry's voice boomed through the walls.

"Larry? Larry! Come in! What's going on?" Viktor kept trying the radio, but no one answered. "We have to go upstairs," he decided.

Jolana didn't move. A red light flashed in her head; she couldn't help the sudden feeling that she'd missed something. Something important.

But what, what was it?

Viktor was almost out in the hallway when the radio started again.

"FROM THE WALL IT STARES BLANKLY AT ME—A DARK HOLE WHERE THE SAFE USED TO BE..."

"What the...," Jolana gasped, but Viktor turned back to the radio, his eyes darting around the room in confusion.

It was then that she realized what she had overlooked.

Ammonia.

Dirt.

Rat bones.

Milk trays, dead flowers, and no one to take care of the house.

Someone to take care of the tenants.

"Viktor, I think I know what's going on here," she breathed in a sudden burst of insight.

As one man, Marek and Pepin pointed their phones at the source of the sound. Light skipped over crates and boxes until darkness swallowed it. Something glimmered at the end of it, though.

"I think I see an exit!" Pepin, who was apparently also beginning to find the environment of the dank, crowded underground quite unpleasant, hissed.

"Great, let's go!" Anka shouted.

Lenora threw out her turn signal and the old Chevy drove sharply onto the gravel road.

"An alder stick, my ass," she snorted contemptuously, glancing at the object the old warehouse worker had given her. He didn't have feathers, but he'd left her a piece of wood instead, meant to protect her from evil forces. She hesitated for a moment, deciding if she should leave it lying on the passenger seat, but in the end she grabbed it with a grunt and stuffed it in her pocket. Better wood than nothing.

"Old fart," Lenora cursed and got out.

She slammed the door maybe a little louder than she had to.

She raced toward the porch, leather pants creaking.

The lights were on in the house and screaming and loud music could be heard.

"You must have started this party without me," she grinned, reaching to her waist for her Glock. Checking the magazine while still walking, she nodded and put it back in place with a click. "Showtime!"

Martens drummed on the ancient parquet floor.

Dust particles swirled in the light around the chandelier.

The eyes under bushy brows were dark and dull as shale.

Larry rubbed his sideburns with a snarl and pointed his shotgun behind another bookcase.

Two steps, three, four, he peered into the aisle behind the shelves.

It was dark in there, and though no one else would probably notice, Larry had exceptionally good hearing. His ears caught a fleeting rustle.

He didn't bother with a warning; he simply fired the shot.

Viktor ran to the machine and slammed buttons with his fist. The divine Karel Gott fell silent.

He pulled his helmet off his head and smoothed his matted hair. "What?" He turned to Jolana. His eyes mirrored his growing frustration; he was like jack-in-box, just waiting for someone to turn the crank and finally let him out of the box.

"I think it's a domovoy," she blurted out. "A housekeeper."

"Like a house elf?"

"Domovoy, housekeeper, lar, penat, lutin, hob, gob, whatever you call it, but I think this one is very old and used to its quiet and its routine—and it's upset that someone invaded its house."

"We would have noticed!"

"Hair. Little tracks like rats. Ammonia. It's not the cats that we can smell, it's him. Empty milk dishes, dry flowers, skeletons... He has no sacrifices, so he eats whatever he can get his hands on, like..."

"... like mice and birds." Viktor swung the helmet in his hand. "But domovoys don't kill people!"

"No, but this one is furious. It's probably very old and hungry and trying to evict the tenants because it doesn't like the changes—and if that doesn't work, then..."

BANG!

An unmistakable shotgun blast echoed upstairs.

"Holy shit," Viktor hissed.

At that moment, the radio started again.

Pepin held the phones while his cousin tossed the junk aside so they could fight their way to the door, which they could already see quite clearly. He was just wrestling with a lawnmower when suddenly Pepin's light slid over the edges of the old garden tool onto something tucked away completely...

Anka felt her stomach tighten.

"Guys, it's ...," she began.

Marek raised his head.

Pepin shone his light closer and in the cone of white light, they saw a black lacquered box with a picture of...

"A swastika!" Pepin exclaimed.

"I knew we'd find it here!" Marek exclaimed.

One over the other they scrambled for the box, Marek tangling himself in the cable of the lawnmower, while Pepin tripped over a bag of plaster. But together they finally got the box with the Nazi insignia on the ground. It thudded with the promise of a lot of weight inside.

Marek cleaned the cobwebs and dust with the back of his hand, and Pepin opened the latch.

Anka squatted down beside them.

"Shouldn't we say something?" Pepin suggested, licking his lips nervously.

"Like what?" frowned Marek.

"I don't know, like 'Sieg Heil'?"

"You're going to heil in a haunted cellar for luck?!"

"It can't hurt, can it?"

Anka unlatched the lid without a word.

The boys fell silent and all three of them tilted their heads to peer inside. Marek and Pepin's foreheads collided, and to Anka's surprise, there was no hollow thud.

Marek frowned.

Pepin swallowed.

"Well," Anka gasped, "this is unexpected."

Then they heard a shot from the floor above them.

Pieces of masonry joined the dust in the air. The buckshot went through the side of the library, shredding the nearest books and carving several dents in the wall. The aged wood tilted aside with a creak and vomited its contents on the floor. The volumes pounded the ground with their spines, corners, pages. The weight and mold-tested shelves finally succumbed to the lure of gravity. *Thud-thud-thud-thud-thud*, one by one they came down like dominoes until it rumbled.

Larry pumped his shotgun again and waited.

Silence. No scurrying, no shuffling, no sounds.

With his left hand, he pulled a plastic case from his pocket and tapped out a thick Ashton cigar. He bit off the tip. He stuck the cigar in the corner of his lips, lit it from the red-hot barrel of the shotgun, and took a long drag.

Still nothing. All the while he waited for the creature in the house to take advantage of his inattention to attack again, but there was no movement, no sound.

"Suddenly you're not such a badass when you see a gun, huh?" grinned Hunter. Taking a drag from his cigar, he brushed past Vlad's crumpled body and stepped out in the hallway.

As he slammed the door behind him, a pair of eyes glittered in the corner of the room.

For the fourth time that evening, the multiple Golden Nightingale award winner interrupted their conversation, and Viktor, who was about to take off upstairs to meet Larry and Vlad, had had enough of the jovial story about the stolen safe. He slammed his fist on the off switch, and when the voice coming from the moldy speakers didn't stop, he angrily reached for the cable.

A flash of recognition passed through Jolana. "No . . . !" she started, but didn't have the time to say any more.

A flash passed through Viktor as well. Unfortunately, without the recognition.

He yanked the power cord to the radio.

Sparks appeared around the cable.

Viktor froze, his already tousled hair standing at attention.

"Viktor!" Jolana yelled.

The bulbs in the mossy chandelier flickered and popped.

Viktor slumped to the floor, and—judging by the sound—took a table full of valuable LPs with him.

The smell of burning flesh filled the air.

Jolana lunged toward him.

"*DO NOT DESPAIR, OH, YEAH, YEAH, YEAH!*" came a mocking voice from the radio.

Lenora stepped up on the porch and opened the door to the house. "Sweethearts? Mommy's home!"

A gunshot echoed from upstairs, the sound of a radio came from the hallway.

The blonde frowned.

She took a step forward.

There was a crash and all lights in the house went out.

They slammed the box shut and looked at each other. Marek finally broke the silence. "I think we can agree that it's not Nazi gold."

"We should have heiled for luck," Pepin complained.

"Anyway," Marek interrupted him, "it's still a Nazi box, and it could be worth something."

"We should take it to the police," Anka said firmly.

The cousins exchanged glances. "Or . . . ," Marek began, but the girl shook her head decisively.

"We will tell the police, end of discussion. This isn't fun anymore, guys."

Marek sighed. "All right. But we're taking the box with us!"

Jolana could still see sparks flashing in front of her eyes.

"Viktor?" She stumbled to where the young Hunter had collapsed to the ground.

She searched for him; there was a moment of uncertainty, and then a realization that she was touching his knee. Quickly she groped further—the hard denim, the soft material of a sweatshirt. She knelt down and hissed. There were shards under her feet and something wet. From the smell, it was urine and probably some chemicals that had shattered in Viktor's bag when he fell.

She finally found his hand, his shoulder, his face.

She bent over his lips.

No breath.

She tried his wrist.

No pulse.

"Shit," she hissed, and started to pull her cell phone out of her pocket. But the display didn't light up. Could the battery be dead?

"Shit, shit, shit!"

She grabbed the radio at Viktor's waist. "Larry! Larry, I need help!" she shouted, but after getting hissing silence instead of a reply, she realized she was alone in this.

No.

She was not alone.

She was here with an aggressive domovoy.

From the darkness, she could hear scratching.

The chandelier went out, but Larry didn't care. The cigar glowed between his lips and he had powerful flashlight at his waist that resembled car headlights. He switched it on.

And all hell broke loose.

Lenora heard the fuses click loudly to her right. Frowning, she lowered the gun and fished in the pocket of her leather jacket for the flashlight.

She didn't notice that the alder twig had fallen out of her pocket in the dark.

"Three, four, five, six..."

Jolana pumped Viktor's chest.

The smell of burnt flesh stung her nose, the shards of precious vinyl cut through her pants, and the fabric was soaked with piss and Viktor's chemicals, but she tried not to think about any of it, just administered CPR with her elbows extended, like she'd learned to do back in school.

When his ribs crunched under her fingers, she felt horror, but knew she couldn't stop.

"... eight, nine, thirty, one, two..." she continued.

Something rustled behind her.

"... six, seven, eight..."

Still no pulse.

Still no breathing.

Just the approaching little steps.

Lenora shone the light on the fuse box and flipped the switches up.

Bang!

All the doors in the corridor opened.

Larry stood there with his shotgun ready.

The hallway lights came on and a chair shot out of the nearest room, a white sheet trailing behind it like a veil. He sent it across the hall with a kick and fired as it skidded around and headed back toward him. The buckshot rattled against the floor. Furniture was blown into splinters.

Unfazed, Larry dropped the shotgun, pulled a massive Ruger revolver from his coat, and took a drag from his cigar. "That's all you can do?" he grinned, but suddenly regretted it.

A velvet stool flew out of the next room.

A pillow followed it.

Another cushion.

A blanket and a moldy fringed shawl.

Several dresses made of frayed fabric, blouses the size of tarp, bras with cups that could have been a soldier's helmet, and other pieces of underwear that Larry decided not to think about because they brushed against his face.

Then the creature apparently realized it needed more dangerous objects, and in quick succession came an antique vase, an old stained glass lamp, and two coat hangers wedged together and swishing like Frisbees. Larry felt like Neo from *The Matrix* as he was narrowly dodging them.

His back was hurting, but he didn't have the time to find out how bad it was.

From the left, spinning plates began to shoot out, *bang-bang-bang*, twelve pieces from a set the owner had apparently been saving for a royal delegation.

Larry threw himself to the ground, thankful that his helmet was still firmly fastened on his head.

The creature continued in the trend started by Italian marriages, and the plates were followed by tiny cups, saucers, a sugar bowl and tongs, and finally a floral teapot that showered the Hunter with a shower of porcelain shards.

"Well, well, someone's angry, eh?"

Larry rolled to the side; the edge of a metal case for thread and needles stuck into the floor. The treadle pedal of a sewing machine whizzed past his head like a stone from a sling, and he avoided a fatal hit to the forehead from an old Singer only by diving to the ground again before a cloud of buttons like projectiles hit the wall at the end of the hallway.

"This is really starting to feel like *The War of The Roses*," the Hunter muttered.

A cupboard traveled out of one of the rooms, rattling and clanking like a skeleton with maracas. The floor buckled and creaked dangerously beneath it. But before Larry could say or do anything, he took an unexpected hit to the stomach.

Comrade Gottwald knocked the wind out of him.

The house shook violently and a shower of dust fell from the ceiling of the cellar.

Pepin covered his mouth with his sleeve. "Wow, what do you think is going on up there?" he said.

"No idea, but I'm glad it's not happening here. Don't just stand there and help me!" Marek said as he was tugging the mower out of way to drag the Nazi box to the exit.

Anka was there already, trying the door leading outside. But it wouldn't budge.

The chandelier over Jolana's head lit up just as she was giving Viktor mouth-to-mouth breathing.

She stood up, blinked, and screamed.

Viktor grabbed the vinyl as he fell, and the Bowie he'd been admiring broke into pieces. One of them was stuck in his windpipe at the end of what was a practically smooth cut across his neck.

The wetness she'd been kneeling in this whole time wasn't just chemicals and urine.

Something rustled off to the side.

Jolana turned her head and screamed for the second time.

Lenora heard a rumble from upstairs, as if the whole house was falling to pieces, but before she could climb the stairs, a scream came from downstairs. Then she saw the Jilemnice chick who'd called them here scrambling out of one of the rooms on her back and elbows.

The blonde gasped and strode after her. "What, did you see a ghost?" she snapped, but even as she said the words she could feel the smile stiffening on her lips.

Jolana was disheveled and covered with blood.

"Holy shit," Lenora gasped and started running.

The girl was shaking and seemed on the verge of crying, but Lenora ignored her and peered into the room. A long red streak glowed in the sea of green as Jolana stumbled out of the room, and at the end of it . . .

"Holy shit apostolic!" Lenora cursed.

Viktor was on the floor.

Viktor's blood was everywhere.

Lenora turned on her heel. "What happened here?!" she barked at the girl, who was curled in a ball, hyperventilating. When Jolana didn't respond, the blonde grabbed her arm and pulled her to her feet. "Hey!" she snapped fingers in front of her face. "What's going on here?"

Jolana's eyes were glossy with shock, most of her clothes were soaked with blood, and her cheeks were smeared with red goo. A string of words that didn't make sense came out of her mouth: "I knew they were made from the souls of slain children, but this one was horrible, it had the body of a rat but the face of a toddler, but not a cute one, more like something out of a horror movie, like when you take one of those ugly plastic dolls with giant eyes and screw it onto a fat rat, that baby was probably eaten by rats, oh God, it was so disgusting and it bared its teeth at me and it was holding the piece of vinyl in its paws that cut through Viktor's . . .

"Jolana!" barked Lenora, shaking her. "What are you talking about? What's going on here?"

The girl finally focused on her. "A domovoy," she gasped.

A crash echoed from upstairs. The ceiling shook.

Lenora lifted her head.

The ceiling shook once more and then caved in.

Larry coughed. He frowned at the picture of the communist leader, which gave him a big punch in the stomach, and without any remorse, he hit the fifth president of Czechoslovakia between the eyes. The glass cracked and Larry scrambled to his feet.

The cupboard wobbled in place and then, with a clatter of cutlery, lurched forward. Forks and knives spilled out of its drawers, doors slammed, dishes clattered on shelves. Larry groaned and fired a full magazine in the furniture.

The cupboard didn't budge.

Facing the rolling sideboard, the Hunter assessed his options. A bookcase with a dead colleague still sounded like a better option than getting smeared across the wall.

He backed up and searched blindly for the door. Even as he grabbed the knob, he realized something was wrong. It was in a different place than it was supposed to be, tipping forward on one rusty hinge, and the handle twisted strangely under his fingers.

He turned his gaze to it.

"Oh, shit," he only managed to stammer out before a giant tentacle pulled him in.

Larry didn't even have the time to cry out. The sideboard slammed into the wall and rolled onto its back with a thud.

The wall, which a moment ago had been a strange doorway, was now perfectly smooth, and a glowing cigar on the floor was the only proof that anyone had ever been there.

A few moments later the floor caved in.

The old ceiling could not handle the excitement of the movement of the massive furniture, and it crashed into the green parlor space. A cupboard, a door, and a large part of the bookcase, including the body of poor Vlad, fell in with a clatter from upstairs. It collapsed in a tangle of dirt and mess, rolled across the broken parquet floor and tripped over the feet of the two women in the hallway.

Jolana found herself knee-deep in foreign bodily juices for the second time that day and couldn't help but scream again.

Lenora turned the dusty corpse around so she could see its face, then jumped away as if bitten by a snake.

"Angel's ass!" she yelled in a falsetto that didn't suit her tough talk one bit.

Jolana was shaking uncontrollably.

Lenora stood up, her pants creaking and a layer of white dust settling on her face that looked like she'd stuck her head in cocaine.

"Girl, get up. Let's get out of here!" she urged Jolana, pulling her car keys out of her jacket.

Jolana stood up shakily. "Larry..."

"Screw him, if he's alive, he'll get out of here too. And I'm not waiting for you either," the blonde snapped, already scrambling away.

Jolana followed her, swaying.

Over their heads, the old Jilemnice house creaked and groaned as if it was in its death throes. Gradually, the ceiling caved in more and more, and Jolana could hear the building moaning behind them, the walls shuddering. It was as if something that held the house together had finally given way.

"Dude, that's heavy as fuck!" Pepin yelled as they tried to lift the box.

"And what do you know about fucking, huh?"

"Dude, I have Pornhub at home, right?"

"Anka, what's taking you so long??" Marek paused as he lifted the other end of the lacquered box with a huff.

Anka turned the handle, but the door didn't budge. "Please, please, please," she breathed like a prayer and slammed into it with all her might.

The rusty hinges came loose. The door brushed against grass and the girl sighed in relief.

The haunted house released them from its clutches.

"Screw this job," Lenora growled as she trotted in the hall, "I don't know what possessed Viktor to come here when we could have been drinking wine in peace and..." She stopped in front of the staircase as if struck by lightning. She saw an alder branch on the ground. The alder branch that was supposed to protect her from evil forces. Frightened, she reached into her jacket pocket.

"The twig," she gasped.

At that moment, Jolana arrived.

And so did the piano, falling down the stairs, picking up speed.

For the third time that day, Jolana was splashed by the bodily juices of one of her colleagues. This time she didn't bother to scream.

When the piano pinned Lenora against the wall, she just lethargically wiped the blood spatter from her face, reached for the car keys in Lenora's agonizingly twisted fingers, and after a brief hesitation, picked up her last word from the floor as well and staggered out the door.

The cellar spat them out in the garden just a few steps from the shed. The box was heavy and slippery, and even with two of them it was hard to carry. Anka tried to persuade the boys to leave the box behind and just carry the contents, but Marek hissed something about the need for evidence and the huge money they would collect as a reward. Anka suspected that no police would give them money for finding a strange thing in someone else's basement, but she didn't want to argue.

Rumbling came from the house, like someone with a sledge-hammer started working inside, and Anka thought the building was shaking at its foundations.

"Just be careful around that car!" Marek hissed as they approached the Impala parked on the green grass off the path.

"Dude, I can't carry it anymore," Pepin complained breathlessly.

"What?!"

"My arms hurt."

"You carry packages at the post office!"

"I carry letters, dude, that's not gonna turn me into Rambo!"

Pepin lifted his end of the box with a grunt and started shuffling backwards towards the car.

"What are you doing?" Marek hissed, following him.

"What do you think, dude? Let's put it on the hood!"

"Are you out of your mind?!"

"If I try to pick it up off the ground again, I'll break my back!"

Thud!

The car buckled a little as the black box was thrown on its hood.

The door of the house opened.

All three of them froze in terror as a lone figure staggered out onto the porch.

It was a woman, and more than anything she resembled Carrie. She was covered from head to toe in a sticky mass which they quickly identified as blood, and she moved with the dreamlike grace of someone trying to crawl out of a nightmare. With unwavering confidence, she headed for her car.

The boys panicked and tried to lift the box, but only achieved dropping it back on the hood.

Anka froze like a pillar of salt.

The female version of Patrick Bateman stopped in front of them, flicking her gaze from one to the others until her gaze landed on the swastika, which even now glittered like Göring's half-shoes in the night.

"We were... uh, looking for treasure," Pepin tried to explain.

"Treasure," the woman repeated, rubbing her eyes. "Do you need a ride?" she asked, unexpectedly calm for someone who looked like she'd just rescued the crew of Serenity.

"It's okay, we..."

"If you could drop us off at Sportovní Street by the housing estate, that would be great," Pepin chimed in.

Anka and Marek shot him significant looks.

Pepin threw up his hands. "What?!"

Marek nodded his head towards the bloodied woman who was just unlocking the car.

Pepin shrugged his shoulders. "And?"

"And... I wonder what your mom would say about hitchhiking!" Marek hissed.

Pepin shook his head. "We're not hitchhiking. She offered!"

"Well, look at the way she looks! She's like someone from *Cannibal Holocaust*!"

"Because she is a larper, dude! I've been saying it all along!"

The blood-covered woman ignored their exchange, unlocked the car and calmly got behind the wheel. She merely asked: "Are you coming?"

The boys pushed each other for a while, but eventually they picked up the box and climbed in the back seat with it. Anka pursed her lips and sighed, but opened the passenger door and climbed in next to the driver from hell. The woman wiped blood from her eyes and slid the keys in the ignition.

With a grunt, the car started and sped forward on the gravel.

The building behind them shook, and then the roof fell in like a house of cards.

"Um . . . a hard night?" Anka suggested cautiously.

Bloody Mary nodded. "Yep."

A short, awkward silence followed.

"What's in the box?" the driver asked as she threw out her turn signal.

"Bones," Pepin answered immediately.

"Bones, huh?" she repeated, taking a slow breath. "Let me guess— baby bones. And rat bones, too."

Pepin's mouth fell open in an admiring O. "How did you know?"

"A lucky coincidence," the woman replied wearily, turning the wheel.

She entered the roundabout a little more abruptly than she probably intended, and the box skidded over the edge off the seat. Pepin and Marek tried to catch it, and though they all heard the crunch of bones, Anka also heard something else—a clink, like metal rubbing against metal.

"That'll do," she blurted, pointing to the street behind the playground. There was a moment of suspense, wondering if the car would actually stop, but by then the driver was pulling over to the side of the road and slowing down.

"Well, thank you!" Pepin thundered, shooting out of the car.

"Yeah, thank you and, uh, have a nice evening," Marek added, quickly stumbling out after his cousin.

The bloody driver turned to Anka, who was just taking hold of the handle.

"Burn the bones," she said in a voice that brooked no objection.

"Sure, sure," Anka nodded, confused.

"That box looked really sturdy. I'd have a good look at it if I were you. The Nazis loved hidden compartments," she added.

"Um, okay. Thanks."

Slamming the door, she felt like she was in a dream. The Impala thundered off into the darkness, and soon its lights left nothing but an afterimage in her eyes. Anka shook her head and turned around. The boys continued to pull the crate, but the impact on the edge seemed to have damaged it a little. When they lifted it again, the bottom had loosened.

"Holy shit, dude!" Pepin yelled.

A huge gold brick fell out onto the pavement in the Jilemnice housing estate.

The car stopped in the parking lot of a closed general store. "A domovoy," Jolana gasped in disbelief and shook her head. The basis of coexistence with the creatures of a home was to appease them and bring offerings—flowers, food, or in the extreme case, prayers and one's own blood. When one angered them, they pulled mischievous pranks, but Jolana had never encountered such violence.

Well, one is always learning.

Maybe it's not too late to change careers. Her cousin was retraining to be a hairdresser, which would be a much more pleasant job. She'll call her tomorrow and ask her about it.

But in the meantime, she'll have to do the paperwork for this bloody mayhem. Three dead, Larry's fate unknown, and three civilians who somehow got involved, God, what a mess...

Jolana rubbed the dried blood out of her eyes. She was almost certain she looked like Samara Weaving at the end of *Ready or Not*.

But then she remembered something. The alder branch she'd picked up in the house shortly after Lenora had been splattered against the wall was still on the dashboard. It didn't look strange or mystical by any means, but there had to be some reason why it was the last thing that went through Lenora's mind—unless she counted the half-ton Petrof piano. Thoughtfully, she put down the stick and flipped off the blinker.

She knew that she should report the events to Fantom, and also that it would be a good idea to contact the relatives of the dead Hunters. Only she was all too aware of what a nightmare those calls would be, so she preferred to turn her attention toward the twig. Lenora had set off for Stará Paka, and from what Jolana could see, she hadn't returned with the feathers. So maybe it would be better if she stopped by now and asked around. There was a chance that someone might try to pull a Lord of the Woods on her, but after tonight she probably wouldn't say no to some beer.

The serpentines were winding through the darkness and the American veteran struggled on the broken road, but in the end Jolana successfully passed a big sign saying STARÁ PAKA. She pulled off at a turnoff separated by a gatehouse and a barrier, beyond which stood a tall, dilapidated building. It was far from perfect; it would have benefited the most from the visit of a bulldozer and a demolition crew.

Jolana stopped the car in front of an abandoned gatehouse, grabbed the twig and stepped outside. She felt the night breeze caress her blood-streaked hair.

She took two steps.

Then there was a crash and the ground shook so violently it knocked Jolana on her butt. When she blinked, the whole world suddenly seemed greener and brighter. She shifted her gaze to the old building.

The good news was that the building no longer needed a bulldozer and a demolition crew—wild, hot flames were shooting out of the windows and roof.

The bad news was that they were a poisonous green color.

Jolana watched the havoc suddenly unfold before her eyes and shook her head. "Typical," she muttered.

Larry opened his eyes. He was lying on his back, it was dark and damp all around him, and he could smell the scent of earth.

"Sir? Sir! Hey!"

He heard footsteps and the someone was shaking him.

He blinked, his eyes beginning to adjust to the darkness, enough that he could make out the outline of a person in it.

"Where am I?" he gasped, sitting up.

"In a sunken town near Jilemnice, sir. Something has pulled you here. Do you have weapons? We need help, there's a monster here that won't let us go . . ."

Larry sighed and rubbed his eyes. A Hunter's work obviously never ends.

He fumbled in his pocket for ammo and loaded his empty revolver.

MICHAELA MERGLOVÁ (* 1990)

When beauty and talent come together, it can never go wrong. Born in Pilsen, Michaela moved to Prague on the verge of adulthood to work in the world of advertising and marketing until she fulfilled her big dream and became a renowned writer. She fell in love with fantasy as a child and creative writing came only a little later.

She first introduced herself to readers as an author with the short story "Three Brothers in Kočas" (Nová vlna, 2015) and continued to win top spots in major fantasy literary competitions, as evidenced by obtaining the title Lady of the Order of Fantasy three times. She excelled as a short story writer in anthologies *The Other Side of the World* (*Odvrácená strana světa*, Straky na vrbě, 2017), *On the Trail of Crime* (*Na stopě zločinu*, Straky na vrbě, 2018), *In the Shadow of Magic* (*Ve stínu magie*, Epocha, 2019), as well as in the pulp-tinged *Beauties and Aliens* (*Krásky a vetřelci*, Epocha, 2021) and the science fiction collection *The Law of the Gene* (*Zákon genu*, Epocha, 2022).

By then, however, she had also already written her debut novel, *Song of Steel* (*Píseň oceli*, Epocha, 2019), a classical heroic fantasy in Gemmell's style, whose heroes, highlander Cuchenan and poet Minangar, would accompany her in two sequels titled *Song of the North* (*Píseň severu*, Epocha, 2021) and *Song of War* (*Píseň války*, Epocha, 2022). Her novel *The Cursed Tower* (*Prokletá věž*, Epocha, 2020), is a slightly different cup of tea, as it delves into the thieving underworld. She most recently proved her versatility with a paranormal science fiction with detective themes titled *The Void* (*Prázdnota*, Epocha, 2023).

Michaela's potential is simply too tempting, which is why the editors of the *MHF* project were as intrigued by her as she was intrigued by the project itself.

How to Deal with Wraiths
Martin Paytok

"What was your name again?" Ruml asked.

"Lenora," the blonde replied emphatically. She was dressed as if she had walked into the Stará Paka SRS warehouse straight from the set of an action movie.

One of those crappy movies where the heroes wear sunglasses inside buildings and run away from the fire at the end, Basil, who was working a Saturday shift with Ruml, added to himself.

Ruml adjusted his cap with the word "Security" on it. "Well, look, Lenora, does this place look like a home furnishings store?"

The action star pulled her hand from the pocket of her leather jacket, pulled her sunglasses down to the tip of her nose, and looked at him as if he was something stuck to the sole of her shoe.

Basil knew what she was thinking.

She thinks it doesn't.

The former factory complex on the edge of the village offered perfect cover. The dilapidated, multilevel building with its spray-painted facade and broken windows was hardly ever glanced at more than once, and the supporters of urban exploration were reliably deterred by the eight feet high fence crowned with rust barbed wire.

In addition, next to the gatehouse, where everyone was at the moment, stood a ground-floor square shack with the most innocent sign over the entrance proclaiming: DAIRY PRODUCTS. A yellowed leaflet, stuck with duct tape in the window, announced the imminent grand opening in a flowery font. It had been hanging there for eight years—exactly from the moment when the flooded Rokytka River washed away the locals' excitement that they would finally witness the opening of the World of Chickens they had been promised for the last eleven years.

It could only be more inconspicuous with a banner saying: Nothing weird is going on here.

So when that woman suddenly walked up to the freight elevator, identified herself as an employee of Fantom, and announced that she came "for the bag of kingfisher feathers," Ruml was thrown off a bit. Basil, however, took it with the grim stoicism of a man who had spent his best years handling objects that could suddenly grow a demonic mouth and bite off his hands. And he wasn't even exaggerating.

Ruml cleared his throat.

"Why did you think you could get something like that here?"

"Your boss promised me that in exchange for letting him stare at me eating spaghetti carbonara."

Basil rolled his eyes. That was the fourth girl this year.

"So much for the reason of my visit," Lenora continued. "As for how I knew to turn this way ..." She didn't finish the sentence. She just looked around and grinned. "I saw this idiot dragging that thing here from across the road."

She pointed her thumb at the tall guy in a sweater and overalls who had been standing next to her the whole time. And next to him was a hand truck loaded with a crudely made dingy coffin tied with a rusty chain.

The guy shrugged his shoulders and explained in a chopped North Moravian accent, "I'm not going to drive a truck all the way to the yard for one box."

"Of course," Ruml nodded ironically. "That's not what this yard's for, is it?"

Basil smoothed his greying moustache and, in a raspy voice as rough as if his vocal cords were made of sandpaper, asked, "Do you have the transfer document for this?"

"Somehow I didn't ... get it."

"What do you mean you didn't get it?"

"They told me to bring it here. So I loaded it up and drove here."

"Then take it back."

"I drove here for five hours. I won't take it back just to get a stupid paper, only to return here tomorrow. Can't they send it to you?"

"Send it?" Basil's younger colleague grinned. "Who do you take us for, postmen? This is a warehouse of paranormal material. If you think we're going to take something from you without documentation that says how to handle it, you're an even bigger idiot than Lenora here thinks you are."

The driver shrugged again. "I threw it on the hand truck and didn't notice any problems."

Ruml shook his head in frustration, but didn't argue further.

Basil tucked his hands into the pockets of his grey overalls and stared at the coffin. It was less than six feet long and, apart from the chains, looked quite ordinary. But so did a lot of the things they stored here, and none of them were really ordinary.

Ordinary or harmless.

He knew that to start treating them as such was the first step to getting into trouble.

Like the one with that deck of cards a year and a half ago.

"I have to make a phone call," he finally announced.

"Go call whoever you want. Just make it quick, bitch. I have to go back to Ostrava today."

Basil, whom nothing irritated more than people from big cities looking down on him, scorned him. "But you're not in Ostrava, *bitch.* So act like it."

The driver was visibly shaken by this level of Stará Paka hospitality.

Without haste, Basil loaded himself in the freight elevator, picked up the controls hanging from a cable from the ceiling, and turned to Lenora.

"Come with me. We'll deal with you both at once."

"How am I supposed to tell you the registration number when you have the papers?" Basil said into the receiver, and while he listened to what the other party had to say, his eyebrows formed a sharp angle. "Why should I care about some newbie? You know very well it's against the regulations."

Lenora slumped down in the uncomfortable chair where he had placed her in a small break room, and put her feet up on the other side of the table than she put her sunglasses. She knew the warehouse clerk's name, because before the elevator grating closed behind them, he remarked to the other yokel: "We'll be right back," and the other yokel replied, "Sure, Basil."

"Sure, blame it on us, that's the best," Basil muttered, hung up and dialed another number. "Paka. I've got some Lenora…"

She wondered how many people in Czechia have such a stupid name, and looked around the small break room in the meantime. Apart from a table with a phone and three chairs, its furnishings consisted of a cupboard, a small fridge, a microwave, a coffee maker, and a bulletin board, to which someone had pinned a note with a hand-scrawled motto next to the schedule of services: HE WHO DOESN'T WORK—SHALL NOT EAT! HE WHO WORKS—SHALL DRINK!

That's probably supposed to be humor. Haha.

"Couldn't you do it from the gatehouse?" she said in a bored tone as the receiver rang in the fork. "Or, I don't know, maybe by cell phone, like a human?"

"This connection is secure," the talkative man replied. "The old man sends his regards. He says we're supposed to cooperate with you." He bent down, pulled out a drawer, tossed a clipboard on the table, wedged a preprinted form into it, scribbled something on it with a pen, and then straightened up again. "I don't have any feathers here, but I think I can find something else."

He pushed her back out into the hallway with the elevator and sent her to the right. The concrete corridor, illuminated by sterile light of fluorescent bulbs here and there, stretched into the distance, lined along its length by dozens of doors, passageways, security gates, and wooden crates of various sizes with numbers printed on them. But they'd only gone past two or three rooms.

"Is this where all the funny things that we who are lucky enough to work outdoors occasionally come across disappear?"

"Hmm."

"How big is this place?"

"That's classified."

She didn't expect anything else. The State Regulatory Service people loved to act as tough guys.

Basil stopped by one of the smaller doors, fished an electronic card out of his breast pocket, and put it close to the obsolete terminal sticking out of the wall under a TALISMANS AND AMULETS sign. Red light shone on it.

"Electronic locks?" she wondered. "I mean, those things have to be out of order all the time in a place like this."

"We didn't design the place," the warehouse clerk replied, as if that explained everything.

The terminal emitted a beep, the red light bulb went out only to turn green, the magnetic lock clicked, and the door swung open. Basil stepped through it, revealing to Lenora a view of a room not much larger than the phone booth where they'd camped earlier, but lined floor to ceiling with metal boxes like a bank vault.

He paused at the opposite wall and squinted at the numbers stamped next to the smoothed handles, then pulled one. The hinges creaked, the door swung open, and the clerk's hand fumbled in the darkness beyond.

Talismans and amulets, Lenora thought. *Real magic. Not carnival props like Vlad was carrying around.*

A triumphant smile spread across her face . . . and then froze when Basil pulled out a withered twig.

"What the hell is that?" she frowned.

"Alder," said Basil, as if that explained anything. But her expression obviously said it all, so he added: "It protects from evil."

"You're kidding, right? I could have grabbed this somewhere along the road."

"I don't know. This one supposedly grew where some saint bled to death."

"Supposedly," Lenora sputtered, pointing a thumb behind her, to the opposite cell, where a golden pipe topped with a gaping dragon's mouth protruded from the box. "You got some Chinese rocket launcher lying around over there, and you give me a piece of wood."

"That's a cursed Vietnamese sky rocket," Basil stated dryly. "It would blow your creepy house to the moon." He shoved a clipboard in front of her face. "Sign this."

She was about to protest further, but when she saw the level of disinterest on his face, she just snorted and snatched that clipboard from his fingers.

"Tell your boss he can forget about another date after this."

A holy twig, for Christ sake, she shook her head before writing her name in the bottom right corner, *Vávra and Vlad will laugh their asses off.*

The coffin messenger had a hard time going into the yard, but five minutes of turning around in a one-way street with the truck apparently seemed fine to him. Thankfully, Lenora had bothered to back her American car up to the gatehouse at least, so she was able to wave them off as soon as she gave them a cordial goodbye with a raised middle finger.

"Ostrava has no idea what this is or who sent it here," Basil remarked. "Until they find out more, we're supposed to quarantine it."

"Amateurs," Ruml snorted.

The driver finally managed to wedge the beeping truck into the drive, where Ruml condescendingly removed the barrier from his path, honked twice, and soon they were both watching its red lights disappearing into the autumn mist.

"Wait, quarantine? You know who's there..."

Basil threw up his hand, took one last drag from the finishing cigar, and ended its misery in the ashtray on the windowsill. "Are we expecting anyone else today?"

"Probably not. The shipment from Liberec will arrive on Monday at the earliest."

"In that case, help me with this."

He and Ruml had known each other for almost twenty years. Ruml had adopted the silent warehouse clerk less than a week after he'd joined, much to Basil's displeasure, and had started deliberately scheduling their shifts so they could work together and he could pop in for a chat on his rounds. And usually it was just him talking. But Basil didn't mind. He could manage a decent pretense of listening, even though he was internally dissociating.

The advantage was that during the one-sided conversations Ruml's body worked on autopilot, which made it enough to hand him things and guide him to where they should be put.

Plus, he played chess.

Best friend I ever had.

The coffin was waiting for them exactly where the driver had left it. He had even left them a hand truck in his noble forgetfulness.

Ruml knocked on the lid and put his ear to it, but no one knocked back.

"Who do you think is in there?" he asked. "Or what?"

"Surely nothing good," Basil grumbled, kicked the hand truck under and wheeled it onto the elevator platform.

"I'd like to have that optimism of yours," Ruml said, pulling the grate behind them.

The elevator began its slow descent into the one hundred sixty feet depths.

"They could do something about this piece of crap by now; even walking down the stairs is faster."

Basil was fairly certain Ruml wouldn't really like the extent of his optimism. He complained about the elevator every time he rode it, each time simultaneously expressing faith that it would one day be replaced by a less outdated model. But he knew it was just a wishful thinking.

After all, they worked for the government.

When the lift finally reached the level of the concrete corridor, Basil pulled the hand truck out of it again and they headed into the four miles long maze that stretched below. The chain jingled like a xylophone on the way.

Ruml impressed him. He managed not to complain about why they hadn't taken the car until almost the fourth turn.

On a normal day, their colleagues with heavier loads transported them through the tunnels on minitrucks, but Basil preferred to walk. He liked the quiet of the more remote parts. The idea that he could wander through them for hours and not meet anyone was comforting.

Not that he would wander often. After nearly twenty years, he was slowly finding his way around them better than on the surface. The last time he'd searched for an ATM it had taken him twenty minutes before he realized that he was not in Stará, but in Nová Paka, but say *Cursed Books* or *Relics and Crucifixes* and he knew exactly the shortest route to a given room.

Behind Unspeakable Horrors on the right.

It took them less than a quarter of an hour to reach the room with the QUARANTINE sign. It was located at the end of a dead-end arm of one of the adjacent corridors, making it the room farthest from the others.

It was one of the smaller ones in terms of size and had a double door entrance—also metal and also with an electromagnetic lock. These, however, were additionally lined with silver plates and painted on the outside with magical symbols and covered in runes, Latin, and Hebrew consonants. All in dried blood.

Basil drew the ancient sign in the air with his fingers and ran the electronic key through the terminal.

Click!

The decoration continued inside, where there was virtually no free space on the walls and ceiling. Where other incantations, protective images and prayers could not fit, specialists in exorcism and dark forces at least added some hieroglyphics.

The eggheads in the research department had designed it to keep any dangerous or otherwise problematic supernatural object inside. Except, of course, the one thing they really needed to keep in there.

A battered packet of mariasch cards, old and faded and a bit bigger than the modern standard, lay where it always had. On the floor in the center of the room, in the middle of a protective pentagram, flanked by five long-burning candles. It seemed harmless enough, but that's what made it so dangerous. Even Basil, who preferred games in which strategy, not chance, was important, had only to look at it to feel a flutter in his stomach caused by the thrill of a gamble. But for the urge to pick it up and outbid someone for a few crowns to get the better of him, he would have to forget how things had gone wrong the last time someone had succumbed to its charms.

For the deck held something else besides the cards. A heavyweight among supernatural beings.

A wraith.

Specifically, a dead gambler from St. Peter's Church in Poříčí, courtesy of his colleagues in Prague. All Basil would have to do was bend down and let him out like a genie from a bottle.

Except this genie only grants wishes to the suicidal ones.

The wraiths had a worse reputation among the Hunters than the Fey. Each was governed by specific rules, and since they existed due to the people's belief in their existence, the usual means of combating paranormal threats showed intermittent effectiveness against them, plus the wraiths had their own off switch that had to be deduced during a confrontation. On top of that, they often played unfair.

Like, for example, the dead gambler who, when activated in the tunnels, would randomly move in clouds of smoke and challenge people to a game of mariasch. He didn't care if his victim didn't know the rules. Anyone who refused or didn't speak up ended up in pieces. Anyone who said yes got screwed anyway, only they lost their money beforehand. On that day, there was a significant reduction in the number of employees at the Stará Paka warehouse. He was only deactivated by the head of maintenance, who had been gambling practically from the cradle. Once he was back in the box, they stuck him in, lit candles, smoked the room with scented sticks and hoped for the best. Or at least that no one would accidentally bump into him.

"They should burn it," Ruml remarked.

Basil maneuvered the hand truck next to the entrance. "Don't look at it and help me with that coffin. We'll put it in the corner over there, next to the box."

There could have been anything in it, and there was probably a reason it was lying there.

"Wouldn't you rather leave it on the hand truck?"

"I don't want whoever comes in after us to be confronted by it as soon as the door opens."

"Some people would deserve it," Ruml muttered, leaning over and lifting the lower end with his back, like a pro, and hissed. "Shit..."

Basil tipped the other side on top of him and immediately understood why. It was heavy. Or rather, the chain that secured it was heavy. There couldn't be much left of the corpse inside, if there was one, and if it was from the same era as the coffin itself.

He backed slowly into the room, careful not to disturb the pentagram in the process.

A careful step or two and...

And then he flinched.

For when he refocused on his colleague, he found that his face had managed to take on the appearance of a red balloon ready to burst.

In his case, a vein in the brain ready to burst.

"Don't...!"

"Shit!" Ruml gasped simultaneously and...

Clang!

The heel of the coffin rumbled on the floor.

Basil didn't wait for anything, dropped his part as well, jumped back, crouched down and covered his head with his hands.

Thud, thud, screech!

They both froze like models in a live painting. In the ensuing silence, all that could be heard was their rapid breathing.

They pretended to be statues for about a minute before Basil decided to assess the situation through the squinted lids of his right eye.

"Sorry," Ruml whispered and showed him his thumb. "I got a splinter."

Basil frowned at him.

The fluorescent light on the ceiling flickered and they both crouched again.

Ordinarily, they wouldn't have found anything odd about it. Paranormal material sometimes leaked through insulation, and power outages were the first manifestation of that. But if this particular paranormal object was leaking...

It could end really badly.

The fluorescent light stopped flashing.

"Perhaps we'd better go."

They moved cautiously into the hallway, and Basil hastily slammed the door shut behind them.

"Jeez," Ruml breathed, running a hand over his face. "That could have turned out badly."

"You think?"

"Yeah. I already saw myself torn to shreds. What are the chances of avoiding him twice?"

Basil was about to remark something about idiots, but he swallowed it down.

"Let's get coffee," he said instead. "And take the damn hand truck with you."

Ruml complained, but obeyed, and soon they were making their way to the break room, accompanied by the rhythmic squeak of unlubricated wheels.

Neither of them noticed that it wasn't just the coffin that hit the floor of the quarantine room, but the padlock in particular—and that the shackle of the medieval-looking relic had popped out as if it had been waiting for that all along.

✦ ✦ ✦

The fluorescent light flickered again. And because it was blinking, it looked like the coffin wasn't opening, but that it was already open. Only the clang of the chain betrayed the movement. That and the cloud of dust that rolled out of the dark gap, which grew larger and larger with each flicker until...

Thud!

The lid fell back on the coffin, but immediately rose again, this time more violently. The chain groaned, the end of it shot out from under the bottom, the dust swirled and the gap widened.

The room was filled with the irritating smell of a dried grave.

Something scraped against the wood inside, and then...

Then four fingers without skin, flesh, blood vessels or blood slid out and wrapped around the edge of the lid like predator claws.

Knock, knock, knock, knock.

The jerk of a bony hand released the rest of the chain and flung the lid across the room as if it weighed nothing. Light poured into the coffin, revealing its ailing occupant. The spotted frontal bone, the empty eye sockets covered in cobwebs, the eternal smile of jaws stripped of lips and a few teeth, the ribs and vertebrae—all old, yellowed, desiccated, and dead.

And yet the joints creaked as the skeleton in the coffin sat up and looked around. Empty sockets stopped on a box in the corner.

Crunch, crunch, crunch.

With the next blink, it was no longer sitting, but standing, and not in the coffin, but beside it. The bones of its feet clicked on the floor like brand new half-shoes, and the phalanx bones pushed under the wooden lid with a squeak.

There were no bones hiding inside that box. It hid a small rumpled book with a dark cross emblazoned on the cover.

The skeleton stooped to pick it up, lifted it to its eye sockets, and looked at it for a moment before opening it, turning it pages down, and shaking it as if trying to knock the Holy Spirit out of it. It didn't succeed, but it did knock something else out.

Suddenly the whole book shattered, the pages slammed shut, and another wraith materialized in that whirlwind.

She was a little taller than five feet, dressed in a nun's habit and missing her head. There were broken blood vessels sticking out of her neck, pumping blood onto the white veil, and a severed spine.

Blood trickled down the garment and dripped on the floor, leaving dark red puddles.

The skeleton dropped the remains of the Bible back into the box and reached out to the nun, palm up. The nun pushed it away with a violent movement, grabbed its pale skull with her hands, and pulled. She slammed it back and forth and side to side, but the skull didn't move.

Pale hands slid down to her hips and the nun's shoulders slumped. The skeleton reached out its palm to her again. This time she didn't push it away, merely pointed to where the human body usually didn't end.

The skeleton gritted its teeth and turned its back on her.

Basil prepared two mugs and brought the coffee machine to life. Ruml, meanwhile, took a chessboard from his cabinet and spread it out on the table. They used to borrow one from *Communications with the Beyond*, but after that gambler debacle they'd decided to buy their own.

The empty gatehouse didn't bother either of them. Most weekends, nobody came here. And if they did, any visitors could always ring the bell.

"Who's playing white today?" Ruml asked.

"Does it matter?" Basil replied, watching as the coffee machine clanked, hummed and vibrated while filling the pot.

Ruml scratched his chin. "I think I started last time."

"So I'm playing white."

"In that case, I won't stand a chance again."

"Then don't ask and keep them," Basil said.

The coffee maker rumbled. Basil pulled the pot from it, poured the lifesaver in the prepared mugs, and put them on the sides of the chessboard where an army of white pieces waited ready for him.

"We're not playing for the last time today, are we?" Ruml chuckled.

A bony leg crossed the edge of the pentagram. The bloody patterns flared, projecting a distorted shadow of its owner onto the ceiling. Nothing else happened. The skeleton stepped in the pentagram with its other foot, stopping near the deck of cards.

It watched it for a few seconds, head cocked to the side, then bent down and picked it up. A picture of a faded monster with its tongue lolling out returned its gaze from the worn deck. The skeleton raised its other hand and scratched the bottom edge of the box with the tip of its index finger—and as it opened, a stack of cards slipped out and scattered across the floor.

The skeleton ruffled them with its foot, but did not deal with them further. Instead, it turned its attention to the case. It shook it, and since nothing else fell out, it put it to its eye socket and peered inside as if it was a kaleidoscope. But there were no strange shapes hiding there. There was nothing there at all.

At least, nothing except black smoke, which rolled out with a hiss and enveloped the surroundings in an impenetrable cloud, but then immediately shrank and formed a humanoid shape. A few moments later, there was no trace of the smoke, and in the center of the pentagram stood a small, hunched man with a round head, bluish skin, receding hair and a moustache of a carnival magician.

On his narrow shoulders hung a rumpled undertaker cloak and he wore a black necktie. In his hand he held a deck, no longer held by a skeleton, and which probably again contained the cards that had disappeared from the floor.

"Hmph," he grumbled at the sight of the pentagram in the middle of which he stood. He scratched his forehead, stepped out of it effortlessly, raised his crooked eyes to the skeleton, and hissed: "A game of cards?"

The skeleton held out its empty palm to him again. The gambler grimaced and laid a card on it. The skeleton raised it to its skull and studied it for a moment before tilting its palm to the side and letting it fall to the floor.

Just before the card touched the floor, it dissipated in a puff of black smoke. The gambler leaned in sharply, sniffed, and wrinkled his nose.

"Dead," he stated.

The skeleton tilted its head and looked at what was left, or rather, what was not left of its earthly vessel. Then the wraiths looked at each other resignedly.

The gambler waved his hand angrily—but stopped mid-movement, for he had spotted the nun through his unreachable victim.

Poof!

He dissolved into smoke and puffed out in a new cloud in front of her.

"A game of cards?"

The nun turned to him stiffly. Maybe to check him out, maybe she was just intrigued by something behind him; it was hard to tell without her head. A stream of blood spurted from her throat directly on the Hebrew text on the wall. It was hard to tell if that meant: "Yes" or "No."

The gambler raised his eyebrows questioningly and waved the fan of cards he had materialized in his fingers at her. The nun, like with the skeleton before, tried to rip his head off, and when that failed, she turned away from him and headed for the door. She paused in front of it, perhaps looking it over for a change.

Whatever she was doing, though, it took her about five minutes before she lifted her arm, the sleeve sliding down to her elbow to reveal a spotted, rachitic arm, and touched the door with her fingers.

The fluorescent light on the ceiling flickered, and with it the lights on the electromagnetic lock.

"Checkmate," Basil announced lethargically after the last move.

"Meh," Ruml grimaced. Lately, he was beginning to feel like he was the only chess player in the world who was getting worse with the increasing number of games he played. "You could let me win again sometime."

"Again?"

"Yeah, like that time when . . ." He frowned as he tried to remember. "That time when . . ."

"You were playing with someone else, huh?" suggested Basil. "It wasn't completely stupid, though. You replicated the Crazy Horse perfectly before the end."

"What's that?"

"1988, Millidge versus Kaniecki. It looked like Millidge was done, but then he shifted the knight to stand between his bishop and Kaniecki's queen. Kaniecki threatened him with a rook from above, and Millidge . . . Well, he surprised everybody by taking his knight and jumping with it completely out of this clash."

"No shit." Millidge. That made Ruml feel a little better. "What good is the Crazy Horse for?"

Basil shrugged. "It's useless. Kaniecki comfortably rode that tower all the way to one and checkmated him."

Ruml sighed, stood up, and set about buckling on his belt with a pepper spray, a flashlight, a radio, a crucifix, a bottle of holy water, a garlic mallet, a yew stake, a kukri knife, a revolver loaded with a variation of bullets from silver to filled with powder from the bones of saints, and other equipment necessary to perform the duties of a security guard at the SRS. "You know what?"

"What?"

"I'd better go on my rounds."

He could never tell if Basil was joking or if he actually found episodes like this from the world of chess interesting.

Or useful.

He didn't slam the door behind him, but it was close. He headed back into the maze. Damn the rounds, he just needed to calm down.

He liked Basil, he really did. He almost saw him as an older brother.

An older, autistic brother who was completely oblivious to the fact that he was pushing someone over the edge.

Shaking his head, he bypassed the section simply titled DOLLS, turned right, and stopped in front of the plain metal door leading to the staircase that descended to the *Archives*.

Technically, it was part of his rounds, but he didn't bother to check it very often—and he didn't bother today.

Rheumatism is coming fast and retirement is still far away. Gotta save your knees, right?

Instead, he turned the next corner and was already reaching for the handle of the restroom door, but...

Flick, flick. Flick.

He looked up at the fluorescent light on the ceiling.

Flick. Flick, flick, flick.

The sign next to the nearest room said: DEMONIC TOYS.

Just typical, he thought grimly, and instinctively rested his palm on the grip of his revolver. During his career with the SRS, he had never taken it out of its holster for any reason other than maintenance or to show it to someone. In fact, he was amazed at how all the trouble had eluded him. Not that he was complaining. But subconsciously, he knew his luck would run out one day.

But ninety-nine percent of the time, the flickering lights are the fault of leaking insulation, so it's not going to happen today! he decided, leaning against the door to the restroom.

And he stopped there.

Ninety-nine percent of the time, he would have ignored it. Dealing with leaking protection wasn't a part of the job of a security guard. That's why the SRS employed professionals. The job of the security guards was to parade around and look menacing in case someone got some funny ideas.

Basically, we're better-paid scarecrows.

Except today, maybe because of that mysterious coffin or the hilarious attempt to store it, he had a bad feeling about it. In fact, it was a really bad feeling.

"Shit," he snorted, pulled out his revolver, checked to make sure it was loaded, flipped the hammer over to open fire with frangible bullets if necessary, pulled an electronic key from his breast pocket, and walked over to the entrance of the section that people were entering only when absolutely necessary and, at best, leaving it only without some fingers.

The red light bulb switched to green, the lock clicked, and a pale glow poured through the crack in the door onto his boots. Ruml took a deep breath and hesitantly pushed it with the barrel of his gun.

The hinges creaked, the gap widened, and he was presented with the view of a room not unlike the one Basil had taken Lenora to. It, too, was lined from floor to ceiling with solid crates, only larger in size and decorated with a plethora of protective markings. Perhaps not as much as in the quarantine, but almost.

Ruml knew that behind every crate lid, there was a little homicidal maniac. Plastic soldiers, knitted dolls, wooden figures, building blocks, stuffed animals, flashing robots—and of course the worst.

Possessed furbies.

He shuddered at the thought. And he shuddered a second time when he noticed that the lid of one of the boxes wasn't fully closed. Cautiously, he crept over to it and reached for the flap. But he hesitated a few inches away from it and clenched his hand into a fist.

I swear to God, if there's one of those furry monstrosities inside . . .

A cold drop ran down his temple. He took a deep breath and . . .

Screw it!

He fumbled for the lid, yanked it open and shoved his revolver inside, ready to put a bullet to anything that might try to eat him. But there was nothing lurking on the other side.

"Jeez," he sighed, running the back of his hand over his sweaty forehead.

All right, all right, false alarm. A simple leak, nothing else.

He still had some luck left after all. With a relieved expression, he lowered his revolver, turned around and strode back into the hallway.

Where the skeleton was waiting for him, palm outstretched.

Basil was just refilling his coffee mug when the first shot was fired. Long story short, not much of it ended up in the mug, unlike the kitchen counter, the cupboard, the wall, the ceiling and Basil.

"Damn, what the . . ." Basil dropped the pot, quickly rubbed the remains of his drink into his shirt, and ran out into the hallway, through which the thunder of the second, third, and fourth shots had already carried—and the other two arrived close behind.

Basil started to run, but slowed down at the first intersection. The echoes traveled far through the tunnels, and he had no idea where exactly the butthurt Ruml might have gone.

"Ruml?!" he bellowed. But only silence answered him.

Damn it, which way?

No, not complete silence. A barely audible thud came from somewhere. He jogged down the main corridor to the next intersection, called out to Ruml again, and again got no answer.

At least, no other than an emergency chemical lighting, immune to the presence of supernatural beings, which replaced the standard one with a loud click and flooded the complex with red light. And the nerve-wracking roar that immediately followed, which made Basil's insides clench.

He didn't try to call out a third time. He just ran. This signal was easy to follow.

He turned the corner to the next corridor, and from there to another corridor, and then passed *Dolls* and *Archives*. He knew what it meant.

That the gate to Hell was around the corner.

Just before he rounded it, a siren belatedly drowned out the roar.

It didn't matter, though, because something liquid and sticky tickled under the soles of his work boots as he turned around another corner.

He didn't see any demonic toys. But he saw Ruml. All over the place, like the spilled coffee.

Basil looked into the dead eye of the severed head that stared at him. "Oh shit. Not again."

In the event of a leak of paranormal material, the protocol called for isolation of the entire facility. The shredded deceased took care of that by setting off the alarm. All exits were now blocked by an armored door with innards similar to the one in the quarantine room.

Certain creatures, such as wraiths, could theoretically still leave the facility, but fortunately they seemed to operate locally and couldn't even get out of a simple maze without being led out by their pursued prey.

Whatever had caused Ruml's death and the isolation, however, meant that Basil was stuck with it down here until the SRT team arrived. That gave him at least a few hours to follow his coworker's example.

For as of last year, Stará Paka was administratively under the jurisdiction of Prague, 70 miles away.

And I'd be surprised if they wasted a helicopter on us.

The regulations clearly stated that in the event of a crisis, warehouse employees were obliged to seek safe shelter to await the arrival of the relevant specialists and not to attempt to leave the premises at any cost. If he wants to survive, he must somehow manage on his own.

Okay, step number one: threat assessment.

He took a deep breath of the air that tasted like rust, and with splashing steps, marched through Ruml's entrails to the open door of the Demonic Toys section.

He had to force himself hard to look inside. But all it took was a cursory inspection to know that nothing had gotten out. The only open box had been in that state since last week, when the occult researchers had taken its contents.

He backed out into the hallway and slammed the door behind him. The siren died that instant, as if out of breath, leaving him in a silence broken only by the dripping of Ruml's remains from the ceiling.

Well, this evaluation sucked.

There were thousands of things stored here that could do something similar to a human, and he could hardly take inventory now. On the other hand, everything had gone smoothly until now.

And today, all we've got was that chained coffin.

He needed to make a phone call. Get in touch with someone on the outside and find out what kind of bastard they sent them. Maybe there was a perfectly simple way to deactivate it or hide from it, but he needed more information to figure out a strategy.

Hopefully the line in the office will work.

He took the shortest route, but took barely two steps before something stopped him. At first he thought it was a part of the dripping Ruml ceiling painting, but once he focused on it, it didn't match. It repeated periodically at about three second intervals, and it didn't sound like drops falling into puddles. It sounded more like a water pistol.

Splash, splash. Splash, splash.

Basil pressed himself against the wall and slowly peered around the corner. For the first second, his brain couldn't even put together what he was looking at. But he knew it wasn't a water pistol. Against the red background loomed what looked like the silhouette of an overgrown penguin, with who-knows-what spraying from its head. That struck him as odd.

Paranormal fauna is stored in Turnov ...

But of course it wasn't an overgrown penguin, and Basil recognized it as soon as the thing swung around and then suddenly moved halfway down the corridor at the speed of a rewinding videotape.

"Oh shit," he whispered.

Splash, splash, came the reply, blood gushing from the neck of the headless nun, who moved again and came to a stop right in front of him.

Basil jerked, pushed himself away from the wall, and was about to make a run for it, but by then bluish rachitic arms, topped with broken nails, were reaching for him. He dodged them before they could rip out his throat. He tried to make a turn, but he took a wrong step, the soles of his boots, covered in a sticky stuff, slipped under him, and he fell into a pool of Ruml's blood, reflecting the scene above it like a black mirror.

Ignoring the dull pain that spilled down his side, he rolled onto his stomach and tried to paddle as far as he could on the slippery surface. His palms slipped and his jumpsuit was heavy with blood, but he managed to lift himself up on his forearms on drag himself forward ... right in front of her bluish, rachitic ankles.

"Oh sh—"

He didn't have the time to finish as fingers with broken nails dug into his skull and dragged him across the floor as if they were going to rip his head off. And maybe not just "as if."

Basil screamed, grabbed the cold knuckles and tried to pull them away, but to no avail. The nun shuffled stiffly across the floor, dragging him behind her like a rag. He groped around and tried to grab something, but all he could feel was the floor and the wall. The latter he felt with his nape first, when the nun slammed him against it.

For a moment, his eyes went dark, but not enough to lose consciousness. Before he could banish the blackout, the nun pulled him the other way.

Blindly he grappled around again, this time feeling something metallic in his palm. He picked it up, together with the severed hand still holding onto it. He pried the fingers off in disgust, pointed it above him, and pulled the trigger four times in quick succession.

The revolver clicked emptily four times.

You have to be . . . !

In a desperate attempt to at least put up some sort of defense, he flung it against the nun's chest.

The revolver bounced and hit him on the forehead.

"Gah!"

Even that false attempt was apparently enough to anger the creature, because she twisted his head and sent him sliding like a curling stone across the bloody pool to the remains of Ruml's body.

Basil's first instinct was to move as far away from it as possible, only before he could, he noticed something. Ruml's duty belt. So, defying his primal instinct, he forced himself, pushed off, jump right between the severed legs and what must have been a pelvis, and slipped the belt onto his arm just before the nun reappeared beside him.

This time a skinny hand gripped him below the neck, lifted him with one quick movement, and pinned him against the nearest wall. He was left hanging just above the ground so he couldn't brush against it with the tips of his boots, blood spurting from the nun's neck in his face. In his face, his bulging eyes, and on his tongue, which was being squeezed out of his mouth by the crushing grip as he tried in vain to suck air into his throat.

The other hand shot up, only to have its fingers dig in his shoulder and pull him down. He felt like he was on a rack, and he knew his neck was bound to snap at any second.

He grabbed the first object on his belt that came to his hand and yanked it from its grip. It was a wooden stake.

Ha!

Sure, the headless nun wasn't a vampire, but if there was one thing he'd learned on this job, it was that few monsters weren't brought down by a stake driven deep enough into their chests.

He gripped it tightly, swung, and...

And the stake slipped from his bloody fingers and rattled on the floor.

If he could have done that, he would have uttered a curse word, but since he had trouble even grunting, he didn't utter anything and went back to pulling the rabbits out of the hat. His cervical spine crunched as the nun gave him the biggest stretch of his life. Something round slipped into his palm. He picked it up and...

Garlic? Christ, if there could be anything less useful!

He dropped it and reached desperately for something else. He didn't have the oxygen to continue being picky. He allowed himself to hope that whatever he pulled out would be worth it.

It wasn't. As soon as he felt the glass under his fingertips, he knew he'd made the wrong choice. But he had to risk it; the pressure on his neck had practically smoothed out his wrinkles.

He could barely see over the blood in his face and the spots in front of his eyes. So he had no choice but to blindly swing and pour the vial of holy water down the nun's throat.

So that's exactly what he did.

A spray of blood spurted from her throat in what might have been a rasping cough, and the hand that had been digging under his jaw finally let go.

He landed on his ass right in a viscous puddle and it splashed everywhere. He rubbed his eyes with the inside of his collar and looked around. Surprisingly, he didn't see the nun anywhere.

Interesting.

He doubted he'd be able to get rid of her for long, but he wasn't going to look a gifted horse in the mouth.

He was sure he could find spare ammo on the belt. He looked around to see if he could see the lost weapon anywhere, but he didn't, and he didn't have the time to look for it. He rubbed the back of his neck, pulled himself to his feet with a muffled groan and a totally unmuffled creak in his knees, and limped away.

"I can't tell you the registration number because I don't have the transfer document," Basil repeated patiently into the receiver. "And I don't have the transfer document because your driver didn't give it to me."

"Our couriers always carry the handover document with them," the curtly speaking woman on the other end dismissed his accusation.

"Apparently not *always*," Basil said, holding the bridge of his nose. "Could you just take a look at exactly what you guys sent here this morning?"

There was a brief silence on the line, followed by a loud sigh and pounding on the keyboard. "We didn't send you any headless nuns."

"What about coffins?"

Clack, clack, clack. Like rain drops smashing against a tin roof. "A coffin with a skeleton in it, tied with a chain, yeah, I see it listed. But I can't tell you much about it. Our operatives brought it back from Prague yesterday. The details are in the enclosed documentation."

On the way to the office, he figured the nun wouldn't be the only paranormal roaming the complex freely. After all, if holy water was enough to drive her away, the relic crumbs loaded in Ruml's revolver would have to work too. He might have missed, but that didn't seem likely given the nun's modus operandi.

But a skeleton?

"In the documentation someone forgot to include?" he asked.

"I don't know what to tell you."

"How about what it says?"

"That's classified information, and I don't have access to that."

Basil glanced at his reflection in the glass of the cupboard. He recognized himself only by his build; he couldn't see much more of himself. His curly hair was plastered to his head with blood, still wet blood was drying on his face, his jumpsuit was soaked through like a sponge, and his boots were squeaking just from shifting his weight from one foot to the other. He looked like a used tampon—and felt about the same. He decided to pull a heavier caliber on the helpful lady.

"My colleague is dead, and it's whatever came out of your box that's to blame. I'd hate to end up the same way."

The woman paused again and all that could be heard from the receiver was her breathing.

"I'll see what I can do," she finally uttered uncertainly.

"I wouldn't dare ask more of you," he assured her, and hung up.

A skeleton, he rolled over in his mind. *No, nothing else had really changed since yesterday.*

Could it have gotten out and activated something else in the process?

He remembered the pack of cards stored not two feet from the coffin, and his stomach did another somersault.

On the other hand, he hadn't run into the gambler before, but a nun.

Which isn't much better, but at least it means that if she didn't come out of the coffin, her documentation must be here.

Having computers in the warehouse didn't make sense given the leaks, so the staff got all the relevant information on paper. And all the files were stored...

In the archives.

Just a few steps from where Ruml died. And where he almost died.

He figured he could barricade himself inside the break room. But then he denounced it as stupid.

Maybe if we had some instinct-driven beasts running around who don't understand the concept of handles and rooms.

But the nun was at best a specter or a ghost, quite obviously exhibiting intelligence, and the skeleton, if it was indeed activated as he suspected, would be no different.

He scratched his wet moustache with a thumb and glanced at the sunglasses Lenora had left behind in the storage room. He wondered how difficult it would be for her to hunt down a headless nun.

It would probably be easy for her. She sure as hell wouldn't even get dirty doing it.

But Lenora couldn't help him, and he still didn't know what had nearly torn his head off.

He went back to the table and found the archive key, a flashlight, and the small bottle of rum he'd gotten from Ruml for his birthday out of the drawers, along with a sampler of cigars.

He pocketed the first two items, took a big swig from the third, and headed for the door.

Headless Nun, proclaimed the label on the faded folder. Despite the flashlight he held in his teeth, Basil smiled, pulled it out of the cardboard box, pushed away the dusty bundles on the nearest table, slapped it down, and opened it.

The creeping journey to the archives had been surprisingly smooth, except for a small crisis when the clack of new half-shoes or walking sticks or something like that came to him from somewhere in the red corridors.

The metal door was followed by metal stairs leading one floor down, into the darkness of a large room where no one had bothered to install crisis lighting. The air was dry and full of dust that made his eyes itch and his throat scratch, and most of the room was filled with a shabby system of rolling shelves that could be bolted together to save space using control wheels, and between which, if one needed to get to a particular section, one had to create an aisle using the same process.

While Basil was torturing the poorly lubricated bearings, he nearly bled out of his ears—and at the same time got the impression that he was doomed.

He could imagine that the footsteps of a skeleton, for example, might sound like the clacking of new half-shoes, and he supposed he would soon find out.

But he didn't. He heard nothing at all. Still, he made an aisle just wide enough for him to slide sideways into and possibly pull out one of the boxes on the shelves.

"A wraith," he read on the cataloguing document inside the file. *Of course it had to be a wraith.*

He rubbed his eyes and turned the page.

"Indecent in life...Convicted of seducing a parish priest... Executed in..."

He didn't need to know any of that. He was only interested in two things: whether she manifested beyond what he had experienced, and how to deactivate her.

"She attacks people and rips their heads off, presumably in an attempt to replace her own. Can be temporary neutralized by using symbols of the Catholic faith, but deactivation only occurs when a 'new' head is acquired."

"Thanks for nothing," Basil grumbled, pushed the file away disgruntledly and circled the archive with his flashlight.

Roller chains, gears and steel rails, desks buried under stacks of boxes and stacks of papers. He could only dream of Catholic symbols.

I'll have to stop by in . . .

Crrrrrrrrrrrrrrrr!

A sharp, rattling sound, like an alarm clock going off nearby. It was a good thing he wasn't holding a mug of coffee, because if he had, he would have spilled it again.

He rushed over to one of the desks and exhumed a ringing phone from under a pile of papers. The caller must have been very patient if they let the office line ring long enough for the machine to transfer them here.

"Paka," Basil announced into the receiver.

"Ostrava," the woman he spoke to first answered back, "Are you still alive?"

"I'm doing my best."

"I managed to find some information on the coffin. You won't like it."

"Humor me."

"It's not much. Nothing definite, just that . . ." She paused. "Just that the skeleton is . . ."

She didn't even need to finish the sentence for Basil to know what she was trying to tell him.

She's trying to tell me I'm completely and utterly screwed.

"That it's a wraith," the Ostrava woman added uncertainly.

Basil didn't know how to respond to that—and apparently neither did she, because the next thing that came out was a curt, "I'm sorry. Good luck."

Then she hung up.

Basil stood there with the receiver, from which only a deaf tone was coming, still at his ear, his gaze fixed on the darkness, his brain focused on one thing.

There are two of them.

If he could get to *Relics and Crucifixes*, he would be perfectly safe from the nun and would only have to wait for the SRT team. Only there were two wraiths, he had no idea how one of them worked or if he could protect himself from it, and he didn't have any means to find out?

At least I can choose to have just my head taken off, or all my limbs, he deduced grimly.

Not that he planned to do it, but he had to include it in his list of possibilities as a part of his critical assessment of the situation. Mainly because there weren't more items on it at the moment.

The receiver was still beeping in his ear. Slowly, he returned it to the fork.

In his reverie, he hadn't even noticed that the flashlight he'd been holding in his clenched hand all this time had been flickering, and that for a while now, the regular clacking of what sounded like new half-shoes or walking sticks had been echoing through the archive.

And that it was getting closer.

In a bizarre moment of mute shock, after forcing the strobe-impaired flashlight to point ahead of him, he and the skeleton remained staring at each other like a pigeon at an approaching cat.

It really was a skeleton. A bone skeleton made entirely of bones, somehow holding together, and covered from forehead to toe-joints in a glistening layer of drying blood.

Basil didn't have to ponder for long whose blood it might be. His heart pounded in a way that seemed as if it would burst with every beat, and instinct told him to make a run for it.

Without moving his eyes, he shifted his focus from the skeleton to the door behind his back. A door that, like the wraith, loomed out of absolute darkness in flashes of white light, only to disappear into it again in a split second.

Basil had no idea if the skeleton was intelligent, but if it could, he couldn't get past the skeleton to the door.

He focused back on it. Its eye sockets returned his gaze with a featureless emptiness, yet there seemed to be something conscious staring back at him from it. Perhaps the emptiness itself.

What could possibly work on a skeleton? Rheumatism?

Ruml had saved his life earlier with the nun, despite his unusual condition. But there was no corpse lying here, purely by chance equipped with the exact thing he'd need to cripple a skeleton. He noticed, however, that something gleamed on the table top. A pair of pointy office scissors.

That would have to do.

He checked to see if the wraith was about to do anything, licked his lips and took a deep breath—and lunged for them.

The skeleton gritted its teeth and lunged after him.

Fragmented by the flickering light, it looked jerky, like a sequence of images, many of which had been lost. Each pose revealed by a flash seemed to take too long, but at the same time it appeared a little closer each time. Suddenly, it was not standing three steps from the table, but right next to it, reaching for Basil's hand.

The warehouse clerk jumped in front of it, swung his scissors and . . .

And he stopped.

The skeleton didn't continue. It didn't lunge at him, didn't try to grab him and paint the room with him. It just stood there, palm up, as if waiting for Basil to put something in it.

"What, what do you want? A coin for the ferryman?"

The skeleton gritted its teeth. Maybe it signified laughter, maybe disapproval, you couldn't quite tell from its expression. But you could read it in its gesture as it turned its palm down, its outstretched fingers curling into five sharp hooks with a wince, and they dug into the table in a flash of light.

Crack!

Splinters shot from the tabletop—and only with that did the skeleton lunge at Basil for real. But the warehouse clerk did not hesitate. As the wraith lurched up, he took advantage of the change in its center of gravity, kicked in the table with his foot, and flipped it over.

Bones rattled on the floor and were covered by stacks of flyers. Basil dropped the scissors, walked over to the shelves and slid back into the space he had created between them.

In the flickering light, he kept himself oriented mostly by touch, and it showed. He bumped his forehead on the corner of the first slightly sagging box, which nearly sent him crashing on the floor. But he caught the shelf in time. If he collapsed here, he probably wouldn't get up again.

Behind him came the sound of wood breaking and bones clacking.

Two more steps, and on the third he was thrown backwards as if a parachute opened. But there was no parachute on his back.

"Damn...!" he huffed.

In the first second, panic flashed through him as he thought the skeleton had got him, but no, his overall just got caught on something. He reached blindly behind his back and...

Dun, dun!

He cocked his head rather than turning it, and his breath hitched again.

The skeleton, unencumbered by such useless things as tissue, muscle, or fat pads, pushed itself headfirst in the passageway and dove after him like a spider after prey trapped in a web. It tore things off the shelves as it did so, each crash of bone against metal eliciting new and new rumbles.

Basil threw himself forward with all his weight, and a bolt, a nail, a sharp edge, or whatever was holding him, took its toll in the form of a piece of torn overall with a loud, "*Ruuup!*" and let him go. He staggered to the end of the shelves, where he was greeted by an even narrower gap between them and the wall.

For Christ's sake.

He wasn't sure he could fit in it, but he didn't have many other options. He blew all the air from his lungs, pulled in his stomach, and pushed into it like a frog under a rock... and immediately regretted it.

As well-preserved as he looked for his age, thanks to his work, the fact remained that his tree-frog days were long behind him and he was slowly becoming an old man. In other words, a fat toad.

Moving through the gap squeezed the last of any oxygen out of him, and whether it was movement at all was up for debate. He felt crammed in there like a cork. But the rapidly approaching rumble gave him the motivation to do something about it.

He reached out, hooked his hand on the edge of the adjacent shelf and pulled.

And nothing happened.

Dun! Dun! Dun!

He pulled again, more strongly. As hard as he could.

He could feel the metal edge cutting through his fingertips, but still it didn't move a millimeter.

Dun! Dun!

"Come on!" he grunted.

A skeleton emerged from around the corner.

Dun!

"Come on!" Basil grunted again, gave one last tug, and . . .

The pressure eased, just as the wraith attacked.

Sharp phalanges flashed just past his face, but missed. Instead, smooth as razor blades, they cut through the overalls and the skin on his arm, and slammed into the wall. The plaster exploded in a white cloud.

Basil collapsed on the floor with a scream. Despite the pain, however, he immediately pulled himself up and slid into the next aisle, a few inches wider, allowing him to move more freely in it. Not by much, but enough that he was able to stand. Thank goodness, because the skeleton wasn't stuck in the narrow gap.

The warehouse clerk grabbed the nearest box and threw it under its feet. The skeleton stepped over it, and as it shifted its weight on the trapped leg, it slid underneath it like it'd stepped on soap.

Crash!

Basil knocked two or three more to the floor and slid out of the space between the shelves. The thought of escape flashed through his mind, but he dismissed it.

It's too fast. I have to paralyze it first. At least for a little while.

The solution offered itself.

He shoved the flashlight between his teeth, took the steering wheel on the side of the nearest rack with both hands, and swung it toward the aisle. The gears groaned and the space he had just emerged from began to shrink. Only it was about as fast as wading through snow.

In other words, it didn't go very well.

The skeleton managed to shake the box off and stand up. But it immediately stepped into another one and slipped again. This time it didn't try to get up. It bent its elbows and started crawling out on all fours over the rest of the obstacles behind Basil. The transformation into a monstrous, overgrown and unnaturally moving spider was complete.

Basil was turning the steering wheel as hard as he could. His arms were burning and a saw of pain was cutting into his left one. He gritted his teeth and kept turning.

He could feel his wounds opening up more. He could feel blood trickling down his arm and sweat running down his back. *A dun dun*

dun sounded through the aisle, approaching too fast! And he knew he didn't stand a chance. He wouldn't make it. That the skeleton would finally get close enough to him to do to him what it'd done to Ruml, and . . .

Dunvrrrrrzskriiiiiiip!

And nothing.

"Shit," he hissed in relief. He gave one last try, but the rack didn't budge. He wouldn't fit through that gap and it looked like the skeleton wouldn't make it either.

At least not right away.

There was a rustling and creaking sound as it wriggled in there, but Basil possessed enough intelligence not to attempt to peer inside. He just turned around and . . .

A bony hand shot out of the gap and fumbled for him.

He didn't manage to jump away this time. Fiery pain shot through his forearm as sharp fingers dug into it like predatory claws.

"Aaaah!" he wailed, dropping to one knee. The flashlight fell out of his mouth and rolled aside. In the flickering light, something glittered on the floor.

He braced his foot on the shelf and tried to wriggle out of the skeleton's grip, but it didn't let him. It was as if a pair of pneumatic pliers were about to snap his arm off.

And that's exactly what it's planning! First this arm, then the other, then everything else!

He shot a glance around to see if he could find anything that might help, but no. Just that shiny thing.

Screw it!

He reached for it, the metal cold on his bleeding fingers.

The scissors!

The realization put a half-crazed smile on his blood-covered face. He picked them up, thrust them right between the wraith's wrist bones, and gave them a good twist. The pneumatic pincers loosened as if he had cut invisible tendons. The bony fingers opened and the button they had ripped from Basil's sleeve clinked on the floor.

Basil rolled aside, picked up the flashlight, and pulled himself to his feet with the aid of the table.

The skeleton groped on the floor, the blades sticking out from under his palm, carving deep grooves in it with an agonizing screech.

It was only when Basil kicked the button between the shelves that the hand disappeared, and peace once again reigned in the archive.

The regulations may have made it clear how to behave in this situation, but this was the second time today that death had reached for Basil, and he wasn't going to wait to see if it would happen a third time.

So screw it. Time to get out.

All that was left was to figure out how to do it.

The SRS functioned like all state institutions—through skillful psychological bullying, which not only distracted from the steadily deteriorating work conditions, but also drove the employees to such a disturbed state of mind that they did not believe they could be better off elsewhere.

That, and through having enough duct tape.

The fact that the word "state" appeared in the institution's name, however, meant that it had to abide by certain rules. Among them, that there must be a freely accessible first aid kit in the workplace and all employees must be properly trained on how to use it.

In other words, Basil reasoned, *to avoid the state institution being held legally liable, only workers with an OHS certificate are allowed to have their heads ripped off.*

At the moment, though, he was mainly interested in the first aid kit.

It was hanging just outside the door to the restroom, and he didn't even bother to rummage through it. He plucked it off the tiled wall and dumped its contents in the sink. Needles of pain ran through his body with every movement, but it warmed his heart to know that he was finally getting a chance to capitalize on the hours and hours of first aid classes he had to take every year. That he knew exactly what to do. That he could treat a potentially life-threatening injury like an expert.

And that's exactly what he did—he unscrewed the cap from a bottle of antiseptic, poured it directly into his wounds, making the pain in his cut fingers and mangled arm much more excruciating, and covered it all with band-aids.

Now for the escape, he thought, as soon as he stopped gritting his teeth, cleaned his hands and face and tied the sleeves of his half-undressed jumpsuit around his waist.

The elevator is without power, but there is a ladder to climb up the shaft. But how to get into the cabin?

When the alarm started, access was blocked by a door inlaid with ceramic plates bearing regularly updated protective verses and bathed in the tears of the Archbishop of Prague, on which a giant eye drawn in virgin blood fixed its potentially scorching gaze on newcomers. The door only opened when the alarm went off, and that could only be done from the outside. The stairs were secured by a similar barrier even at the top; he would certainly not get through those, and the only other alternative was to dig his way out.

He leaned against the basin and stared at the red swirl rotating above the drain.

Layered armor . . .

He could hardly open something like that with a crowbar. He'd need a proper welder, or maybe thermite. Something that could cut or burn through.

Something that would blow the door to the moon.

In sudden realization, he looked up at the mirror and stared in his own eyes.

"Yeah," he muttered between the thoughts that flew through his head, "that might work."

A triumphant grin played on his lips as he did so—but it didn't last long after he headed back into the dark corridors.

The cursed Vietnamese sky rocket, in the form of a shiny, though now red rather than golden dragon, was still in the same place: in a box in a room opposite of the break room, where the warehouse workers put material that was not in acute danger of coming to life and killing everyone, and which was therefore in no hurry to be processed.

The paradox of the situation was that if he had rushed to process it, he could have picked it up in one of the unlocked cells on the way and would never have been in the situation that awaited him.

Or maybe I would be, but at least I would have been holding the most powerful flamethrower in history.

But he was holding nothing but a flashlight. A flashlight that thankfully managed to start blinking again before he walked into the arms of a hunched guy in crumpled clothes.

Flick, flick, flick.

Promptly, he turned it off, quietly reaching the corner and peering cautiously in the main tunnel.

His stomach twisted and the world rocked with him like a boat on the ocean.

The dead gambler walked back and forth in front of the elevator, one hand smoothing his mustache, the other shuffling his cards and repeating neurotically, "A game of cards? Shall we have a game of cards? What? What do you say? A game of cards?" There was an occasional *poof* as he disappeared in a puff of black smoke, only to materialize again a few steps away.

Basil stepped back so the wraith couldn't see him and ran a palm over his face.

Of course, this one must be here too. Because nothing can be easy around here.

He might have cursed, but he felt like a deflated balloon. With the nun and the skeleton, he used all his luck, but the gambler?

Luck had never saved anyone from him.

As soon as the gambler notices Basil, he'll end up just like Ruml, if not worse.

With a quiet sigh, he slumped in a squat and rubbed the bridge of his nose.

Ruml, his favorite colleague, who had been buying him his favorite brand of rum and cigars for his birthday.

And to whom I always gave the pickle coffee the vendor recommended because I never thought to pay attention to what type he was actually drinking.

What did he really know about him?

That he suffered from a fear that he would one day perish under an avalanche of possessed furbies.

He rubbed his eyes.

At least that prediction hadn't come true. Though it's hard to say if he would have appreciated it. Either way, he'd be eager to kick the ass of that idiot who brought that damn coffin without papers.

Basil could still do that for him.

All right then.

He shook his head, took a deep breath, pulled himself to his feet, and looked out toward the elevator again.

"A game of cards! A game of caaaaards!" the gambler moaned. *Poof, poof, poof!*

But that wasn't all. He was already pulling back when the familiar *splash, splash, splash, splash* was added to the mix, and the nun shuffled in the red light from the darkness behind the lift.

Basil clenched his jaw. In the end it didn't matter, though; the original plan flew out the window. Maybe if he could lure them somewhere. Use the way they operated against them . . . It would have to work long enough for him to get to the surface, though. He didn't like the idea of a wraith puffing into the elevator.

But that would require a trap—and more importantly, bait. Or three, rather, since each wraith was interested in something different, and while there were only two currently in his way, he wasn't going to risk them being replaced by the skeleton after a successful diversion.

Fortunately, Ruml could help him with that.

The problem with the gambler was that the SRS staff had long been unable to pry any information about his origins from folklorists, beyond the legend of a churchman from St. Peter's church with a passion for mariasch who was deprived of all his opponents by the plague. One evening, he supposedly have asked in the morgue if the dead would play with him, and they got up and granted his wish—or at least carried it out before they all fell to the ground at midnight. Probably including the gambler, who had haunted that place from then on until the Prague staff sent him to Stará Paka.

Of course, the story lacked any grounding in reality, and no dead churchman found in the cellar of the church in question was mentioned in any relevant historical documents. In this, the gambler was no different from other wraiths. Unlike them, however, it was impossible to find a way to turn his behavior against him. His creation did not involve trading a soul to Hell, a connection to any religion, or even occult rituals, and although he was dead, he was not technically speaking, undead.

While the nun's mechanics were documented quite clearly, the only thing that could be said for sure about the gambler was that he liked cards and that only a few people survived his offer to play, whether accepted or declined. Which, at the same time, was more than Basil had been able to find out about the skeleton.

He realized that what he was about to do was risky, perhaps even ill-advised or downright foolish.

But still better than doing nothing.

It's been almost two hours since the alarm went off. Despite emergency regulations, the SRT team was in no hurry, and the chances of him being accidentally cut off by one of the paranormals again were steadily increasing. So, foolishly or not, as Basil made his way, heart pounding and a cardboard box in hand, through the middle of the hallway directly to the gambler, who had once again become a lonely guardian of the elevator while Basil had been making certain arrangements, he only had one thought:

That he finally understood what Millidge had been up to.

If he'd fooled Kaniecki enough, he could have ended the game within two moves.

And while it didn't quite work, none of the wraiths were chess grandmasters, so Basil might have been able to pull it off.

"A game of cards, a game of caaaards!" the gambler was shouting, shifting back and forth briskly, scratching his head with a clenched fist as he did so. "Hhhh, a game of cards!"

Maybe he's trapped in a loop and will soon deactivate without an outside prompt, Basil thought. Of course, by then the dead gambler had already noticed him and didn't bother with puffing over this time.

"Shall we play a game?" he grunted right in Basil's face while waving a deck of cards. "What? What do you say? Just one game!"

In the red light, he looked like he'd bathed in blood too, and the smell of carrion wafted from his mouth, equipped with shark-pointed teeth instead of the standard ones, overpowering even the acrid smoke.

Basil's insides protested. Their owner swallowed hard.

"Come on, man!" The gambler cut a smile worthy of a less than honest insurance man. "What do you say?"

What does he say? He'd rather say nothing.

But since that's not a good response either, I guess I'll have to say something after all. So he put the box on the floor, took a deep breath, cleared his throat, and...

"Screw you," he said—and with that, he fumbled for the deck, snatched it out of the surprised wraith's hand, and ran off with it.

He really must have surprised him, at least as far as he could tell from the fact that almost three seconds had passed before he could hear an angry "Hhhhhh!" behind him, followed by a machine-gun *poof poof poof*.

Basil didn't look back. He ran like the sky was falling on him, the floor was caving in beneath him, and his lungs were about to burst. He ran, seeing every cigar he had ever smoked before his eyes.

At the third intersection, he darted to the left, into the next corridor, which was no different from any of the others. Except that there was a minitruck waiting for him with a doorless cab and a spinning orange beacon. The beacon started to go off in the presence of a wraith, but the diesel engine kept purring.

Basil jumped behind the wheel, stepped on the accelerator and sped into the depths of the warehouse at a deadly speed of fifteen miles per hour.

Crazy horse, bitch!

Poof, poof! Poof, poof, poof! Poof!
Screech!

The vehicle careened out of the turn so hard that it was a miracle it didn't flip over. Basil clutched the steering wheel as momentum tried to throw him out of the cab. The minitruck shuddered beneath him as if it was about to crumble. The beacon and the halogens flashed frenetically, yet he didn't let it slow down. In the rearview mirror, he could clearly see the red phantom approaching and receding again— and receding only as long as he kept the throttle to the floor. Fortunately, he continued down a long straight corridor.

If he could, he would have jammed the pedal even lower, maybe through the floor. But he couldn't, so he had no choice but to squint his eyes and hope for the best.

But still, better to get a head start than ...

He didn't finish the thought, because just then the room he needed to hit appeared in front of him. The door secured by wedges was wide open, but the passage was just wide enough for the tractor to fit through.

Basil didn't dare slow down. He either gets through, or he won't have to worry about the wraiths anymore.

He gritted his teeth, gripped the steering wheel tighter, and ... drove through.

The storage room marked *Miscellaneous* was the largest storage space in the complex. It covered nearly half a square mile and its innards more than anything else resembled a game of jenga out of control. Crates of all materials and sizes were stacked to the ceiling on massive shelves. Side by side, behind each other, stacked neatly on pallets and sticking over the edge, some perfectly stable, others held in place only by an absolute abuse of the laws of physics. Exactly how many crates there were would probably be impossible to trace even in the archive, and each box held paranormal material inactive long enough to be labeled safe.

Basil jerked the steering to the left to avoid hitting a support column, and tried to straighten it again. The tires squealed, leaving a wavy trail behind them as the front and the rear of the vehicle swayed side to side, but the minitruck keep going. Right up to the pyramid of boxes blocking most of the path in the middle of the room. He stomped on the brakes right in front of them. Thanks to the preparations he made in advance, he knew they were empty. But the momentum tossed him mercilessly on the steering wheel anyway, the back of the car skidding as if it was on ice, turning him sideways and...

Eeeeeecrrrrh!

The smell of burnt rubber, the dull ache in his ribs, the jerk as if someone wanted to knock every bone out of him. He collapsed in the seat, his thinning curls caressing the strut supporting the shelves just inches from his fragile skull.

His heart pounded, his muscles quivered, and his thoughts mulled over each other in his head, but the purpose of his visit here shone like a neon sign in the dark night above all that mess. And even if it didn't, his reminder was still in his hand.

He slid out of his seat like an earthworm and collapsed to the floor, but immediately braced himself against the fender, pulled up on his feet, and staggered over the remains of the pyramid.

He wasn't as fast as he would have liked. The sides of his chest throbbed and he couldn't take a full breath without feeling pressure somewhere inside, but he didn't stop. Though he couldn't hear the gambler, he knew he was on his way. Good thing he was only a few steps away from his destination.

Once he reached the folding table he'd set up with three chairs before the chase started, he opened the deck of cards with trembling fingers and quickly dealt for a three-player mariasch.

Before leaving again through the opposite exit, he sacrificed two more seconds for one last thing. "Sorry, buddy," he said to Ruml's head, which lay on the coffee table next to a pile of plastic buttons.

✧ ✧ ✧

When the gambler appeared in the storage area just a short while later, accompanied by proper sound effects, the minitruck was dying, and the wraith's presence didn't help. The halogens flickered, a swarm of sparks erupted and went out, the engine breathed its last breath and the space was swallowed up by blackness and silence.

The gambler looked around, but did not see the bag of meat that had robbed him of his cards. He felt, however, that at least the tool of his trade was not far away.

Poof, poof!

The aisle stretching between the rows of shelves was empty, but roughly in the middle...

Poof, poof!

As soon as he saw what was laid out on the table, an expression of pure malice spread into a cruel smile. Ignoring the head, watching him with its one remaining eye—a trickle of blood, oily and black as ink, oozing from the cracks of its torn off lower jaw—he picked up the empty box and reached for the cards as well, but just before he could scoop them up, the wail of hinges rang through the room. He turned his head sharply in that direction.

Nothing happened for a few moments. Then the headless nun emerged from the shadows. The gambler grinned, reached for his cards again, and this time was disturbed by a sound from the other side.

Clack, clack, clack.

The skeleton didn't take its time with its arrival and went straight to investigate the table. The nun followed it, and soon they were all gathered around it, sizing each other up for some time. Then the skeleton held out its hand, from which the knife was still sticking out, and raked the buttons in a not entirely controlled movement.

The gambler, who still hadn't picked up his cards, straightened up, tapped the ones lying in front of him with his forefinger and grunted, "Bet."

The skeleton ignored him, scooped a few in its palm and raised them to its eye sockets. Or at least it tried to, only for the gambler to come over and knock them out of its hand.

"A bet, I say!" he snapped, picking up the cards prepared beside the pile of buttons and shoving them between the bones of the skeleton's fingers instead.

The skeleton let them fall to the floor and gritted its teeth, but by then the nun, touching the squinting head with her rachitic fingers, had already attracted the gambler's attention.

The gambler's left hand flickered like an attacking snake, nails digging in her forearm. She tried to pull away from him, but he wouldn't let her. Her upper body twisted menacingly in his direction and a stream of blood spurted from her throat.

Splash.

The skeleton reached for the buttons again, its forearm grabbed the gambler's right hand again. "First, a game."

The coffin's occupant didn't seem to agree though, because its arm jerked with such force that it pulled close the gambler, who took the nun with him, who, like a tube of tomato paste squeezed too quickly, spilled blood all over everyone.

And then it went fast.

The nun wrapped her fingers around the gambler's neck, the skeleton bit his face, and the three of them collapsed in a heap on the table.

The flimsy piece of furniture broke. Cards, buttons and Ruml's head flew around and the fighting wraiths fell to the ground.

Just as he landed, an open door entered the gambler's view. The last thing he saw before he lost his view again was a red-lit silhouette, the one he had followed here earlier, retreating down the corridor.

Basil ached with every step. Even his every breath hurt. But he knew he couldn't slow down—and that if he got out of here, he'd have to stuff something green down his throat every now and then, because by the time he reached the elevator, he was nearly hyperventilating.

But he got there and nothing came up to paint the hallway with his guts, which made him conclude that his plan had worked. He allowed himself three or four breaths, and after that he kicked the box, which rattled disapprovingly in response, closer to the armored door and limped into the office, where he equipped himself with work gloves and Lenora's sunglasses, and . . .

He sighed.

The chessboard was still spread out on the desk.

Basil had never considered himself an overly sentimental person. Things just were, or they weren't. People came and went. But Ruml somehow managed to find a loophole even in this.

"Ruml, dude," he sighed, but decided to leave the internal struggle for another day, preferring instead to pick up the chessboard straight away, gather the pieces into it and stuff it in the back pocket of his overalls.

The cursed sky rocket was waiting for him. He pulled it out from under a pile of other objects and examined it. Up close like this, it looked perfectly ordinary. More than that, it looked cheap. The dragon's mouth was made of a not very detailed plastic casting and the golden body was covered by glossy paper. It measured over two feet in length and maybe five inches in diameter, but it weighed no more than two pounds.

In short, there was nothing to distinguish it from the ordinary pyrotechnics one could buy at any market.

Except, of course, that it burned its marketplace with such heat that in the end you couldn't tell human remains from melted sneakers.

He grinned.

I never said it was a good plan.

He returned to the corridor, took up a position about five meters from the armored door, and put on Lenora's sunglasses. The already low visibility turned to near absolute darkness, but he didn't expect it to last long. He pointed the dragon's mouth directly in front of him and struck a match.

The incendiary cord, which he could have sworn hadn't hung from the sky rocket a minute ago, sputtered like an angry cat and vanished with a hiss. A streak of smoke rolled out of the hole left by it and pinched his nose. And then ... nothing.

Basil shuffled his feet.

"What the hell?" he muttered, shaking the sky rocket, but it didn't seem to have any effect. He grunted in frustration, moved his glasses to his forehead, and ...

And it turned out that maybe something was happening after all, because suddenly, *everything* was happening.

The dragon started shaking in Basil's hands so hard he nearly dropped it, its mouth glowing green and shooting out not only equally colored flames, but most of all an irregular sphere, green around the edges, completely white inside, hot as a small sun, leaving a rippling trail in the air behind it, whizzing by at the speed of a speeding car.

In a blinding flash, it splashed across the top of the door. Basil was enveloped in a heat wave that baked his mucous membranes, cooked his lungs, and peeled off his skin—or at least that's how it felt. It heated the alloy in the affected area to the point that it began to melt.

Basil bared his teeth in a triumphant smile and pointed the sky rocket lower.

Whoosh!

The moisture from his gums evaporated and the sweat that was running down his face never reached his chin, but another ball splattered just where he needed it. And a third one, too. And a fourth one right next to it.

The metal boiled, hissed, bubbled like gas escaping from a swamp, and dropped to the floor. The tunnel was filled with stifling, radiant heat and the stench of burning. Basil's head throbbed, his eyes burned, and the world rippled before him, but he didn't let up. Unless he needed to adjust his course of fire, he didn't move, just watched the magical fire burn through. The glowing depression became a fist-sized hole, and then it grew into a somewhat narrow but large enough hole for a man to squeeze through.

Basil waited for the sky rocket to spit out the thirteenth, usually last, projectile. The edges of the hole in the armor glowed orange and smoke rose from the dragon's mouth.

"I suppose that would do," he stated, his vocal cords rubbing together like brake pads as he spoke. He took off the sunglasses, staggered slightly unsteadily to the storage room, stuck the sky rocket where he'd taken it from earlier, and made his way to the elevator.

But he had barely taken two steps when something stopped him.

Something he hoped he had managed to escape.

"What about our game of cards?"

"Last chance," the gambler warned him, standing a few feet away, almost exactly in the same place where Basil had robbed him of his deck of cards.

The warehouse clerk sighed in resignation, lowering his shoulders. He really hoped the diversion would work and it wouldn't come to this. A chess player, however, has to think a few moves ahead to be able to react just in case things don't go according to plan—and that's exactly what he had done with the purring box.

He didn't want to do it. No one deserved this, in his opinion.

Not even a killer wraith.

But the gambler gave him no choice. He couldn't bring him to the surface.

They'd tried nearly everything to eliminate him: silver bullets, explosives, showers of holy water, ancient rituals, exorcism ... but not something as cruel as being swallowed up by an avalanche of possessed furbies.

Which was exactly what came out of the box after Basil had knocked it over with his foot.

About ten multicolored furry owl-bat hybrids, whose bodies were often chosen by the dark forces as their Earth suits because they weren't so different from their own, rolled across the floor with a panicked *"Boo, boo!"* But soon they were using their three-toed feet to lift themselves up.

The gambler watched them curiously.

The mechanical eyes, which certainly did not have any light bulbs from the factory, yet shone like searchlights, returned his gaze.

"Ya, ta, ra, ta, ra, ta!" the furbies proclaimed in unison, pricked up their ears and ran forward.

The wraith grinned and turned to Basil. That was a mistake. For as soon as he opened his mouth, the first of the little demons leapt right at him. He tried to shake them off of himself, but the sharp beaks held firm, slicing through clothes and skin.

Poof, poof!

The gambler disappeared and reappeared a few feet away—to his and Basil's surprise, still surrounded by the attacking toys.

"La, la, la, la, la," the ones still marching on the ground started, and scattered after him.

The gambler backed up in front of them, still trying to get rid of the ones that had already mounted him. He spun on the spot, pounding on them, trying to tear them away, even throwing himself against the wall to crush them, but to no avail. And others were coming.

Basil didn't wait for what would follow. He'd seen plenty of unpleasant things today, but he didn't need a mental picture of this one.

Careful not to touch the hot metal, he crawled through, lifted the door in the cabin ceiling, grabbed the edges, and pulled himself up the shaft.

In the entire history of the universe, there was nothing more pleasant than the cool air that enveloped him. Unfortunately, he couldn't stop to savor it. Too many people died because they stopped trying just before the end, and he wasn't about to become one of them.

The rungs of the ladder clinked under his heavy boots as Basil started to climb.

"*Pam pam, brm brm brm!*" echoed behind him, accompanied by the worst scream he'd ever heard.

The problem with the Vietnamese sky rocket was that it was cursed. And that its fire sequence might usually end with the thirteenth projectile, but it wasn't 100% reliable.

So the explosion, followed by a green flash that lit up the shaft, didn't surprise Basil much. But he sped up anyway, just in case.

Except for his injured arm and the throbbing pain in his ribs, it went surprisingly well. No one chased him, he climbed steadily, and soon he had to agree with Ruml.

Even this is faster than that stupid lift.

If only he'd known how much faster it was going to be.

He was almost at the top when a second, bigger explosion came and shook the ladder. And not just that. The whole complex had shaken. His bleeding left hand slipped off the rung. His right hand held on, but as his own weight swung him around, he saw what was happening below him.

"Oh shit!"

The shaft was engulfed in flames. Green waves spilling over each other, vivid, wild, expanding, glowing like high-temperature plasma, and climbing dangerously fast behind him.

With a groan, he pulled back and tried to squeeze the last of his strength from his aching body and turn it into the best performance anyone had ever given in short-distance ladder climbing.

There were barely ten rungs left. The flames began to melt his soles.

Five rungs.

Three.

Last one.

No sooner had he rolled over the edge and curled into a ball than a column of unnaturally colored fire shot out of the shaft and burned through the ceiling and into the first floor.

And from there, probably higher.

✦ ✦ ✦

The firefighters were late—but still not as late as the SRT team, which still hadn't arrived. Basil sat on the curb by the gatehouse and watched the warehouse burn. The fire was, of course, green. He assumed he was going to get yelled at for both; he just didn't know what would have pissed them more.

On the other hand, if some people did their jobs properly, none of this would have happened, so they can kiss my ass.

He spat into the grass, poured the rest of the tea from Ruml's thermos in himself, and fished around in his overalls. The cigars had taken their toll during the previous escapades, but he found the aluminum case hiding one of the cigars his friend had given him a few months back.

He smiled reluctantly, freed it from its plastic wrapping and lit it. Dry tobacco aroma filled his mouth.

"Don't you worry," he muttered as the smoke came out, "I'll find that guy, even if I have to go all the way to Ostrava for it."

I'll probably have plenty of free time now anyway.

He wondered what he could do in that case. Maybe find a new hobby?

Or a girlfriend.

As if on cue, an engine roared from the driveway, and a foreign car he hadn't seen in nearly three hours—as well as the person who would be getting out of it—came to a screeching halt in front of the barrier. At least, that's what he thought, until the driver got close enough for him to make out her features under the bloody paint.

"You're not Lenora," he stated.

"I'm not," the person said, sitting on the curb beside him. "I'm Jolana." T-shirt, jeans, a lithe figure. Could have been thirty at most, more likely less; he couldn't tell through the red crust.

"Basil," he introduced himself. "Rough day?"

She grinned and nodded her chin toward the building, which was slowly beginning to collapse in on itself. "Compared to yours, probably not so much."

Well, he'd managed to set the bar pretty high on that one.

"Who did this to you?" he asked.

"A domovoy, a falling ceiling, Lenora exploding," Jolana calculated on her fingers. "In that exact order. And you?"

"Wraiths."

"Really?" she opened her eyes wide. "As in plural?"

"Yeah. A dead gambler, a headless nun, and a button-collecting skeleton. The order doesn't matter."

"Credit where credit's due," she said approvingly. Then she paused. "Buttons?"

Basil shrugged. "At least, that's what it looked like to me. It kept reaching out to me like it wanted something, and it ripped one off."

Jolana frowned. "That almost sounds like the begging skeleton from Karolinum. Although that one pulls money off people."

Basil took a thoughtful drag from his cigar.

Yeah, that made a lot more sense.

"Prague people," he snorted.

Jolana fumbled in her pocket, and when she pulled out her hand, she was holding an alder branch. "I brought this. Lenora came back with it from you instead of feathers. I don't know what it's for, but she devoted her last words to it. I suppose it's important."

Basil shrugged. "She wanted something against the chorts. That usually works on them."

"Not so much against falling pianos."

"Yeah, as you would expect."

Jolana shook her head and scrambled to her feet. "You're the closest place. I thought I could report what happened in Jilemnice here, that maybe you'd take over, but . . ." She gestured eloquently to the flames shooting from the roof. "But I'd like to hear that wraith story sometime."

He watched her walk back to the car, and was surprised that he wanted her to stay. That for once he'd appreciate the company, even if it was in the form of a complete stranger and just until someone from the SRS finally comes to scold him.

"Wait," he shouted after her before he could stop himself.

"Huh?"

He pulled a checkered box from his pocket and waved it in the air.

"Do you by chance play chess?"

MARTIN PAYTOK (* 1993)

Some people you just like at first sight. Unfortunately, Martin is not one of them. As a joker with a very specific type of black humor and a horror fan, he needs to be given some time as an author to have a chance to get under your skin. And if he gets there, we can guarantee you won't forget him.

He spent a number of years writing about games and movies for *inGamer*, *CDR*, *Bloody-Disgusting*, *XB-1* magazine's website, and magazines *SCORE* and *Pevnost*. Meanwhile, his love of all things decadent bears clear influences and fascinations with Donald E. Westlake, Garth Ennis, and the whole Kulhánek action school. This is also evident in his first printed story, "The Best Enemy" in anthology *Fantastic 55* (*Fantastická 55*, Hydra, 2013). This was followed by a few other delicate pieces in collections like *One Step Before Hell* (*O krok před peklem*, 2018) from the world of Hammer of Wizards; *God of the Black Forest* (*Bůh Černého lesa*, Gorgona Books, 2018); and *Beauties and Aliens* (*Krásky a vetřelci*, Epocha, 2021). The author has not neglected genre magazines, where he has shone with his short stories like "Hard Night" (*Pevnost*, 9/2019) and "Professionals" (*Pevnost*, 9/2020). In both cases, these were heavyweight pieces with horror motifs and dark jokes.

Just a year later, he added his first novel, *Curses for Everyone* (*Prokletí pro všechny*, Epocha, 2021), a noir detective story with several fantastical themes, including a serial killer with a bag full of meat cleavers, a talking puppet, and a strange artifact. And it was a scene of one closed door and a few knocks from this book that catapulted him into the *MHF* ranks.

Golden Ferns
Oskar Fuchs

The unit moved forward as fast as the terrain allowed. According to coordinates from a drone, contact with the subjects should be made soon. The *Międzylesie* team tactically split into five-member groups with the intention of attacking simultaneously from multiple sides and catching the designated targets in crossfire. They acted quietly, only gesturing to each other for communication. One last time, out of habit, they checked the magazines of their automatic weapons and set off.

The third group was led by Jacek Klackowitcz. His men were able to work together exemplarily well; the result of years of hard training could be recognized at a glance even by a complete layman. They moved quickly and confidently among the ancient spruces, covering each other and making excellent use of the terrain. Klackowitcz moved to the front position of the triangle formation, raised his hand and clenched his fingers into a fist. He leaned his shoulder against the trunk of a massive spruce tree to keep from staggering and stared at the scene before him, unable to speak, paralyzed by its sheer brutality.

Corpses of his fellow Hunters lay in an unnatural position on the reddened pine needles, limbs either twisted out of joint or even severed. The contents of their abdominal cavities were scattered about, and their shattered rib cages testified to the incredible destructive power of their attackers. The extent of the injuries was consistent with an anti-personnel mine or artillery attack, but that was out of the question here. The surrounding forest was completely silent; they had not heard a single shot or scream.

Then the wind blew against the branches and shook them furiously. Jacek decided not to break radio silence for now. He attached a thermal imaging clip-on to the optics of his weapon and used it to scan the area. The bodies of the killed Hunters were still warm; they must have died a short time ago. Nothing. He looked around again, only to suddenly freeze, cold sweat beginning to trickle down his back. Very slowly, he raised his head and looked above him, where the rapidly darkening evening sky was visible through the branches of the spruce.

They were there. He didn't count them, but there were at least a dozen. They attacked in a split second. Jacek had no time to think about anything, reflexes taking over his body. He dodged, took aim and fired. He hit the first hunched figure mid-jump. The projectiles shook her muscular body, but didn't stop her. Klackowitcz cursed and hit his target with two more rounds.

A short stocky figure with incredibly dirty and matted hair stopped in front of Jacek and bared sharp, yellowed teeth. She was nearly naked, except for a primitive loincloth, so the hits were clearly visible. Only the wounds stopped bleeding immediately, and the creature's body expelled the bullets, healing the last traces of the hits only a second later.

"*Kurwa*," Klackowitcz whispered in disbelief, emptying the rest of the clip as well. That was all he could manage. The figure reached him in a single, nearly twenty-feet leap and lunged at him. He felt his bones snap and screamed in pain as the tremendous force ripped his arms from his shoulder joints. His own brain betrayed him as Jacek remained completely conscious instead of merciful unconsciousness. He saw several ugly faces above him, a cruel sneer on their lips.

Then the world went black, and the great loss of blood finally brought Klackowitcz into the arms of merciful death.

An icy wind shook the leafless birch trees and lightning bolts came down from the sky. The symbolic drizzle turned into a regular thunderstorm. I still held the shovel in my hand and looked at the too-fresh grave breaking the monotony of the yellowed leaves. Around me, sharpened, about three feet-high pikes were stuck into the ground. I smelled the scent of wet fur and noticed light-footed shadows with green glowing eyes moving between the white-black trunks.

"No," I answered their unspoken question. "Your time is yet to come. Be on guard for now. I'll be back soon." The rain beat on the broad brim of my hat, running down it in cold trickles. A muddy puddle formed under my heavy boots. The ground exhaled mist.

My mouth went dry and bile rose up my throat, choking me, as did the growing anger that gripped me like a straitjacket. This was personal. With a snap of my fingers, I crushed the handle of the shovel and threw it away. The longer I looked at the grave, the more I wanted to do some really nasty things to whoever was responsible for this. I had more than enough experience with this. They wanted it; they would get it. I'll figure out who did it.

"Uncle, will you go get Daddy now?" A little girl with long blonde hair and innocent blue eyes tugged on my sleeve.

"It's early, he'll be very weak," I replied, even forcing myself to smile.

"But I have a very bad feeling," she said grimly, wrinkling her nose.

"All right. I'll go there, you wait here. It's dry and warm here." I took her hand and led her to a big cabin.

"What if they come when you're not here?" she worried.

"They won't, Katie," I assured her. "I give you my word on that."

She nodded contentedly. "Mommy said that once you make a promise, you never break it."

I stood by and watched the hospital. Raindrops drummed on the windows of the buildings, reporting to me whether the ones I was looking for were inside their rooms or not. But then I saw them.

Two nurses were hurrying across the parking lot at a fast pace. I recognized them immediately. They couldn't outsmart me. But this was a complete novelty in their otherwise very straightforward strategy. They could disguise themselves as people! It crossed my mind that if those two were going to feed, they would leave a terrible mess behind them as usual. I created an electrostatic field over the hospital and let it discharge. The nurses became two charred, smoking statues. Asphalt boiled around them and sprayed out into the surrounding area. Several nearby vehicles caught fire. The boiled water enveloped everything in a cloud of steam within moments.

I transported myself to a quiet room on the first floor. At the same time, a large dose of static electricity was released into the wiring, destroying the CCTV system throughout the building. The man on the bed was deeply asleep. His arms were laid along his body and several tubes led from them to the IV stands. I closed my eyes and concentrated fully. The patient and the reclining bed slowly transitioned from a material state to an ectoplasmic spirit and dissolved. The vital signs monitors began to beep, confused and unnecessarily loud.

There was a long scream from the corridor, and then many more. Suddenly, however, there was an uncomfortable silence. A good ten seconds later, the door flew open and a burned nurse stood in it. I decided to call her Crispy. Although she had already partially recovered, she didn't look good at all. She immediately lunged at me, but a hit of my fist threw her back. I felt her bones loosen under my fist, which was an unexpectedly pleasant sensation. She hit the wall hard, fell to the ground, but immediately rolled to her feet and attacked again with a deep guttural growl. By that time I had taken out an acacia stake, cut to a sharp point, as long as my forearm. Only a second later I thrust it between the fake nurse's shoulder and neck. She dropped to the floor, giving me a hateful look. The fluids leaking from her body began to spread around her.

"Uughm?" Crispy wondered as she found her body refusing to obey and her regeneration completely halted. She gritted her pointed teeth and grunted. Then she began to choke. For to most magical creatures, acacia wood was violently poisonous, and the same was true of the acacia honey that coated the tip of the stake. Her companion appeared in the doorway only a split second later. She screamed until the window panes cracked, and the displays of all the instruments did the same. At least the annoying beeping had stopped.

"Hi, Crusty," I greeted her and smiled. Because she looked like burnt toasted bread. It was better that they came to me after all. Chasing them through the woods would have been much harder. Besides, they always formed packs.

The air rippled as a hypnotic attack swept through the room. I deflected it easily. This could work on the common folk; I, on the other hand, couldn't be counted among them. On the contrary. Crusty, however, was quite annoyed by this. She bared her teeth at me, and a piece of her charred lip fell off in the process. It left a disgusting pink stain. The nurse crouched down, and even through her thick dark hair, I could see the strong muscles in her legs tense up. Then she lunged for me.

I moved out of the way and checked on her collapsed sister. A large dark puddle had spread beneath her, red bubbles were forming at her nose, foam was coming out of her mouth, and her eyes were rolled back. She wasn't acting it out, so I could give my full attention to her friend. She swung her hand at me, missed, but her long fingernails tore the plaster off the wall and revealed the bricks. I blocked the next blow, grabbed her wrist and crushed it. She screamed, tried to bite me, and then kicked me too. I caught her leg and backed away. The nurse lost her balance and fell.

I grabbed her ankle with both hands and pulled her towards the door. She struggled; her fingernails carved deep furrows in the linoleum. She grabbed a chair and immediately threw it at me. The furniture may have missed its target, but the creature managed to kick me, throwing me into the hallway, where my body hit the wall so hard that my imprint was left in it. I staggered back, knocking fallen plaster and chunks of broken brick off my shoulders. And then I saw it.

Dead bodies in hospital gowns and medical uniforms covered the entire corridor. Among them I saw two overturned material carts, and a little further on there were crutches, walkers or IV stands. From the door I flew out of, a head peeked out, and then the nurse was out. I threw what was closest at her. Coincidentally, it was a wheelchair. It was a perfect hit. It crashed with the nurse mid-leap, which would put a panther to shame. The collision went better for the wheelchair; Crusty rolled over onto her stomach, but before she could get up, I kicked her in the ribs with a run. She skidded almost twenty feet across the blood-slick floor. She lay helpless and whimpering—I must have damaged her spinal cord with the kick. By the time I reached her, she had recovered enough to start moving her left arm again. I pulled out another acacia stake and finished the job.

I looked around. One thing was clear: this was a cardinal screw-up. The quiet times were over. I wondered how they were going to cover up this massacre and who they were going to put in charge at TEFLON, the acronym for the Secret European Fund for Hunter Bounties and Reparations.

I grabbed the ugly fake nurses by their ankles and disappeared from the hospital.

It was raining hard. I stood again in front of the grave and at my feet lay Crusty and her sister Crispy. They weren't pretty names, but I hated it when things got mixed up, so I had a compulsive need to somehow distinguish them from each other, even with made-up nicknames.

I tore off Crispy's head and impaled it on one of the pikes. Her eyelids fluttered and her blackened lips moved slightly. She also got a tic under her right eye. Crusty was much calmer. I watched them intently for several long moments.

I figured I had plenty of time, so I decided to go see Katie and her father. But I didn't leave the sisters unattended, even though they were technically dead. I didn't trust them that much.

I went back to the cabin. There was a large fireplace opposite the entrance and a bed with a patient to the left of it. He was holding Katie's hand and crying. When he saw me, he looked up and fear appeared on his face. I didn't know how much his wife had told him about me, but apparently enough to start worrying.

"Why are the yezinkas after your family?" I asked him without any attempt at politeness. Because I never liked him.

"I don't know, I swear I don't know!" he groaned.

Katie looked at me reproachfully. I ignored it. He was there and he didn't protect my sister. That was all I needed to know. I considered it an injustice that he survived. It should have been the other way around. That's it. End of discussion.

"Then why did they try to kill you twice? The first time could have been an accident, but they came straight to the hospital to get you," I said bluntly. At the same time, I checked the situation at the grave through the wolfish eyes of my guards. So far, it looked all right. The vicious forest animals had just begun to feast on the two headless bodies. And they came to eat in abundance.

Katie's father, unable to bear my reproachful look, averted his eyes and his bearded face twisted. "I really don't know. And why isn't...?" He couldn't finish his sentence and shuddered. Then he collapsed back onto the pillow and fell asleep.

"You sure helped me," I grumbled.

I took a needle and thread from a drawer under the table and headed back to the grave. It was high time. Crispy and Crunchy were beginning to wake up. Nervous twitches ran across their swollen faces. I didn't want to be cursed, so I secured myself against them and sewed the first yezinka's eyelids and lips shut. Several magpies perched on nearby branches began to loudly scold me for interrupting their feast.

"Uncle, may I?" Katie asked, holding out her hand.

After a moment's hesitation, I handed her the thread and needle. "Tighten the stitches properly," I warned her.

She didn't answer me, but instead got to work. I had to admit that she was doing much better and also faster than me. I looked at my niece and lost myself in thoughts. She never once looked up from her work, finishing stitching the right eye with a professional knot.

The word spread quickly that two elite teams of Hunters were massacred by the yezinkas in Poland. It actually happened on the other side of mountains. Then they ran here. But this wasn't their preferred hunting ground. Someone deliberately sent them here and then told them where to go on their various expeditions. The question was who and why. I haven't even found the main camp of the yezinkas yet; they were able to camouflage themselves really well. Or they were being camouflaged. Also, at the hospital, I only gained a lot of new questions and a minimum of answers. My brother-in-law didn't know anything, or kept it to himself. Which, to me, was all the same.

I frowned and shook my head to shut out the intrusive thought of Katie's father. A double grave would have looked much more romantic to me. Yezinkas, as far as I knew, didn't clean their teeth, and my bitten brother-in-law could, with a little luck, die of sepsis . . . It made me feel better. But it didn't last long.

A fat jay perched on a nearby branch. It tilted its head to the left and burped so hard its feathers fluffed up. "Sorry, these earthworms are getting too fat lately. It's making me sick to my gallbladder," it apologized demurely. "But that's not why I'm here."

"Well, out with it," I sighed.

"Hunters are camped at Štírovník," it declared importantly.

I cast a critical glance at Crispy and Crusty. Katie had done an excellent job.

"Yes, I know that," I assured the jay.

The bird shrugged cheekily and burped again. "It's none of my business, but you should go see them. Or they'll soon burn the place down to ashes and level the whole forest."

"You're a professional denunciator, not Sibyl," I warned the jay distantly, but at the same time I spread my mind wider.

What I saw made me curse. The bird wisely remained silent. But it didn't last long.

"Ranger? Are you going to crack down on the Hunters and yezinkas like you did with Hansmichl when he was chasing after your sister?" the jay wanted to know, hopping excitedly on a branch. "It's been quiet for too long!"

The jay really made me angry with that remark. It knew instantly that it had gone too far, because my eyes began to glow green, as did those of my guardian wolves.

"I have to do something somewhere else," it peeped, and then, unexpectedly quick for its size, it disappeared from sight.

Katie turned to me. "Who is this Hansmichl and what did he have to do with my mom?"

I cleared my throat. "That's not a story for little girls."

"And when will I be old enough to hear it?"

"Never."

That story happened a long time ago. It took place in times when there were no Hunters, and therefore the law of the mightiest was in effect. Both among humans and among the creatures now called supernaturals, or more simply, monsters.

My sister Katherine has grown into unusual beauty. And since she was to receive almost half of the Eagle Mountains as a dowry, she had no shortage of suitors. To put it very politely, not all of them had honorable intentions. The most annoying and also the most troublesome was a mountain spirit who called himself Hansmichl. He was a rather powerful being, full of mischief and greed. My sister was stalked and terrorized by this Hansmichl. Each time she refused him, his behavior got worse. But the final straw was when he brazenly followed her to my house. He broke down the door, came in and sat down at my table. He claimed to be Katherine's husband and behaved very arrogantly. He wore expensive clothes, iron rings on his fingers, and spat on the floor. He had always been used to being feared by everyone.

I asked him to give me a written promise that he would never speak to Katherine again and would avoid her until he died. He refused, became angry, and wanted to strike me with the heavy club he always carried. But he didn't realize that these mountains belong to me and he has no power or rights here. So I took him on a little trip. I tied him to a tree at the top of the peak called Palice, and then all I had to do was wait for the wild pigs to leave their wallows for their evening meal. Hansmichl scolded me at first, thinking I was just trying to scare him. But when the boars and sows were eating the meat off his legs, his attitude quickly changed and he began to beg for mercy. I only took him up on his offer when the hungry wild boars got higher up and chewed out his testicles. Afterwards, he was more than happy to sign a paper promising to give up Katherine for good. From then on, Hansmichl wore a long coat and high boots, so that it would not be obvious how he was affected by the feast of the wild pigs.

For a long time this story was told even among the common people, and that was enough to keep the peace in my woods. I, Ranger, guardian of the Eagle Mountains, had become forgotten as time passed. People were much fonder of Katherine, whom they loved and worshipped as a princess. It suited me. I rarely appeared among the people. Mostly in the rain and when it was necessary to punish poachers and those who would destroy the forest. But I never spoke to them. Katherine got married in the meantime, to Rampušák. We didn't click well; he was a dry and obnoxious nag, laughing at his own jokes. Eventually they moved to Deštná in the Eagle Mountains and we gradually broke off all contact. They only got in touch a few years ago, when their daughter was born. They asked me to be her godfather. After long hesitation, I accepted the offer. I found that they were now living among humans and trying to be as inconspicuous as possible. They managed to do that until they were attacked by the yezinkas.

Katherine called me for help, but unfortunately I got there too late. She died in my arms; she only had enough time to tell me who did it. Rampušák became a widower and ended up in the hospital, badly bitten. So I buried my beloved sister and took Katie in temporarily to protect her while her father was recovering.

And now it was time for me to go see those Hunters.

If there was one thing I really hated, it was someone destroying my forest. The government-hired Hunters of nonhumans reveled in it. They deployed their special photo traps capable of scanning the surroundings in several different spectrums, laying motion detectors and landmines or remote-controlled shooting nests. And above it all flew drones designed not only to monitor but also to destroy live targets. Snipers took over high ground and specialist soldiers measured the signal strength in controlled segments where their teams were to advance. This place wasn't as lively even when Emperor Franz Josef came here for maneuvers.

The Hunters took a meadow for themselves near the railroad from Rudoltice to Česká Třebová and set up their big black SUVs and operational tents covered with camouflage nets. I watched all this with considerable displeasure. I wasn't afraid that they might be able to discover my cabin, but they could have done a lot of damage to the trees and the land.

A man walked past me with a spectrum detector. He stopped and looked around. He couldn't physically see me. Unless it was raining, I was perfectly intangible. His device still found me. The man tapped his finger several times on the display and frowned. I stood close behind him and looked over his shoulder. I saw myself as a blue dot that glowed prettily in the very center of the screen.

"Damned piece of junk, it must be broken again," the guy muttered. "You can't rely on these technicians. It shows someone standing right here." He looked around again, then restarted the machine.

When the machine started up again, the blue dot—that is, me— was still there. But then a large group of other dots appeared. Blood red and pulsating. They were closing in fast. The man pulled out a phone with a shaky hand and tried to punch in a number. His fingers wouldn't listen.

Nearby, I heard shouting and then gunfire. I moved over there; it was only two hundred yards away. There were already three yezinkas feeding. They had managed to gouge out their victims' eyes, as was their custom, and were now stuffing them in their wide mouths. They were blissfully munching away, thick saliva running down their chins. The eldest of them stiffened and sniffed. She had a face full of deep wrinkles, a bald spot on the top of her conical head, and very crooked legs. She looked in my direction and growled something to her younger sisters.

The ground began to tremble, broken trees cracked, and then suddenly a tank swept across the yezinkas at tremendous speed. I stared at it in disbelief. What kind of a madman had the courage to drive a tank through my forest and spray a completely stupid sign saying *Ostrava* on it? The yezinkas pushed in the dirt were certainly even more surprised than I was. The weight of the multi-ton war machine crushed their joints and bones to a pulp. I decided to try to make something of the situation for myself. The creatures would regenerate in minutes and all the efforts of the mad driver, whoever they were, would be completely wasted.

I summoned the rain, and materialized with the first drops. I pulled the yezinkas out of the trail of tracks, laid them on top of each other and rolled them up like pancakes. I then banded everything very tightly with the blackberry tendrils that grew just a few steps to the left, and pierced the whole package with three acacia stakes for good measure. Gunfire, booming explosions and roars filled the forest. It was high time to get out.

I returned home with my catch. The wolves greeted me enthusiastically, rubbing against my legs, sniffing the flat little yezinkas and poking them with their wide, wet snouts. They were demanding a hunt. I promised them that their time would come soon. I didn't waste time and got to work. First the sewing, then the fun. I wanted to see for myself how our famous and praised Hunters fared in battle. Because the ones in Poland ended up in pieces.

And I was also going to make sure that no one ever drove a tank through my woods again.

I stitched up the last yezinka's eyes. The skull had managed to grow back, but it hadn't been able to recover its original shape, so what I'd impaled on the stake next to the grave was more suited to a museum of curiosities, a panopticon of freaks, or a nightmare.

It was dark. The moon was rising in the sky, showering the forests with silver light. A small piece of dirt on the grave lifted and pushed away a pebble that rolled down. Then a long, shiny stem slid out and unfurled. More followed, and in a few minutes the grave was covered with golden ferns. I took that as a good sign. My sister used to love them.

I headed for the meadow where the Hunters had camped earlier. There was an almost imperceptible misty haze hovering over it. The result did not please me in the least. In spite of careful preparation and undeniable technical superiority, the humans got brutally beaten. Not again. I walked among torn and fallen tents, burnt blast spots, overturned vehicles and partially gnawed corpses with no eyes. I noticed that a large number of the bodies had been bitten by something much larger than yezinkas. So they had an ally. The bites themselves exhibited abnormal dental patterns and grip strength. I also found traces of the creature. The prints were very large, humanoid, but quite unlike orc or ogre prints.

I finished examining the site. I was quite surprised to find several magical weapons. I'd heard there were a few among the Hunters, but I'd thought it was just a rumor until now. I examined them carefully, but didn't touch them. These things were extremely expensive, very effective, but also highly whimsical. And from a purely practical point of view, if they proved they couldn't stop the yezinkas, they were useless to me anyway. I'll let the cleanup team take them when they arrive.

In the meantime, I decided to change my tactics from observation to intervention, because as long as the yezinkas were wandering through the woods, they were attracting Hunters. I therefore adopted a wolf form, the only physically tangible form I used when it wasn't raining. I didn't need rain now, for it would wash away the scents and the tracks. The sounds of the forest were suddenly louder, the air brought a lot of interesting information, and the grass was cold under my paws. I bent down to the big print, sucked in the air and tasted it. I smelled of a yezinka, a corpse, and three kinds of magic. Earth, sign and control. There was a very faint human scent attached to the last one. I stored it in my memory. Now I'll never forget it in any of its forms.

Long-legged shadows with green glowing eyes stepped out of the forest. There were many of them, almost a hundred and a half. I smiled and greeted them. It was shaping up to be a good hunt today. A young owl perched a little uncertainly on a nearby spruce and watched me with atypically bright blue eyes.

She was very talented. She figured out how to do it all by herself... just like her mom.

The hunt started.

I ran with the pack among the trees that cast their long shadows in the moonlight. The cool air carried many interesting smells, but we were only interested in one. The prey couldn't be far away; the tracks were getting fresher. We finally caught up with the yezinkas and surprised them while feeding. They dragged the bodies of the Hunters to a place called Dubina and were feasting on them. It looked like some kind of victory banquet. Nearby lay the reddened rocks and sticks with which they had smashed their victims' heads to get at the brains, their second favorite delicacy after the eyes. In the same primitive way, they had broken ribs and chests to get to the hearts. With sickle-shaped claws, they now opened the bellies of the dead to eat the liver. This must have been at least the fourth course.

The yezinkas stared in disbelief at the great beasts that had emerged from the night in utter silence. The cold air formed clouds of steam at the wolves' mouths, and their long pink tongues hung over their sharp teeth.

The pack attacked at once, their superiority overwhelming. And though the yezinkas thrashed and bit and scratched around them, it was no use. A few tried to climb the nearest trees, but didn't make it that far. Except for one. She climbed to what she thought was a safe height, then made a wailing sound that could have easily been a warning or a cry for help. But at that moment, the owl's talons scratched her face. The yezinka lost her balance and tumbled backwards, where the wolves claimed her after she hit the ground.

This was a great success. Twelve yezinkas. Not bad at all. I waited for the wolves to feed and called in the rain. We needed to move the trophies and prevent the yezinkas from telling their sisters what happened here.

There was a surprise waiting for me at the grave. Katie stood there, visibly grown and matured. A needle and thread were in her hand, more sharpened pikes for heads were impaled in the ground, and new acacia spears were leaning against a nearby twisted large birch tree. I impaled the heads of the yezinkas on the pikes and looked again at my niece. "Really, just like your mother," I murmured, just to cover my embarrassment and say something.

"I'll take care of it, Uncle," she smiled, tossing a strand of long blond hair out of her face. "I'll come back to you after I sew them up."

"I don't know if that's appropriate. Your father probably wouldn't approve of you wanting to get involved."

The wind ruffled the golden ferns on the grave. "He might not, but as you can see, Mommy doesn't mind," Katie didn't give in and began stitching together the first set of eyelids.

✤ ✤ ✤

I returned to the pack. Now I was going to solve the rest of the problems. And for that, I needed some perspective. On a sudden impulse, I opted for a physical move to the location, not a magical one. A little movement never hurt anyone, quite the opposite. And in wolf form, movement was one of the greatest joys. So I ascended a rocky trail copying a contour line in the hilly terrain. It followed a forest path with a raised grassy central strip created by passing heavy cars of foresters. I stood still and listened.

The distant rumble was getting closer. I retreated among the trees and watched curiously to see what would happen. From around a bend, a harsh glare cut through the darkness and a thundering roar shook the forest. Then screaming yezinkas ran past. They were running very fast indeed, and with good reason.

They were being chased by a tank. The dark green armor was worn down by the years, the paint peeling in many places, exposing rust spots of various sizes. The forward movement of the machine, though very brisk, was accompanied by a ghostly creaking and deafening screeching, indicative of neglected or inadequate maintenance.

I immediately remembered that this was also one of the things I intended to solve. No Hunters were going to be driving around my woods in this vehicle with a totally stupid name. Ostrava! Phew. It didn't even really exist! That rolling, stinking piece of iron could have been called Brno or Balanced State Budget and it would have worked out the same.

The tank disappeared around the bend in the road. I felt droplets of badly burnt diesel landing on my skin. It made me angry. Morally and environmentally, it was absolutely necessary to disable this vehicle. Even if someone was using it to hunt yezinkas.

First, the vehicle had to be stopped. I looked up at the sky, which immediately clouded over, and a storm like no one had seen in years began. In a few minutes, the roads here became torrents, but of mud instead of water. As I already knew, neither tractors and Tatras nor foresters' V3S could pass through it.

There was as much light as if it was still daytime, the sky was struck by one lightning bolt after another, and no words could be heard over the downpour. I liked it.

I returned to my human form, took off my hat and turned my face toward the rain.

✦ ✦ ✦

I found the tank two turns away. It had cut a path up a steep hill, flipped on its side and slid down the hillside. It broke several trees in the process, and the turret hit a large beech with five trunks twisted together. The armored vehicle left a deep trough in the hillside resembling a brown scar. Nearly twenty deranged yezinkas were running around the tank, hysterically pounding it with sticks and stones. A few even climbed on top of the overturned war machine, jumping on it and hurling obscene insults. Every now and then, however, one of them slipped and ended up on her back in the mud next to the armored vehicle, hitting herself on the protruding, twiggy roots.

I haven't laughed so hard in a long time.

After a good hour of frantic assault, the yezinkas got tired. They stood near the tank and discussed it vividly. I gathered this from the expressive gesticulation that supplemented the monsters' speech. And just at that moment one of the hatches opened, a small hand appeared and threw two round things in an arc in the middle of the yezinkas. Night immediately turned into day after the hatch closed again.

The incendiary grenades sprayed their content all over and created a cloud of burning phosphorus. The glowing gelatine clung to any surface and emitted a great deal of heat. Grass, leaves, trees and pines were burning despite the torrential rain. Then four figures in black Hunter armor emerged from the tank. There were two men and two women. I heard somewhere that if four people come out of a tank, there must be a dog as the fifth crew member. But I never saw anything like that, so either they didn't have one, or they ate it a long time ago. But maybe the poor animal committed suicide in time so that it wouldn't have to be locked up with them in a tank with *Ostrava* written on it. Personally, I leaned towards the latter version; it seemed the most likely of all.

The hunters happily fired a few short bursts among the yezinkas and seemed very satisfied with the result of their actions.

"This is an elite Fantom team, living legends, not some Polish losers, you understand?" a tall man with a short beard shouted at the fallen yezinkas. But he stopped boasting quickly, as the yezinkas began to regenerate. They stood up, and the projectiles gradually fell out of their bodies with a subtle hiss.

"Shit," the bearded man said, using his Milkor rotary grenade launcher without hesitation. "Martin, don't just stand there like capital Y and do something!" he shouted.

A short, fat man with a big belly nodded, let out a war cry, and his flamethrower roared like a swarm of angry forest bees. The long flame engulfed several yezinkas, which ran in all directions like great fireballs on legs. They crashed into trees and bushes, or tripped over roots, and then rolled down the hillside. But as soon as they stopped burning, they came back to take revenge on the Hunters who had tried to kill them. "Libor, they're like some kind of crazy Terminators!" the flamethrower guy complained wryly.

"Pick up is in thirty-seven minutes at the earliest! And the extraction point is out of the woods according to the coordinates," the smaller of the two women with an earpiece in her ear shouted over the gunfire and screaming of the yezinkas, while busily tapping something into her tablet. "We have to get there and then survive until they arrive! Do you hear me? I need a few minutes to activate Fantom's emergency backup!"

"You'll get 'em, Alex!" A tall blonde climbed up the side of the overturned tank at the urging of her teammates, holding the machine gun she had removed from its rack. She threw the strap over her shoulder and tossed her head defiantly. The long cartridge belt ended somewhere down by her feet.

"Thanks, Petra," Alexandra nodded, continuing to focus on her tablet.

A large fiery flower bloomed at the end of the barrel the moment a screaming yezinka leapt at the blonde. She literally cut the attacker in half and her body hit the ground with a splash.

However, I knew from experience that even this was unfortunately not enough. In fifteen, twenty minutes at most, the yezinka would be running around again as if nothing had happened. The machine gun chewed through the entire cartridge belt in less than a minute and fell silent. The last of the fired brass cartridges hit the wet ground with a hiss, inaudible because of the barking of the shots.

Setting up the second belt was a matter of moments, but the yezinkas partially regenerated during that time. They announced their determination to continue the fight with a roar and a new mass frontal assault.

"How many more grenades do we have?" Libor wanted to know.

"Looks like if we cut these monsters in pieces, they'll give up for a little while!"

"Don't worry about it," Alexandra told him. "Everybody get in the tank right now! The drones should be here in... three! Two!" She slipped into the tank first and everyone else followed her as fast as they could.

Multiple quiet, buzzing sounds came in overhead, similar to when bats fly. This was followed by loud clicks of electric motor switches, and then small-caliber overhead rotary machine guns began their deadly chant. The yezinkas were caught in the crossfire. Projectiles tore chunks of flesh from their bodies, shattering bones and tearing ligaments. The show was ended by air-to-surface missiles, smaller in size but no less devastating than their larger counterparts.

Humans and Hunters in particular have obviously worked on their weapons and equipment in recent years. With that kind of tenacity, they might be able to beat the yezinkas after all. The massacre lasted almost eight minutes. All the while, hundreds and thousands of red-hot bullets rained down from the dark sky, hissing like a squashed viper on contact with the rain. As silently as the drones flew in, they disappeared again.

The team climbed out of the tank. Again there were four of them, and again they had no dog.

"We're out of here, there's no better chance," the blonde announced. "Take only the bare essentials, we're running for our lives. It's all about speed. We'll come back for the rest in the daylight and much better armed."

"That goes for your scrap too, Martin! Throw it away! It's got an empty tank anyway, and you're having trouble running even a mile straight!" his big bearded teammate warned the little man.

"Don't call my flalalalalamememethrower scrap!" the little man retorted, stammering with indignation.

The yezinkas may have been a mass of mush at the moment, but even that was beginning to come together.

"Move it!" Alex urged them impatiently.

"I should have stuck to cleaning nuclear reactors," Martin sighed, reluctantly dropping the flamethrower from his back.

"Woe is me, why didn't I marry Keanu Reeves?" laughed Petra.

Martin was offended. "You mean I'm whining?"

"You're not whining," Alex replied instead of the blonde. "Instead, you're always making up stuff like an old fart." One of the lying yezinkas squealed, arching her back, and they hear the sound of her bones grinding together. At the same time, heavily deformed projectiles began to pop out of her body.

"Even the silver didn't work, they're already regenerating," Libor noticed. "So the fun is over, kids, let's go! You can argue later. The GPS says to go that way." He waved his hand to indicate the direction and ran first into the darkness.

A blue-eyed owl fluttered in front of me. I raised my left arm and she sat on it.

"Uncle, you must help them," she told me urgently.

"Why?" I wanted to know.

"They don't know how to kill the yezinkas! They will lose! The yezinkas will catch them before they get out of the forest!"

"It's very likely," I nodded. "But you don't have to worry about anything; I'll catch the yezinkas then."

"Uncle, please, please, help them! You can't let them die."

"There's nothing to be done, Katie. I help them, and then they'll put me at the top of their TEFLON list and hunt me. I'm glad my existence has been forgotten, and that's the way it will stay."

"But they are the good guys! Just like you. Will you think of something to help them? They don't even have to see you. Please!"

She must have inherited this humanity from my sister, otherwise I couldn't explain it. Okay. For once in my life, I could afford to be the good guy.

But really, just once.

The Fantom team had a huge advantage in that the route to its destination, the pick-up point, was mostly downhill. They were not very good at running anyway, stumbling over branches, losing their balance on the roots and snorting like a pig leaving a beechmast feast. My guards and I had a lot of fun at that. We kept a safe distance from them and watched their every move. A wolf's run was economical, light and fast compared to that of a man.

"Libor huffs the most!" Martin hissed during one brief slowdown.

"Me?" the bearded man protested, rubbing his drooling chin. "Do you want to lose your bonuses?"

"Oh, I was wrong, it was Alex!" the fat man decided on the lesser of two evils, trying at all costs to distract from his poor physical condition.

"You're not huffing because you are basically rolling all the way for now, fatty," retorted the heavily panting Alexandra, standing in a slight hunch with her palms resting on her knees.

That's when I got word from the guards that the first yezinka was catching up to us. I switched from my wolf form to a human form, prepared an acacia stake, and stood in the middle of the path.

"Hello, Roasty," I said politely as she approached. Instead of starting to brake, she accelerated, jumped, and attacked with bared teeth and outstretched fingers, which on most yezinkas ended in long, dirty fingernails, so that in addition to scratching, they threatened their victims with several kinds of nasty infections and diseases, such as tetanus and jaundice. I let a long zigzag green bolt of lightning strike her down, illuminating the area with a ghostly light for a few seconds. I pierced the charred body, carried her to the grave, and there I severed her head, which went very well in her roasted state. So much, in fact, that the ears of the yezinka remained in my hands. I sniffed my dirty hands and frowned.

"It smells like burnt frying oil," I said in disgust, and stuck her head on the nearest available pike. In the soft glow of the golden ferns, an owl appeared, flying silently. Just above the ground, it transformed into a human form and Katie gracefully hopped on the grass. Then she clung to my neck.

"You're wonderful, Uncle, I'll sew her up right now..."

I didn't say anything. I picked up some new acacia stakes and four spears and went to finish what I had started.

The Hunters haven't run nearly as far as I would have expected. The human race may have risen technically since the time of Maria Theresa, but it has clearly decayed physically, which does not bode well for its future. I joined the wolves again. In the meantime, they've torn apart two yezinkas. I stabbed them and carried them off. I had plenty of acacia stakes, which was a good thing, but I still didn't enjoy cutting them. Hopefully this was the last yezinka invasion for a long time.

The Fantom team stopped because the fat man couldn't continue, holding his side and making noises similar to braying. Libor and Petra tentatively took him between them and forced him to run again.

Alexandra was two steps ahead of them. She stopped suddenly. A yezinka jumped down from a tree in the team's path, having outrun us on the branches. She rolled her eyes and then blood spurted from her gaping mouth instead of a scream. She grabbed her stomach, which is where the spear I threw at her came out. The slippery blood prevented her from properly grasping the carefully smoothed shaft, so she couldn't pull the toxic wood from the wound. Smoke trailed from her hands as the acacia honey reacted with her skin, eating it away. I added three more spears. It wasn't a waste; I needed the team to have something to defend themselves with. I wasn't going to clear the path completely, they also had to show some effort to survive. As the saying goes, a wise man needs just a hint...

The yezinka I used to catch the spears, which now looked like a large pincushion, collapsed very quickly. I've decided to call her Needle. Poisoning through the abdominal cavity progressed quite fast. Instead of blood, Needle was now vomiting gastric juices, fell on her side, and was seized with tremors. Ten seconds later she fell unconscious.

"She should be regenerating, but she can't," Petra remarked. She cautiously approached the yezinka and wrinkled her nose. "I smell acacia," she said, squashing Needle with a heavy boot and pulling out one of the spears. She looked around, trying to pierce the inky darkness with her gaze. The red aura of witches surrounded her. She didn't see me, but my snarling wolves certainly didn't escape her attention. While they were holding a yezinka by the throat to keep her from screaming, they were making such distinct sounds as they butchered her that they were impossible to miss.

"Thank you for your help and advice," the blonde spoke aloud, adding a deep bow. I could appreciate that.

"Who are you talking to?" Libor whispered, adjusting his ballistic vest.

"Probably the ruler of the local forest. At least I think so. I can see their demonic pack of wolves protecting us. And they also showed us how to kill the yezinkas..."

"I guess the rest of us should bend our backs real quick too, huh?" the bearded man asked.

"That would be good. After that let's take the spears they gave us and get out of here fast. Their good mood may not last long."

Young and rather wise, I assessed the blonde witch with the red aura. Katie wasn't wrong to want me to help them. According to the wolves, though, they had a few more yezinkas in their path who had outran them and were now lying in ambush.

I was very curious to see how they would handle them.

The Fantom squad proceeded cautiously to the edge of the forest. The muddy field in front of them did not promise an easy walk, but this was the path to their rescue.

"Helicopter!" Martin shouted. "Do you hear that? They're actually flying to get us even in this terrible weather!"

This morale boost came at just the right time. The team's running speed picked up considerably, but the yezinkas got in their way. Two of them. They were sizing up the Hunters with disdain; they had enough experience with them already and knew they were not difficult prey.

The first yezinka grinned and lunged for Alexandra. The latter didn't hesitate, bracing her long spear on the ground and pointing the tip at the yezinka who could no longer change the direction of her jump. Her eyes widened in horror and she gave a terrible shriek as the acacia wood passed just below her left collarbone.

Libor immediately rushed to Alex's aid and stabbed the raging yezinka in the side. This knocked her out of the fight for good.

The other yezinka lunged at Martin. Unfortunately, he stumbled and fell on his back, but to his credit he did not drop the spear. He clutched the shaft convulsively, grimacing, his eyes closed. Petra thrust her weapon between the yezinka's protruding shoulder blades, paralyzing her hands, which threatened to gouge out the corpulent man's eyes. There was complete silence for several long moments, then uncontrollable laughter rumbled through the drenched forest.

For the yezinka was sitting, straddling Martin, and he was writhing beneath her to get rid of the dead weight in what looked like copulatory movements. When he saw his colleagues having fun at his expense, he started to get angry, but it didn't help.

"You're idiots, I'm not banging her!" the fat man yelled uncomfortably. A few flashes coming from his colleagues' mobile devices, however, let him know that there would be an aftermath.

A helicopter appeared over the field, its nose light on. It swooped down just above the ground and lowered a rope ladder. The team ran heavily towards it, their feet encased in soggy soil. I looked after them with some satisfaction. This wasn't a bad bunch. In the end, I was even glad that I had given in to Katie and helped them.

When the helicopter disappeared, the wolves surrounded me and demanded to be petted. They poked me with their cold snouts and gave me their big, scraggly paws. It was a good hunt today. I got rid of the yezinkas' heads and transport myself home.

The rain had stopped and the first subtle hint of dawn appeared in the east.

I finished the last stitches, made a knot and stretched my stiff back. The door of the cabin opened, and there stood Rampušák, leaning on a twisted stick. He headed toward me. He stood silently by the grave for a long time, his tired, haggard face showing a lot of emotion.

"We're going home," he announced to me then, trying to sound firm.

"I won't stop you," I told him. "You know your limits."

His gaze swept over the impaled yezinka's heads and his face contorted in disgust. "I could handle it. But I have to take care of my mountains, just like you. Winter's around the corner, and it's going to be a lot harder this year, so I want to get started as soon as possible. Thanks for everything, brother-in-law."

But I knew there was something else. He wasn't the only one who heard those heavy creeping footsteps skirting the magical boundary that had always separated my home from the outside world. He didn't want to be here when the last clash of forces will happen. And he wanted his daughter to be here even less.

Katie came out of the cabin, carrying her backpack and other belongings.

The goodbyes were quick. When she hugged me, she whispered in my ear that she'd come visit soon. I led them past the boundary and watched as they disappeared into the rays of the morning sun.

I waited a few more minutes, and then bent to the ground. The large tracks were hard to see after the rain, but I recognized the smell immediately. It must have been the same creature that had destroyed the Hunter on Štírovník. My olfactory memory confirmed it. I had to stop this from continuing to spread through my forest at all costs.

I thought about it. The solution to this problem was really simple.

I went back to my sister's grave. The golden fern waved a greeting.

"What do you think?" I asked. A soft glow spilled from the plants into the surrounding area.

"All right, I'll do it, little sister."

"You guys wait among the trees for now," I temporarily banished the wolves from the main stage, where the final part of the show would soon take place. "You'll have my back when it gets tough."

The rain came.

I set up a few places with prepared spears, pikes, and stakes. It took me almost an hour and a half. I was in no hurry to get anywhere, and I worked extra carefully. I checked everything repeatedly. It was time to act.

First, I let the border fall temporarily, and then I took a knife with a deer antler hilt from my pocket and cut the stitches on Crusty's mouth. The dead yezinka immediately opened her mouth and screamed. Just as I expected and needed. The only thing I hadn't counted on was the foul smell that wafted out of Crusty's mouth. In the meantime, the tongue and surrounding tissues had been fully engulfed by the decay and putrefaction processes, making the smell almost unbearable. I had to retreat a good twenty paces. The other heads began to make deep grunting noises, many of them wobbling on their stakes. However, the wrist-thick pikes were stuck deep into the soil and held firm. I looked around.

Shards of thick grey mist, looking like a giant snake and smelling like three-day-old carrion, appeared among the trees. I smiled. It worked.

It wasn't long before a startled jay flew by. It rolled its eyes and gasped. Its obese body was propelled forward through the thick rain like a feathered ball shot from a catapult or a giant slingshot. It didn't even say hello and hurried away as far as its wings would take it. The ground began to shake as something large and heavy approached.

I restored the boundary and secured it with several insidious and unpleasant spells. The whole point of my plan was that no one could get in or out without my knowledge. And it worked. Whatever the outcome of our duel, I made sure it would never get out again. That realization brought a very pleasant sense of peace and balance to my soul that I had long lacked.

The best laid plans were always simple.

Then I grabbed one of the spears and checked the tip. It was coated with a mixture of acacia honey and bogbean, two of the most toxic plants to yezinkas. The fog reduced visibility to barely ten paces. And then two figures stopped at the golden glowing grave.

The first was an older fat man with grey hair, three chins and an aura that looked like a badly mopped floor rag, typical of necromancers. No surprise there. But the other one... It was ugly, much taller than any human, and shriveled. It resembled an overgrown mummy, with sunken cheeks, large protruding knuckles, and large muscles beneath the bald, dark grey, wrinkled skin. I estimated its height at just under ten feet, and the monster had sharp claws instead of fingernails, a backward-arching skull, and thick, protruding jaw full of sharp teeth. The creature's eyes had no whites; they were emotionless and all black as asphalt pools.

Crusty screamed again. With a wave of its long arm, the monster dispersed the fog in its immediate vicinity, and in that moment it also saw the impaled heads of the yezinkas.

The large creature took Crusty's head in its palm and put it to its ear. It shook it, as if it that could let it hear what the dead yezinka was saying better. Meanwhile, the fat man concentrated on the grave with the golden fern. He stared at it in fascination, and then raked his sparse, greasy hair. He tried to touch the ferns, but they dodged and then attacked. "It... bit me!" the necromancer said, surprised. He examined the wound, but it was apparently nothing serious. "Katherine, do you really think you can stop me with such circus tricks?" he said in a deep voice. "You are mistaken, and this time you will not refuse my advances. I'll dig you out, partially revive you, and then you'll experience something special."

The monster uttered a wail so long the necromancer had to put his hands to his ears. He shook his head and frowned. He finally took note of something other than the golden fern.

"No, I really don't know who this Ranger is, I've never heard of him. I understand that he killed all your children, but there's nothing I can do about it when there are only disembodied heads. To be resurrected, the person in question has to be whole, you know that yourself," he snapped at the wailing mummified creature. "Then find the guy, if he's here, and kill him. What else can I tell you, Jadwiga?" he finished his monologue and took a folding shovel off his belt.

The monster stuttered again. The sounds was long and anguished.

"I revived you to help me, Jadwiga. Do you remember our agreement? I command you and you command the yezinkas, because you are their mother and queen. You will kill the proud Katherine and all her family, and I will give you your freedom in return. I only see one grave here. Not three. Those are the facts. Now shut up. Or you might as well go back to your tomb in the rock for another few centuries, what do you say, Jadwiga?"

The great creature crouched and fell silent. So the necromancer's threat hadn't fallen on deaf ears. He turned his attention back to the grave. I weighed the spear, inspected its tip, and estimated the distance and, more importantly, the angle at which it would penetrate its target. He confessed, the bastard. That was all I needed.

"So, Katherine, you will soon be mine. And remember once and for all, my golden-haired princess, when you refuse the amorous advances of a necromancer, never say 'over my dead body,'" the fat man laughed at his own joke.

Two seconds later, I was the one laughing because the necromancer was pierced by the spear I threw at him. It landed exactly as I'd intended, entering his body through his solar plexus and exiting through his tailbone. The kinetic energy knocked the necromancer to his knees and knocked the wind out of him. The tip of the spear dug into the forest floor and prevented the mage from toppling over. The impaled body shuddered. The man now resembled a fish, opening and closing his mouth without a sound coming out.

The howls of a pack of my guards sounded quite close. Jadwiga turned around several times in confusion. At that, she casually crushed Crusty's head with a single squeeze. Then, with lightning speed, she bent down and bit off the dying fat man's head. Now the monster was completely free, severing all ties with the necromancer that had been formed before the revival and allowing him to control Jadwiga.

I gripped my spear, moved behind Jadwiga, and struck the point where kidneys used to be. Because of our height difference, I guided the stab from below. Dark green blood spurted out, reeking of decay and rot. I leaned on the shaft with full force. The acacia wood groaned and broke the front of the large Jadwiga's ribcage. She roared and bent her long arm. The curved claws missed me by the proverbial hair and knocked my hat off my head. I moved to a safe distance and took another spear. The birch tree, behind which I had hidden myself behind so that I could attack at the right moment, flew away into the distance with its root ball still attached. Behind the deep hole left by the uprooted tree loomed Jadwiga. She grabbed the spearhead I had thrust into her a moment before and pulled. She pulled the whole spear out, threw it away, and no sooner did I realize that the acacia's toxicity didn't apply to her than she lunged at me.

I escaped by a mere half a step; the impact of the heavy body would surely have driven me into the ground. I stabbed at her exposed flank and leaned on the shaft to drive the spear as deep as I could.

It sliced through flesh and tore through guts, at least as far as I could tell from the stench that wafted from the wound. Jadwiga reared up, thrashing around furiously, her claws tearing up the ground and breaking trees. I was able to avoid four such blows. But then someone turned out the lights and my world suddenly disappeared.

I woke up to the pain as magic repaired my broken bones and also a feeling on my face. A wolf's tongue ran over my cheek again. I gently pushed the large grey and black beast aside and staggered to my feet. This was one hell of a blow; I had possibly never received such a blow before, and I had driven heavyweights like golems, warlocks, and ogres out of my forest. Through the long corridor of broken birch trees created by the passage of my body, I caught sight of Jadwiga. She was angrily fending off the attacking wolves that prevented her from reaching me. They grabbed at her heels, nipped her calves and pretended to bite, only to retreat to safe distance.

I stretched out my arms and sucked in the ancient power of the Eagle Mountains. It was everywhere beneath the surface, a slow flow of raw magical energy, accumulated over long eras. The Třebov Walls had never had a master; they had always stood alone, but their rugged beauty mesmerized me. That's why I took over them. I left managing the Eagle Mountains to my sister and Rampušák, but it was still I, Ranger, who was their true ruler.

The sky turned black, the icy wind howled and it became dark. In the depths of the earth something huge overturned and shook the land.

Magic was in the air; its crackling could be clearly heard. In the form of green sparks and small lights, it was discharging on tall objects. The mountains themselves came to my rescue.

When Jadwiga and I collided a few seconds later, it was she whose bones rattled and who flew backwards. She waved her long arms helplessly, and when she landed, she cried out in pain and slid back a good twenty yards. She broke through mature trees in the process, carved a deep furrow in sodden grass, and stopped within reach of the golden fern. She lay there for a moment, but then rolled heavily on her stomach to get up. I took a spear from the nearest post and threw it at Jadwiga. It went deep under her right shoulder blade, pinning her hard to the ground, and before she could do anything about it, three more pierced her. The wolves, eyes blazing, rushed to my aid again, hanging onto the monster's arms and legs, making even the slightest defense impossible.

I headed for the grave at a brisk pace, picking up my hat in the process. The yezinka s' heads kept mumbling and Jadwiga seemed to be taking strength from them. For all the spears in her body began to rot in an instant, and if it hadn't been for the wolves, she probably would have gotten back on her feet and the fight could have continued anew. I knelt down on Jadwiga's back, interlocked my fingers under her neck, let out a long breath, and at the same time leaned back sharply. The monster's tendons and spine clenched, but did not snap. Meanwhile, Jadwiga had grown strong again, and her injuries had healed. She even threw off some of the wolves, freeing her left arm. Everything in the vicinity was once again infested with grey, sticky smelling mist. The threads preventing the yezinkas from speaking suddenly grew thinner, and they began to recite their incantations en masse.

I resisted their magic, fumbled to catch the monster's head better, and pulled again. Jadwiga beat her arms around me, and raked the grave in the process. A blinding golden glow spilled around. The heads of the yezinkas instantly burst into flames and fell silent as either their lips melted together or their tongues charred. Their eyes popped with a loud snap, spilling out through the gaps between the stitches holding their lids together.

"Try again," my sister's voice rang in my ears. I obeyed and used all my strength. My head was buzzing, black spots appearing before my eyes from the exertion. I felt like I was trying to break a steel anchor rope. But I refused to give up and continued to stubbornly pull the predator's head towards me. Suddenly her vertebrae and ligaments loosened under my hands, as did the rest of her tissue. I rolled backwards and inadvertently dropped the morbid trophy. The monster's body shuddered, air escaped whistling from its lungs, and then it began to burn. The same fate befell the head of the great Jadwiga.

The flames also engulfed the necromancer's fat body, slumped nearby.

I sat down on the ground, leaned my back against a broken birch tree and breathed in deeply. The wolves lounged near me, watching their surroundings with squinting eyes or licking wounds they had suffered in their fight with Jadwiga. At least an hour passed. I stood up heavily. The ferns on the grave had wilted, the stalks were withered and lay on the soggy dirt.

"Brother!"

She stood there, three paces from me, her golden dress flowing to the ground.

"Sister?"

She waved me over. Then she underwent a quick transformation, turned into a large owl, hooted, and disappeared into the trees. A single golden feather fell from her wing to the ground. I bent over, picked it up and stared at it for a long time.

The precious moment of magic and power was spoiled by an obese jay. It perched on the towering roots of the uprooted tree, puffed itself up, hiccupped twice, and shook its head gravely. "Well done, Ranger. We really gave them hell together, didn't we?"

OSKAR FUCHS (* 1982)

He is a stocky guy with a big heart and an even bigger imagination, whose favorite mascot is a fox. (Don't ask why.) He's just as cunning as one and can handle the strangest situations in life and in stories. Although he graduated from a technical school, he has always been interested in the history and legends of his native Lanškroun, as well as the entire Hřebečsko/Schönhengstgau region, which is reflected in his work. He discovered creative writing by accident. His first attempts were pure fantasy or science fiction, but later he switched to a combination of these genres mixed with elements of action fiction. He is one of the few Czech authors who skipped the short story and writing contests phase to jump straight into novels.

The first one was a short-ish fantasy novel *Frost* (*Frost*, Epocha, 2017), where Fuchs added a few splatterpunk-themed action scenes. The protagonist is a tough war mage who is not fazed by a little spilled blood. The following novel, *Hitokiri* (*Hitokiri*, Epocha, 2018), a brutally insane action ride full of gunpowder, bullets, and battle magic, unfolds in a similar vein. And *Leichenberg* (*Leichenberg*, Epocha, 2020), spiced up with themes of betrayal and revenge, also has the distinctive features of hard action. On the other hand, his latest novel *The Hell Shepherd* (*Pekelný pastýř*, Epocha, 2021) is of a different kind, as it plays with the motif of Hell and sheep in an absolutely brilliantly twisted story.

In the *MHF* project, Oskar was an obvious choice for the editors ever since his short story "Stuhač" (*Pevnost*, 4/2021), an action sci-fi where he introduced a very specific hunting agency that can provide an extraordinary adrenaline experience—if the client has enough money and courage.

In Harmony with Nature
František Kotleta

A sharp whistle flew through the trees and pierced Kateřina's ears.

"Assholes," she sighed, her right hand shooting into the air, not intending to turn around after the source of the whistling. In doing so, her fingers curled and straightened in the international gesture known in Czechia as *fakáč*.

The only response was loud male laughter.

"Go screw yourself," she hissed, but in doing so she did exactly what she didn't want to do—thoughts of whistling lumberjacks and a raised hand diverted her attention from the bushes she was just pushing her way through. So she tripped over a large spruce branch and fell on it. She felt sharp pain in her knee on impact, and her mouth subsequently became the proof of how well she could curse.

"Shit!" she gasped, rolling onto her back. She closed her eyes in pain, a few tears escaping from them.

"Do you need help, Red?"

The man's raspy voice sounded genuinely concerned.

"Not from you," she growled. She didn't have the courage to open her eyes at the same time. She could just make out the three figures above her, casting shadows. Beyond that, she could smell them. They carried the scent of a mixture of gasoline, sap, and fresh sawdust.

"You're bleeding," the voice informed her again, then added: "Bob, get the medkit."

Bob trotted off somewhere. His heavy boots shook the surrounding ground, making her head pound. She opened her eyes and saw two lumberjacks. The one whistling and talking was Old Pávek. She'd never called him that in her life, but no one in the village called him anything else, so that's what she called him in her mind at least. Standing next to Old Pávek was Young Pávek, a boy of barely eighteen who had graduated from the forestry school in Olomouc a few months ago and looked a bit like a pimpled copy of his father. But unlike him, he had no baldness and no muscles built not in a gym but by daily hard work. She hated to admit it, but Old Pávek looked a bit like Bruce Willis in *The Last Boy Scout*, a movie she loved and would watch whenever she was feeling blue. She felt that way a lot the last few weeks.

"Aah!" she yelled as the returning Bob sprayed her bloody knee with disinfectant without warning. She held the edge of her skirt tightly at the same time, so that the men wouldn't see that she hadn't put on panties for her trip in the woods.

Bob was Roma. But Kateřina Hodková was probably the only person in the entire Jeseníky Mountains who called him that, because the others—even himself—referred to him as the Gypsy. During her studies of andragogy at the Faculty of Arts, she took a semester of Romani studies, and so she tried to speak Romani to him once. He didn't understand a single word and subsequently told her that she had nice tits. That was the end of all their interaction.

"You wanna bend over, Red?"

"What?"

"You wanna bend that leg so I can bandage it?" Bob grinned. He was grinning like a teenager, not just now, but all the time, even though he was apparently in his late twenties. The double entendre was, of course, rewarded by the other two lumberjacks with a grin.

"You don't have neither the guts nor the tools for that," she snapped angrily. Even she was surprised at how sharp she was. But the whole situation was driving her crazy. Without their whistling, she wouldn't have scraped her knee and she wouldn't be in such an undignified situation in the first place. She gritted her teeth and jumped to her feet. Her knee stung again, but she managed to ignore it. She could think of about a dozen ways to explain to the men that their behavior was not only unacceptable, but more importantly, it showed what village primitives they were, but then she just waved her hand mentally. She'd given up long ago. After moving to Jeseníky in a foolish hope that she would be closer to nature as well as the people who live there, she had to reconsider her ideas quickly.

She rolled up the bottom of her blue and white batik skirt, tucking the end into her waistband so she wouldn't get blood on it, ignored their stares at her knees and thighs, took the two wicker baskets—the reason why they called her Little Red Riding Hood—and just left. She was being damn careful not to trip again.

When she was out of their sight and heard the chainsaw whirring again, she finally sat down on the stump and swore for a long time.

The evening was close. It took a few hours, but she was in a better mood. Mostly because both her baskets were full. In one of them were several kinds of boletes and two parasol mushrooms. She loved mushrooms. Maybe that was the only reason why she was still staying in that house after all.

The other basket held a mixture of blueberries and raspberries. She had an important meeting to attend over Zoom tomorrow, and when lemon balm tea wasn't helping, it was berries that she used to chase away the depression of her work. Fruit sugar was the only sugar she indulged in. She and Boris had been living a healthy, organic and eco lifestyle, and she still clung to it, as if it was the only thing between her and sinking into absolute futility.

"Dianthus carthusianorum sudeticus," she breathed enthusiastically. Indeed, there was the Sudeten carthusian, an endemic pink flower as delicate as Kateřina herself, fluttering in the light breeze. Boris would have always been telling her about botany, and especially about the endemics of Jeseníky. While she'd been studying andragogy and sociology, he had completed his doctorate in botany. He showed her the world of plants and mountains. He brought her to the Jeseníky Mountains, where they began to live together in harmony with nature. Kateřina left the walls of corporations and start-ups to follow her love and his dreams.

And then he died of a heart attack at forty because the ambulance didn't get to him in time because of the snow. Since then she's been gritting her teeth and trying to keep her cabin and especially her home office job in a Prague marketing agency where she was bossed by girls ten years younger and with much less experience just because they could talk to senior managers face to face and not via a webcam. The bold neckline and short skirt, traditional tools for career growth, worked rather poorly via a webcam.

She resisted the urge to pluck the flower, preferring to walk a few more steps to discover any others. But endemics weren't as easy as mushrooms—they didn't grow in a circle.

Help.

She turned instinctively at the sound. That it might mean something didn't occur to her. She was standing in a clearing where several spruce trees had been freshly cut down in an effort to prevent the spread of the bark beetle. Looking at the rusty needles of the nearest trees, she knew immediately that the effort was as pointless as it had been all over Jeseníky. Nothing could stop the bark beetle's spectacular march through the forest.

Help.

Only now did she realize it was a man's voice and that he was indeed calling for help. She dug into the basket of mushrooms and pulled out a folding knife.

"Who's there?"

She wasn't afraid. She'd encountered strange types of existences in the woods before, but none tried to harm her. There was only one danger in the woods, and that was breaking a leg and not being able to reach anyone.

Help.

The voice definitely belonged to a man. Yet it sounded strangely whispery. Like it had been strained through old fallen leaves.

She placed both baskets on a big stump and resolutely set off among the nearest trees. It grew darker immediately. While there was still plenty of light in the clearing, it was already dark among the forest giants.

"Hello? What's your name? Are you lost?"

The voice echoed through the forest as it made its way through moss and ferns. Even though it didn't look that way because of those *stupid* lumberjacks, Kateřina knew how to walk through a forest. She could dodge potholes, leap over rotting stumps, see and step over moss-covered puddles. She couldn't remember the last time she had worn heeled boots, but she walked through the forest as if she had been born in it. At least during the day.

Help.

Finally, the voice sounded clearer than something that pops into one's head on its own. She picked up the pace. She assumed that if someone was lying here with a broken leg, they'd already spent at least one evening here. And despite the summer, it tended to be near zero at night this high in the mountains. The first frozen puddles usually appeared in the second half of August.

Here I am.

Finally, something other than a simple "help." Kateřina pushed away young birch trees, walked through them, and when she lowered both hands, the tree barrier closed behind her again like a subway door. She could see nothing. Only a massive oak tree that was covered with a group of white polypores. It had a blackened cavity in the middle that smelled of rot.

Here I am.

It came straight out of the tree.

"Hello?!" she called, a little unnecessarily, and took a step towards the tree.

She finally recognized it—a human face. It was sticking out of the tree like the polypores. The man's face was black with dirt, but the whites of his eyes were shining. Otherwise, they were a brown color reminiscent of the sky shortly before dawn. His mouth was open and his teeth were also white.

Kateřina remained standing and just stared at the man. Her brain tried for a moment to convince her that there was a body along the head, but it finally gave up. The body—if the man had one at all—had to be in the middle of the trunk.

"Please call for help. Call Fantom. My name is Martin, tell them that the SRS totally screwed up. It's important because at midnight there will be a..."

The voice trailed off as the woman retraced her steps. She walked through the birch trees, which soon blocked her view of the man's face, and then simply ran towards the clearing. In her hand she still clutched the knife in front of her. Strangely enough, it gave her a bit of confidence that if she encountered anything else, she would kill it with her five-inch blade. She skipped past the last of the trees and spotted her baskets.

Come back!

She picked them up and ran down the forest path below the ridge.

Expertly aiming for where the fewest trees grew, she knew she would find the most light there. Her mind was clear, completely blank. She focused only on the path, step by step, skipping over puddles, logs, branches, rocks, and holes. She was in great shape, so she didn't even get out of breath and made the four miles to her house in less than an hour. As soon as she heard the familiar whirr of a chainsaw, the tension lifted.

"I need to start taking antidepressants," she decided aloud when she finally arrived at her cabin. Still, she locked the door behind her, used the latch that otherwise only swung next to the lock on the door like a prop for an old cobweb, and turned on all the lights in the house. She left the baskets on the floor, the knife still clutched in her hand.

She cursed. Several times. Only then did it finally dawn on her what she needed. She ran up to the second floor, with two attic rooms. One served as a storage room, the other as a guest room. The last time someone had used it was for Boris's funeral. That someone was Jasmine, and in addition to a crumpled thong, she had left an open pack of Marlboros there. They were still on the bedside table. She grabbed them and ran to the kitchen with them. She was cold, so she pulled a sweatshirt over the T-shirt she'd headed out into the woods in before scrabbling for the lighter on the stove and managing to light one cigarette on her third try. The dried tobacco burned faster than she remembered, but the first drag made her feel like she could do it. She felt a little dizzy, but she just considered that a nice bonus. She opened her laptop, turned it on, expertly punched in the password *Boris12345*, and quickly opened Facebook. Jasmine's Messenger screen glowed green. She hovered with the mouse right over the camera icon and then pressed it.

Her friend only picked it up as she lit her second cigarette. By then the first puff had made her a little nauseous.

"You smoke?"

Jasmine's appearance matched her name. Her mother had met her father while working as a nurse in Saudi Arabia. She left her lucrative job early, but with something of a trust fund that guaranteed Jasmine money during her childhood, her studies and a decent start in life. They met at university and also started their first job together. Throughout all the complex escapades of their lives, they were and have remained each other's support system, although in recent years they have communicated mainly via Messenger using memes.

"I'm losing my mind!" she blurted out.

"Explain."

Typical Jasmine. Smart, brusque, straight to the point. Only now did Kateřina realize she was only wearing her underwear. And quite sexy, too. She probably distracted her from something important. But the thought just flitted through her mind as she was trying to concentrate on her own state of mind.

"I was in the woods. Someone was calling for help. I found a big tree and saw a human face in it. The guy was mumbling something about SRS, Fantom, screw-ups, and that something was going to happen at midnight. Total mess."

With a shaking hand, she put half a cigarette in a saucer. She was sure she'd take one more drag and throw up.

"Are you drunk?"

"I don't have any alcohol, Jas. You know we live ... I live healthily."

"Have you eaten?"

"Yeah. Mushrooms and tofu this morning."

At the word tofu, Jasmine shuddered. She preferred bacon, caviar, and port, though with her figure she looked more like she was living off air.

"Those mushrooms, weren't they liberty caps?"

Still matter-of-fact and calm. She even started giving herself a manicure during the interview.

"I know my way around mushrooms," Kateřina argued. But she turned to the basket on the floor anyway, suspiciously checking the pile of mushrooms. She raked through them, making sure there were no liberty caps or toadstools.

"Are you tired? Are you sleeping well?"

"I sleep for ten hours straight, thanks to that bloody fresh air around here!" she retorted, but then lowered her eyes. She couldn't be mad at someone who was helping her. Jasmine generously waved off her outburst. She was like that.

"Jesus, I'm sorry. You're probably right. It's too much for me. Those bitches at work are bossing me because I didn't send a presentation to a client last week because a tree fell here and damaged a 5G mast. Those idiotic lumberjacks dropped some spruce on it."

She reached over to the other basket and scooped out a handful of raspberries and two blueberries. This would do her good. She remembered that she and Jasmine used to organize raids to the cake shops. They called it looting. Once a month they indulged in tiramisu, panna cottas, harlequin cakes and cream puffs. Another pillage usually followed at a bar. She realized she'd do almost anything for a cream puff and a bottle of gin now. Hungrily, she scooped up another handful of forest fruits.

"Are you still dreaming about Boris?"

Kateřina shook her head. She had indeed dreamed of him often since his death. She saw him in various situations, especially at their cabin or in the woods he loved. A few times she had even spoken to him in her dreams. But about a month ago, all the dreams stopped. Unexpectedly and suddenly. She'd slept soundly every night since.

"Do you think I could have gone crazy? The loneliness, the loss of Boris..."

Jasmine turned away from the monitor and Olaf came into view. The tall blond man was actually named Jarmil. He said his parents apparently hated him, so he had taken to calling himself Olaf. He was only wearing shorts. As a mockery of Kateřina's situation, there were yellow ducks on them.

"Hi," Kateřina mouthed through a mouthful of raspberries. She didn't like Olaf. He was a consultant for the government, which could mean anything. But Jasmine was happy with him.

At least someone was doing well.

"You don't look like a nutcase, Kat. I'd say you're just missing a good steak."

Typical Olaf. Not only was he the only one who called her Kat, but he'd also teased her when she'd gone vegan for Boris.

"Thanks, Jarmil, I'll take that as a credible diagnosis from you," she growled. She knew very well how to return his teasing.

Before he could react, there was the sound of shattered glass.

She turned and saw something knock three window panes out of the window. She had a double-glazed window, so only one pane remained whole; the others scattering shards to the floor. Jasmine screamed something, Olaf asked in a calm voice what happened. Kateřina just stared out, startled. Several branches came through the window.

"Bastards."

"Who?!" Jasmine yelled.

Kateřina had no doubt that Old Pávek and company were behind this. The window was across from a small herb and vegetable garden. The nearest trees grew maybe a hundred yards away. The forest was on the other side of the house. The branches had nowhere to fall from. And certainly not with enough strength to destroy the window. The wind blew in through the fresh holes. It was very strong. The air smelled of rain, yet Kateřina was sure there wasn't a cloud in the sky when she turned on the computer. What's more, she didn't hear the usual pounding of drops on the roof.

Instead, there was pounding on the door.

"Kat, should I call the police?"

Olaf finally said something that made sense. She didn't have the time to answer. All the electricity in the house had gone out. Only the blue light of the laptop screen illuminated the room. She skipped over to the basket of mushrooms, on top of which lay a still-open knife. She grabbed it in her hand and pointed it in front of her, as if the knife could actually protect her from whoever was pounding so hard on the door.

It didn't take long for the door to break open.

Someone must have knocked it out with tremendous force. They didn't break the lock; the door just fell in. It split in the hinges as well as around the lock. It hit the floor with a loud thud and clatter. The figure that stood in the entrance certainly didn't look human.

Jasmine's voice screamed from the laptop. Olaf's voice, still calm, echoed in the background, but the noise of the door slamming and the wind whistling changed it to a murmur that Kateřina couldn't perceive. Her hand was shaking, and despite the sudden cold, sweat was running down her forehead. She wiped it off with her free hand and spread the salty drops through her short hair. She'd cut her hair short once she'd moved here. It was practical.

"I'm back, my love."

The man had the voice of Boris, but he certainly didn't look like him. His whole figure seemed to have grown and thickened. His skin was black, covered with hair and something else—as if, like the hair, it was growing needles. A huge penis swung between his legs. He'd never had one like it, nor had he ever had testicles shaped like pine cones. This was a strangely disgusting masquerade.

"This is a crime, you idiots. The police are on their way!" she yelled.

The figure took a few steps toward her. It reached out a hand, unnaturally long, slender, with skin resembling tree bark, and grabbed her left hip. It finally dawned on her that this was no Pávek prank. She grabbed the laptop with her free hand, and while Jasmine's screams rumbled out of it, she whacked the figure over the head with it. She didn't believe for a moment that it was Boris. He was dead, after all.

The laptop crackled and Jasmine stopped screaming. The blue light disappeared and the terrifying figure let go of her. At that moment, she stabbed the knife in it. All the way in. It wasn't very deep, but she stabbed it with all the force she could muster. The computer ended up on the floor and she jumped onto the table. She then flipped it over onto the dark figure.

"Don't run away from me, my love," it growled.

Kateřina ran through the kitchen and up the stairs, old floorboards buckling under her. Before that, she gracefully zigzagged between the mushroom, apple and herb dryers in the hallway. She knew the house even in the dark. After all, she was usually moving around in darkness. Considering her expenses, she tried to conserve electricity at all costs. After dark, the only light in the house was usually the laptop with a screen saver on.

While she was running up the stairs, her attacker crashed into them. Drying racks and wooden boxes full of dried berries fell to the ground. So did the attacker. But it didn't take it long to get up. When the first step made a creaking sound under its weight, the door to the guest room slammed shut. She ran past the bed, still unmade after Jasmine's visit, and pushed it towards the door. She then picked up the rickety nightstand and placed it on the bed so that it formed another counterweight to the door.

It didn't take long for it to fall into the covers, knocked down by the kinetic energy of the blows torturing the door.

✦ ✦ ✦

Kateřina was breathing heavily. She searched all the drawers and cabinets. Each one looked different. Some had been left by the previous owners, others had been bought by her and Boris at an antique shop so they could put in things that they no longer needed, but didn't want to give up. While that thing was banging on the door, which only resisted thanks to the heavy bed, she was throwing clothes, old books and notebooks on the floor. Soon, her certificates were on the floor too—coaching, digital marketing, presentation specialist, social wizard ... All that marketing crap materialized on paper was now worthless.

"My love, don't run away from me."

The voice sounded as real as Boris's, at least from what she remembered. It made no sense. Nothing made sense. Ever since she'd seen that terrifying human face in the tree, her world had turned upside down.

The door had turned to rubble. The thing with Boris's voice pushed the bed away and stepped into the room.

"Leave me alone!" she shouted. She abruptly realized the absurdity of it all. A command, a shout, a plea, nothing could change it. That creature had come for her.

She leaned against the dresser and heard the clink of bottles. They were filled to the brim with an alcoholic tincture with her pickled herbs—mint, chamomile, lemon balm, plantain and several others. Some she had for her own use, others she planned to sell, through an upcoming e-shop.

"Don't be afraid, my love. This is what we've always wanted—to become one with nature."

She knew about the lighter in her pocket the whole time. She put it there when she lit the first cigarette in Jasmine's pack. There was a wobbly table between her and the intruder. She poured five glasses on it. The whole room was filled with the smell of herbs. The lighter flared with a bright red flame.

"Whoever you are, leave me alone," she said.

The creature took two steps forward. A wall of fire rose between it and Kateřina.

She ran through the darkness, feeling every footfall. The moment she fell after jumping, she lost the warm socks she had pulled on when she got home; pine needles, twigs and small stones bit into her bare feet. But there was no other way down to the settlement. And that way was too damn long. She only looked back once. She could see the terrifying figure in the window, and the alcohol-drenched table burning behind it. She didn't want to see if the fire had spread. She firmly believed it hadn't, but she preferred to play Schrödinger on this one and didn't want to find out. In addition to the pain in her feet, she could feel her left knee. When she had jumped out of the window and landed in the compost below, it had snapped, and now the sharp pain in her knee alternated with the sharp pain in her feet. Still, she didn't stop. She knew she couldn't. She could handle it. She'd built up a decent body by walking in the mountains. It was finally doing her some good.

She saw the light of *civilization* before she reached the first house. It was coming from a construction trailer. She knew too well who it belonged to, or rather, who was currently living in it. According to the faded sign, it was the property of the *Forestry of the Czech Republic js* and probably maybe *c*, but it no longer had corners and the letter had disappeared with one of them.

"Hey! Help!"

She was screaming from a distance. With no success because of sport commentator Robert Záruba shouting from the open windows of the trailer. She stumbled about fifty yards from the trailer and rolled to the ground. Her left foot was bleeding. It must have been cut by a rock. She landed on her knee, which Bob had treated that morning. The scab had worn off and she was now bleeding from two places. The grass was wet with evening dew. It cooled her and stuck to her at the same time. She realized that the sweatshirt she had thrown on at home was torn. She had no idea from what. Maybe from that ... guy who'd broken into her house.

She looked back. Her cabin was drowning in darkness. It was maybe even darker than it should have been. At least that was good news.

And then she just started crying. With exhaustion, pain, fear, and utter confusion at what was happening around her. Her tears fell straight into the grass. She couldn't remember the last time she'd cried. Not even after Boris's death. Back then she had simply been her gritting her teeth and doing whatever it took to fulfill his last wish.

After a while, a strange sound penetrated her ears. She looked up and saw Bob standing in the open doorway of the trailer on the highest step of the three, urinating. In the darkness she couldn't see the details—and she certainly wasn't interested in them—she only saw the powerful stream of fluid arcing to the ground where it broke up in droplets that sprayed out into the wide open.

It woke her up. Something as natural, common and normal as emptying one's bladder brought her back to sanity. She stopped crying, took a deep breath, and stood up. She felt pain in her knee and foot, but it was nothing that would prevent her from getting up. Finally, Bob noticed her, too. That he should stop urinating because of it didn't occur to him.

"Hey, guys, it's Red," he shouted. The stream of urine finally stopped on its own. Bob performed a "shaking" and finally buttoned up the fly of his pants. Only then did she make her way over to him. She bypassed the impact zone of the urine in an appropriately wide arc.

"Dude, what happened to her?"

The voice belonged to Old Pávek. She looked him in the eyes and started crying again.

She stared hesitantly at the clear liquid in a red cup marked Nescafé for a moment, then drank it. The slivovitz burned her throat, but did her good before it could even be absorbed into her system. She had a brown blanket thrown over her. She had no idea why, and the lumberjacks probably didn't either, for the trailer was warm as the sunlight roasted it during the day. Plus, someone had been cooking on the gas stove recently, judging by the smell of sausages. Throwing a blanket over someone in need was probably a tradition, so she didn't refuse it.

They didn't pressure her to talk, which was unexpected. Old Pávek surprised her the most. He dragged her inside, made her sit down, gave her a blanket, and with Bob's help, they cleaned her wounds with disinfectant. They even pulled out a clean bandage and bandaged both her foot and knee.

"Can I have another one?" she asked.

Young Pávek smiled and poured her a drink from the bottle. The faded letters on the label claimed "Domestic Rum." Fortunately, the contents didn't match it.

She kicked the second shot back as well before looking at the faces of the lumberjacks. They looked unexpectedly human. And caring. She had to tell them what had happened. But at the same time, she was afraid of how absurd it would sound. Here in the warmth of the trailer, with the TV off, and after the second drink, she felt like she'd lost her mind and none of this had happened. For a moment she even thought about borrowing the phone from them, calling Jasmine and having her confirm that she hadn't even spoken to her today so she could go straight to a madhouse.

She shook her head. She wasn't crazy. She was sure of what she had experienced. Still, the whole event was incredibly absurd.

"Someone broke into my house. He beat me up and I ran away."

Actually, that was true.

"Who? It was Blažek, wasn't it?"

Young Pávek clenched his hands into fists. Blažek was an infamous alcoholic from the other end of the village, but Kateřina had never had a problem with him. In fact, he limited himself to beating his own wife. She shook her head.

"I don't know who he was. Maybe he's still in the house."

She stared at the ground as she spoke. She couldn't lie, but now she just had to. They'd think she was crazy.

"Try putting these on."

Old Pávek tossed a pair of shabby army boots at her feet. They must have been a good thirty years old. She went straight to putting them on. At least she could keep staring at the ground. They were about three sizes too big for her, but she didn't mind. As long as she had solid support for her feet. Bob took off the blanket and handed her a light, dark green coat. It smelled of smoke, wood, and male sweat. She buttoned it up and rolled up the sleeves so her arms stayed free. She wanted to say thanks, but somehow, she couldn't. These guys still struck her as a bunch of primitives after all the teasing, mouthing and whistling.

But she was grateful anyway.

They went fast. Old Pávek and Bob led the way, with the youngest member of the expedition following behind. They all had axes in their hands. Bob called his axe a hamaxe, but Kateřina could not tell the difference. She wrapped herself in her borrowed coat. Not that she was cold. She had a strange feeling that the extra layer of clothing would protect her from...

If only she knew what it was. Definitely not Boris.

The door remained open and the house was dark. Old Pávek went inside and tried turning on the light. It didn't work.

"Whew," she sighed in relief, maybe louder than she wanted to. Bob turned to look at her in disbelief. At least the loss of electricity wasn't her invention. The fact that they'd get there and find that nothing had happened to the house at all scared her more than whatever had tried to *hunt her down*. Maybe a little more. That she was going to go crazy was a much worse idea than some masquerading bastard who might be trying to rape her or maybe just rob her.

The cone of light from a powerful flashlight illuminated the entry room, the hallway, and then the kitchen. Shards of glass and a broken laptop lay on the floor. Something rustled under her feet.

"Leaves?"

They were indeed everywhere.

"Probably blown in through the broken window," she explained to Old Pávek, pointing up the stairs. He went first, Bob following Kateřina. Young Pávek stayed outside. Bob shoved the flashlight in her hand to shine under their feet. The door to the guest room remained closed. Old Pávek pushed them open and her flashlight began to lick the room hungrily. The charred table, the pushed back bed, the open window. Everything reminded her of her frantic flight and feeble defense.

"What the hell happened here?"

Her throat tightened. What if she'd really made this up and made this mess because she was hallucinating? She shook her head as she tried to convince herself, but she could almost believe it.

"Why are the leaves dry?"

That question came from Bob. He wasn't stupid at all. And he was right. Dry oak leaves were lying up here too, in a room smelling like a burned table. It was damn summer. There was no place to get dry leaves. Before she could think of a coherent response, a whistle came through the open window. Everyone looked out. Young Pávek stood there with a lighted headlamp.

"Hey, you gotta see this."

✧   ✧   ✧

The electrical box was on the floor. Someone ripped it off with brute force and tore out the wires.

"I'm not crazy," Kateřina was relieved. Someone really was after her.

"Dude, what cutters did he use?" Bob looked at the case and shook his head.

"I'd probably call the cops and the dicks from ČEZ[8] . The former will be here tomorrow, the latter in a month," Old Pávek grinned and pulled out a pack of Chesterfields. He nonchalantly slung an axe over his right shoulder and with one hand pulled a cigarette from the pack. In doing so, he offered the pack to the others. His son just waved his hand, but the others took one. Kateřina coughed at the first drag, but steadied herself and took another. The head of the lumberjack party pocketed the pack, as well as the lighter.

"I'd lock everything. If you're worried, Red, my boy could sleep here on the couch."

He may have called her Red, but his usual *piggish* grin was gone. This was an unexpectedly serious offer.

"Or you can sleep in our trailer. Just expect farting and snoring," Bob added. Yeah, his grin was back.

"Did you hear that?"

Young Pávek turned around. They were standing at the back of the cabin. That part was the one closest to the woods. Not even ten yards away, the first spruce trees were already growing. The light of his flashlight licked a few trees.

"I didn't hear anything," Bob stated.

"It's like someone's talking, really," uttered the fresh graduate, taking a few steps closer to the woods. The sturdy boots on his feet crushed the grass, drops of night dew falling from its stalks.

The wind picked up. Kateřina looked up at the sky, which now glowed with the first quarter moon. Not a single cloud drifted across it. She tried to wrap herself more tightly in her coat, but she couldn't.

"I'd rather wait for the cops," she whispered. She was afraid. Thanks to the broken electrical box, she was sure she wasn't crazy and hallucinating. But now she was more afraid of who had actually attacked her.

Rightfully so.

✦ ✦ ✦

---

[8] ČEZ—the main Czech producer and supplier of electricity

Young Pávek went down screaming. He threw up his arms and fell on his back before he disappeared from everyone's sight. The burning cigarettes immediately flew to the ground.

"Help!"

She didn't see him. The light of his torch had gone out. Fortunately, he was still shouting, so they knew he was moving toward the woods. The lumberjacks ran after him, Kateřina with them. The woods scared her, but she was more afraid of being left alone in the darkened cabin.

"Dad!"

Heavy boots hit the grass of an uncut meadow. It wasn't long before they caught up with him. Young Pávek grabbed the trunk of the nearest fir tree and held on to it. His axe lay beside him. Something was pulling him into the woods by his legs. Kateřina shone a light on them. They flailed three feet in the air, wrapped in ropes. Black, maybe brown; they looked like wood. She shone her light behind them and saw a figure like the one that had attacked her in the cabin. The man, perhaps six feet tall, was covered in pine needles, leaves, and twigs. The massive hands had turned into branches instead of fingers, the ends of which were wrapped around the young man's legs.

"Virgin Mary, intercede on our behalf! It's the devil!" Bob screamed. He stopped dead in his tracks; Kateřina almost bumped into him. But Old Pávek flew past them. Still running, he drew his axe and stuck it in the guy's chest. The smell of resin wafted through the area.

The branches let go of the young man and a second later knocked Old Pávek to the ground. His axe remained lodged in the strange monster. Just as he hit the ground, the light of the torch showed the branches pounding the man on the ground. Moments later, one wrapped itself around his neck. Pávek flew in the air, flailing its legs and grunting. He tried to tear the branch apart with his hands, but judging by the grunting, he wasn't that successful.

The hamaxe dug into the creature's right arm. Kateřina was standing close enough to see droplets of pitch fly out from the point of impact. A few landed on her face. She wiped them off and shone her flashlight on them. The red blood still smelled of resin. Old Pávek hit the ground, panting heavily, while Bob delivered a blow after blow with practiced movements. As he withdrew his hand, the creature screamed. But it did not move from its place. The second branch struck Bob in the face. This time, his blood spurted in the air.

But by then, old Pávek had already pulled his axe out of it, and at his side appeared his son, to whom Kateřina handed his lost tool.

"One!" the oldest lumberjack shouted, swung and plunged his axe deep into the body of the attacker. From the other side, his son did the same.

"Two!" he shouted. They both pulled their trusty axes from the body and chopped again.

"Three!" Old Pávek bellowed again, and then they were slashing furiously at the man's body.

It wasn't a human body. No human could have lasted that long. And it didn't even look like one. It fought back. Even as they hacked chunks of flesh from its body, even as its thick blood spurted everywhere, it kept attacking with its remaining arm. It punched Old Pávek a few times, but he didn't care. He just staggered, yelled a foul curse, and continued hacking at the wooden body. It wasn't long before the creature fell to the ground. The Páveks cut it in half. The two parts were now lying close together, still twitching. Thick blood oozed from both.

All the time she had been shining a light on the monster to be of some use to them. The others' torches had either gone out or they had simply lost them somewhere. Now she was looking for Bob. He was lying in the grass, holding a hand to his face. Blood was running between fingers. She ran over to him, took off her jacket, and gently pulled his hand away. A gaping wound peeked out at her.

"We need to stitch it up, quick," she uttered expertly. In doing so, she frantically removed her sweatshirt. She wore a T-shirt underneath and nothing else. She pulled it over her head and wrapped it around Bob's face. She didn't care that she was naked from the waist up.

"Uh, what's wrong with him?"

Old Pávek didn't know whether to stare at Bob or at her. His son acted like a gentleman, picked up her sweatshirt from the ground and handed it to her.

"I've got disinfectant and sutures at home. It only looks awful, but the sooner I sew it up the better," she replied.

"We have medical equipment in the trailer. Lumberjacks need it all the time," Old Pávek nodded his head down toward the village, where some of the houses were peacefully lit.

"Hehe, nice tits," Bob said through his shirt.

✦ ✦ ✦

They went fast. The Páveks held Bob's hands and together they looked for the easiest way. Fortunately, it was easier to get into the valley than out of it. Kateřina carried the axes and the hamaxe. Soon she overtook them and helped Bob into the caravan. There she finally disposed of the bloody tools. Old Pávek opened the couch and pulled out a green first aid kit. He was right—the lumberjacks really did have great equipment.

Bob had made it through without so much as a scream. Not just the sewing, but the disinfecting too. Kateřina patched his gaping wound professionally, while Old Pávek got two shots into Bob and the others, then hid the rest of the bottle as a precaution.

"Maybe you shouldn't smoke with that wound open," she growled nervously.

"Maybe you shouldn't talk when he's got the wound open," he retorted, but took two steps away. He picked up his cell phone, fiddled with it for a moment, but in the end put it back on the shelf.

"What the hell was that?" he finally asked.

"The devil," Bob replied. Kateřina cleaned the blood off the rest of his face and checked his eyes. They looked fine. She'd tried really hard at stitching him, but he'd still be left with a big scar.

"Was that the guy who broke into your house, Red?" Old Pávek ignored Bob's mutterings about the devil.

She shook her head.

"Similar, but not this one."

She was sure of it. This creature wasn't claiming to be her deceased Boris. And after all, he looked a little different.

"Why did you lie to us?"

The young Pávek didn't look angry, just very scared.

"I was afraid you wouldn't believe me. I also thought I was hallucinating, that I was going crazy from . . . everything." She wrung her hands.

"I've never seen something like this in the woods before. I've been cutting damn trees since the commies. I ran into Soviet troops on a training exercise once, saw two bearded nimrods banging each other in the moss and ferns, kicked a bunch of lost Prague idiots out of the woods, but this, this has never been here," Old Pávek uttered.

"I . . ." Kateřina looked around at their faces. Bob had his eyes closed, Young Pávek was tapping the floor with his right foot, and his father was lighting another cigarette. "I saw something similar up below the ridge. A guy trapped in a tree. He said something about midnight tonight..."

"The same monster?"

She shook her head.

"Someone else. He wasn't moving. Really, it was like the tree trapped him. Maybe he could help us. What if he was right about midnight and something terrible happens?"

"Worse than this?" Bob pointed to his freshly stitched wound.

Old Pávek looked at his watch. It was half-past ten.

"It's at least an hour's walk up the ridge," she sighed.

"That's all right. The young one will start the Lakatosh. In the meantime, the Gypsy and I will take everything we need."

LKT was an abbreviation for *Lesní Kolový Traktor*—a Forest Wheel Tractor. It's been produced in Slovakia since the 1970s and one of its more modern versions was standing on the edge of the forest. It was used by a logging crew. Like everyone else, they called it Lakatosh because of the official abbreviation. This one had a metal plough and a hydraulic loading arm. It probably lived its best years around the turn of the millennium, but it was still a reliable servant. The loggers loaded it with all their equipment, so there wasn't much space left inside the cabin. It could only fit the driver and Kateřina, who had to stand next to the driver's seat. The other two passengers were outside holding onto the metal fencing protecting the glass of the cabin. It was necessary. Old Pávek stomped hard on the gas. The headlights shone out into the deep night, which was taking on a much darker and more eerie quality in the forest, and the tractor's engine rumbled out into distance. Few people could drive that fast at night, but the lumberjack knew the whole area better than his own boots. They reached the clearing where she had first heard the strange *help* in less than a quarter of an hour. The men jumped out of the tractor, Kateřina checked Bob's bandaged wound, and then everyone grabbed their axes and flashlights.

"Damn," she cursed when her foot got stuck in a muddy puddle. The whole area looked different at night than it did during the day. And Kateřina didn't go in the woods after dark. She loved it when the sun was shining. She was always in the cabin after sunset. She had a strange feeling about the dark. Probably like every person who grows up in a city that is actually always lit and never as dark as a village or a forest.

"This way, maybe," she pointed between the trees when Young Pávek helped her pull her foot out of the mud. She finally wasn't wearing a skirt, but his overalls, which she only needed to tuck in a little and tighten the belt properly. They were now taking the brunt of the mud.

She stepped over a stump that looked familiar and then slipped through the trees, the lumberjacks behind her. Torch light licked the tree trunks, moss and mature ferns.

Help.

"There!" she pointed. Everything looked different in the dark, but she was sure she knew where to go now. She stepped over stumps, a rotting trunk of a fallen young spruce, and parted the veil of birch trees.

"Please, don't shine light in my eyes."

She recognized the man's voice, but didn't turn off or lower the flashlight. She couldn't. She was still staring at what she'd seen a few hours ago, and it made her question her sanity. The man's face did indeed look like it had grown into the tree.

"The devil!" Bob exclaimed.

"Screw you and your devil. Whatever it is, it doesn't have goddamned horns or a tail."

Old Pávek walked up to the trunk and stood between it and the torchlight. As he did so, he raised his axe hand. He was obviously waiting for one of the branches to move so he could chop it in defense. But the tree did not move at all. Moreover, it looked quite different from the creature they had killed at the cabin. Kateřina was right about that.

"I'm from the Fantom company. I was hired by the SRS to help them with an awakened leshen. But they screwed up. Most of their agents are dead, the rest will soon turn into leshens themselves. At midnight, the summoner wants to perform an ancient spell to awaken the forest. We wanted to stop it."

"Lewhat?" asked Pávek.

"The devil, dammit," Bob spat.

"A leshen. An ancient woodland creature. It's also called a *mochovik* or a *polisun*. All of them that lived here were put to sleep before the First World War. But some imbecile woke them up to get their power."

For a guy completely covered in trees, he spoke with unexpected directness, though neither Kateřina nor the lumberjacks understood the details of what had happened here.

Old Pávek pulled out a pack of cigarettes. He scratched his head and then lit one up. Kateřina squared up and walked over to him to take one as well. She wasn't as sick of smoking as she had been a few hours ago. And she wasn't as scared either.

"We killed one," Young Pávek joined the conversation.

"That's not enough. We have to stop whoever woke them up. The mage. Apparently he had prepared some sort of a spell, which he triggered by his own sacrifice. He died and rose again as a leshen. That woke the others."

"What?!" Kateřina exclaimed.

She crushed the filter of her cigarette.

"A mage. Self-sacrifice is the most powerful magical tool. Tonight, he will become the lord of the leshens. He will control all the ancients and be able to create new ones. We underestimated him a bit."

"Boris...," she gasped.

It was crazy, but in the light of what she had experienced, the man's words made sense to her. Boris had spoken to her about his funeral shortly before he died. He'd insisted that—*if I ever died, my love*—she bury him in the woods. Plus, she had to bury his bag with him. He claimed it contained the seeds of trees and plants and he wanted to serve some good purpose when it all grew from him. With Jasmine's help, she bribed the guys at the crematorium to give her a receipt that Boris had been burned. She then *officially* scattered his ashes in a meadow by the cemetery in Olomouc.

"...that fucking bastard," she added. The creature in her house was indeed her *late* husband.

"Are you all right, Red?"

She turned to Old Pávek with a mad expression and an angry curl of her bottom lip. But then she returned her gaze to the guy in the tree. She realized she was embarrassed in front of the lumberjacks. She'd despised them all along, hated them, and now it turned out that biggest bastard was her husband and *they* were saving her ass.

So no, she wasn't all right. Plus, she had this weird intense feeling in her head that she needed to apologize to them.

"He came to my house. Boris. The one who came back from the dead as a leshen."

It was really hard for her to say the name.

"He wanted to add you to his pack. You'd be just like him."

She cursed. She swore so nastily that Young Pávek raised an eyebrow in surprise.

"Where can we find these woodies?" Old Pávek finally asked, straightforward.

"According to the map, it's called Červeňák."

The old lumberjack looked at his watch. It was after eleven o'clock.

"Okay, let's go. It's half an hour, even with the Lakatosh," he finally announced. Kateřina just grunted something, turned on her heel, and went through the birch trees. The lumberjacks followed her.

"Hey, wait a minute, you don't know how to stop him!"

But no one was listening to the man in the tree anymore.

The tractor sped through the darkness over potholes as if it were a freshly paved road. Mud splashed from under the wheels, branches crunched and rocks flew. Young Pávek and Bob were struggling to stay on it. But they made it, just like the Lakatosh. Kateřina's legs tingled and her calves cramped as she stood in the driver's compartment behind the single seat. At times she closed her eyes; that was when Old Pávek lit his umpteenth cigarette while driving with one hand, or when they drove into terrain that seemed impassable to her. They drove through several dense areas and freshly cleared clearings. The closer they got to Červeňák, the stronger the wind blew. The cloudless sky glowed with the moon and stars, as if perhaps beckoning for a nighttime romantic picnic. But just as they entered the last of the dense undergrowth, she saw the treetops buckle under the strong wind.

"To the left. Something's shining there!"

She waved her hand at Pávek, who was in the process of dropping another cigarette butt on the floor.

"The moon?"

She shook her head. The light looked like moonlight. Theoretically it could have been reflecting off something, but it was shining too strongly to be a reflection. He turned to follow the light. Carefully this time. He figured that the hands of the two passengers clinging spasmodically to the cage around the cabin must be frozen to the bone. The tractor groaned as it pulled out of a pothole filled with dirty water, and that's when the country radio started playing.

"Shut up," the lumberjack shouted at Michal Tučný and turned the radio off.

Then he finally focused on driving. He went off the road and had to continue through the trees. Fortunately, they became more and more spaced out until they reached a clearing dominated by several stray rocks. It wasn't Červeňák. The well-known hiking spot was about four hundred yards higher up the ridge.

The Lakatosh stopped and Kateřina jumped off. She held a flashlight in her hand, but it was useless. The whole place literally glowed. That's why Pávek turned off the lights.

"Devils."

Bob dropped to the ground beside her and was rubbing his hands. Old Pávek then helped his son jump down.

"Wait here," she said and took off. She didn't look back at the lumberjacks. She took a few steps and only now did she see the whole scene. There were eight leshens standing there. Boris was at their head. In the line to his left... *branch*..., one was missing. Her throat tightened. It wasn't just the leshens, it was the source of light. Skulls. Twenty, maybe thirty, she found it hard to count them, spread out on the stones, glowing as if each one had a full moon inside. Beneath the stones lay a pile of human bones. Beside them sat a group of people. She counted them quickly—nine. Seven men, two women. Bruised, dirty, and most importantly, immobilized by flexible, but surely strong branches. She saw it when the lumberjacks had killed that leshen near her cabin. They could hardly move. She assumed they were the SRS people, whatever that meant.

She pulled the cigarette she had got from Pávek from her pocket. She needed four tries to light it. Her hand was unexpectedly steady, but the wind all around her was extinguishing the flame, even as she tried to hide the cigarette and lighter under her coat. Eventually, though, she took a triumphant drag and kept walking.

Despite the smoke, she could smell rot and dampness, just as she had when Boris had *visited* her at their house.

"My love, you came!"

She looked at him. No longer with fear, more with interest. She detected several familiar features in his face. It made him look even scarier. In the light of the skulls, she examined his strange body covered in hair and needles, and the creepy thing that was wobbling between his legs. He wasn't the only one, they all had such *jewels*. She noticed there was a difference between Boris and the other leshens—his humanity. Boris looked more human. They looked like trees, as if, it occurred to her, he had become a tree from a human, and they had gone through the opposite process, as if something had once transformed them from a tree to something more human-like.

"You lied to me. It wasn't a heart attack," she said.

"Of course it wasn't. I stumbled upon a way to awaken these powerful guardians of the forest. But I had to become one of them. This is what we believed in—living in harmony with nature."

His voice rustled like leaves, and the other leshens nodded as if in agreement.

No, I've believed all my life in making a pile of money to afford a loft apartment in Prague. I gave it up for you.

"...and now I'm here."

She didn't realize she'd spoken the last part of the thought that ran through her head out loud.

"Yes, you're here now. You'll merge with nature. You will become a powerful being of the forest," Boris said and added: "But first there must be more of us. Behold."

The people sitting by the bones began to move without wanting to. The leshens, whose branches imprisoned them, drew them together. While they fumbled and muttered something, the tree creatures dragged them among the others. Kateřina finally saw up close how exhausted and bruised they were.

"You want to kill them?!"

She shouted. But not hysterically. More like angrily. She took a drag from her cigarette as she did so.

"I'll show you what you'll become. They will belong with us."

Boris raised his hands to the moon. The wind, already strong enough, picked up. The people on the ground began to thrash and scream in pain. The first one had needles growing out of his body.

Kateřina threw down her cigarette, put her fingers to her mouth and whistled loudly. Behind her, the lights came on and the Lakatosh started up.

The front plow picked up the nearest leshen and threw it to the ground. Only then did the door open and Old Pávek jumped to the ground. In a moment, the other two lumberjacks were standing by him. This time they held whirring chainsaws in their hands instead of axes.

"These guys know their job, Boris," she grinned and ran over to them.

Old Pávek took a few steps toward the prone leshen and plunged the chainsaw into it. The leshen roared, but it couldn't drown out the chainsaw. Sawdust and sap-like blood flew out of it. Boris swung his branches, the wind whined, and all the leshens ran towards the Lakatosh.

They attacked mostly with their branches that had held a group of strangers at bay only moments ago. They tried to whip them, beat them, or wrap around them and knock them down, but all the lumberjacks had to do was set their chainsaws and the branches became stumps.

It was literally the Jeseníky chainsaw massacre.

But Kateřina didn't run to the lumberjacks. Something grabbed her legs and knocked her down. She screamed in pain and tried to turn around so she wouldn't be lying on her stomach on the ground. It didn't work. Instead, something pulled her as far away from the lumberjacks as possible. She had just seen Bob cut off a branch and then expertly cut one of the leshens in half. The engine seemed to hum happily as it did so.

She hit a few bones and then whizzed past the thrashing people. They seemed to be better off than they had been a moment ago. Some were touching themselves, but their transformation was interrupted.

"You can't escape me, my love."

Only now did she turn around—dirty, wet, her overall covered in dirt, twigs and pine needles. Boris towered over her. The branches that held her legs shortened—as if they had been sucked into his body—and strengthened. Then they crawled under her body—one wrapped around her hip, the other under her arms—and lifted her into the air. She hovered only a few inches off the ground, but it still felt like she was literally flying. She tried swinging her legs, but she wasn't having much success. She couldn't reach solid ground no matter how hard she tried.

"I'm going to make you into a being just like myself. The tree killers won't stop us, my love."

She looked at his woody, limp penis with horror in her eyes and thought of the worst. She tried to scream for help, but the end of one of the branches clamped around her throat and choked her. She just grunted. The end of the other arm extended and slipped into her mouth. She gagged, became nauseous and finally tried to vomit. There was nothing but her gastric juices oozing out around the branch. It didn't last long, maybe a few seconds. But at the same time, with even more horror, she heard the whirring of the chainsaws cease and screams of the lumberjacks could be heard instead.

She hit the ground. Boris pulled the end of his hand out of her mouth and released his grip at the same time. She felt cold, a strong chill in her insides, and at the same time it felt like something was awakening there. She looked down at her hands. A leaf was growing between her index and middle finger.

"I planted my acorn in you. It has already begun to sprout. Your transformation has begun," he said with satisfaction.

"You son of a bitch," she said.

"You'll thank me later," he chuckled hoarsely, and headed for the lumberjacks. She watched his back. Old Pávek was on the ground. Bob waved the chainsaw furiously, trying to free Young Pávek. The youngest lumberjack was entangled by several leshens' branches.

She stood up. She took an arc around the stray rocks. She jumped over the bones, and even though her insides clenched and she could feel something happening to every cell in her body, she kept running. She pushed past two dead leshens cut into several pieces, splashed into a thick pool of their blood, and then finally ran to the Lakatosh. She sat down on the seat, slammed the door and started the engine. The tractor lights illuminated the whole scene.

There were only five leshens left. The others were dead. But things weren't looking good for the loggers. Fortunately, Bob managed to free Young Pávek, who was crawling towards his father. His forehead was surrounded by a pool of blood.

She took off and the radio came back with country music. Someone was furiously playing the banjo and singing about *how beyond the blue mountain, the blue woods, there's my home, there lies Tennessee.*

She ran into Boris. The plow blade threw him back a few yards, but she caught up with him, didn't let him rest and hit him again. This time she managed to impale him.

"You bastard, you bastard," she muttered to the tune of the country song, still stomping on the gas. She ran over the remains of several leshens and headed straight for the stray rocks.

But Boris didn't wait for anything. He stretched his twiggy arms out to the door of the Lakatosh again, and even opened it. But at that moment the plow blade hit a rock. The Lakatosh stopped, but kept trying to push forward. She jumped out, ignoring the flailing branches, and out of the corner of her eye, she saw the blade sink a few inches into Boris's body. He was a tough son of a bitch.

"It's too late, my love. Soon you'll be like me. And so will they, look."

He smiled at her, wanting her to look at the people they were trying to turn before her. She felt something start to grow out of her nose. But she wasn't going to let it distract her. She pulled a canister of gasoline from the cabin, the kind that lumberjacks used to refill their chainsaws, and poured it on Boris.

Only now did he start to get scared.

"My love, what are you doing? Remember what you promised me. Loyalty..."

"Shut up, really, Boris, shut the fuck up. I knew there was something really wrong with you," she snapped and then she simply flicked her lighter.

The sun was shining.

"A smoke?"

She shook her head. Her stomach clenched. From hunger, dehydration, nerves, and probably cigarettes. She sat next to the charred Lakatosh, still unable to look away from Boris's ashen body. While the other dead creatures had been removed by the SRS agents, this one was still here. When Boris had caught fire, the others seemed to have lost their strength and Bob easily turned them into firewood. When he ran out of gas in his chainsaw, he thoroughly shredded them all with his hamaxe. Right then, not only did her transformation stop, but everyone else's as well. Now she and Bob were alone. Old Pávek was taken to the hospital by a helicopter, and his son flew with him. The SRS agents arranged it. Not the ones who were supposed to end like leshens, but new ones. They arrived at around 3 a.m.—all-terrain vehicles, helicopters, a bunch of guys in bulletproof vests and with equipment the purpose of which they couldn't even guess.

Olaf called them. He worked for the government, and when he saw what was coming at Kateřina in her house, and heard her mention the SRS on top of that, he figured out who to call. She made a mental note to thank him later.

It was strange that no one was talking to them. They just took them aside and started cleaning up the mess she and the lumberjacks had made. In doing so, they photographed, filmed and documented every part of the dismembered bodies as well as the bones.

It wasn't until dawn that they were approached by a guy in a brown jumpsuit.

His brown eyes looked familiar to her.

"A smoke?" Bob asked him.

He too shook his head.

"It'll be a while before I stop being afraid of fire," he chuckled. "I still feel like a piece of wood," he added by way of explanation.

"Hey, it's you! How did you get out of that tree?" Kateřina asked.

"You don't want to know, miss."

"Widow. For the second time," she nodded her head towards the charred Boris.

"Yeah, actually," he rolled his eyes at not figuring that out sooner.

"I wanted to thank you and reach an agreement to keep it quiet. You see, neither we nor the SRS are entirely eager for anything that happened here to become public."

Kateřina and Bob nodded their heads. They knew that no one would believe them anyway.

"Sure thing, boss. And will anything come of it? Maybe a new Lakatosh?" asked Bob.

"Well, considering how many monsters you've killed, you're due a decent reward. I'm guessing it'll be enough to buy five of them." The guy scratched his beard and a wide grin spread across his face. A magical protective medallion swung around his neck. He instinctively squeezed it tightly. It visibly calmed him down. He exhaled deeply. It was the only thing that saved him from the fate of eternal woodenness.

Kateřina was surprised by the gesture, but she was too tired to think about it.

"Is there anything I can do for you now? Anything?" he asked.

"Yes," she nodded. "Take us somewhere for a proper steak. Ideally an Argentina one. Because I'm definitely done with organic, eco, and the rest of this bullshit," she stated firmly, with a glance at the charred leshen.

FRANTIŠEK KOTLETA (* 1979)

He is a phenomenon of Czech fiction and the rougher alter-ego of a writer, journalist and science popularizer Leoš Kyša. At the beginning of his work stood his great role model Jiří Kulhánek. Fascination with Kulhánek's work is already evident in Kotleta's first book *Hardcore* (*Hustej nářez*, Klub Julese Vernea, 2010), full of blood, sex and explicit violence, where aliens and vampires fight each other for the fate of the Earth. The author followed that up with several more volumes to finally bring the story to the end in *Stalingrad* (*Stalingrad*, Epocha, 2019). In the meantime, Kotleta went among the gods in the *Perun's Blood* trilogy (*Perunova krev*, Epocha, 2013-2014). But he didn't stop there—he combined urban fantasy and detective themes in *A Too Long Swingers Party* (*Příliš dlouhá swinger party*, Epocha, 2014), and took a superheroic approach to an existential account of real people's lives in *The Hunters* (*Lovci*, Epocha, 2015). He offered his own version of a post-apocalyptic world in the tetralogy *Fallout* (*Spad*, Epocha, 2016-2018), and he did not forget to include several sequels to *A Too Long Swingers Party*, which he concluded with *Dark Blues in New Orleans* (*Temné blues v New Orleans*, Epocha, 2022).

The cyberpunk-themed *Underground* (*Underground*, Epocha, 2020) and *Underground: The Revolution* (*Underground: Revoluce*, Epocha, 2021) make a separate series. Both books became bestsellers in Poland and were also published in U.S. by Royal Hawaiian Press.

The most ambitious project so far, however, is a series of space operas called Legion, set in a universe which he shares with Kristýna Sněgonová. He opened it with the novel *Operation Thümmel* (*Operace thümmel*, Epocha, 2020) and continued with *Red Sparrow* (*Rudý vrabčák*, Epocha, 2021), *Aga* (*Aga*, Epocha, 2022), and *Operation Petragun* (*Operace petragun*, Epocha, 2023).

The *MHF* project is exactly what Kotleta loves most about fiction, so he was immediately welcomed on board!

Bestiary

Black Lady—the antithesis of the usually benevolent spirit known as the White Lady. The Black Lady committed serious crimes while alive, most often the murder of her husband, and was sentenced to an eternal haunting as punishment.

Bludiczka—similarly to the will o' the wisp, they lure pilgrims from the roads deeper into the forest, but in Czech folklore they often take the form of beautiful ethereal women who lure travellers in a swamp or dance them to death.

Bosorka—one of the many Czech words for a witch, who can be either human or a forest fairy.

Brno dragon—one of the two famous medieval stuffed crocodiles in Czechia; the other, also mentioned in this anthology, is located in the town of Budyně. While the origin of the Brno dragon is uncertain, the Budyně one was brought back from an expedition to Egypt in 1522 by the adventurer Jan IV. Zajíc of Hazmburk and the crocodile made the entire journey across the Mediterranean Sea and half of Europe alive.

Chort—basically a devil—a creature with horns, black fur, a tail and hooves; but in Czech legends they do not live only in Hell, but also in abandoned houses, sawmills and mills, where they haunt travellers, offering to grant them wishes in exchange for their souls or making bets; if humans lose a bet, they also lose their souls or are taken straight to Hell.

Deadlings—the ghosts of children, killed at birth by unwed mothers who then secretly buried them without a proper burial. According to legends, deadlings then weep piteously at their graves until someone gives them a shirt or says the Lord's Prayer backwards to them.

Domovoy—a Slavic house spirit ("domov" meaning "home"), which brings prosperity to the family if they give him sacrifices, and harms them if this sacrifice is denied.

Durandl—see **Mountain spirits**

Fayermon—a fiery wraith that usually appears in the form of a burning man or a dog, but there are more curious stories where it takes the form of a flying burning sheaf of grain or a shoe, for example. Usually it is the ghost of a farmer who was secretly moving boundary stones to enlarge his fields.

Fext—one of the modern monsters appearing hand in hand with technological advancement. The first legends date back to the Thirty Years' War, one of the first major conflicts fought with firearms. Because some soldiers emerged unscathed from even the worst firefights, they came to be called fexts, a name derived from the German *kugelfest*—bulletproof—and even a few generals were considered to be fexts in addition to ordinary soldiers. In the end, however, it was always the bullet that killed them; it just had to be made of glass.

Hastrman—see **Vodnik**

Heykal—woodland creatures that provoke travellers at night with their loud shouts . . . and if anyone dares to answer them in the same loud voice, a heykal would come running and tear them to pieces.

Leshen—a male forest shapeshifter that considers himself a protector of the forest and game and hates humans. He would chase hunters and poachers out of the forest, kidnap women, and replace human children with his own offspring, who then return to his forest when they grow up. Humans can protect themselves from him by wearing their clothes inside out or by swapping their shoes.

Lord of the Woods—see **Mountain spirits**

Melusine—in the original French legend, Melusine was a cursed woman who turned into a half-serpent every Saturday. In the Czech lands, however, she eventually became a wind wraith that wails mournfully in the chimneys.

Mountain spirits—protectors of mountains, neither good nor bad, who often help people in need, but at the same time severely punish those who do not show proper respect to the mountains.
The most famous is Krakonoš, the protector of the Giant Mountains, sometimes nicknamed the Lord of the Woods. He appears as a tall man with a beard, a long cloak and a wide-brimmed hat. Sounds familiar? According to one theory, it was a postcard with a picture of Krakonoš that inspired Tolkien when he created Gandalf.

On the other hand, Durandl shows up in the form of a small man. He resides in the Bohemian Forest to the south and helps local glassmakers because he fell in love with their craft.

The Eagle Mountains are an exception, because they have not one, but two protectors. The older one is the brave and beautiful Katherine, whose origins derive from St. Katherine, who was a popular saint in the local mountains. In modern times she was joined by her husband Rampušák.

And Ranger? As he said, he's already forgotten.

Mura—a nocturnal creature that sits on the chest of sleepers, suffocating them and disturbing their sleep. Its name can also be found in English—the "mare" in "nightmare" is of the same origin as mura. Its descriptions vary, with mura being described as a small devil-like creature, a white cat, or a pale woman, but there are also more bizarre descriptions, such as the one used in this anthology.

Noonwraith—a wraith from Slavic mythology that walks the fields at noon, because noon is considered the hour of spirits, just like midnight. It punishes people who are working at that time or gives them unsolvable riddles, and abducts children who are playing in the fields without their parents.

Permonik—a small creature inhabiting mines and shafts in large numbers, similar to gnomes and kobolds. Their sighting usually heralds impending mining misfortune, but when sacrifices are offered to them, they can alert miners to ore veins. On the other hand, violations of mining traditions such as the ban on whistling in a mine usually anger them.

Plivnik—like a domovoy, it serves the owner of a house and ensured their well-being, but mostly it is a creature with an evil nature. The house owner can find it or raise it by carrying a black hen's egg in their armpit for nine days without washing or praying, but then they have to pay for seven years of happiness with their soul.

Print gremlin—a mischievous creature that is supposedly responsible for all the typos, smudges, flipped pages and other printing defects you can find in books.

Rarach—according to legends, they are feral domovoys who started harming humans. They take on the form of children or small people, spreading disease and setting houses on fire, but if a person is able to tame them again, they bring their owner luck in gambling.

Rusalka—a Slavic water demon. Usually living in a group, they rise from young girls who died by drowning, either by accident or suicide. They lure young men into rivers and lakes, where they envelope them with their hair and drown them, and by combing their hair they cause floods.

Slibka—another Slavic demon preying on young men. Her name is derived from the word *slib* (promise), because during night in the woods she promises love games with her singing, only to dance the whole night with men at best or kill and eat them at worst.

Stodolnik—a relative of a domovoy, but while a domovoy lives in a farmer's house, a stodolnik lives in a barn, where he guards the crops.

Striga—a Slavic name for a witch, usually of inhuman or demonic origin.

Strigoi—a vampire creature that was not created by another vampire, but was cursed as a human to rise from the grave and drink blood after death. During the day they return to their grave or tomb, to get rid of them, they have to be staked and beheaded.

Voden—see **Vodnik**

Vodnik—a water demon that resides in rivers, ponds and lakes. They drown people and collect their souls in cups in their underwater hideout. They especially target young girls, who they lure in with colored ribbons and small mirrors hanging in the reeds or on branches above the water's surface.

Yezinka—in Old Slavic, their name literally means "evil women." They are ugly, humped creatures covered with long hair, who hunt travellers in forests and feed on their flesh. They are also sneaky and manipulative. In the most famous story about yezinkas, they coax a little boy through the door to let them into the house so they could warm themselves, only to kidnap him afterwards.